THE GRAPHIC NOVEL
William Shakespeare

ORIGINAL TEXT VERSION

Script Adaptation: John McDonald
Character Designs & Original Artwork: Jon Haward
Coloring & Lettering: Nigel Dobbyn
Inking Assistant: Gary Erskine

Associate Editor: Joe Sutliff Sanders
Design & Layout: Jo Wheeler & Greg Powell
Publishing Assistant: Joanna Watts
Additional Information: Karen Wenborn

Editor in Chief: Clive Bryant

Macbeth: The Graphic Novel
Original Text Version

William Shakespeare

First US edition published: November 2008
Reprinted: August 2009, December 2010, August 2012, January 2014, June 2015, February 2017
September 2019, July 2021, June 2022

Library bound edition published: August 2011
Reprinted: September 2019, July 2021, June 2022

Published by: Classical Comics Ltd

Acknowledgments: Every effort has been made to trace copyright holders of
material reproduced in this book. Any rights not acknowledged here will be
acknowledged in subsequent editions if notice is given to Classical Comics Ltd.

Images on pages 3 & 6 reproduced with the kind permission of
the Trustees of the National Library of Scotland. © National Library of Scotland.
Images on page 141 reproduced with the kind permission of The Shakespeare Birthplace Trust.

All enquiries should be addressed to:
Classical Comics Ltd.
PO Box 177
LUDLOW
SY8 9DL
United Kingdom

info@classicalcomics.com
www.classicalcomics.com

Paperback ISBN: 978-1-906332-44-0
Library bound ISBN: 978-1-907127-36-6

This book is printed by Graphy Cems, Spain using environmentally safe inks, on paper
from responsible sources. This material can be disposed of by recycling,
incineration for energy recovery, composting and biodegradation.

The rights of John McDonald, Jon Haward, Nigel Dobbyn and Gary Erskine
to be identified as the artists of this work have been asserted in accordance with
the Copyright, Designs and Patents Act 1988 sections 77 and 78.

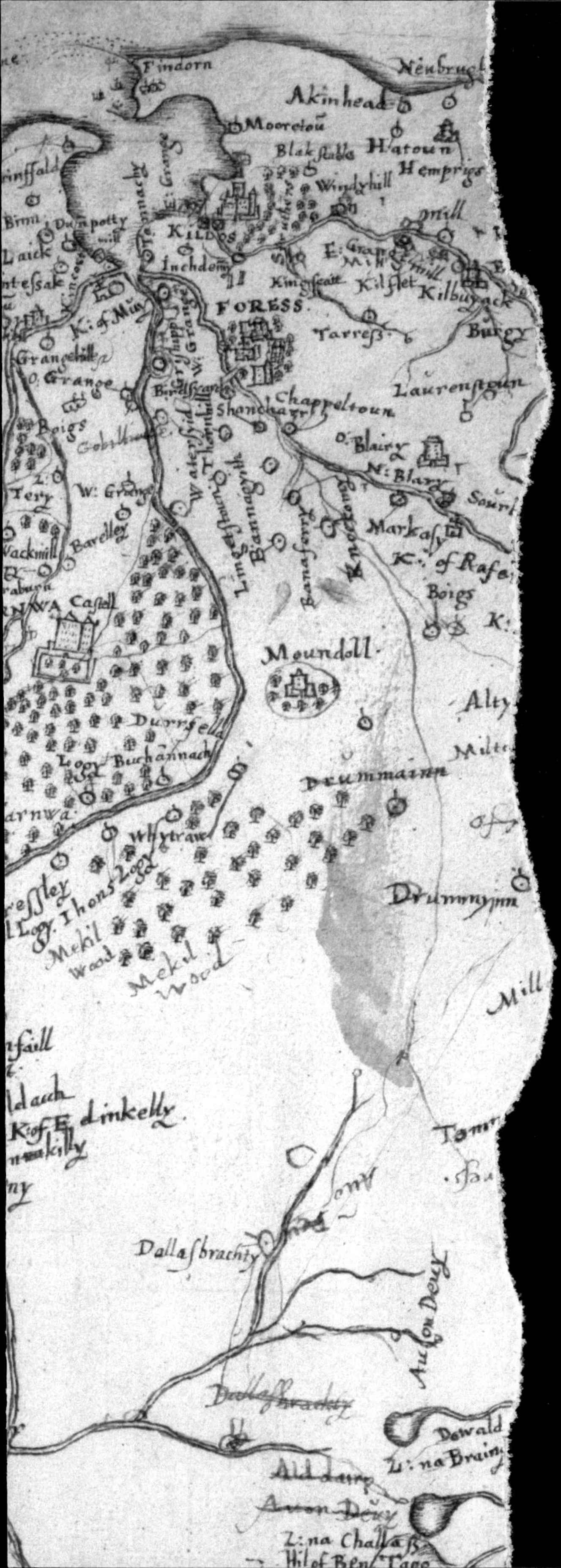
Findorn
Akinhead
Moorcoul
Hatoun
Hempriggs
Windyhill
Kildos
Inchdom
Foress
Tarres
Kilflet
Kilbuyack
Burgy
Laurenstoun
Chappeltoun
O: Blairy
N: Blairy
Markasy
Boigs
Moundoll
Durrsell
Logy Buchannach
Whytraw
Drummainn
Drumnyn
Mekil Wood
Mill
Edinkelly
Dallasbrachty
Dowald

Contents

Dramatis Personæ

Duncan
King of Scotland

Malcolm
Son of Duncan

Donalbain
Son of Duncan

Macduff
Nobleman of Scotland

Lenox
Nobleman of Scotland

Rosse
Nobleman of Scotland

Lady Macbeth
Wife of Macbeth

Lady Macduff
Wife of Macduff

Siward *Earl of Northumberland,
General of the English forces*

A Gentlewoman attending
to Lady Macbeth

Seyton
An officer serving Macbeth

An English Doctor

A Scottish Doctor

A Porter

An Old Man

Murderer 1

Murderer 2

Murderer 3

Dramatis Personæ

Macbeth
General in the King's Army

Banquo
General in the King's Army

The Ghost of Banquo

Menteth
Nobleman of Scotland

Angus
Nobleman of Scotland

Cathness
Nobleman of Scotland

Young Siward
Son of Siward

Fleance
Son of Banquo

Boy
Son of Macduff

Witch 1

Witch 2

Witch 3

Hecate
The "Queen" Witch

and Lords, Ladies,
Officers, Soldiers,
Messengers, Attendants
and Apparitions.

Prologue

Scotland in the year 1040.

King Duncan has ruled the land for six years, ever since the death of his grandfather, Malcolm II. Duncan is a good king, but even under his kind and gentle ruling, Scotland is far from being a settled nation.

For centuries, following the departure of the Romans, the land has been split in two – with bands of Vikings in the north and tribes of Saxons in the south. It's a barbaric land. Both local tribes have strong leaders: men who rely on the strength of their sword arm for honors and often have to fight for their very survival.

But the country is changing. With the reign of King Duncan comes a rare promise of unity amongst the tribes to create a single, Scottish nation ruled by a single Scottish King. However not everyone welcomes this peace. Some chieftains want to maintain their independence and continue to rebel against the King, often joining forces with warriors from other tribes and from other countries such as Ireland and Norway; and there are even some chieftains who would like to claim the title of King of Scotland for themselves.

To defend his crown, and to maintain order in his land, King Duncan commands a powerful army, led by noblemen who are experienced in the ways of war - and the mightiest and most trusted of these noblemen is King Duncan's cousin, the Thane of Glamis, otherwise known as…

…Macbeth.

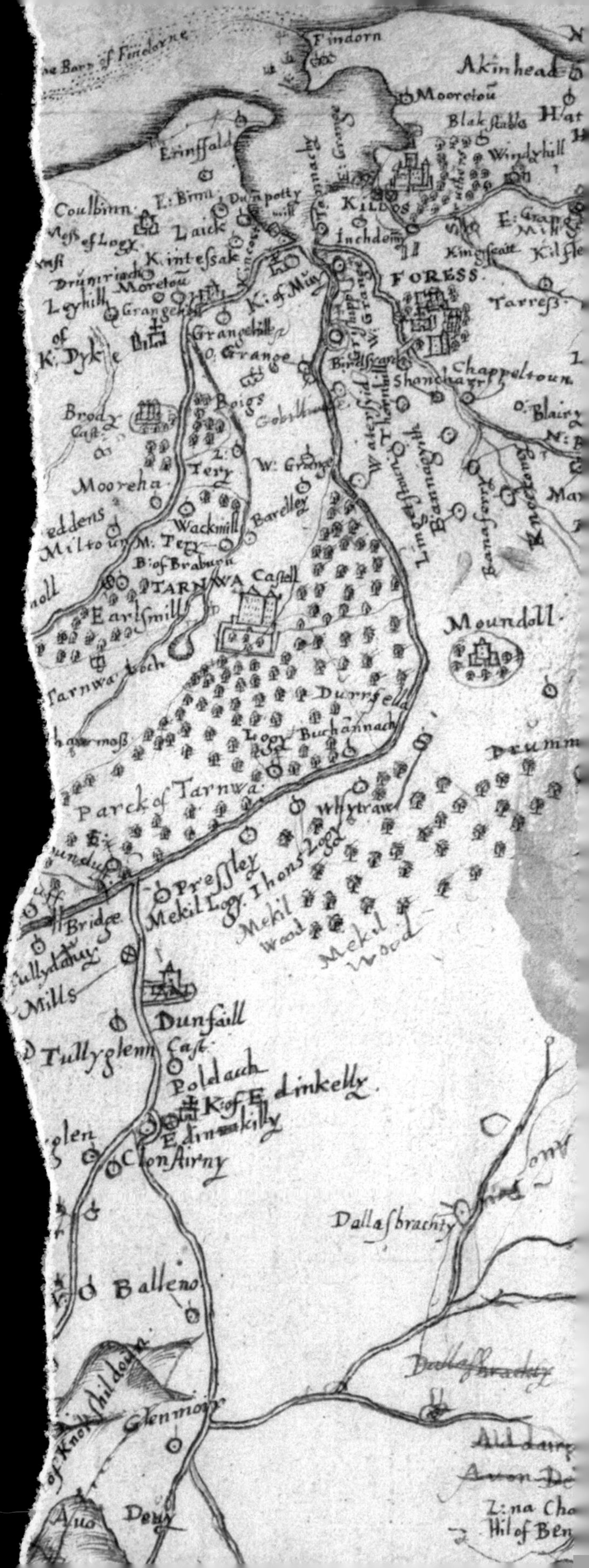
Findorn
Akinhead
Moorcotou
Windyhill
Erinsfald
Coulbinn
Laick
Kintessak
Inchdom
FORESS
Tarress
Chappeltoun
Grangehill
Mooreha
Wackmill
TARNWA Castell
Earlsmill
Moundoll
Park of Tarnwa
Whytraw
Pressley
Mekil Logy
Bridge
Mills
Dunfaill
Tullyglenn
Poldach
Edinkelly
Dallasbrachty
Balleno
Glenmore

A Note on Pronunciation

As you go through this Original Text version, you will notice how some words that usually end in "-ed" are written "-'d" whereas others are written out in full.

Shakespeare wrote much of his plays in verse, where the rhythm of the speech formed strings of "iambic pentameters", each line being five pairs of syllables, with the second syllable in each pair being the most dominant in the rhythm.

To help with enunciation and voice projection in early theaters, words that ended with "-ed" had that last syllable accented — unless to do so would have spoiled the iambic rhythm, in which case it was spoken just as we say the word today.

This speech by Macbeth:

"Accursed be that tongue that tells me so,"

would have been said as:

"Accurse–ed be that tongue that tells me so,"

so that the syllable pairs (five of them in the line) are correct in number and in emphasis (if you say it as "accurs'd" you'll see how the rhythm of the line is destroyed).

Whereas:

"And damn'd be him that first cries, 'Hold enough!'"

cannot be pronounced "dam-ned" because to do so would give eleven syllables in the line, and would not allow the right emphasis to be placed on each syllable.

In short, whenever you see a word ending "-ed" it should have its "e" pronounced to preserve the rhythm of the speech.

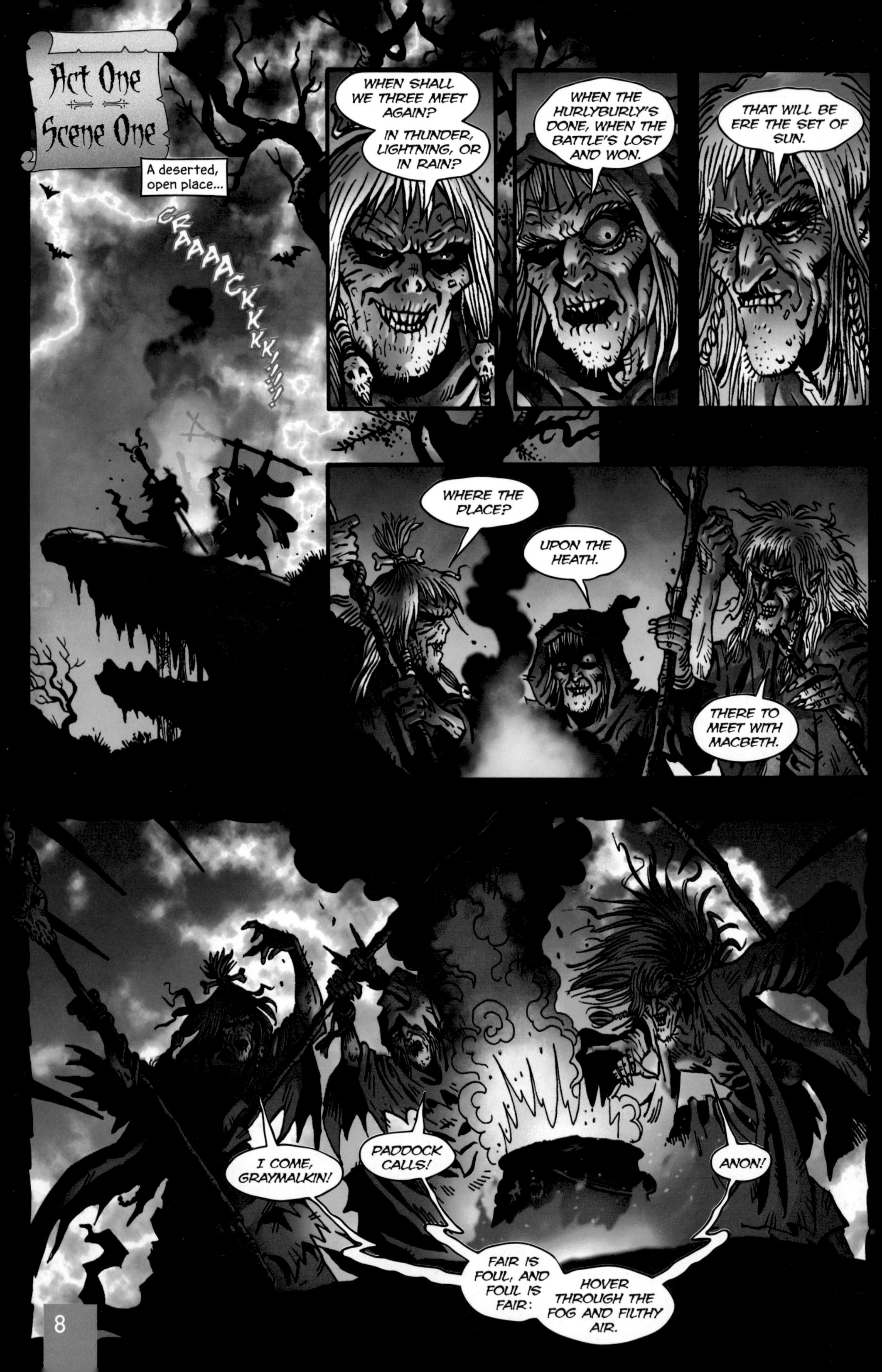
Act One
Scene One
A deserted, open place...
CRAAAACKKK!!!
WHEN SHALL WE THREE MEET AGAIN?
IN THUNDER, LIGHTNING, OR IN RAIN?
WHEN THE HURLYBURLY'S DONE, WHEN THE BATTLE'S LOST AND WON.
THAT WILL BE ERE THE SET OF SUN.
WHERE THE PLACE?
UPON THE HEATH.
THERE TO MEET WITH MACBETH.
I COME, GRAYMALKIN!
PADDOCK CALLS!
ANON!
FAIR IS FOUL, AND FOUL IS FAIR:
HOVER THROUGH THE FOG AND FILTHY AIR.

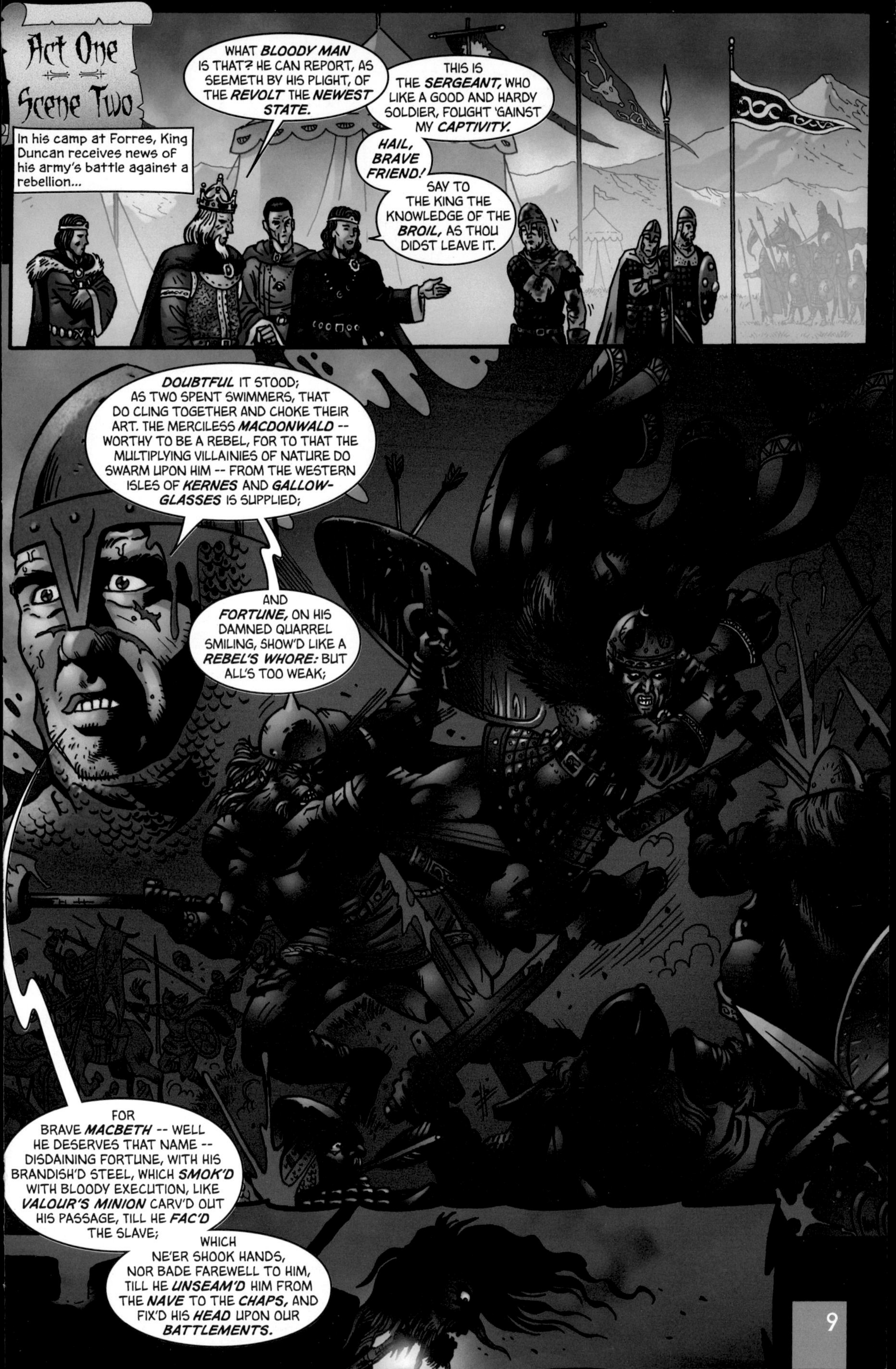

Act One
Scene Two
In his camp at Forres, King Duncan receives news of his army's battle against a rebellion...
WHAT BLOODY MAN IS THAT? HE CAN REPORT, AS SEEMETH BY HIS PLIGHT, OF THE REVOLT THE NEWEST STATE.
THIS IS THE SERGEANT, WHO LIKE A GOOD AND HARDY SOLDIER, FOUGHT 'GAINST MY CAPTIVITY.
HAIL, BRAVE FRIEND!
SAY TO THE KING THE KNOWLEDGE OF THE BROIL, AS THOU DIDST LEAVE IT.
DOUBTFUL IT STOOD; AS TWO SPENT SWIMMERS, THAT DO CLING TOGETHER AND CHOKE THEIR ART. THE MERCILESS MACDONWALD -- WORTHY TO BE A REBEL, FOR TO THAT THE MULTIPLYING VILLAINIES OF NATURE DO SWARM UPON HIM -- FROM THE WESTERN ISLES OF KERNES AND GALLOW-GLASSES IS SUPPLIED;
AND FORTUNE, ON HIS DAMNED QUARREL SMILING, SHOW'D LIKE A REBEL'S WHORE: BUT ALL'S TOO WEAK;
FOR BRAVE MACBETH -- WELL HE DESERVES THAT NAME -- DISDAINING FORTUNE, WITH HIS BRANDISH'D STEEL, WHICH SMOK'D WITH BLOODY EXECUTION, LIKE VALOUR'S MINION CARV'D OUT HIS PASSAGE, TILL HE FAC'D THE SLAVE;
WHICH NE'ER SHOOK HANDS, NOR BADE FAREWELL TO HIM, TILL HE UNSEAM'D HIM FROM THE NAVE TO THE CHAPS, AND FIX'D HIS HEAD UPON OUR BATTLEMENTS.

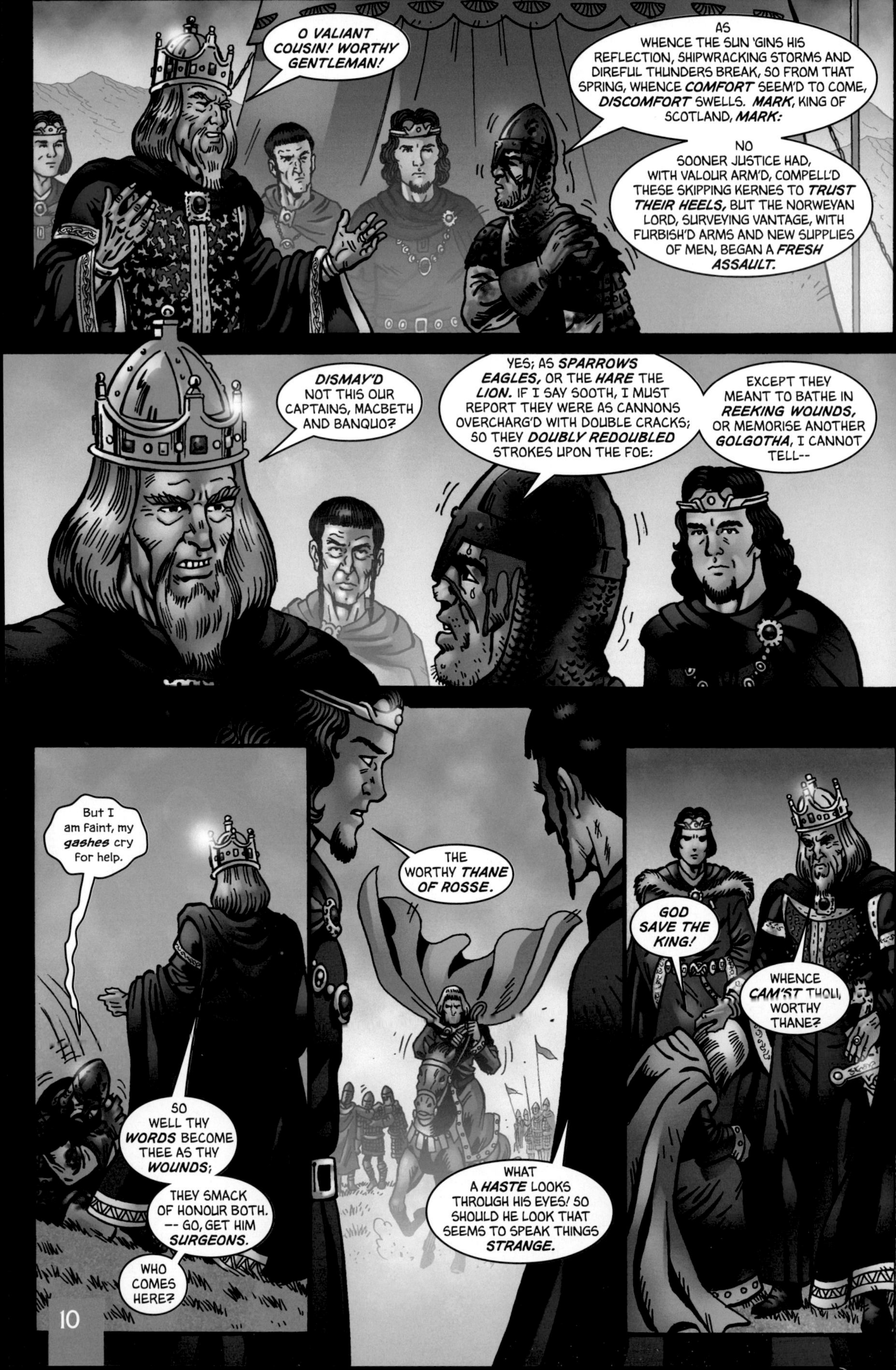
O VALIANT COUSIN! WORTHY GENTLEMAN!
AS WHENCE THE SUN 'GINS HIS REFLECTION, SHIPWRACKING STORMS AND DIREFUL THUNDERS BREAK, SO FROM THAT SPRING, WHENCE COMFORT SEEM'D TO COME, DISCOMFORT SWELLS. MARK, KING OF SCOTLAND, MARK:
NO SOONER JUSTICE HAD, WITH VALOUR ARM'D, COMPELL'D THESE SKIPPING KERNES TO TRUST THEIR HEELS, BUT THE NORWEYAN LORD, SURVEYING VANTAGE, WITH FURBISH'D ARMS AND NEW SUPPLIES OF MEN, BEGAN A FRESH ASSAULT.
DISMAY'D NOT THIS OUR CAPTAINS, MACBETH AND BANQUO?
YES; AS SPARROWS EAGLES, OR THE HARE THE LION. IF I SAY SOOTH, I MUST REPORT THEY WERE AS CANNONS OVERCHARG'D WITH DOUBLE CRACKS; SO THEY DOUBLY REDOUBLED STROKES UPON THE FOE:
EXCEPT THEY MEANT TO BATHE IN REEKING WOUNDS, OR MEMORISE ANOTHER GOLGOTHA, I CANNOT TELL--
But I am faint, my gashes cry for help.
SO WELL THY WORDS BECOME THEE AS THY WOUNDS;
THEY SMACK OF HONOUR BOTH. -- GO, GET HIM SURGEONS.
WHO COMES HERE?
THE WORTHY THANE OF ROSSE.
WHAT A HASTE LOOKS THROUGH HIS EYES! SO SHOULD HE LOOK THAT SEEMS TO SPEAK THINGS STRANGE.
GOD SAVE THE KING!
WHENCE CAM'ST THOU, WORTHY THANE?

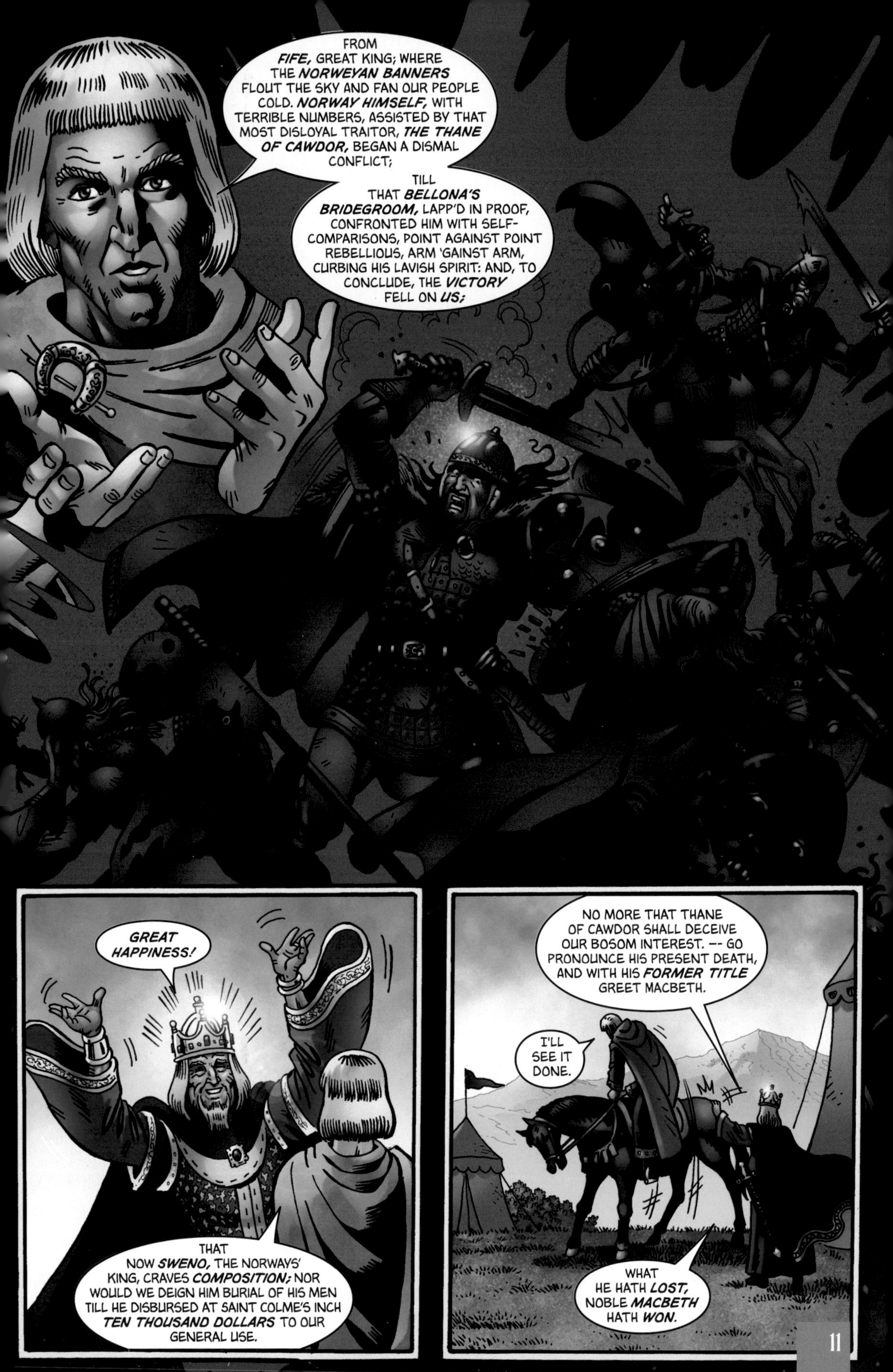
FROM FIFE, GREAT KING; WHERE THE NORWEYAN BANNERS FLOUT THE SKY AND FAN OUR PEOPLE COLD. NORWAY HIMSELF, WITH TERRIBLE NUMBERS, ASSISTED BY THAT MOST DISLOYAL TRAITOR, THE THANE OF CAWDOR, BEGAN A DISMAL CONFLICT;
TILL THAT BELLONA'S BRIDEGROOM, LAPP'D IN PROOF, CONFRONTED HIM WITH SELF-COMPARISONS, POINT AGAINST POINT REBELLIOUS, ARM 'GAINST ARM, CURBING HIS LAVISH SPIRIT: AND, TO CONCLUDE, THE VICTORY FELL ON US;
GREAT HAPPINESS!
THAT NOW SWENO, THE NORWAYS' KING, CRAVES COMPOSITION; NOR WOULD WE DEIGN HIM BURIAL OF HIS MEN TILL HE DISBURSED AT SAINT COLME'S INCH TEN THOUSAND DOLLARS TO OUR GENERAL USE.
NO MORE THAT THANE OF CAWDOR SHALL DECEIVE OUR BOSOM INTEREST. -- GO PRONOUNCE HIS PRESENT DEATH, AND WITH HIS FORMER TITLE GREET MACBETH.
I'LL SEE IT DONE.
WHAT HE HATH LOST, NOBLE MACBETH HATH WON.

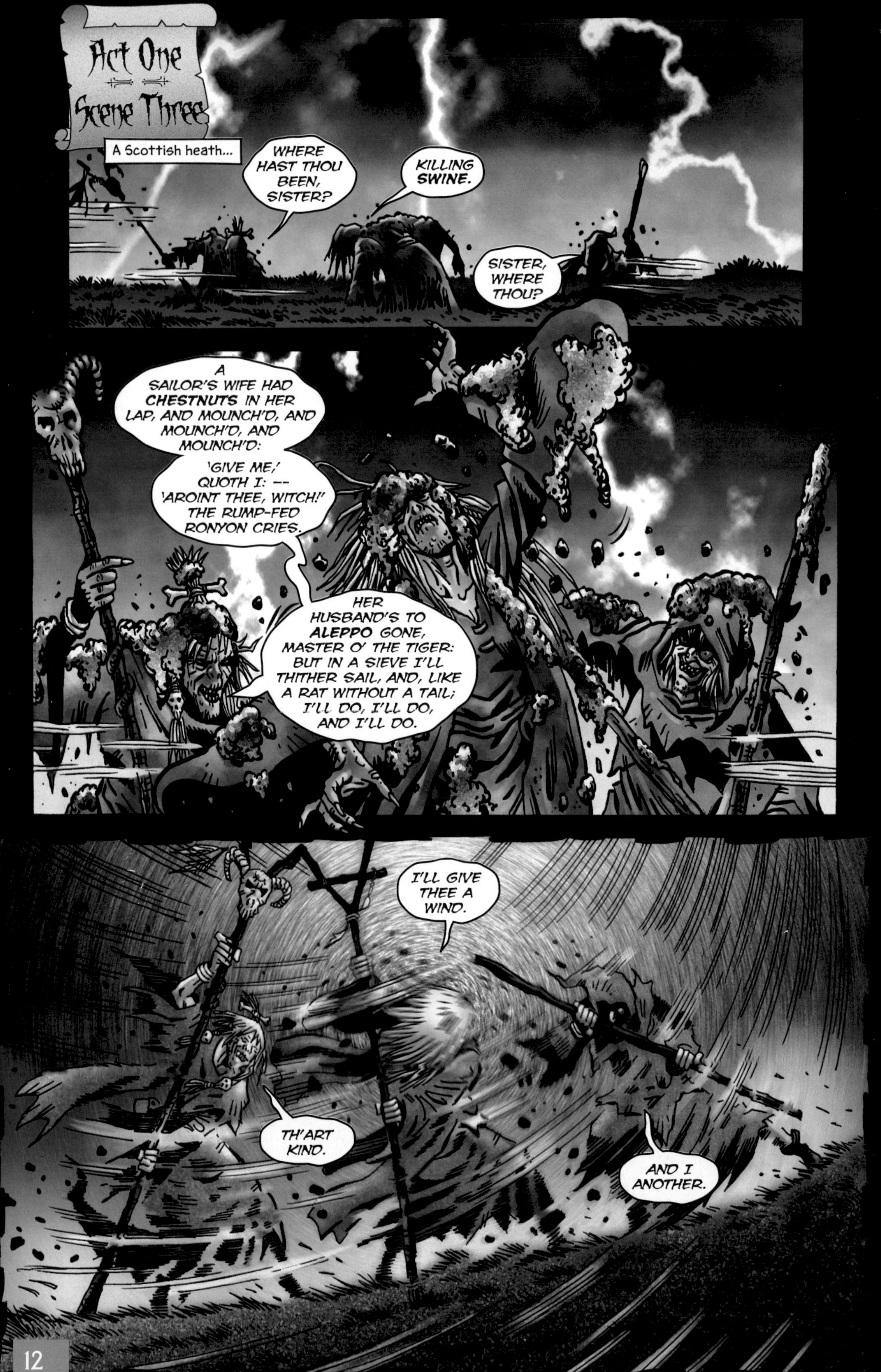
Act One
Scene Three
A Scottish heath...
WHERE HAST THOU BEEN, SISTER?
KILLING SWINE.
SISTER, WHERE THOU?
A SAILOR'S WIFE HAD CHESTNUTS IN HER LAP, AND MOUNCH'D, AND MOUNCH'D, AND MOUNCH'D:
'GIVE ME,' QUOTH I: -- 'AROINT THEE, WITCH!' THE RUMP-FED RONYON CRIES.
HER HUSBAND'S TO ALEPPO GONE, MASTER O' THE TIGER: BUT IN A SIEVE I'LL THITHER SAIL, AND, LIKE A RAT WITHOUT A TAIL; I'LL DO, I'LL DO, AND I'LL DO.
I'LL GIVE THEE A WIND.
TH'ART KIND.
AND I ANOTHER.

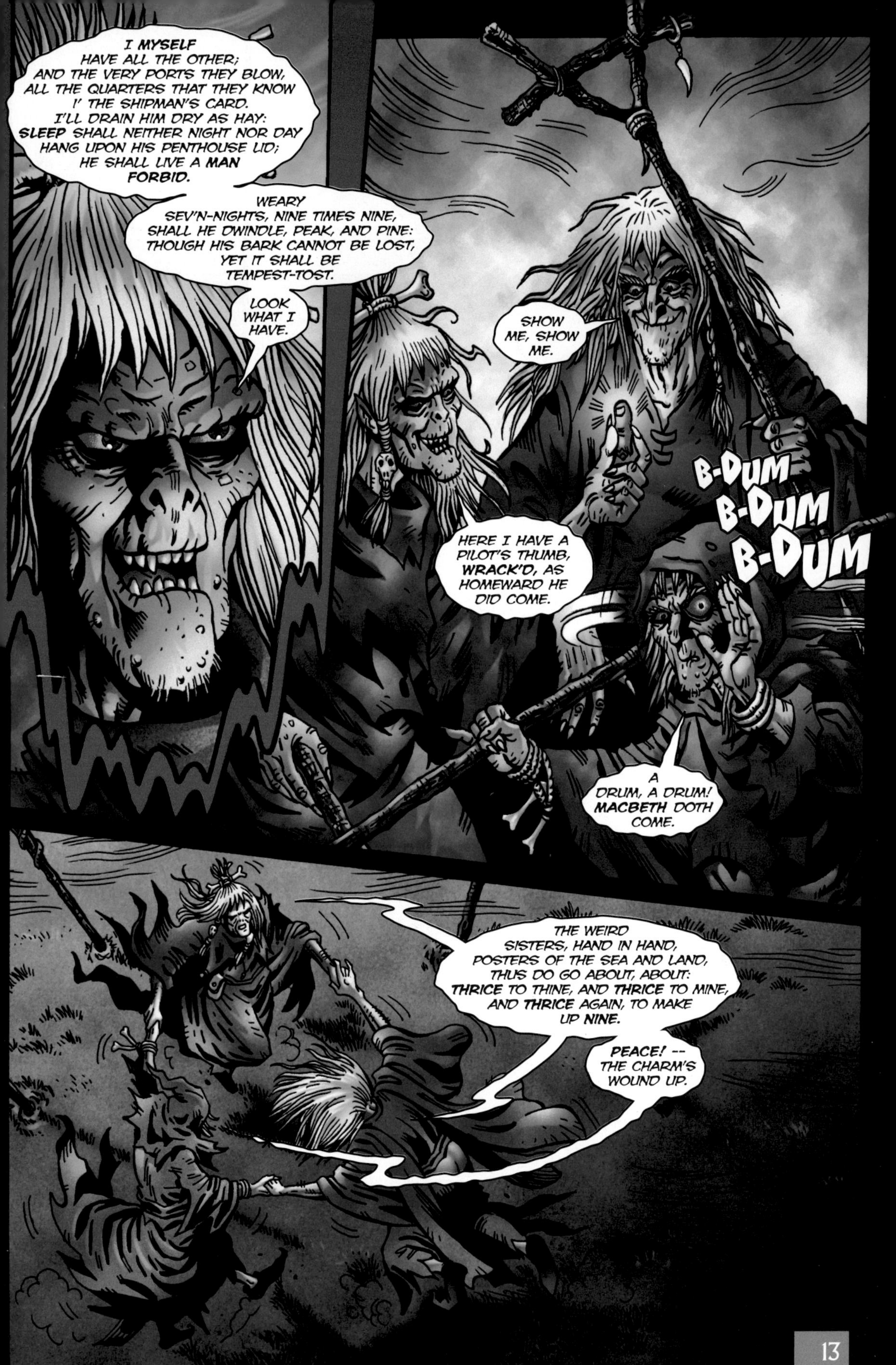
I MYSELF HAVE ALL THE OTHER; AND THE VERY PORTS THEY BLOW, ALL THE QUARTERS THAT THEY KNOW I' THE SHIPMAN'S CARD. I'LL DRAIN HIM DRY AS HAY: SLEEP SHALL NEITHER NIGHT NOR DAY HANG UPON HIS PENTHOUSE LID; HE SHALL LIVE A MAN FORBID.
WEARY SEV'N-NIGHTS, NINE TIMES NINE, SHALL HE DWINDLE, PEAK, AND PINE: THOUGH HIS BARK CANNOT BE LOST, YET IT SHALL BE TEMPEST-TOST.
LOOK WHAT I HAVE.
SHOW ME, SHOW ME.
HERE I HAVE A PILOT'S THUMB, WRACK'D, AS HOMEWARD HE DID COME.
B-DUM B-DUM B-DUM
A DRUM, A DRUM! MACBETH DOTH COME.
THE WEIRD SISTERS, HAND IN HAND, POSTERS OF THE SEA AND LAND, THUS DO GO ABOUT, ABOUT: THRICE TO THINE, AND THRICE TO MINE, AND THRICE AGAIN, TO MAKE UP NINE.
PEACE! -- THE CHARM'S WOUND UP.

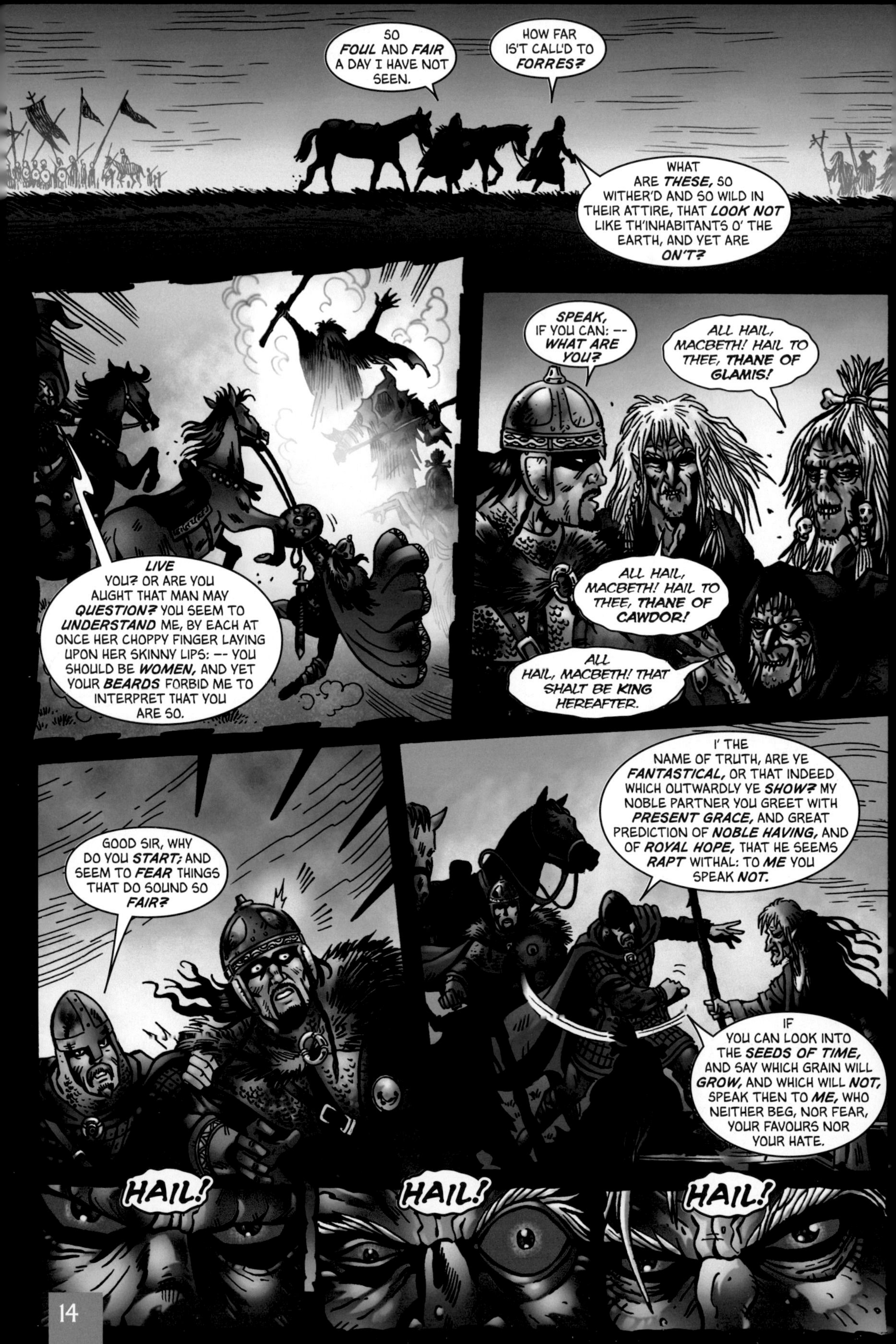
SO FOUL AND FAIR A DAY I HAVE NOT SEEN.
HOW FAR IS'T CALL'D TO FORRES?
WHAT ARE THESE, SO WITHER'D AND SO WILD IN THEIR ATTIRE, THAT LOOK NOT LIKE TH'INHABITANTS O' THE EARTH, AND YET ARE ON'T?
LIVE YOU? OR ARE YOU AUGHT THAT MAN MAY QUESTION? YOU SEEM TO UNDERSTAND ME, BY EACH AT ONCE HER CHOPPY FINGER LAYING UPON HER SKINNY LIPS: -- YOU SHOULD BE WOMEN, AND YET YOUR BEARDS FORBID ME TO INTERPRET THAT YOU ARE SO.
SPEAK, IF YOU CAN: -- WHAT ARE YOU?
ALL HAIL, MACBETH! HAIL TO THEE, THANE OF GLAMIS!
ALL HAIL, MACBETH! HAIL TO THEE, THANE OF CAWDOR!
ALL HAIL, MACBETH! THAT SHALT BE KING HEREAFTER.
GOOD SIR, WHY DO YOU START; AND SEEM TO FEAR THINGS THAT DO SOUND SO FAIR?
I' THE NAME OF TRUTH, ARE YE FANTASTICAL, OR THAT INDEED WHICH OUTWARDLY YE SHOW? MY NOBLE PARTNER YOU GREET WITH PRESENT GRACE, AND GREAT PREDICTION OF NOBLE HAVING, AND OF ROYAL HOPE, THAT HE SEEMS RAPT WITHAL: TO ME YOU SPEAK NOT.
IF YOU CAN LOOK INTO THE SEEDS OF TIME, AND SAY WHICH GRAIN WILL GROW, AND WHICH WILL NOT, SPEAK THEN TO ME, WHO NEITHER BEG, NOR FEAR, YOUR FAVOURS NOR YOUR HATE.
HAIL!
HAIL!
HAIL!

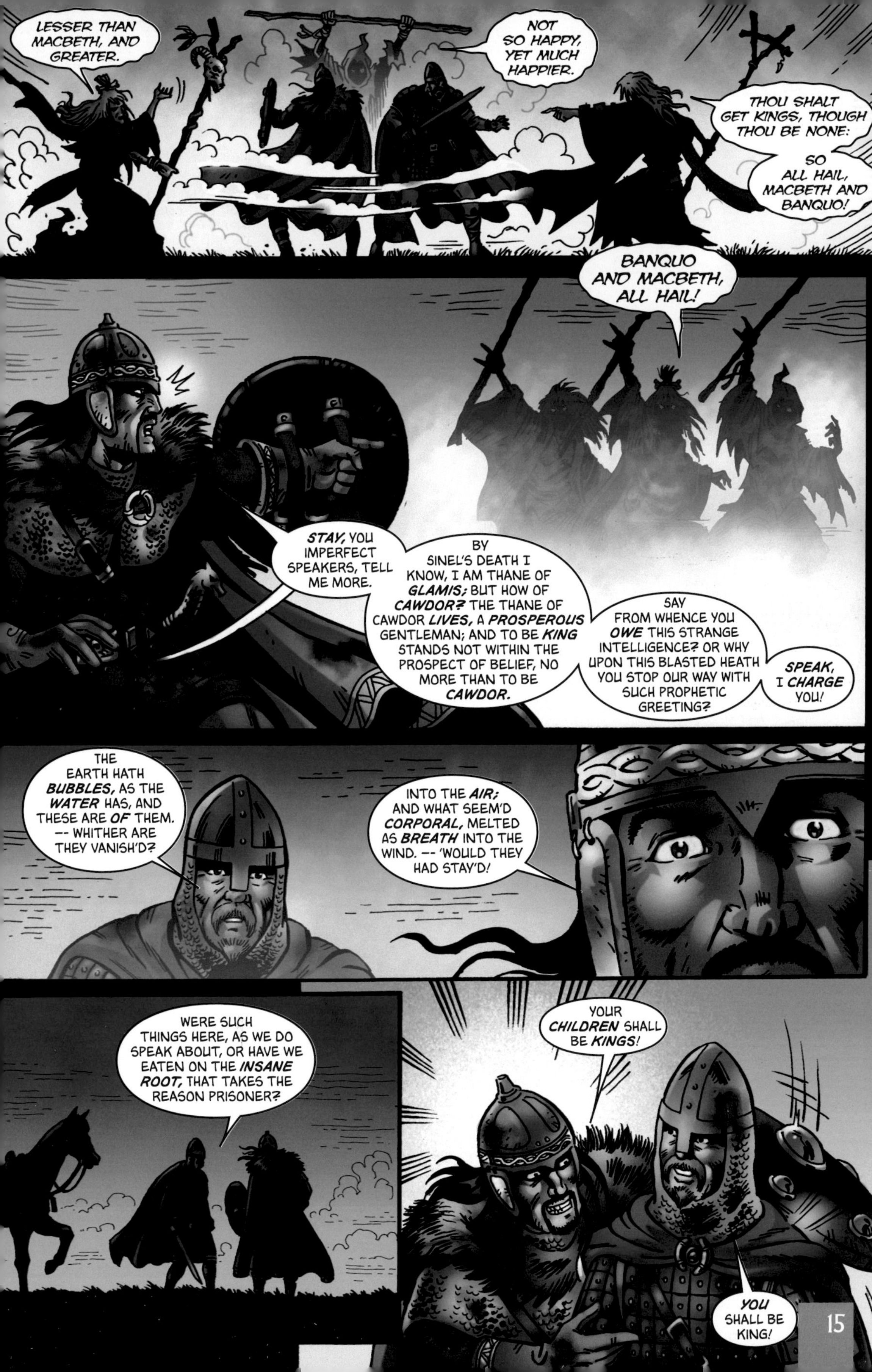
LESSER THAN MACBETH, AND GREATER.
NOT SO HAPPY, YET MUCH HAPPIER.
THOU SHALT GET KINGS, THOUGH THOU BE NONE:
SO ALL HAIL, MACBETH AND BANQUO!
BANQUO AND MACBETH, ALL HAIL!
STAY, YOU IMPERFECT SPEAKERS, TELL ME MORE.
BY SINEL'S DEATH I KNOW, I AM THANE OF GLAMIS; BUT HOW OF CAWDOR? THE THANE OF CAWDOR LIVES, A PROSPEROUS GENTLEMAN; AND TO BE KING STANDS NOT WITHIN THE PROSPECT OF BELIEF, NO MORE THAN TO BE CAWDOR.
SAY FROM WHENCE YOU OWE THIS STRANGE INTELLIGENCE? OR WHY UPON THIS BLASTED HEATH YOU STOP OUR WAY WITH SUCH PROPHETIC GREETING?
SPEAK, I CHARGE YOU!
THE EARTH HATH BUBBLES, AS THE WATER HAS, AND THESE ARE OF THEM. -- WHITHER ARE THEY VANISH'D?
INTO THE AIR; AND WHAT SEEM'D CORPORAL, MELTED AS BREATH INTO THE WIND. -- 'WOULD THEY HAD STAY'D!
WERE SUCH THINGS HERE, AS WE DO SPEAK ABOUT, OR HAVE WE EATEN ON THE INSANE ROOT, THAT TAKES THE REASON PRISONER?
YOUR CHILDREN SHALL BE KINGS!
YOU SHALL BE KING!

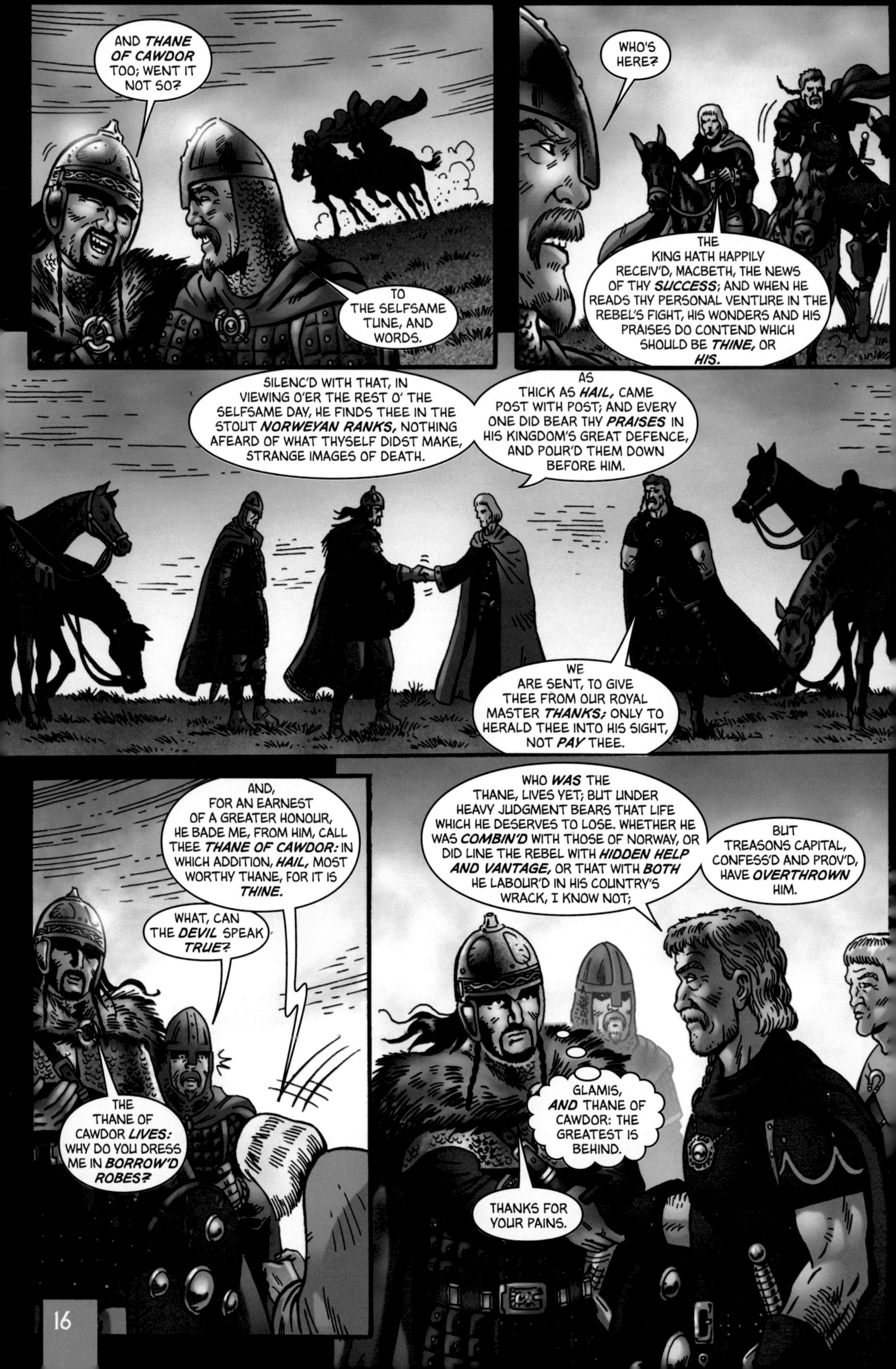
AND THANE OF CAWDOR TOO; WENT IT NOT SO?
TO THE SELFSAME TUNE, AND WORDS.
WHO'S HERE?
THE KING HATH HAPPILY RECEIV'D, MACBETH, THE NEWS OF THY SUCCESS; AND WHEN HE READS THY PERSONAL VENTURE IN THE REBEL'S FIGHT, HIS WONDERS AND HIS PRAISES DO CONTEND WHICH SHOULD BE THINE, OR HIS.
SILENC'D WITH THAT, IN VIEWING O'ER THE REST O' THE SELFSAME DAY, HE FINDS THEE IN THE STOUT NORWEYAN RANKS, NOTHING AFEARD OF WHAT THYSELF DIDST MAKE, STRANGE IMAGES OF DEATH.
AS THICK AS HAIL, CAME POST WITH POST; AND EVERY ONE DID BEAR THY PRAISES IN HIS KINGDOM'S GREAT DEFENCE, AND POUR'D THEM DOWN BEFORE HIM.
WE ARE SENT, TO GIVE THEE FROM OUR ROYAL MASTER THANKS; ONLY TO HERALD THEE INTO HIS SIGHT, NOT PAY THEE.
AND, FOR AN EARNEST OF A GREATER HONOUR, HE BADE ME, FROM HIM, CALL THEE THANE OF CAWDOR: IN WHICH ADDITION, HAIL, MOST WORTHY THANE, FOR IT IS THINE.
WHAT, CAN THE DEVIL SPEAK TRUE?
THE THANE OF CAWDOR LIVES: WHY DO YOU DRESS ME IN BORROW'D ROBES?
WHO WAS THE THANE, LIVES YET; BUT UNDER HEAVY JUDGMENT BEARS THAT LIFE WHICH HE DESERVES TO LOSE. WHETHER HE WAS COMBIN'D WITH THOSE OF NORWAY, OR DID LINE THE REBEL WITH HIDDEN HELP AND VANTAGE, OR THAT WITH BOTH HE LABOUR'D IN HIS COUNTRY'S WRACK, I KNOW NOT;
BUT TREASONS CAPITAL, CONFESS'D AND PROV'D, HAVE OVERTHROWN HIM.
GLAMIS, AND THANE OF CAWDOR: THE GREATEST IS BEHIND.
THANKS FOR YOUR PAINS.

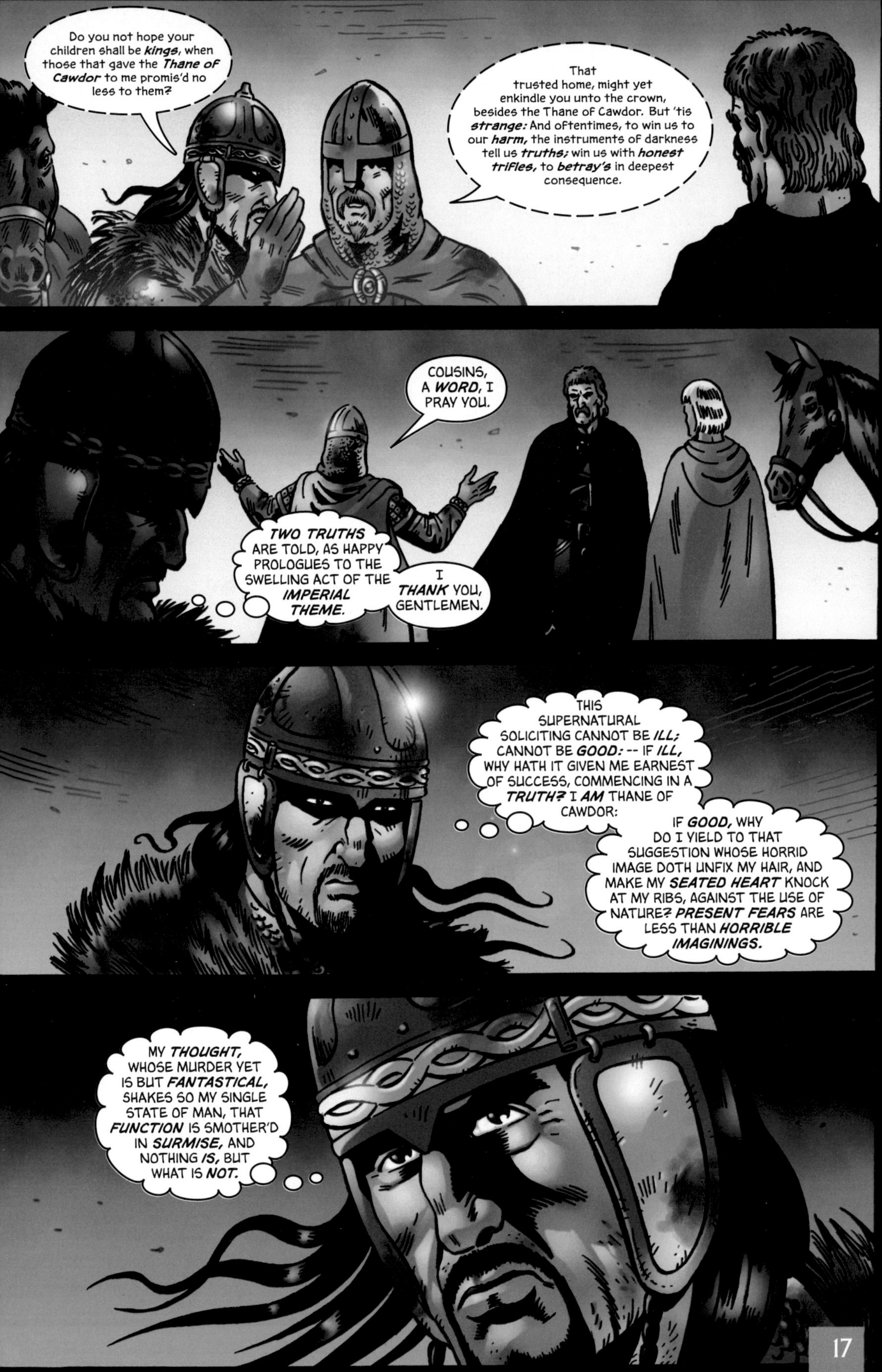

Do you not hope your children shall be *kings*, when those that gave the *Thane of Cawdor* to me promis'd no less to them?
That trusted home, might yet enkindle you unto the crown, besides the Thane of Cawdor. But 'tis *strange:* And oftentimes, to win us to our *harm,* the instruments of darkness tell us *truths;* win us with *honest trifles,* to *betray's* in deepest consequence.
COUSINS, A *WORD*, I PRAY YOU.
TWO TRUTHS ARE TOLD, AS HAPPY PROLOGUES TO THE SWELLING ACT OF THE *IMPERIAL THEME.*
I *THANK* YOU, GENTLEMEN.
THIS SUPERNATURAL SOLICITING CANNOT BE *ILL;* CANNOT BE *GOOD:* -- IF *ILL,* WHY HATH IT GIVEN ME EARNEST OF SUCCESS, COMMENCING IN A *TRUTH?* I *AM* THANE OF CAWDOR:
IF *GOOD,* WHY DO I YIELD TO THAT SUGGESTION WHOSE HORRID IMAGE DOTH UNFIX MY HAIR, AND MAKE MY *SEATED HEART* KNOCK AT MY RIBS, AGAINST THE USE OF NATURE? *PRESENT FEARS* ARE LESS THAN *HORRIBLE IMAGININGS.*
MY *THOUGHT,* WHOSE MURDER YET IS BUT *FANTASTICAL,* SHAKES SO MY SINGLE STATE OF MAN, THAT *FUNCTION* IS SMOTHER'D IN *SURMISE,* AND NOTHING *IS,* BUT WHAT IS *NOT.*

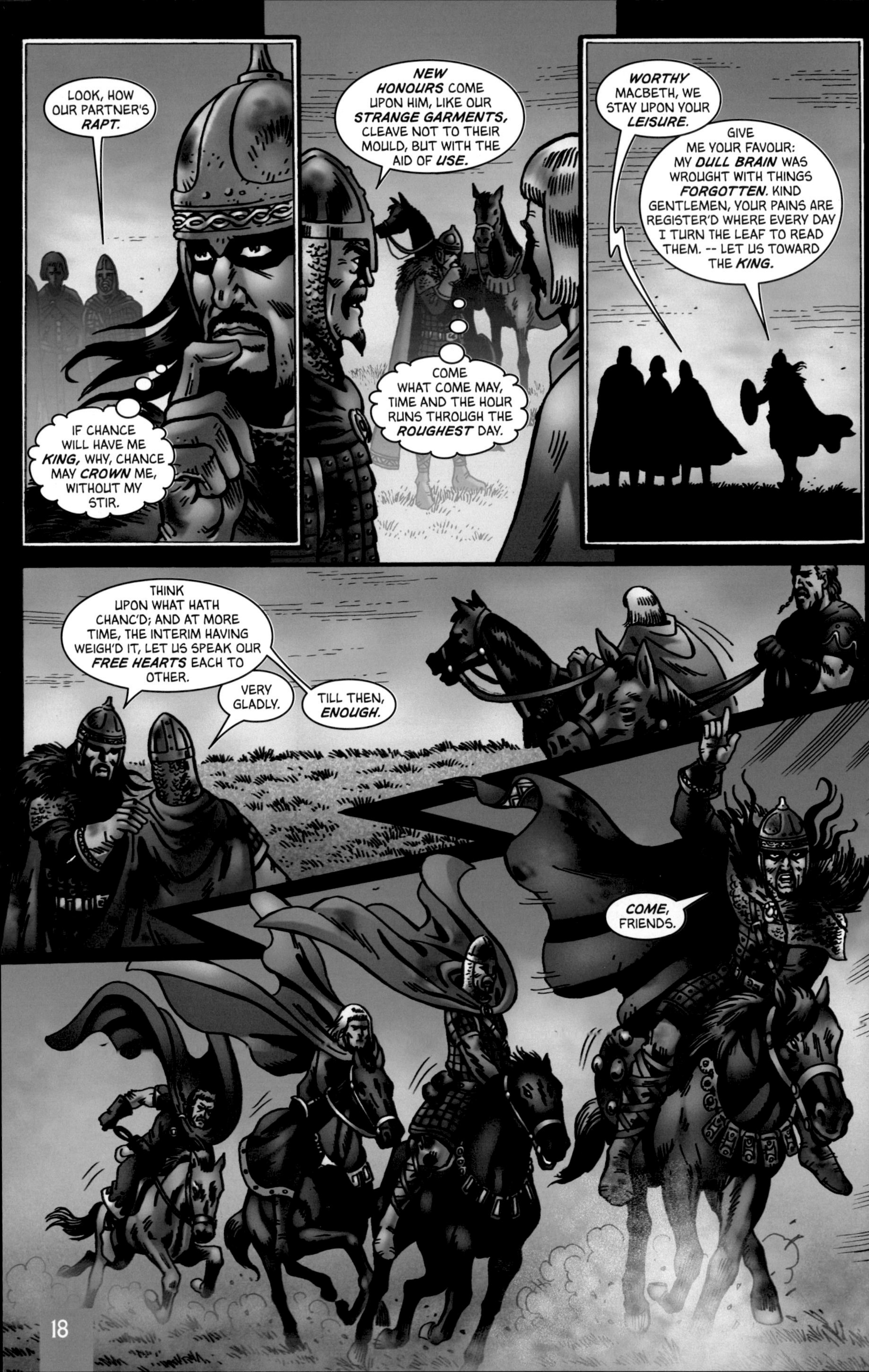
LOOK, HOW OUR PARTNER'S RAPT.
IF CHANCE WILL HAVE ME KING, WHY, CHANCE MAY CROWN ME, WITHOUT MY STIR.
NEW HONOURS COME UPON HIM, LIKE OUR STRANGE GARMENTS, CLEAVE NOT TO THEIR MOULD, BUT WITH THE AID OF USE.
COME WHAT COME MAY, TIME AND THE HOUR RUNS THROUGH THE ROUGHEST DAY.
WORTHY MACBETH, WE STAY UPON YOUR LEISURE.
GIVE ME YOUR FAVOUR: MY DULL BRAIN WAS WROUGHT WITH THINGS FORGOTTEN. KIND GENTLEMEN, YOUR PAINS ARE REGISTER'D WHERE EVERY DAY I TURN THE LEAF TO READ THEM. -- LET US TOWARD THE KING.
THINK UPON WHAT HATH CHANC'D; AND AT MORE TIME, THE INTERIM HAVING WEIGH'D IT, LET US SPEAK OUR FREE HEARTS EACH TO OTHER.
VERY GLADLY.
TILL THEN, ENOUGH.
COME, FRIENDS.

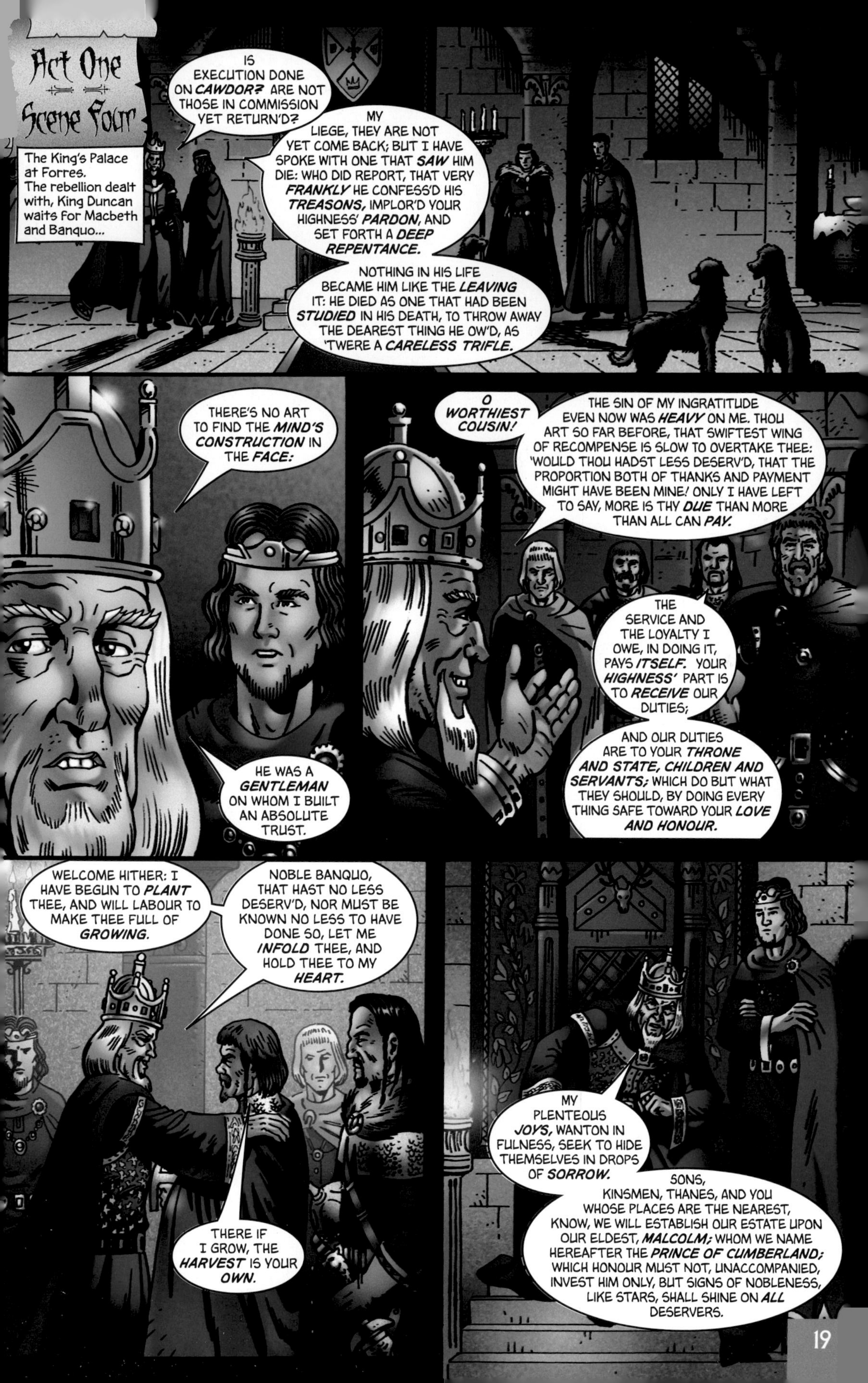
Act One
Scene Four
The King's Palace at Forres. The rebellion dealt with, King Duncan waits for Macbeth and Banquo...
IS EXECUTION DONE ON CAWDOR? ARE NOT THOSE IN COMMISSION YET RETURN'D?
MY LIEGE, THEY ARE NOT YET COME BACK; BUT I HAVE SPOKE WITH ONE THAT SAW HIM DIE: WHO DID REPORT, THAT VERY FRANKLY HE CONFESS'D HIS TREASONS, IMPLOR'D YOUR HIGHNESS' PARDON, AND SET FORTH A DEEP REPENTANCE.
NOTHING IN HIS LIFE BECAME HIM LIKE THE LEAVING IT: HE DIED AS ONE THAT HAD BEEN STUDIED IN HIS DEATH, TO THROW AWAY THE DEAREST THING HE OW'D, AS 'TWERE A CARELESS TRIFLE.
THERE'S NO ART TO FIND THE MIND'S CONSTRUCTION IN THE FACE:
HE WAS A GENTLEMAN ON WHOM I BUILT AN ABSOLUTE TRUST.
O WORTHIEST COUSIN!
THE SIN OF MY INGRATITUDE EVEN NOW WAS HEAVY ON ME. THOU ART SO FAR BEFORE, THAT SWIFTEST WING OF RECOMPENSE IS SLOW TO OVERTAKE THEE: 'WOULD THOU HADST LESS DESERV'D, THAT THE PROPORTION BOTH OF THANKS AND PAYMENT MIGHT HAVE BEEN MINE! ONLY I HAVE LEFT TO SAY, MORE IS THY DUE THAN MORE THAN ALL CAN PAY.
THE SERVICE AND THE LOYALTY I OWE, IN DOING IT, PAYS ITSELF. YOUR HIGHNESS' PART IS TO RECEIVE OUR DUTIES;
AND OUR DUTIES ARE TO YOUR THRONE AND STATE, CHILDREN AND SERVANTS; WHICH DO BUT WHAT THEY SHOULD, BY DOING EVERY THING SAFE TOWARD YOUR LOVE AND HONOUR.
WELCOME HITHER: I HAVE BEGUN TO PLANT THEE, AND WILL LABOUR TO MAKE THEE FULL OF GROWING.
NOBLE BANQUO, THAT HAST NO LESS DESERV'D, NOR MUST BE KNOWN NO LESS TO HAVE DONE SO, LET ME INFOLD THEE, AND HOLD THEE TO MY HEART.
THERE IF I GROW, THE HARVEST IS YOUR OWN.
MY PLENTEOUS JOYS, WANTON IN FULNESS, SEEK TO HIDE THEMSELVES IN DROPS OF SORROW.
SONS, KINSMEN, THANES, AND YOU WHOSE PLACES ARE THE NEAREST, KNOW, WE WILL ESTABLISH OUR ESTATE UPON OUR ELDEST, MALCOLM; WHOM WE NAME HEREAFTER THE PRINCE OF CUMBERLAND; WHICH HONOUR MUST NOT, UNACCOMPANIED, INVEST HIM ONLY, BUT SIGNS OF NOBLENESS, LIKE STARS, SHALL SHINE ON ALL DESERVERS.

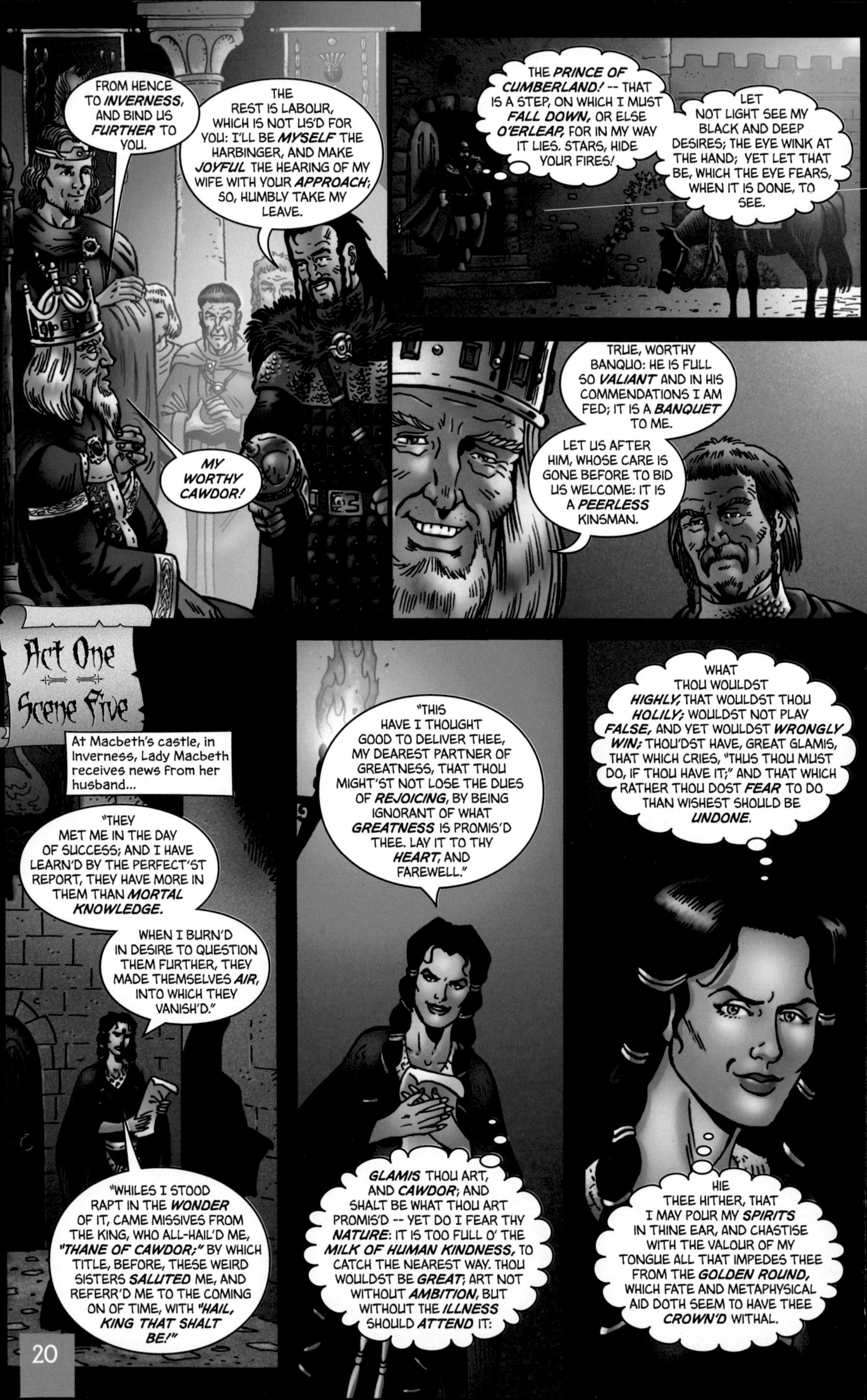
FROM HENCE TO INVERNESS, AND BIND US FURTHER TO YOU.
THE REST IS LABOUR, WHICH IS NOT US'D FOR YOU: I'LL BE MYSELF THE HARBINGER, AND MAKE JOYFUL THE HEARING OF MY WIFE WITH YOUR APPROACH; SO, HUMBLY TAKE MY LEAVE.
MY WORTHY CAWDOR!
THE PRINCE OF CUMBERLAND! -- THAT IS A STEP, ON WHICH I MUST FALL DOWN, OR ELSE O'ERLEAP, FOR IN MY WAY IT LIES. STARS, HIDE YOUR FIRES!
LET NOT LIGHT SEE MY BLACK AND DEEP DESIRES; THE EYE WINK AT THE HAND; YET LET THAT BE, WHICH THE EYE FEARS, WHEN IT IS DONE, TO SEE.
TRUE, WORTHY BANQUO: HE IS FULL SO VALIANT AND IN HIS COMMENDATIONS I AM FED; IT IS A BANQUET TO ME.
LET US AFTER HIM, WHOSE CARE IS GONE BEFORE TO BID US WELCOME: IT IS A PEERLESS KINSMAN.
Act One
Scene Five
At Macbeth's castle, in Inverness, Lady Macbeth receives news from her husband...
"THEY MET ME IN THE DAY OF SUCCESS; AND I HAVE LEARN'D BY THE PERFECT'ST REPORT, THEY HAVE MORE IN THEM THAN MORTAL KNOWLEDGE.
WHEN I BURN'D IN DESIRE TO QUESTION THEM FURTHER, THEY MADE THEMSELVES AIR, INTO WHICH THEY VANISH'D."
"WHILES I STOOD RAPT IN THE WONDER OF IT, CAME MISSIVES FROM THE KING, WHO ALL-HAIL'D ME, "THANE OF CAWDOR;" BY WHICH TITLE, BEFORE, THESE WEIRD SISTERS SALUTED ME, AND REFERR'D ME TO THE COMING ON OF TIME, WITH "HAIL, KING THAT SHALT BE!"
"THIS HAVE I THOUGHT GOOD TO DELIVER THEE, MY DEAREST PARTNER OF GREATNESS, THAT THOU MIGHT'ST NOT LOSE THE DUES OF REJOICING, BY BEING IGNORANT OF WHAT GREATNESS IS PROMIS'D THEE. LAY IT TO THY HEART, AND FAREWELL."
GLAMIS THOU ART, AND CAWDOR; AND SHALT BE WHAT THOU ART PROMIS'D -- YET DO I FEAR THY NATURE: IT IS TOO FULL O' THE MILK OF HUMAN KINDNESS, TO CATCH THE NEAREST WAY. THOU WOULDST BE GREAT; ART NOT WITHOUT AMBITION, BUT WITHOUT THE ILLNESS SHOULD ATTEND IT:
WHAT THOU WOULDST HIGHLY, THAT WOULDST THOU HOLILY; WOULDST NOT PLAY FALSE, AND YET WOULDST WRONGLY WIN; THOU'DST HAVE, GREAT GLAMIS, THAT WHICH CRIES, "THUS THOU MUST DO, IF THOU HAVE IT;" AND THAT WHICH RATHER THOU DOST FEAR TO DO THAN WISHEST SHOULD BE UNDONE.
HIE THEE HITHER, THAT I MAY POUR MY SPIRITS IN THINE EAR, AND CHASTISE WITH THE VALOUR OF MY TONGUE ALL THAT IMPEDES THEE FROM THE GOLDEN ROUND, WHICH FATE AND METAPHYSICAL AID DOTH SEEM TO HAVE THEE CROWN'D WITHAL.

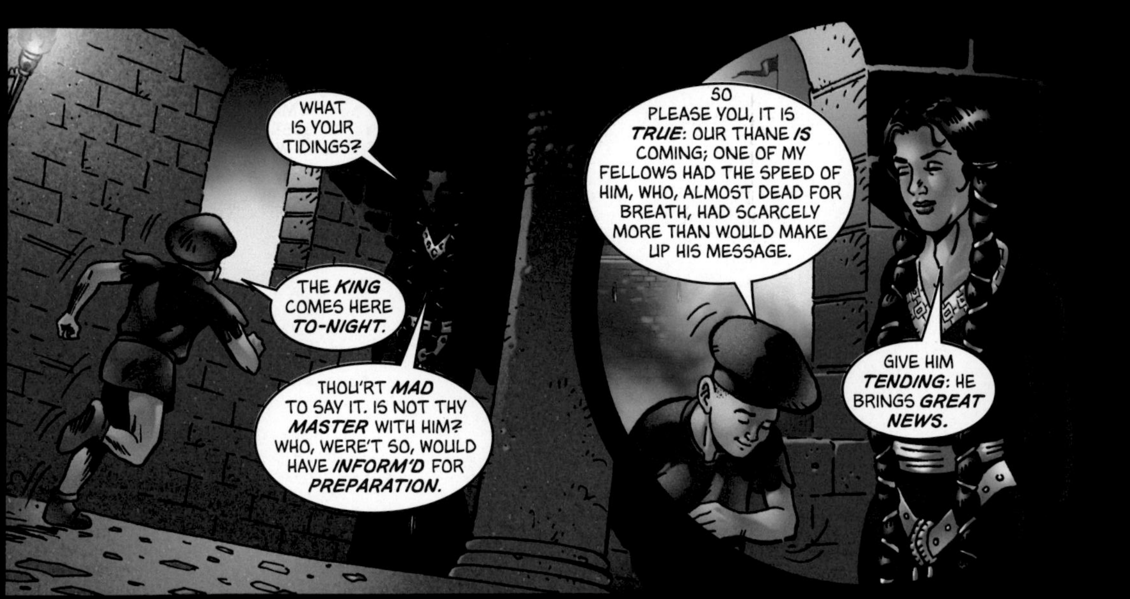
WHAT IS YOUR TIDINGS?
THE *KING* COMES HERE *TO-NIGHT.*
THOU'RT *MAD* TO SAY IT. IS NOT THY *MASTER* WITH HIM? WHO, WERE'T SO, WOULD HAVE *INFORM'D* FOR *PREPARATION.*
SO PLEASE YOU, IT IS *TRUE*: OUR THANE *IS* COMING; ONE OF MY FELLOWS HAD THE SPEED OF HIM, WHO, ALMOST DEAD FOR BREATH, HAD SCARCELY MORE THAN WOULD MAKE UP HIS MESSAGE.
GIVE HIM *TENDING*: HE BRINGS *GREAT NEWS.*

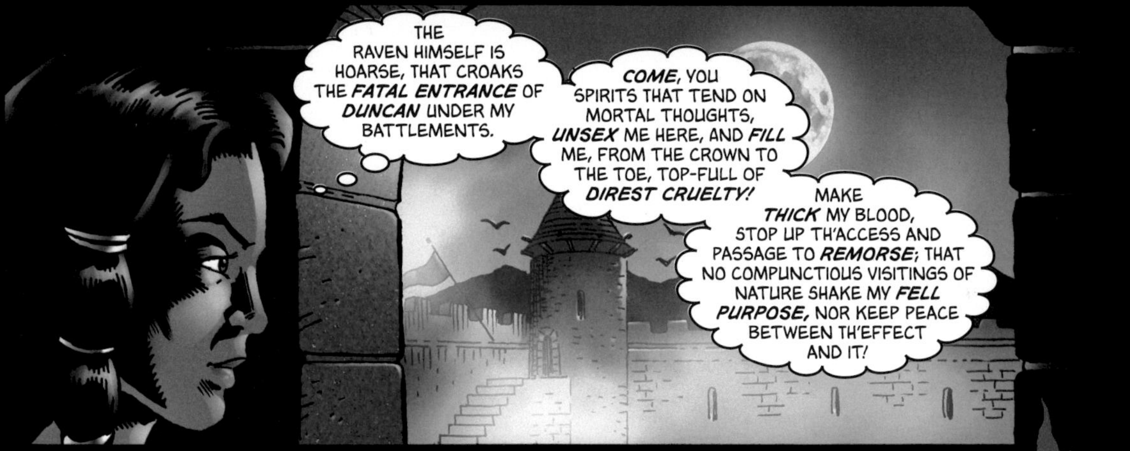
THE RAVEN HIMSELF IS HOARSE, THAT CROAKS THE *FATAL ENTRANCE* OF *DUNCAN* UNDER MY BATTLEMENTS.
COME, YOU SPIRITS THAT TEND ON MORTAL THOUGHTS, *UNSEX* ME HERE, AND *FILL* ME, FROM THE CROWN TO THE TOE, TOP-FULL OF *DIREST CRUELTY!*
MAKE *THICK* MY BLOOD, STOP UP TH'ACCESS AND PASSAGE TO *REMORSE*; THAT NO COMPUNCTIOUS VISITINGS OF NATURE SHAKE MY *FELL PURPOSE,* NOR KEEP PEACE BETWEEN TH'EFFECT AND IT!

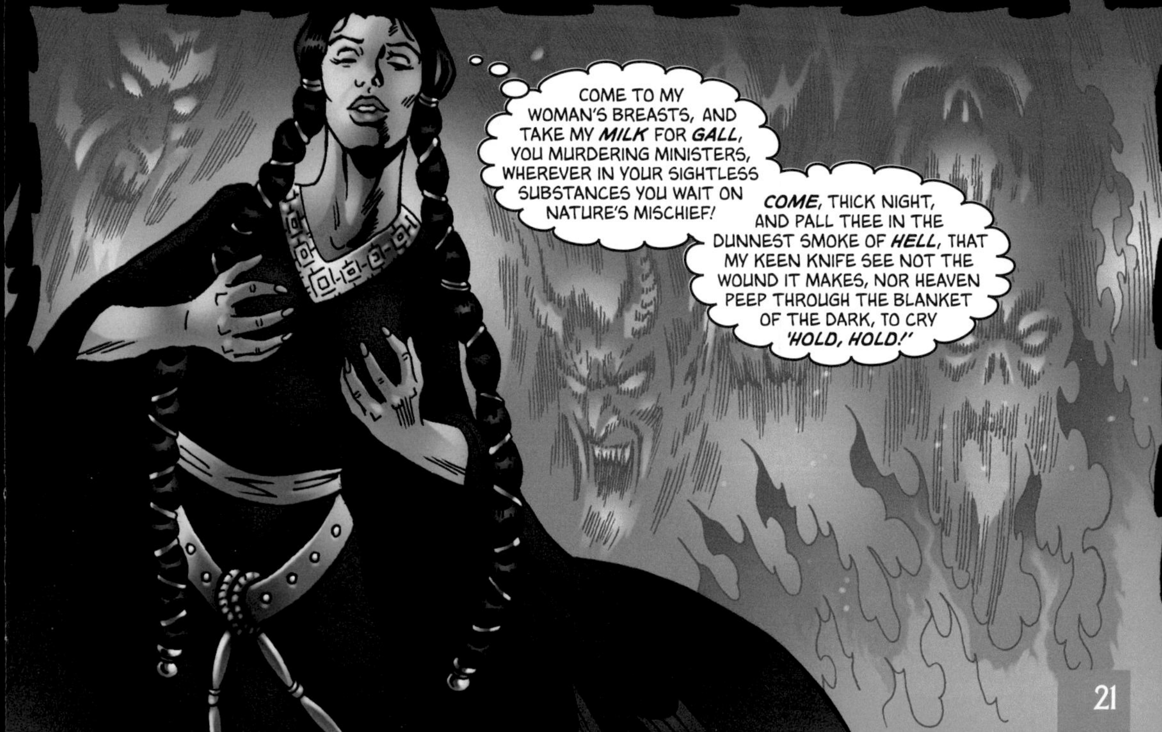
COME TO MY WOMAN'S BREASTS, AND TAKE MY *MILK* FOR *GALL*, YOU MURDERING MINISTERS, WHEREVER IN YOUR SIGHTLESS SUBSTANCES YOU WAIT ON NATURE'S MISCHIEF!
COME, THICK NIGHT, AND PALL THEE IN THE DUNNEST SMOKE OF *HELL*, THAT MY KEEN KNIFE SEE NOT THE WOUND IT MAKES, NOR HEAVEN PEEP THROUGH THE BLANKET OF THE DARK, TO CRY *'HOLD, HOLD!'*

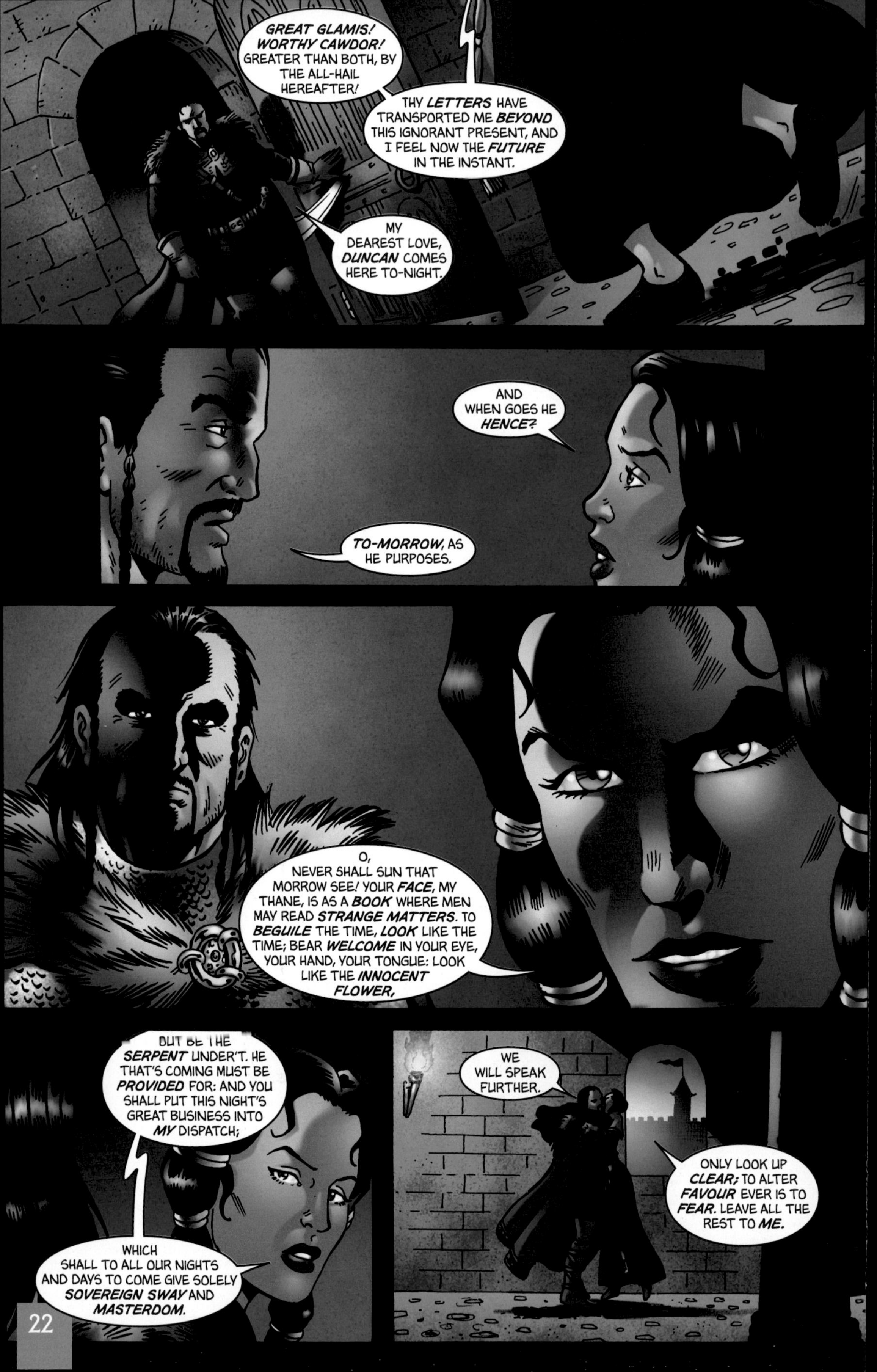
GREAT GLAMIS! WORTHY CAWDOR! GREATER THAN BOTH, BY THE ALL-HAIL HEREAFTER!
THY LETTERS HAVE TRANSPORTED ME BEYOND THIS IGNORANT PRESENT, AND I FEEL NOW THE FUTURE IN THE INSTANT.
MY DEAREST LOVE, DUNCAN COMES HERE TO-NIGHT.
AND WHEN GOES HE HENCE?
TO-MORROW, AS HE PURPOSES.
O, NEVER SHALL SUN THAT MORROW SEE! YOUR FACE, MY THANE, IS AS A BOOK WHERE MEN MAY READ STRANGE MATTERS. TO BEGUILE THE TIME, LOOK LIKE THE TIME; BEAR WELCOME IN YOUR EYE, YOUR HAND, YOUR TONGUE: LOOK LIKE THE INNOCENT FLOWER,
BUT BE THE SERPENT UNDER'T. HE THAT'S COMING MUST BE PROVIDED FOR: AND YOU SHALL PUT THIS NIGHT'S GREAT BUSINESS INTO MY DISPATCH;
WHICH SHALL TO ALL OUR NIGHTS AND DAYS TO COME GIVE SOLELY SOVEREIGN SWAY AND MASTERDOM.
WE WILL SPEAK FURTHER.
ONLY LOOK UP CLEAR; TO ALTER FAVOUR EVER IS TO FEAR. LEAVE ALL THE REST TO ME.

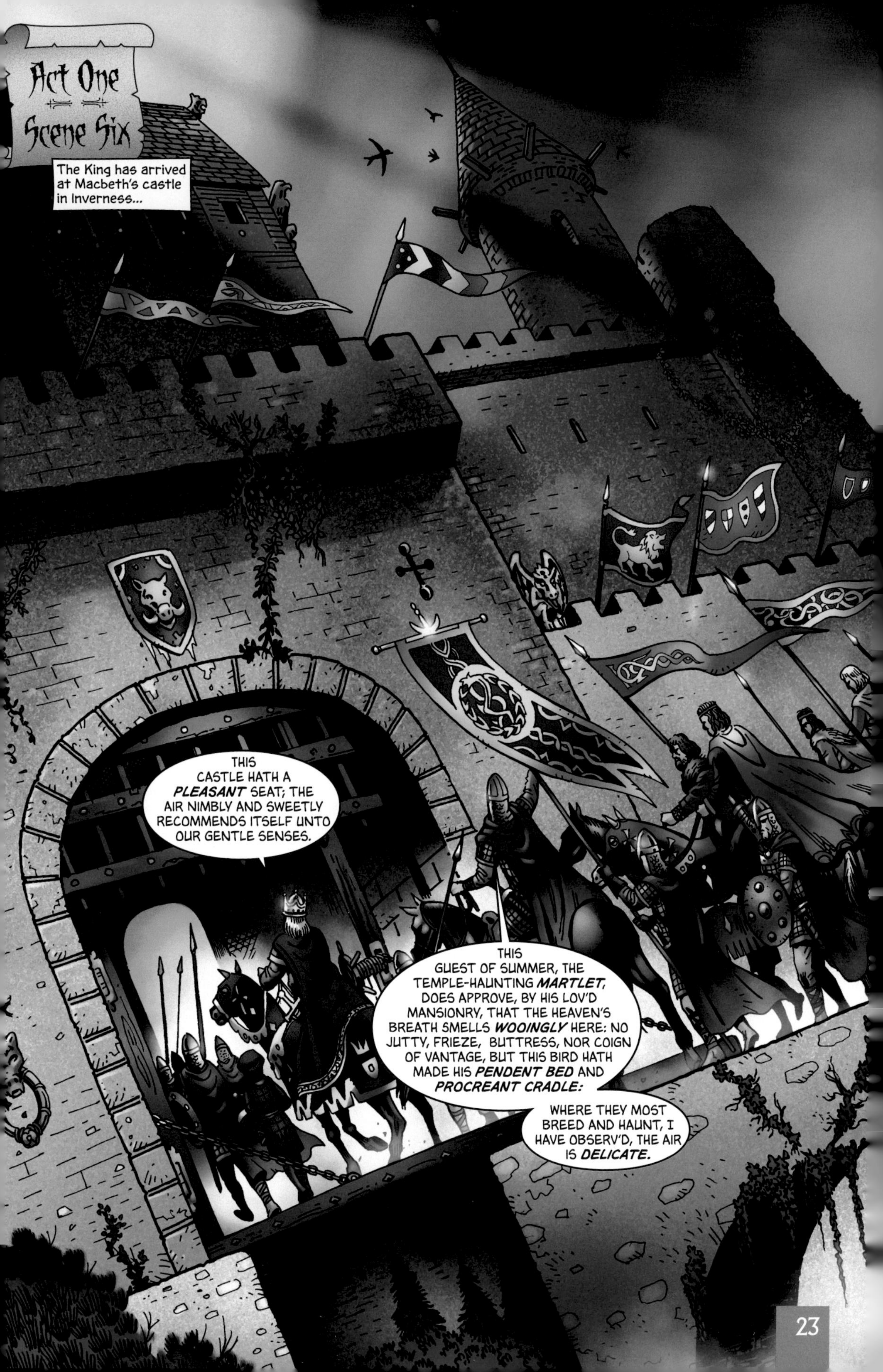
Act One
Scene Six
The King has arrived at Macbeth's castle in Inverness...
THIS CASTLE HATH A *PLEASANT* SEAT; THE AIR NIMBLY AND SWEETLY RECOMMENDS ITSELF UNTO OUR GENTLE SENSES.
THIS GUEST OF SUMMER, THE TEMPLE-HAUNTING *MARTLET,* DOES APPROVE, BY HIS LOV'D MANSIONRY, THAT THE HEAVEN'S BREATH SMELLS *WOOINGLY* HERE: NO JUTTY, FRIEZE, BUTTRESS, NOR COIGN OF VANTAGE, BUT THIS BIRD HATH MADE HIS *PENDENT BED* AND *PROCREANT CRADLE:*
WHERE THEY MOST BREED AND HAUNT, I HAVE OBSERV'D, THE AIR IS *DELICATE.*

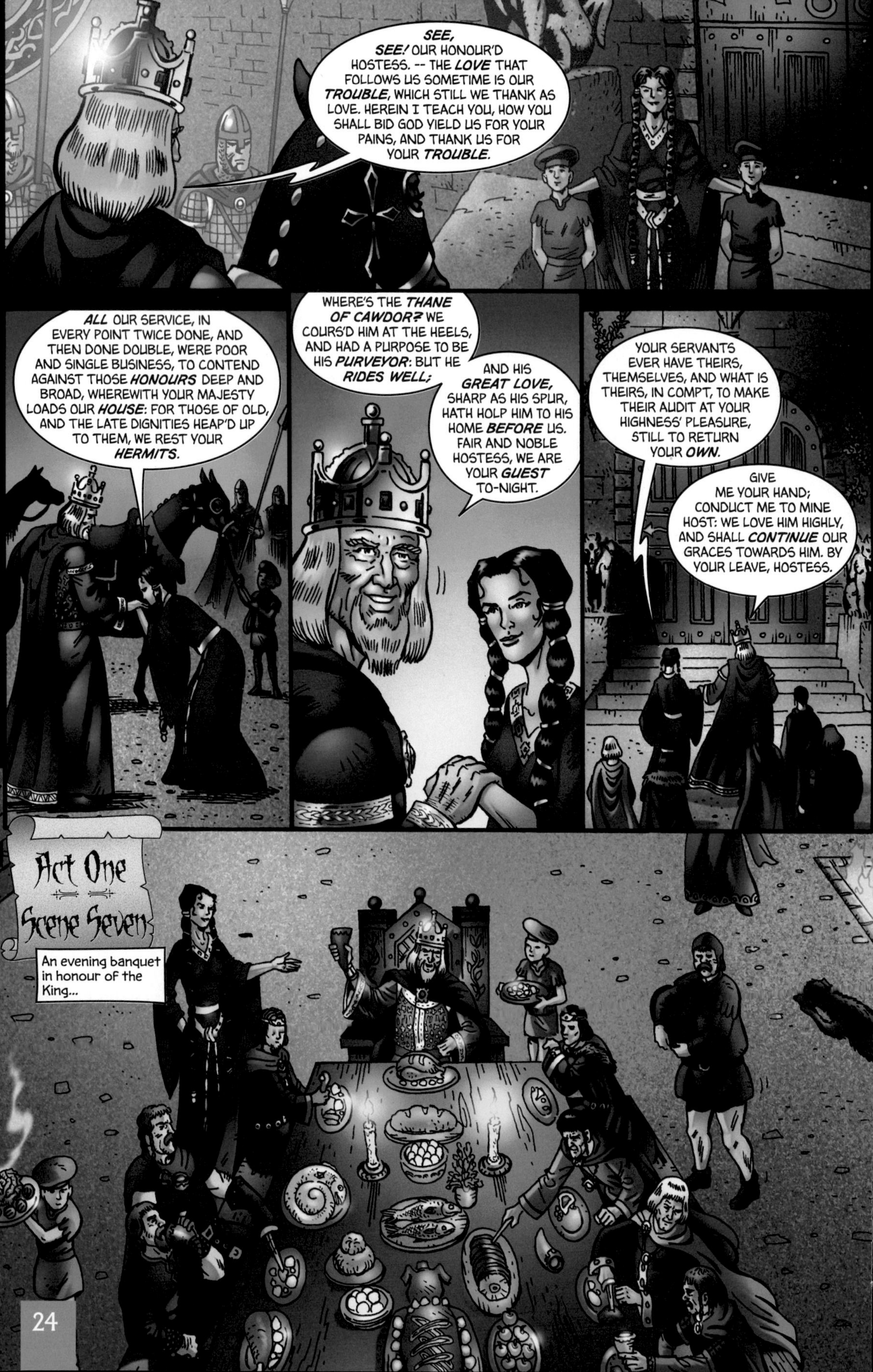
SEE, SEE! OUR HONOUR'D HOSTESS. -- THE LOVE THAT FOLLOWS US SOMETIME IS OUR TROUBLE, WHICH STILL WE THANK AS LOVE. HEREIN I TEACH YOU, HOW YOU SHALL BID GOD YIELD US FOR YOUR PAINS, AND THANK US FOR YOUR TROUBLE.
ALL OUR SERVICE, IN EVERY POINT TWICE DONE, AND THEN DONE DOUBLE, WERE POOR AND SINGLE BUSINESS, TO CONTEND AGAINST THOSE HONOURS DEEP AND BROAD, WHEREWITH YOUR MAJESTY LOADS OUR HOUSE: FOR THOSE OF OLD, AND THE LATE DIGNITIES HEAP'D UP TO THEM, WE REST YOUR HERMITS.
WHERE'S THE THANE OF CAWDOR? WE COURS'D HIM AT THE HEELS, AND HAD A PURPOSE TO BE HIS PURVEYOR: BUT HE RIDES WELL;
AND HIS GREAT LOVE, SHARP AS HIS SPUR, HATH HOLP HIM TO HIS HOME BEFORE US. FAIR AND NOBLE HOSTESS, WE ARE YOUR GUEST TO-NIGHT.
YOUR SERVANTS EVER HAVE THEIRS, THEMSELVES, AND WHAT IS THEIRS, IN COMPT, TO MAKE THEIR AUDIT AT YOUR HIGHNESS' PLEASURE, STILL TO RETURN YOUR OWN.
GIVE ME YOUR HAND; CONDUCT ME TO MINE HOST: WE LOVE HIM HIGHLY, AND SHALL CONTINUE OUR GRACES TOWARDS HIM. BY YOUR LEAVE, HOSTESS.
Act One
Scene Seven
An evening banquet in honour of the King...

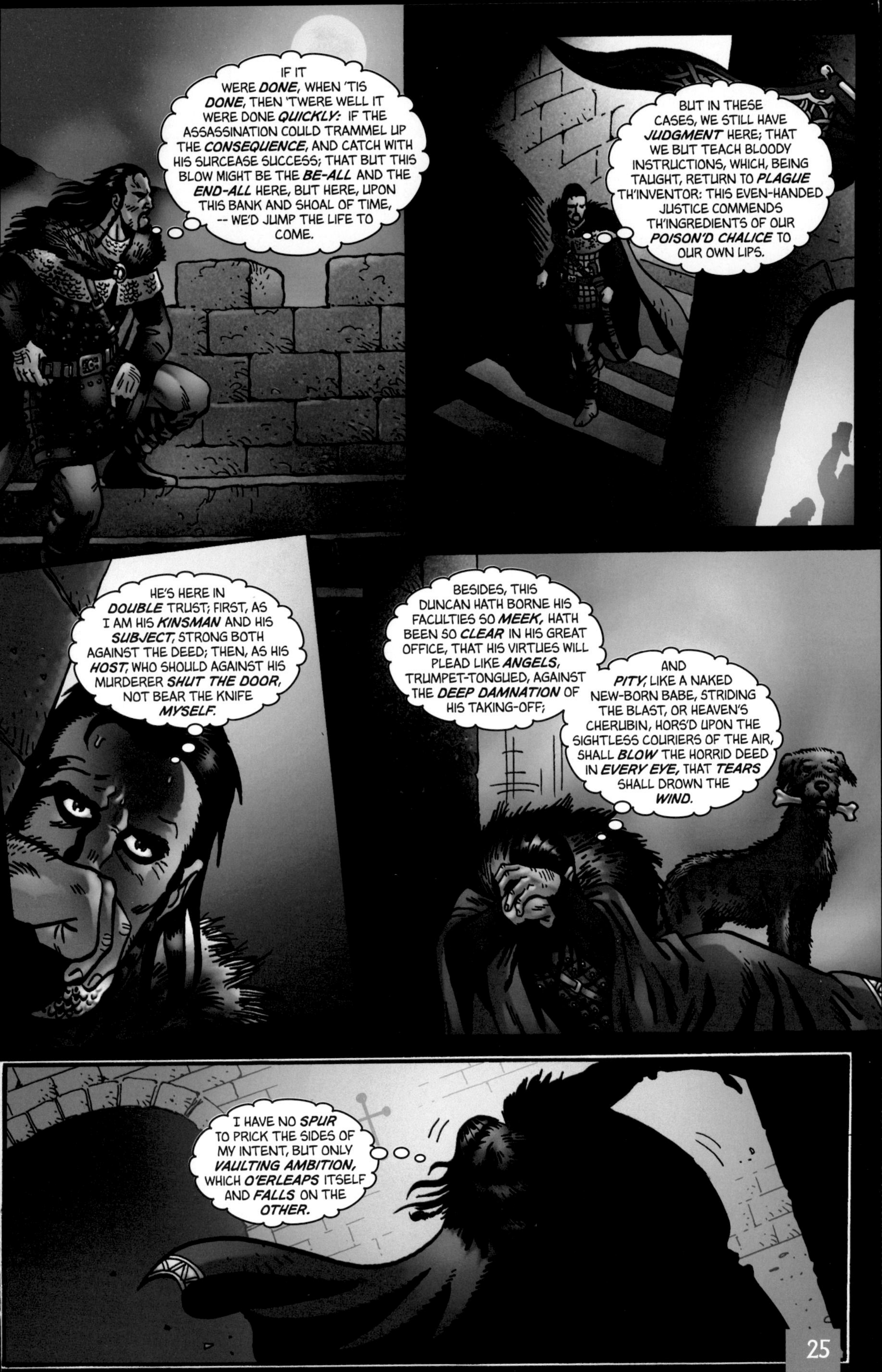
IF IT WERE DONE, WHEN 'TIS DONE, THEN 'TWERE WELL IT WERE DONE QUICKLY: IF THE ASSASSINATION COULD TRAMMEL UP THE CONSEQUENCE, AND CATCH WITH HIS SURCEASE SUCCESS; THAT BUT THIS BLOW MIGHT BE THE BE-ALL AND THE END-ALL HERE, BUT HERE, UPON THIS BANK AND SHOAL OF TIME, -- WE'D JUMP THE LIFE TO COME.
BUT IN THESE CASES, WE STILL HAVE JUDGMENT HERE; THAT WE BUT TEACH BLOODY INSTRUCTIONS, WHICH, BEING TAUGHT, RETURN TO PLAGUE TH'INVENTOR: THIS EVEN-HANDED JUSTICE COMMENDS TH'INGREDIENTS OF OUR POISON'D CHALICE TO OUR OWN LIPS.
HE'S HERE IN DOUBLE TRUST; FIRST, AS I AM HIS KINSMAN AND HIS SUBJECT, STRONG BOTH AGAINST THE DEED; THEN, AS HIS HOST, WHO SHOULD AGAINST HIS MURDERER SHUT THE DOOR, NOT BEAR THE KNIFE MYSELF.
BESIDES, THIS DUNCAN HATH BORNE HIS FACULTIES SO MEEK, HATH BEEN SO CLEAR IN HIS GREAT OFFICE, THAT HIS VIRTUES WILL PLEAD LIKE ANGELS, TRUMPET-TONGUED, AGAINST THE DEEP DAMNATION OF HIS TAKING-OFF;
AND PITY, LIKE A NAKED NEW-BORN BABE, STRIDING THE BLAST, OR HEAVEN'S CHERUBIN, HORS'D UPON THE SIGHTLESS COURIERS OF THE AIR, SHALL BLOW THE HORRID DEED IN EVERY EYE, THAT TEARS SHALL DROWN THE WIND.
I HAVE NO SPUR TO PRICK THE SIDES OF MY INTENT, BUT ONLY VAULTING AMBITION, WHICH O'ERLEAPS ITSELF AND FALLS ON THE OTHER.

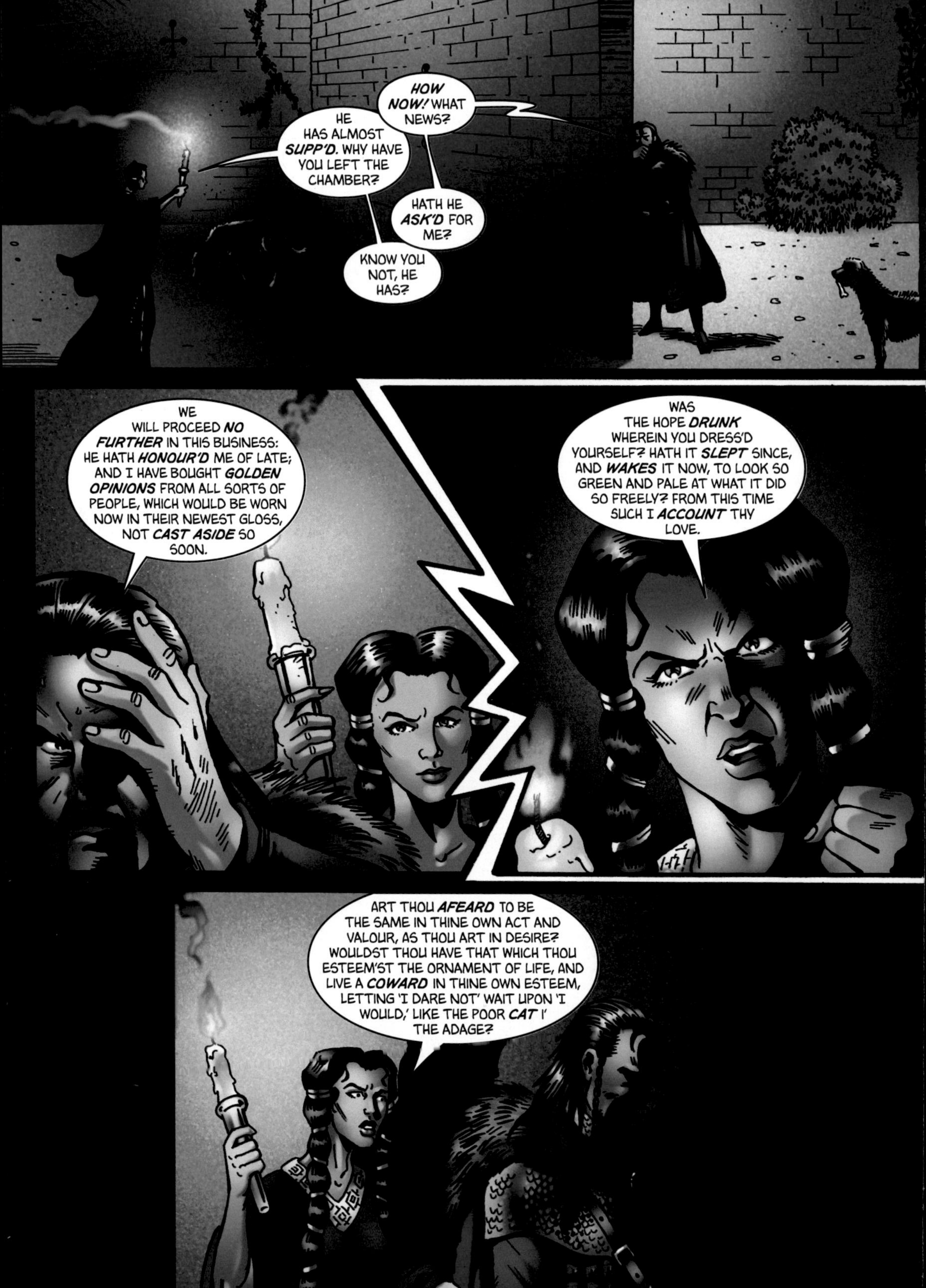
HOW NOW! WHAT NEWS?
HE HAS ALMOST SUPP'D. WHY HAVE YOU LEFT THE CHAMBER?
HATH HE ASK'D FOR ME?
KNOW YOU NOT, HE HAS?
WE WILL PROCEED NO FURTHER IN THIS BUSINESS: HE HATH HONOUR'D ME OF LATE; AND I HAVE BOUGHT GOLDEN OPINIONS FROM ALL SORTS OF PEOPLE, WHICH WOULD BE WORN NOW IN THEIR NEWEST GLOSS, NOT CAST ASIDE SO SOON.
WAS THE HOPE DRUNK WHEREIN YOU DRESS'D YOURSELF? HATH IT SLEPT SINCE, AND WAKES IT NOW, TO LOOK SO GREEN AND PALE AT WHAT IT DID SO FREELY? FROM THIS TIME SUCH I ACCOUNT THY LOVE.
ART THOU AFEARD TO BE THE SAME IN THINE OWN ACT AND VALOUR, AS THOU ART IN DESIRE? WOULDST THOU HAVE THAT WHICH THOU ESTEEM'ST THE ORNAMENT OF LIFE, AND LIVE A COWARD IN THINE OWN ESTEEM, LETTING 'I DARE NOT' WAIT UPON 'I WOULD,' LIKE THE POOR CAT I' THE ADAGE?

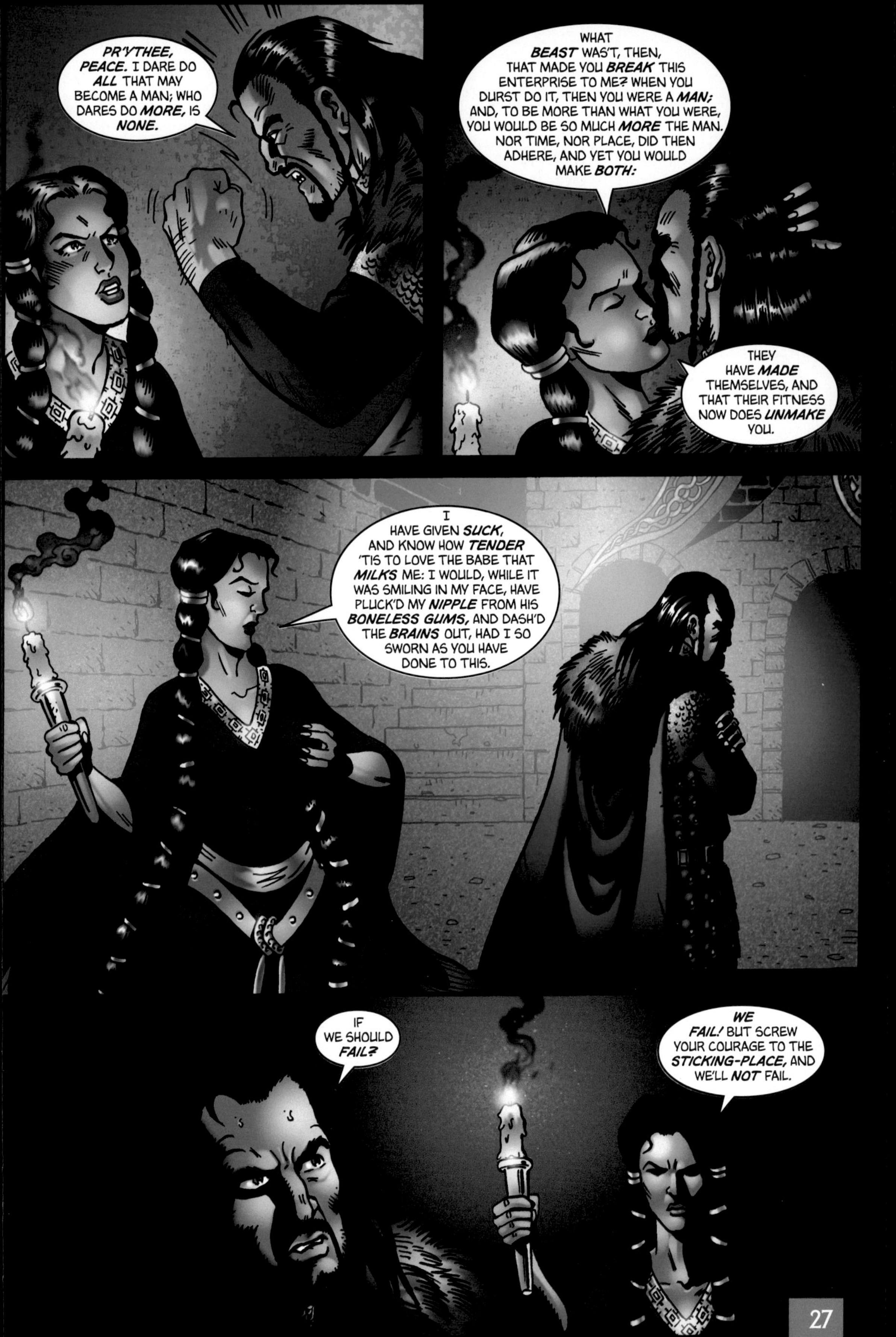
PR'YTHEE, PEACE. I DARE DO ALL THAT MAY BECOME A MAN; WHO DARES DO MORE, IS NONE.
WHAT BEAST WAS'T, THEN, THAT MADE YOU BREAK THIS ENTERPRISE TO ME? WHEN YOU DURST DO IT, THEN YOU WERE A MAN; AND, TO BE MORE THAN WHAT YOU WERE, YOU WOULD BE SO MUCH MORE THE MAN. NOR TIME, NOR PLACE, DID THEN ADHERE, AND YET YOU WOULD MAKE BOTH:
THEY HAVE MADE THEMSELVES, AND THAT THEIR FITNESS NOW DOES UNMAKE YOU.
I HAVE GIVEN SUCK, AND KNOW HOW TENDER 'TIS TO LOVE THE BABE THAT MILKS ME: I WOULD, WHILE IT WAS SMILING IN MY FACE, HAVE PLUCK'D MY NIPPLE FROM HIS BONELESS GUMS, AND DASH'D THE BRAINS OUT, HAD I SO SWORN AS YOU HAVE DONE TO THIS.
IF WE SHOULD FAIL?
WE FAIL! BUT SCREW YOUR COURAGE TO THE STICKING-PLACE, AND WE'LL NOT FAIL.

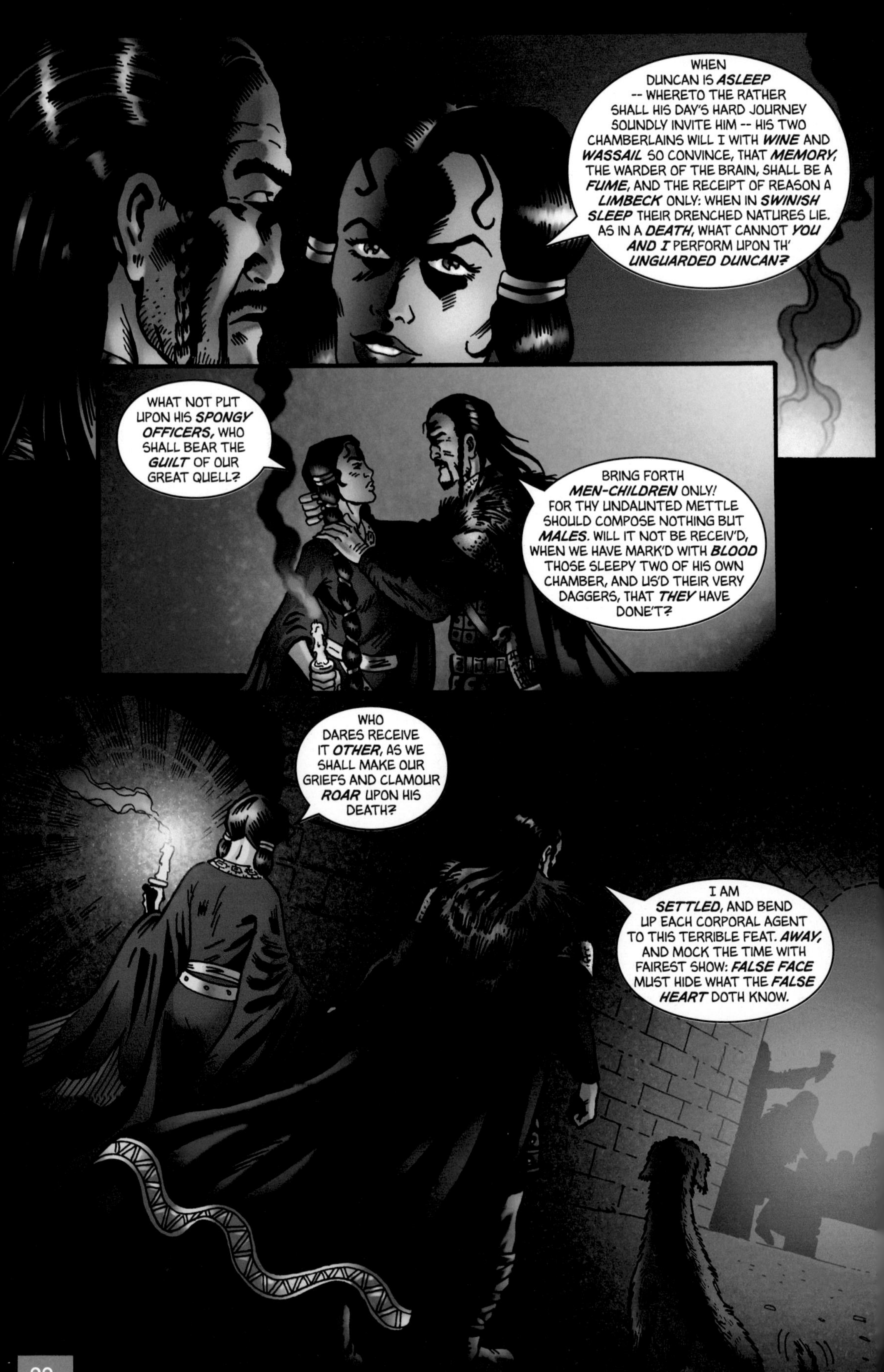
WHEN DUNCAN IS ASLEEP -- WHERETO THE RATHER SHALL HIS DAY'S HARD JOURNEY SOUNDLY INVITE HIM -- HIS TWO CHAMBERLAINS WILL I WITH WINE AND WASSAIL SO CONVINCE, THAT MEMORY, THE WARDER OF THE BRAIN, SHALL BE A FUME, AND THE RECEIPT OF REASON A LIMBECK ONLY: WHEN IN SWINISH SLEEP THEIR DRENCHED NATURES LIE. AS IN A DEATH, WHAT CANNOT YOU AND I PERFORM UPON TH' UNGUARDED DUNCAN?
WHAT NOT PUT UPON HIS SPONGY OFFICERS, WHO SHALL BEAR THE GUILT OF OUR GREAT QUELL?
BRING FORTH MEN-CHILDREN ONLY! FOR THY UNDAUNTED METTLE SHOULD COMPOSE NOTHING BUT MALES. WILL IT NOT BE RECEIV'D, WHEN WE HAVE MARK'D WITH BLOOD THOSE SLEEPY TWO OF HIS OWN CHAMBER, AND US'D THEIR VERY DAGGERS, THAT THEY HAVE DONE'T?
WHO DARES RECEIVE IT OTHER, AS WE SHALL MAKE OUR GRIEFS AND CLAMOUR ROAR UPON HIS DEATH?
I AM SETTLED, AND BEND UP EACH CORPORAL AGENT TO THIS TERRIBLE FEAT. AWAY, AND MOCK THE TIME WITH FAIREST SHOW: FALSE FACE MUST HIDE WHAT THE FALSE HEART DOTH KNOW.

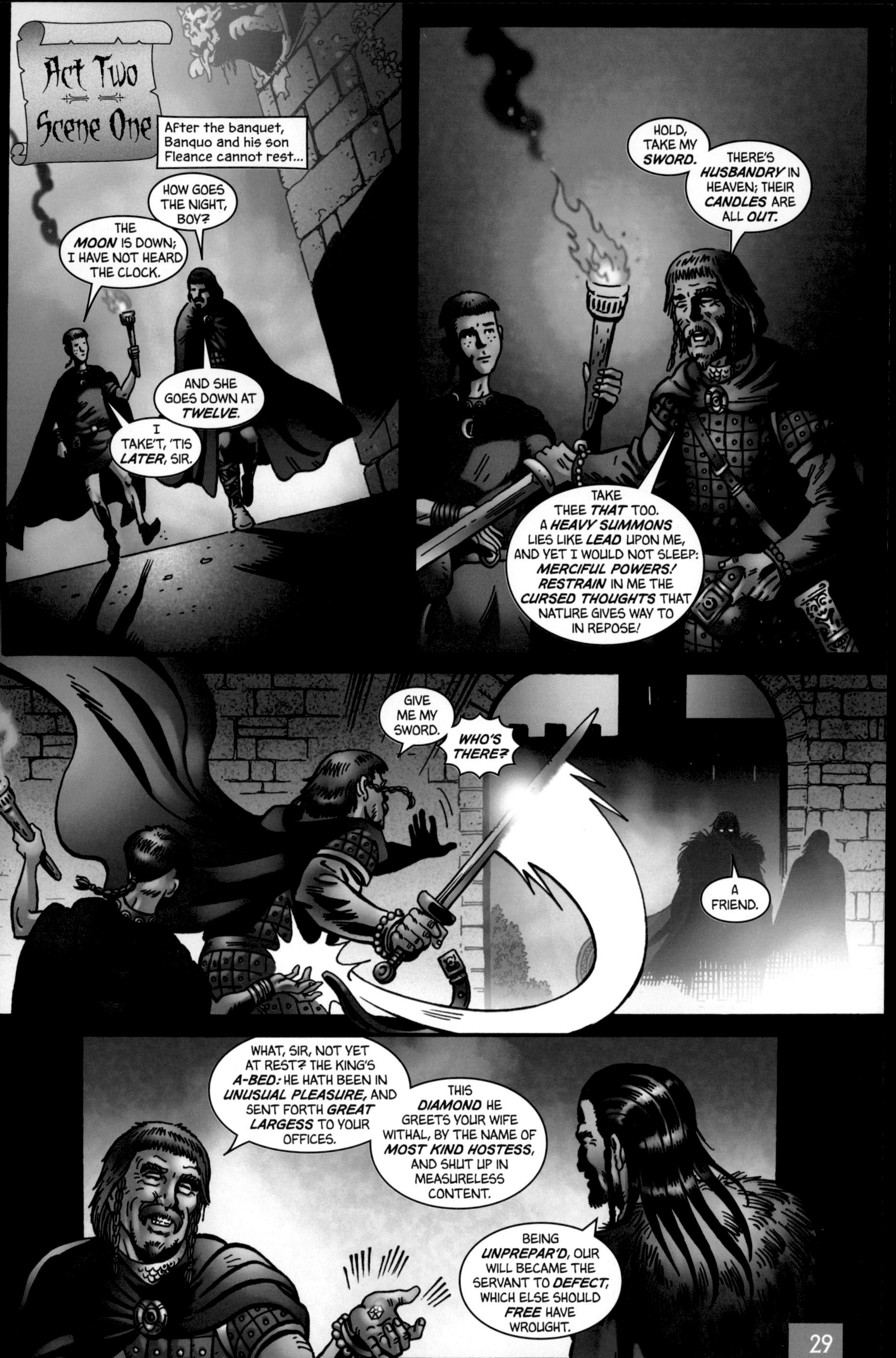
Act Two
Scene One
After the banquet, Banquo and his son Fleance cannot rest...
HOW GOES THE NIGHT, BOY?
THE MOON IS DOWN; I HAVE NOT HEARD THE CLOCK.
AND SHE GOES DOWN AT TWELVE.
I TAKE'T, 'TIS LATER, SIR.
HOLD, TAKE MY SWORD.
THERE'S HUSBANDRY IN HEAVEN; THEIR CANDLES ARE ALL OUT.
TAKE THEE THAT TOO. A HEAVY SUMMONS LIES LIKE LEAD UPON ME, AND YET I WOULD NOT SLEEP: MERCIFUL POWERS! RESTRAIN IN ME THE CURSED THOUGHTS THAT NATURE GIVES WAY TO IN REPOSE!
GIVE ME MY SWORD.
WHO'S THERE?
A FRIEND.
WHAT, SIR, NOT YET AT REST? THE KING'S A-BED: HE HATH BEEN IN UNUSUAL PLEASURE, AND SENT FORTH GREAT LARGESS TO YOUR OFFICES.
THIS DIAMOND HE GREETS YOUR WIFE WITHAL, BY THE NAME OF MOST KIND HOSTESS, AND SHUT UP IN MEASURELESS CONTENT.
BEING UNPREPAR'D, OUR WILL BECAME THE SERVANT TO DEFECT, WHICH ELSE SHOULD FREE HAVE WROUGHT.

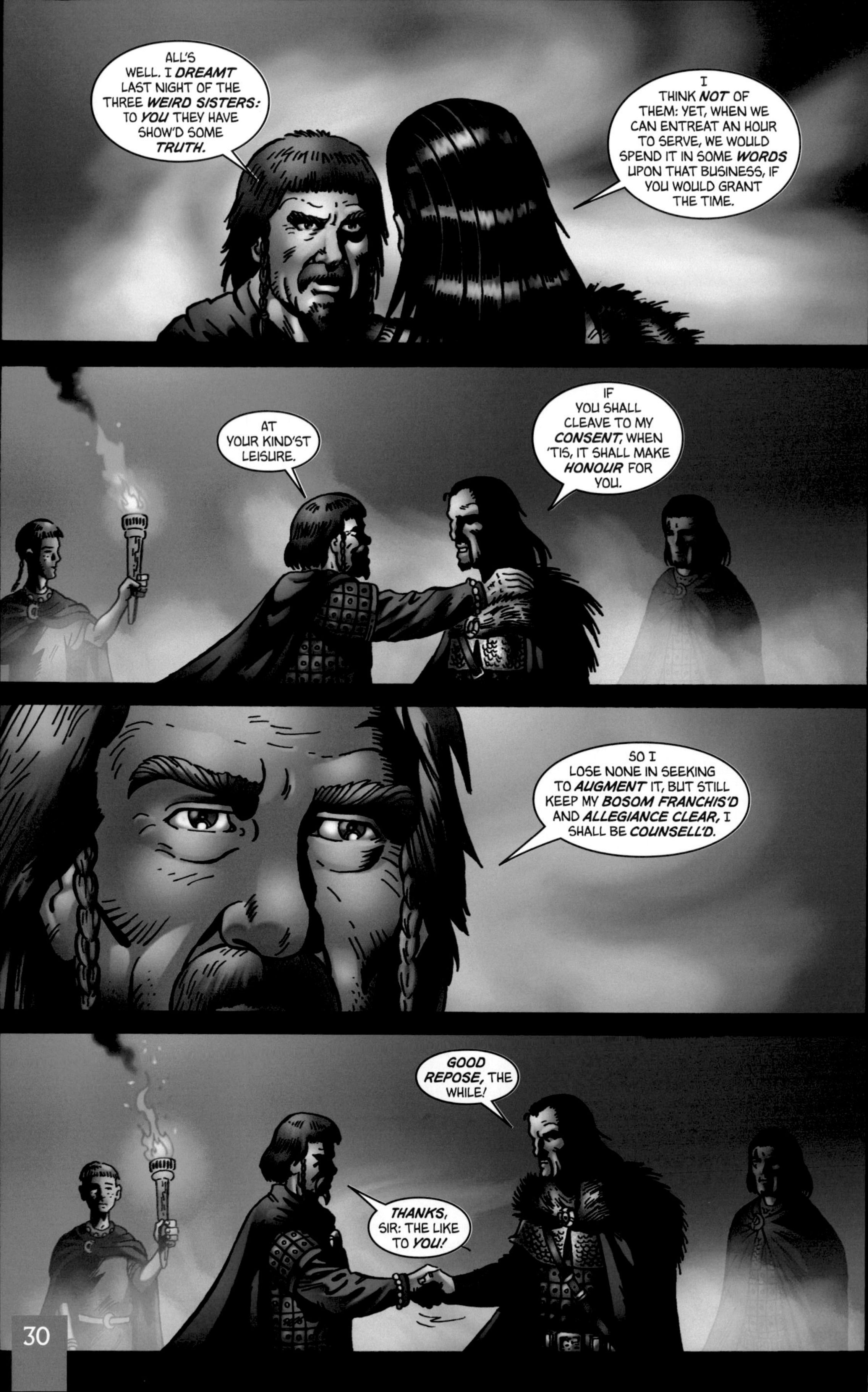
ALL'S WELL. I DREAMT LAST NIGHT OF THE THREE WEIRD SISTERS: TO YOU THEY HAVE SHOW'D SOME TRUTH.
I THINK NOT OF THEM: YET, WHEN WE CAN ENTREAT AN HOUR TO SERVE, WE WOULD SPEND IT IN SOME WORDS UPON THAT BUSINESS, IF YOU WOULD GRANT THE TIME.
AT YOUR KIND'ST LEISURE.
IF YOU SHALL CLEAVE TO MY CONSENT, WHEN 'TIS, IT SHALL MAKE HONOUR FOR YOU.
SO I LOSE NONE IN SEEKING TO AUGMENT IT, BUT STILL KEEP MY BOSOM FRANCHIS'D AND ALLEGIANCE CLEAR, I SHALL BE COUNSELL'D.
GOOD REPOSE, THE WHILE!
THANKS, SIR: THE LIKE TO YOU!

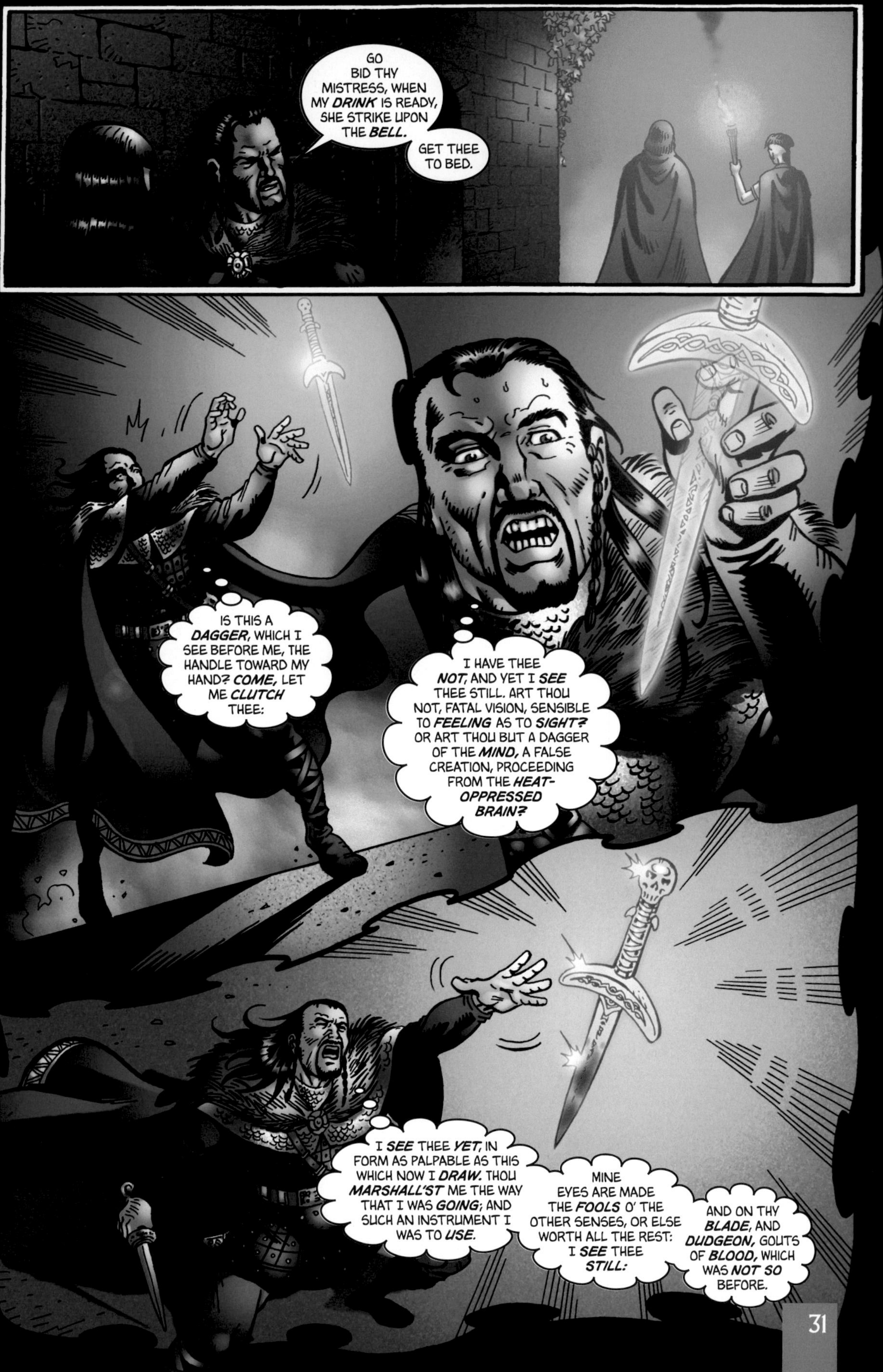
GO BID THY MISTRESS, WHEN MY DRINK IS READY, SHE STRIKE UPON THE BELL.
GET THEE TO BED.
IS THIS A DAGGER, WHICH I SEE BEFORE ME, THE HANDLE TOWARD MY HAND? COME, LET ME CLUTCH THEE:
I HAVE THEE NOT, AND YET I SEE THEE STILL. ART THOU NOT, FATAL VISION, SENSIBLE TO FEELING AS TO SIGHT? OR ART THOU BUT A DAGGER OF THE MIND, A FALSE CREATION, PROCEEDING FROM THE HEAT-OPPRESSED BRAIN?
I SEE THEE YET, IN FORM AS PALPABLE AS THIS WHICH NOW I DRAW. THOU MARSHALL'ST ME THE WAY THAT I WAS GOING; AND SUCH AN INSTRUMENT I WAS TO USE.
MINE EYES ARE MADE THE FOOLS O' THE OTHER SENSES, OR ELSE WORTH ALL THE REST: I SEE THEE STILL:
AND ON THY BLADE, AND DUDGEON, GOUTS OF BLOOD, WHICH WAS NOT SO BEFORE.

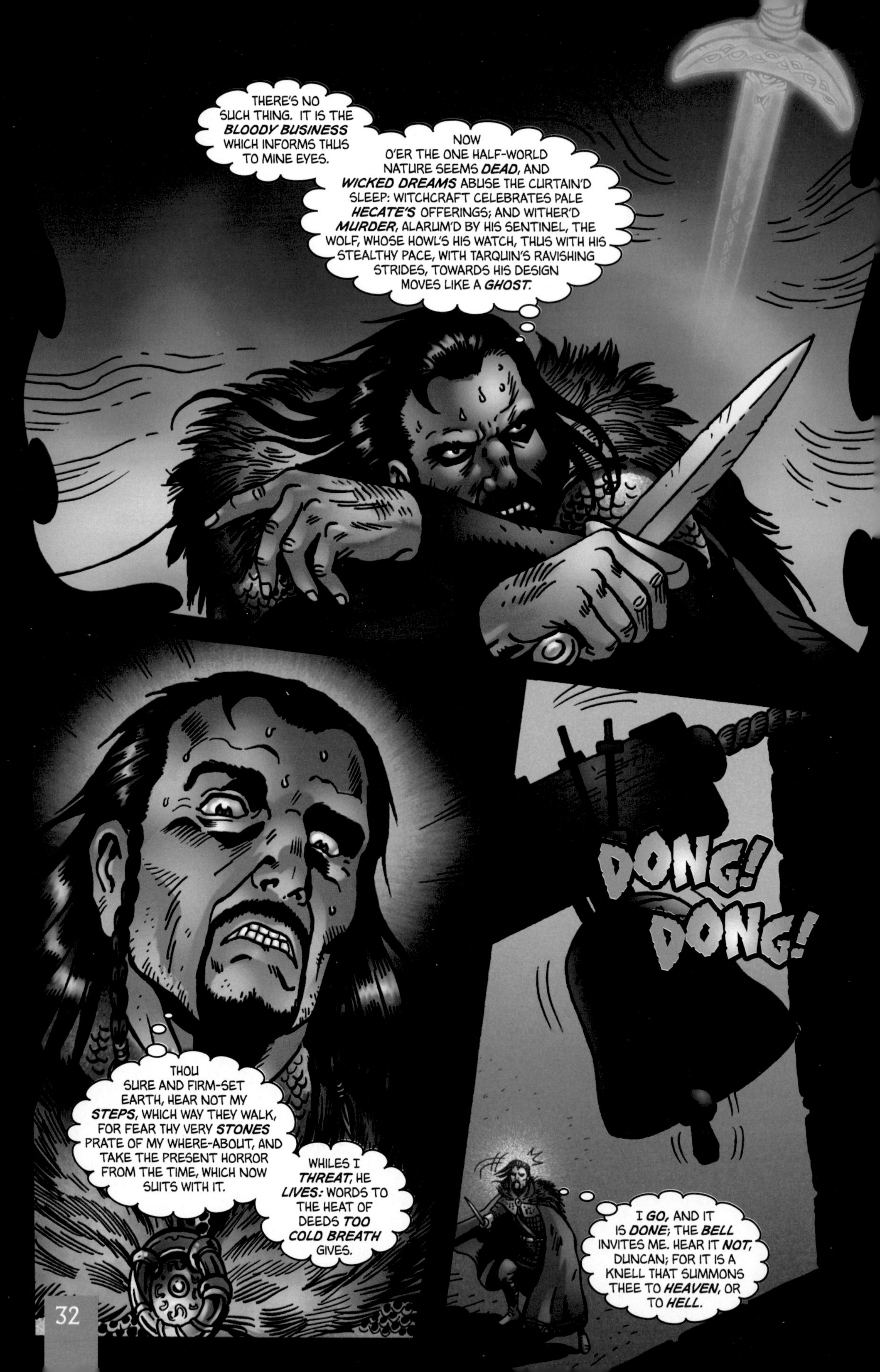

THERE'S NO SUCH THING. IT IS THE BLOODY BUSINESS WHICH INFORMS THUS TO MINE EYES.
NOW O'ER THE ONE HALF-WORLD NATURE SEEMS DEAD, AND WICKED DREAMS ABUSE THE CURTAIN'D SLEEP: WITCHCRAFT CELEBRATES PALE HECATE'S OFFERINGS; AND WITHER'D MURDER, ALARUM'D BY HIS SENTINEL, THE WOLF, WHOSE HOWL'S HIS WATCH, THUS WITH HIS STEALTHY PACE, WITH TARQUIN'S RAVISHING STRIDES, TOWARDS HIS DESIGN MOVES LIKE A GHOST.
THOU SURE AND FIRM-SET EARTH, HEAR NOT MY STEPS, WHICH WAY THEY WALK, FOR FEAR THY VERY STONES PRATE OF MY WHERE-ABOUT, AND TAKE THE PRESENT HORROR FROM THE TIME, WHICH NOW SUITS WITH IT.
WHILES I THREAT, HE LIVES: WORDS TO THE HEAT OF DEEDS TOO COLD BREATH GIVES.
DONG! DONG!
I GO, AND IT IS DONE; THE BELL INVITES ME. HEAR IT NOT, DUNCAN; FOR IT IS A KNELL THAT SUMMONS THEE TO HEAVEN, OR TO HELL.

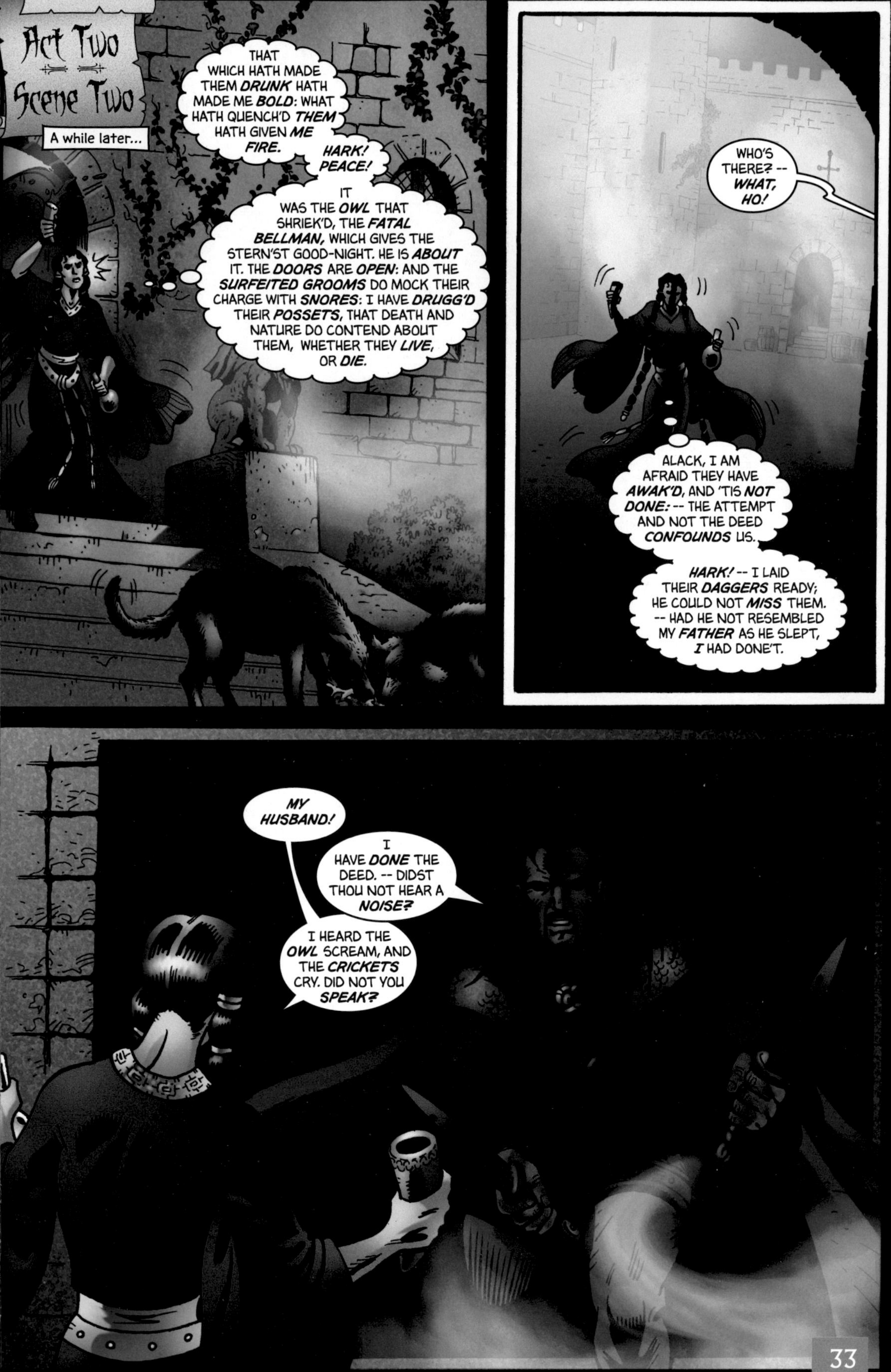
Act Two
Scene Two
A while later...
THAT WHICH HATH MADE THEM DRUNK HATH MADE ME BOLD: WHAT HATH QUENCH'D THEM HATH GIVEN ME FIRE.
HARK! PEACE!
IT WAS THE OWL THAT SHRIEK'D, THE FATAL BELLMAN, WHICH GIVES THE STERN'ST GOOD-NIGHT. HE IS ABOUT IT. THE DOORS ARE OPEN: AND THE SURFEITED GROOMS DO MOCK THEIR CHARGE WITH SNORES: I HAVE DRUGG'D THEIR POSSETS, THAT DEATH AND NATURE DO CONTEND ABOUT THEM, WHETHER THEY LIVE, OR DIE.
WHO'S THERE? -- WHAT, HO!
ALACK, I AM AFRAID THEY HAVE AWAK'D, AND 'TIS NOT DONE: -- THE ATTEMPT AND NOT THE DEED CONFOUNDS US.
HARK! -- I LAID THEIR DAGGERS READY; HE COULD NOT MISS THEM. -- HAD HE NOT RESEMBLED MY FATHER AS HE SLEPT, I HAD DONE'T.
MY HUSBAND!
I HAVE DONE THE DEED. -- DIDST THOU NOT HEAR A NOISE?
I HEARD THE OWL SCREAM, AND THE CRICKETS CRY. DID NOT YOU SPEAK?

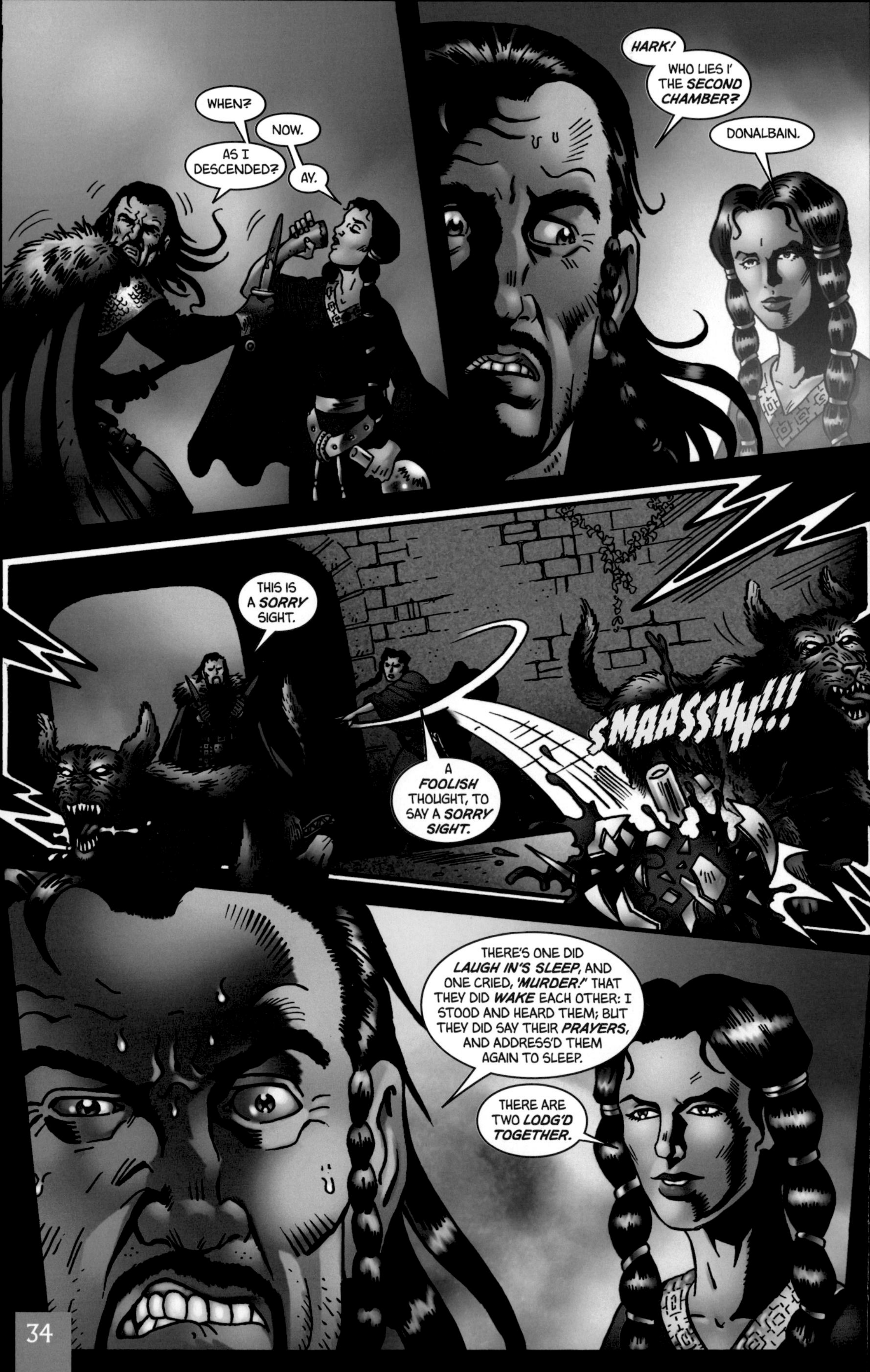
WHEN?
NOW.
AS I DESCENDED?
AY.
HARK!
WHO LIES I' THE SECOND CHAMBER?
DONALBAIN.
THIS IS A SORRY SIGHT.
A FOOLISH THOUGHT, TO SAY A SORRY SIGHT.
SMAASSHH!!!
THERE'S ONE DID LAUGH IN'S SLEEP, AND ONE CRIED, 'MURDER!' THAT THEY DID WAKE EACH OTHER: I STOOD AND HEARD THEM; BUT THEY DID SAY THEIR PRAYERS, AND ADDRESS'D THEM AGAIN TO SLEEP.
THERE ARE TWO LODG'D TOGETHER.

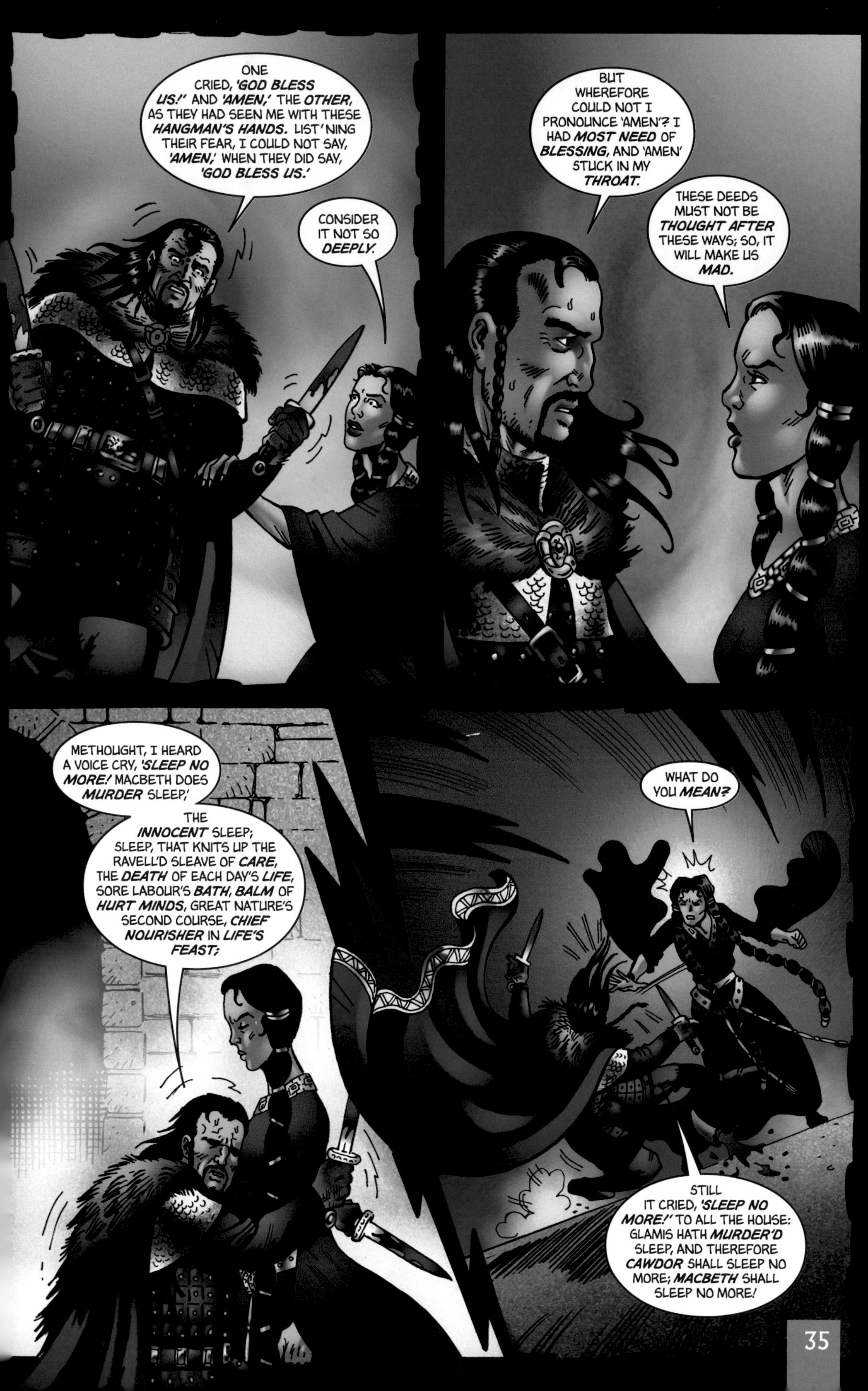
ONE CRIED, 'GOD BLESS US!' AND 'AMEN,' THE OTHER, AS THEY HAD SEEN ME WITH THESE HANGMAN'S HANDS. LIST'NING THEIR FEAR, I COULD NOT SAY, 'AMEN,' WHEN THEY DID SAY, 'GOD BLESS US.'
CONSIDER IT NOT SO DEEPLY.
BUT WHEREFORE COULD NOT I PRONOUNCE 'AMEN'? I HAD MOST NEED OF BLESSING, AND 'AMEN' STUCK IN MY THROAT.
THESE DEEDS MUST NOT BE THOUGHT AFTER THESE WAYS; SO, IT WILL MAKE US MAD.
METHOUGHT, I HEARD A VOICE CRY, 'SLEEP NO MORE! MACBETH DOES MURDER SLEEP,'
THE INNOCENT SLEEP; SLEEP, THAT KNITS UP THE RAVELL'D SLEAVE OF CARE, THE DEATH OF EACH DAY'S LIFE, SORE LABOUR'S BATH, BALM OF HURT MINDS, GREAT NATURE'S SECOND COURSE, CHIEF NOURISHER IN LIFE'S FEAST;
WHAT DO YOU MEAN?
STILL IT CRIED, 'SLEEP NO MORE!' TO ALL THE HOUSE: GLAMIS HATH MURDER'D SLEEP, AND THEREFORE CAWDOR SHALL SLEEP NO MORE; MACBETH SHALL SLEEP NO MORE!

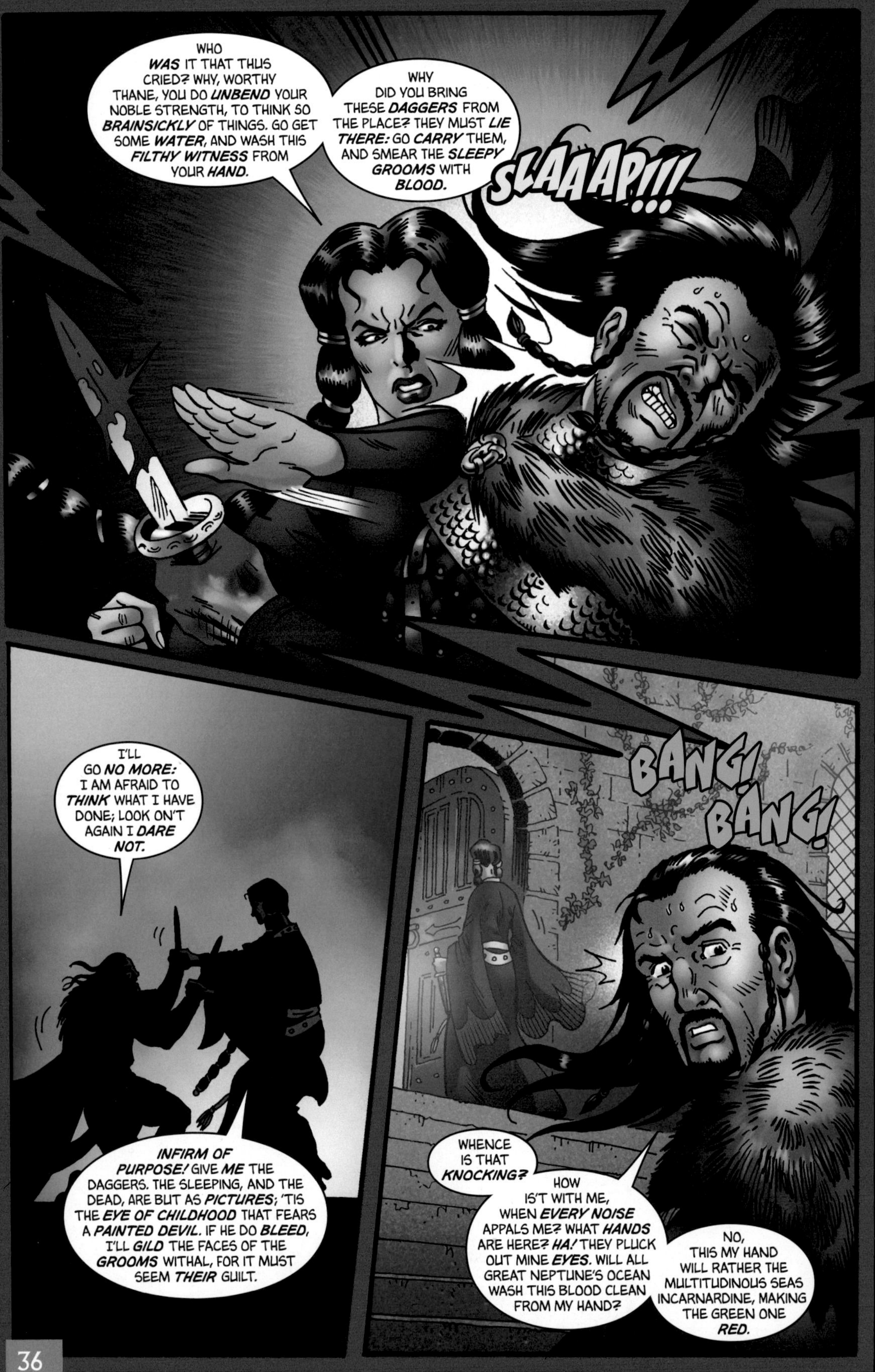
WHO WAS IT THAT THUS CRIED? WHY, WORTHY THANE, YOU DO UNBEND YOUR NOBLE STRENGTH, TO THINK SO BRAINSICKLY OF THINGS. GO GET SOME WATER, AND WASH THIS FILTHY WITNESS FROM YOUR HAND.
WHY DID YOU BRING THESE DAGGERS FROM THE PLACE? THEY MUST LIE THERE: GO CARRY THEM, AND SMEAR THE SLEEPY GROOMS WITH BLOOD.
SLAAAP!!!
I'LL GO NO MORE: I AM AFRAID TO THINK WHAT I HAVE DONE; LOOK ON'T AGAIN I DARE NOT.
INFIRM OF PURPOSE! GIVE ME THE DAGGERS. THE SLEEPING, AND THE DEAD, ARE BUT AS PICTURES; 'TIS THE EYE OF CHILDHOOD THAT FEARS A PAINTED DEVIL. IF HE DO BLEED, I'LL GILD THE FACES OF THE GROOMS WITHAL, FOR IT MUST SEEM THEIR GUILT.
BANG! BANG!
WHENCE IS THAT KNOCKING?
HOW IS'T WITH ME, WHEN EVERY NOISE APPALS ME? WHAT HANDS ARE HERE? HA! THEY PLUCK OUT MINE EYES. WILL ALL GREAT NEPTUNE'S OCEAN WASH THIS BLOOD CLEAN FROM MY HAND?
NO, THIS MY HAND WILL RATHER THE MULTITUDINOUS SEAS INCARNARDINE, MAKING THE GREEN ONE RED.

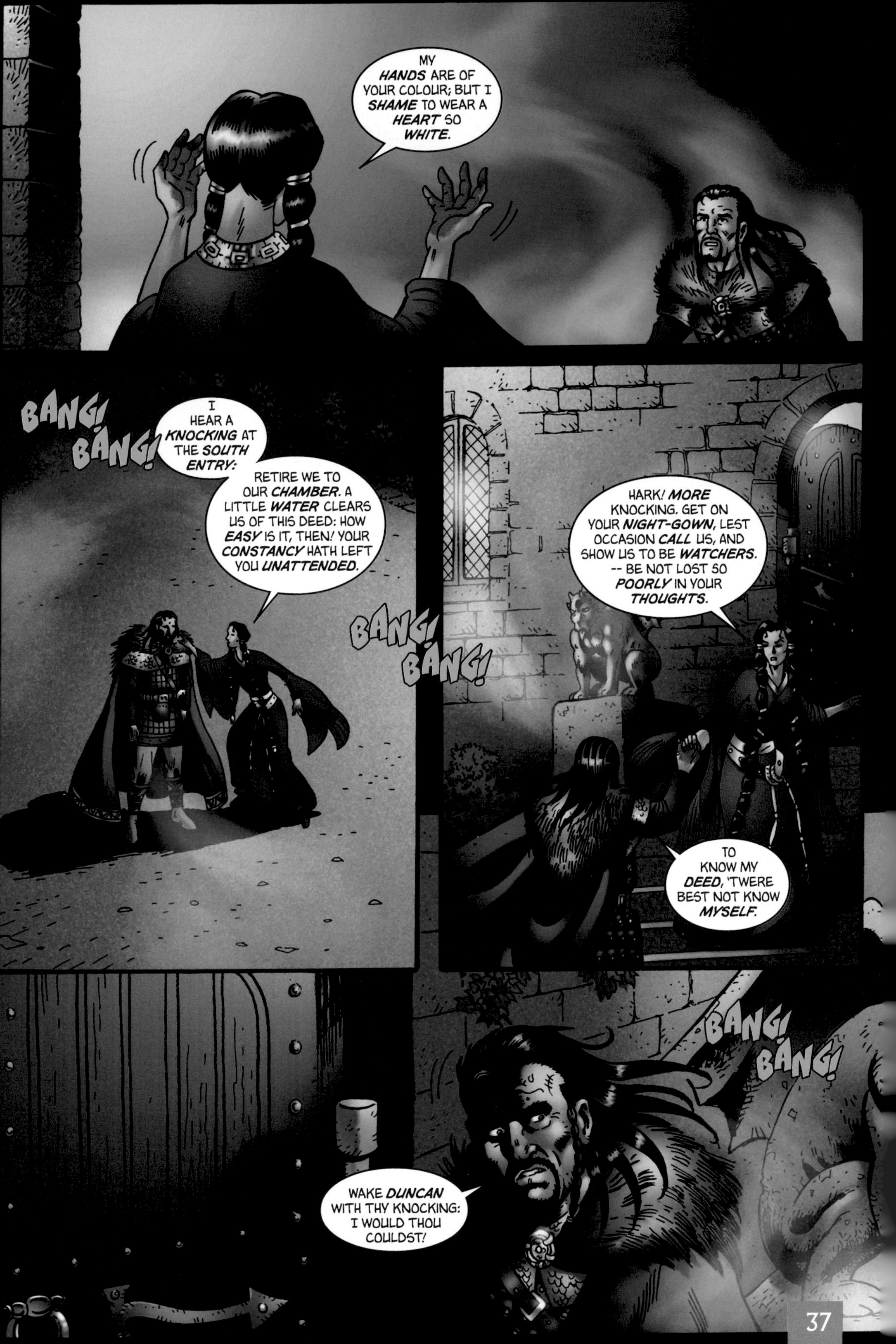
MY HANDS ARE OF YOUR COLOUR; BUT I SHAME TO WEAR A HEART SO WHITE.
BANG! BANG!
I HEAR A KNOCKING AT THE SOUTH ENTRY:
RETIRE WE TO OUR CHAMBER. A LITTLE WATER CLEARS US OF THIS DEED: HOW EASY IS IT, THEN! YOUR CONSTANCY HATH LEFT YOU UNATTENDED.
BANG! BANG!
HARK! MORE KNOCKING. GET ON YOUR NIGHT-GOWN, LEST OCCASION CALL US, AND SHOW US TO BE WATCHERS. -- BE NOT LOST SO POORLY IN YOUR THOUGHTS.
TO KNOW MY DEED, 'TWERE BEST NOT KNOW MYSELF.
BANG! BANG!
WAKE DUNCAN WITH THY KNOCKING: I WOULD THOU COULDST!

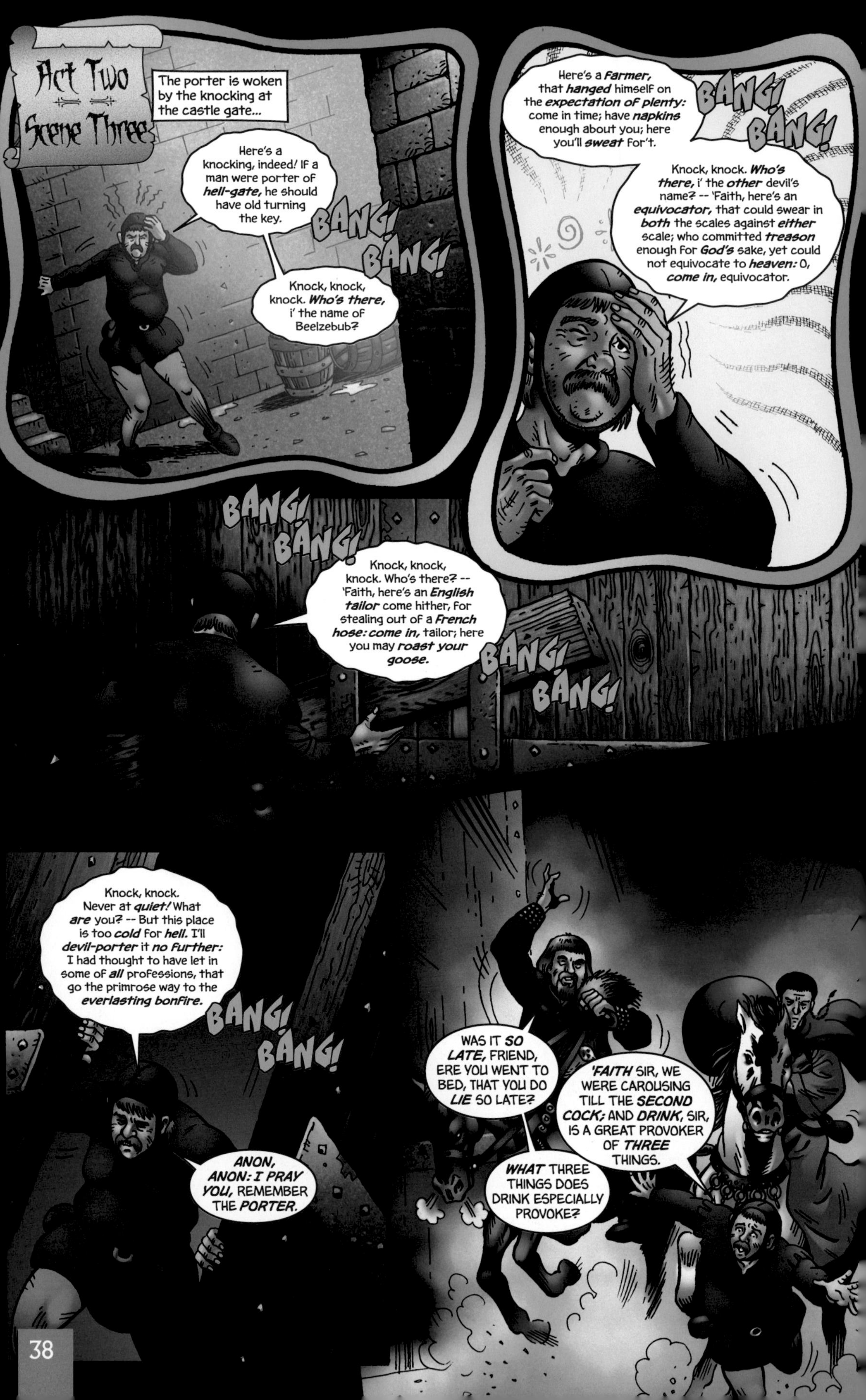
Act Two
Scene Three
The porter is woken by the knocking at the castle gate...
Here's a knocking, indeed! If a man were porter of hell-gate, he should have old turning the key.
BANG! BANG!
Knock, knock, knock. Who's there, i' the name of Beelzebub?
Here's a farmer, that hanged himself on the expectation of plenty: come in time; have napkins enough about you; here you'll sweat for't.
BANG! BANG!
Knock, knock. Who's there, i' the other devil's name? -- 'Faith, here's an equivocator, that could swear in both the scales against either scale; who committed treason enough for God's sake, yet could not equivocate to heaven: O, come in, equivocator.
BANG! BANG!
Knock, knock, knock. Who's there? -- 'Faith, here's an English tailor come hither, for stealing out of a French hose: come in, tailor; here you may roast your goose.
BANG! BANG!
Knock, knock. Never at quiet! What are you? -- But this place is too cold for hell. I'll devil-porter it no further: I had thought to have let in some of all professions, that go the primrose way to the everlasting bonfire.
BANG! BANG!
ANON, ANON: I PRAY YOU, REMEMBER THE PORTER.
WAS IT SO LATE, FRIEND, ERE YOU WENT TO BED, THAT YOU DO LIE SO LATE?
'FAITH SIR, WE WERE CAROUSING TILL THE SECOND COCK; AND DRINK, SIR, IS A GREAT PROVOKER OF THREE THINGS.
WHAT THREE THINGS DOES DRINK ESPECIALLY PROVOKE?

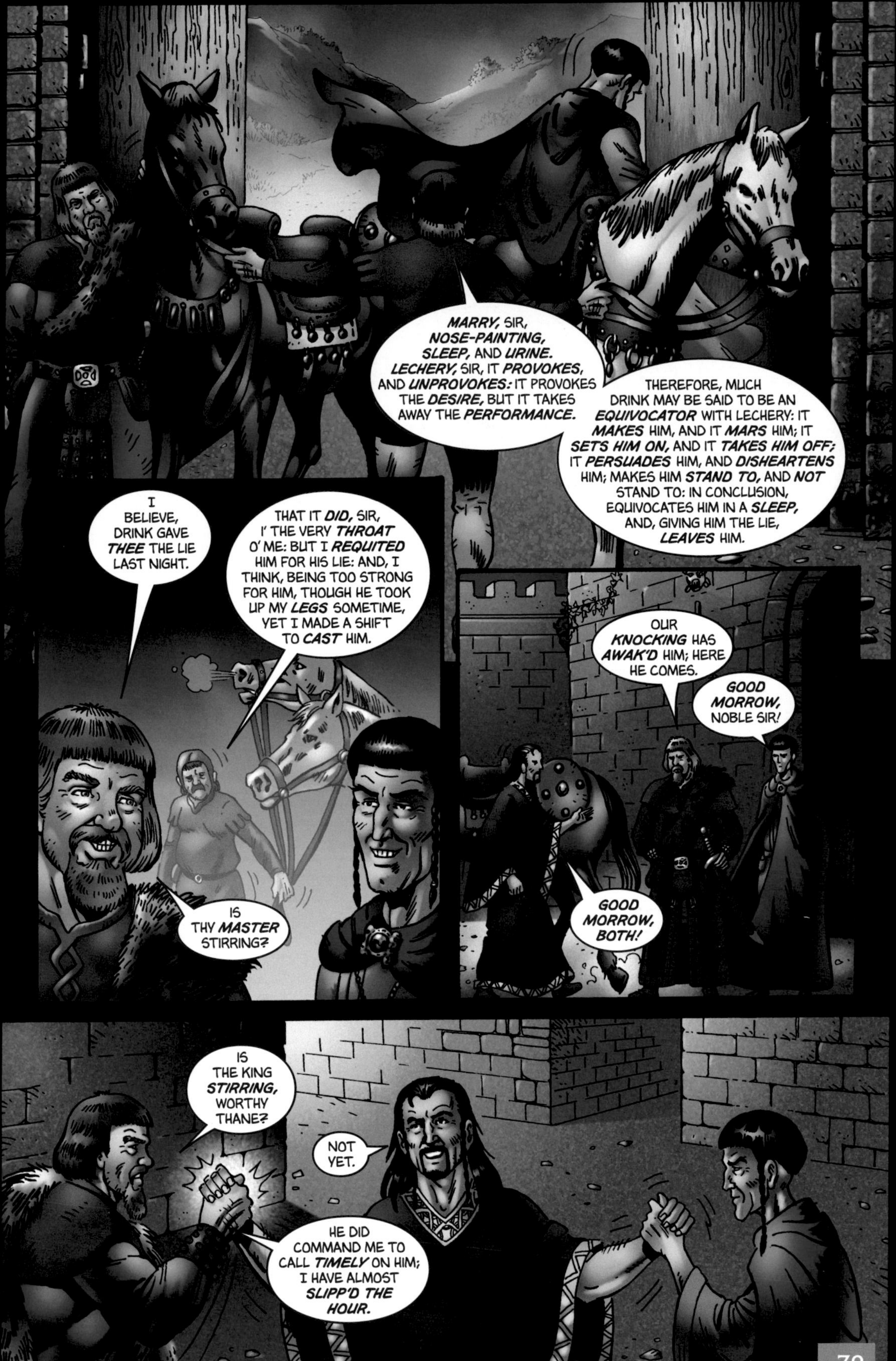
MARRY, SIR, NOSE-PAINTING, SLEEP, AND URINE. LECHERY, SIR, IT PROVOKES, AND UNPROVOKES: IT PROVOKES THE DESIRE, BUT IT TAKES AWAY THE PERFORMANCE.
THEREFORE, MUCH DRINK MAY BE SAID TO BE AN EQUIVOCATOR WITH LECHERY: IT MAKES HIM, AND IT MARS HIM; IT SETS HIM ON, AND IT TAKES HIM OFF; IT PERSUADES HIM, AND DISHEARTENS HIM; MAKES HIM STAND TO, AND NOT STAND TO: IN CONCLUSION, EQUIVOCATES HIM IN A SLEEP, AND, GIVING HIM THE LIE, LEAVES HIM.
I BELIEVE, DRINK GAVE THEE THE LIE LAST NIGHT.
THAT IT DID, SIR, I' THE VERY THROAT O' ME: BUT I REQUITED HIM FOR HIS LIE: AND, I THINK, BEING TOO STRONG FOR HIM, THOUGH HE TOOK UP MY LEGS SOMETIME, YET I MADE A SHIFT TO CAST HIM.
IS THY MASTER STIRRING?
OUR KNOCKING HAS AWAK'D HIM; HERE HE COMES.
GOOD MORROW, NOBLE SIR!
GOOD MORROW, BOTH!
IS THE KING STIRRING, WORTHY THANE?
NOT YET.
HE DID COMMAND ME TO CALL TIMELY ON HIM; I HAVE ALMOST SLIPP'D THE HOUR.

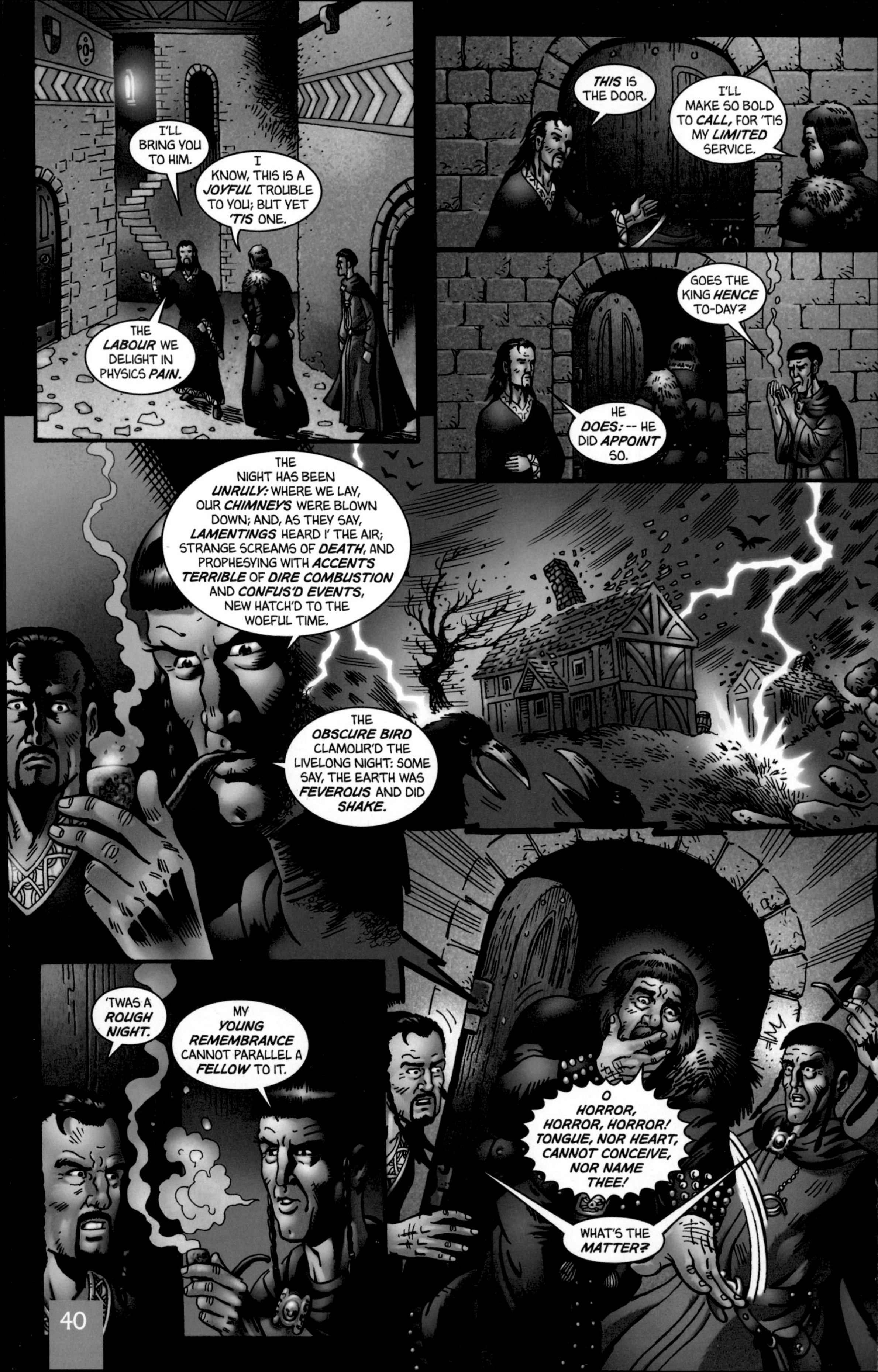
I'LL BRING YOU TO HIM.
I KNOW, THIS IS A JOYFUL TROUBLE TO YOU; BUT YET 'TIS ONE.
THE LABOUR WE DELIGHT IN PHYSICS PAIN.
THIS IS THE DOOR.
I'LL MAKE SO BOLD TO CALL, FOR 'TIS MY LIMITED SERVICE.
GOES THE KING HENCE TO-DAY?
HE DOES: -- HE DID APPOINT SO.
THE NIGHT HAS BEEN UNRULY: WHERE WE LAY, OUR CHIMNEYS WERE BLOWN DOWN; AND, AS THEY SAY, LAMENTINGS HEARD I' THE AIR; STRANGE SCREAMS OF DEATH, AND PROPHESYING WITH ACCENTS TERRIBLE OF DIRE COMBUSTION AND CONFUS'D EVENTS, NEW HATCH'D TO THE WOEFUL TIME.
THE OBSCURE BIRD CLAMOUR'D THE LIVELONG NIGHT: SOME SAY, THE EARTH WAS FEVEROUS AND DID SHAKE.
'TWAS A ROUGH NIGHT.
MY YOUNG REMEMBRANCE CANNOT PARALLEL A FELLOW TO IT.
O HORROR, HORROR, HORROR! TONGUE, NOR HEART, CANNOT CONCEIVE, NOR NAME THEE!
WHAT'S THE MATTER?

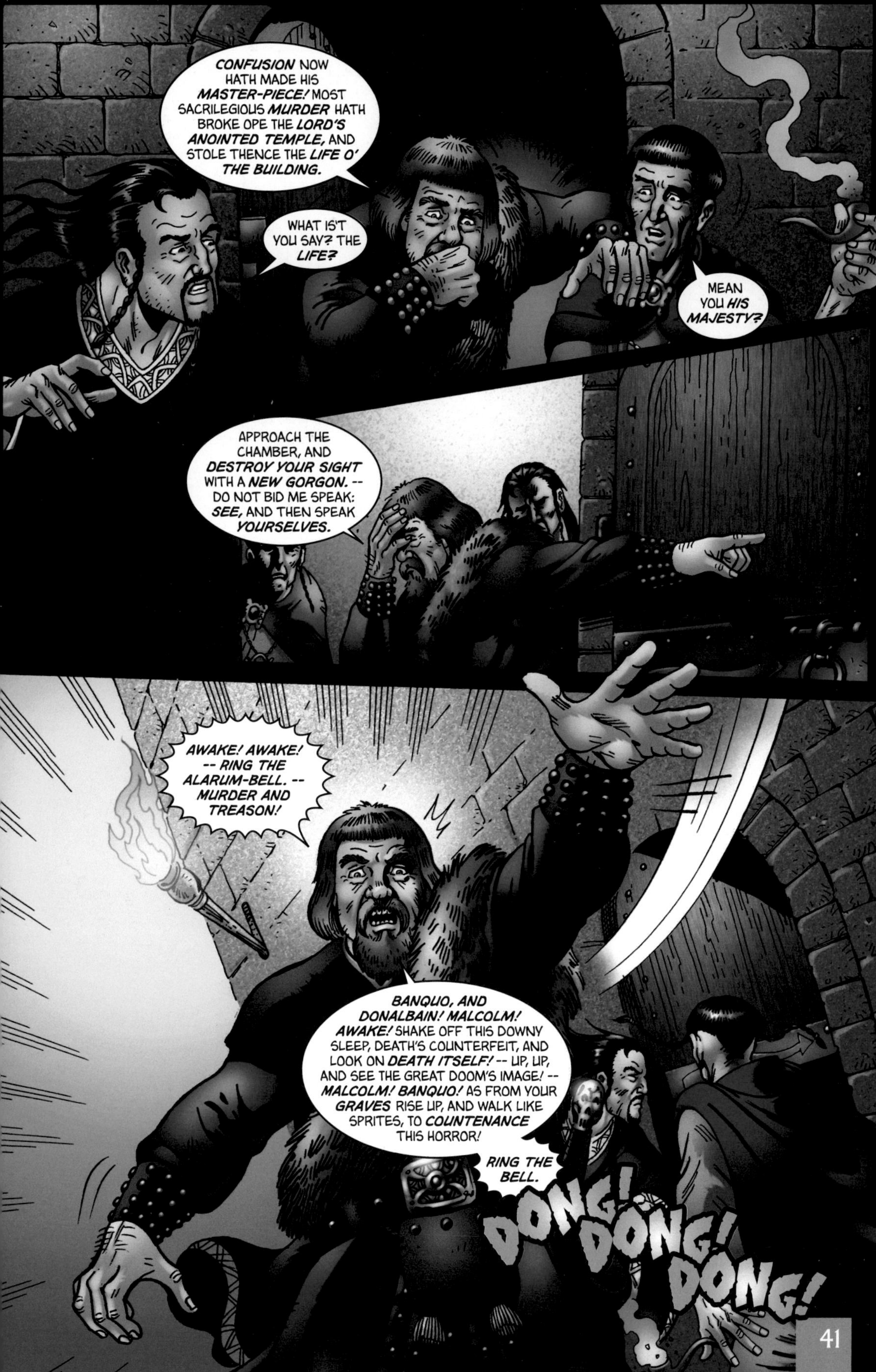
CONFUSION NOW HATH MADE HIS MASTER-PIECE! MOST SACRILEGIOUS MURDER HATH BROKE OPE THE LORD'S ANOINTED TEMPLE, AND STOLE THENCE THE LIFE O' THE BUILDING.
WHAT IS'T YOU SAY? THE LIFE?
MEAN YOU HIS MAJESTY?
APPROACH THE CHAMBER, AND DESTROY YOUR SIGHT WITH A NEW GORGON. -- DO NOT BID ME SPEAK: SEE, AND THEN SPEAK YOURSELVES.
AWAKE! AWAKE! -- RING THE ALARUM-BELL. -- MURDER AND TREASON!
BANQUO, AND DONALBAIN! MALCOLM! AWAKE! SHAKE OFF THIS DOWNY SLEEP, DEATH'S COUNTERFEIT, AND LOOK ON DEATH ITSELF! -- UP, UP, AND SEE THE GREAT DOOM'S IMAGE! -- MALCOLM! BANQUO! AS FROM YOUR GRAVES RISE UP, AND WALK LIKE SPRITES, TO COUNTENANCE THIS HORROR!
RING THE BELL.
DONG! DONG! DONG!

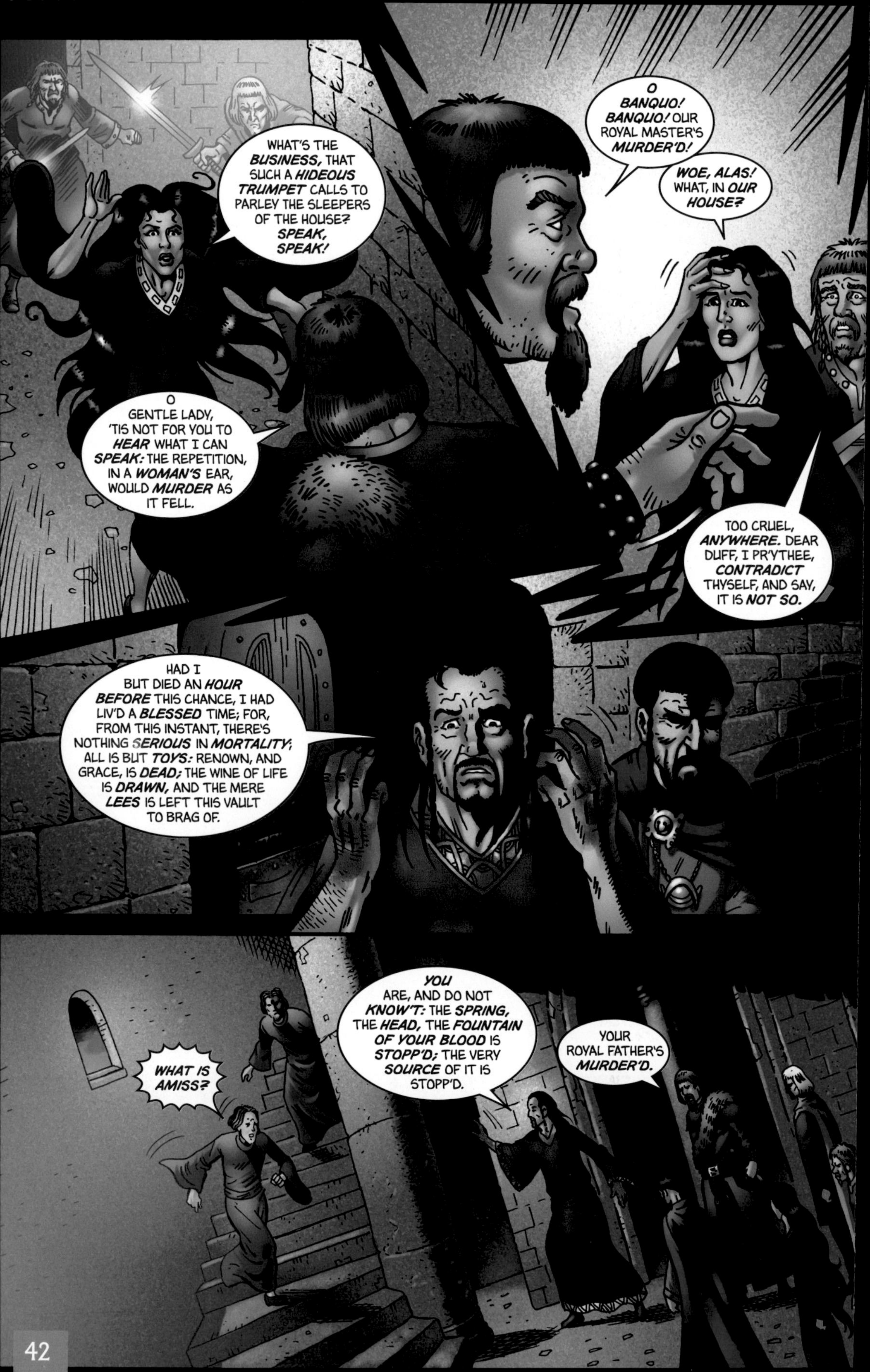
WHAT'S THE BUSINESS, THAT SUCH A HIDEOUS TRUMPET CALLS TO PARLEY THE SLEEPERS OF THE HOUSE? SPEAK, SPEAK!
O GENTLE LADY, 'TIS NOT FOR YOU TO HEAR WHAT I CAN SPEAK: THE REPETITION, IN A WOMAN'S EAR, WOULD MURDER AS IT FELL.
O BANQUO! BANQUO! OUR ROYAL MASTER'S MURDER'D!
WOE, ALAS! WHAT, IN OUR HOUSE?
TOO CRUEL, ANYWHERE. DEAR DUFF, I PR'YTHEE, CONTRADICT THYSELF, AND SAY, IT IS NOT SO.
HAD I BUT DIED AN HOUR BEFORE THIS CHANCE, I HAD LIV'D A BLESSED TIME; FOR, FROM THIS INSTANT, THERE'S NOTHING SERIOUS IN MORTALITY; ALL IS BUT TOYS: RENOWN, AND GRACE, IS DEAD; THE WINE OF LIFE IS DRAWN, AND THE MERE LEES IS LEFT THIS VAULT TO BRAG OF.
WHAT IS AMISS?
YOU ARE, AND DO NOT KNOW'T: THE SPRING, THE HEAD, THE FOUNTAIN OF YOUR BLOOD IS STOPP'D; THE VERY SOURCE OF IT IS STOPP'D.
YOUR ROYAL FATHER'S MURDER'D.

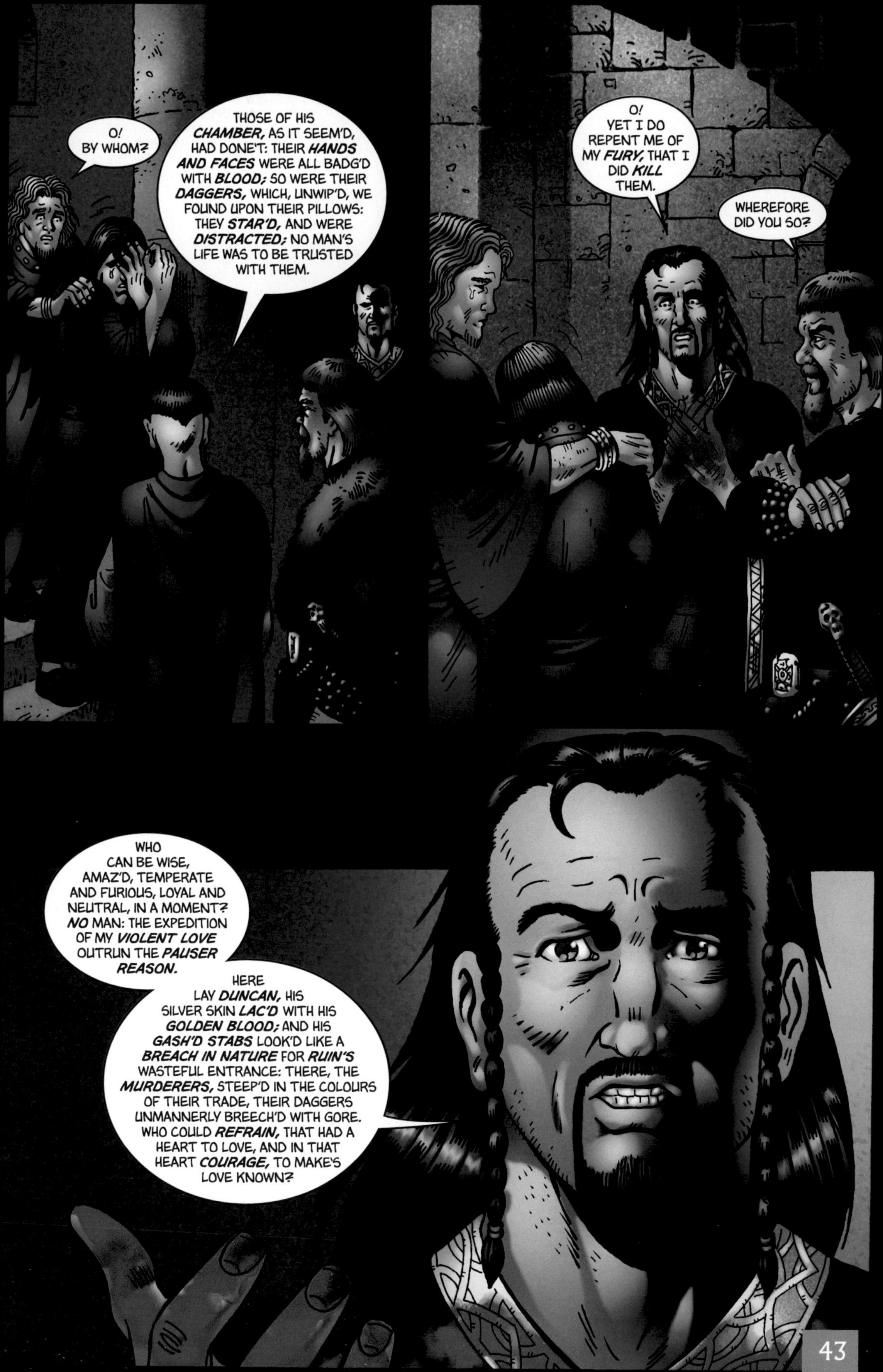
O! BY WHOM?
THOSE OF HIS CHAMBER, AS IT SEEM'D, HAD DONE'T: THEIR HANDS AND FACES WERE ALL BADG'D WITH BLOOD; SO WERE THEIR DAGGERS, WHICH, UNWIP'D, WE FOUND UPON THEIR PILLOWS: THEY STAR'D, AND WERE DISTRACTED; NO MAN'S LIFE WAS TO BE TRUSTED WITH THEM.
O! YET I DO REPENT ME OF MY FURY, THAT I DID KILL THEM.
WHEREFORE DID YOU SO?
WHO CAN BE WISE, AMAZ'D, TEMPERATE AND FURIOUS, LOYAL AND NEUTRAL, IN A MOMENT? NO MAN: THE EXPEDITION OF MY VIOLENT LOVE OUTRUN THE PAUSER REASON.
HERE LAY DUNCAN, HIS SILVER SKIN LAC'D WITH HIS GOLDEN BLOOD; AND HIS GASH'D STABS LOOK'D LIKE A BREACH IN NATURE FOR RUIN'S WASTEFUL ENTRANCE: THERE, THE MURDERERS, STEEP'D IN THE COLOURS OF THEIR TRADE, THEIR DAGGERS UNMANNERLY BREECH'D WITH GORE. WHO COULD REFRAIN, THAT HAD A HEART TO LOVE, AND IN THAT HEART COURAGE, TO MAKE'S LOVE KNOWN?

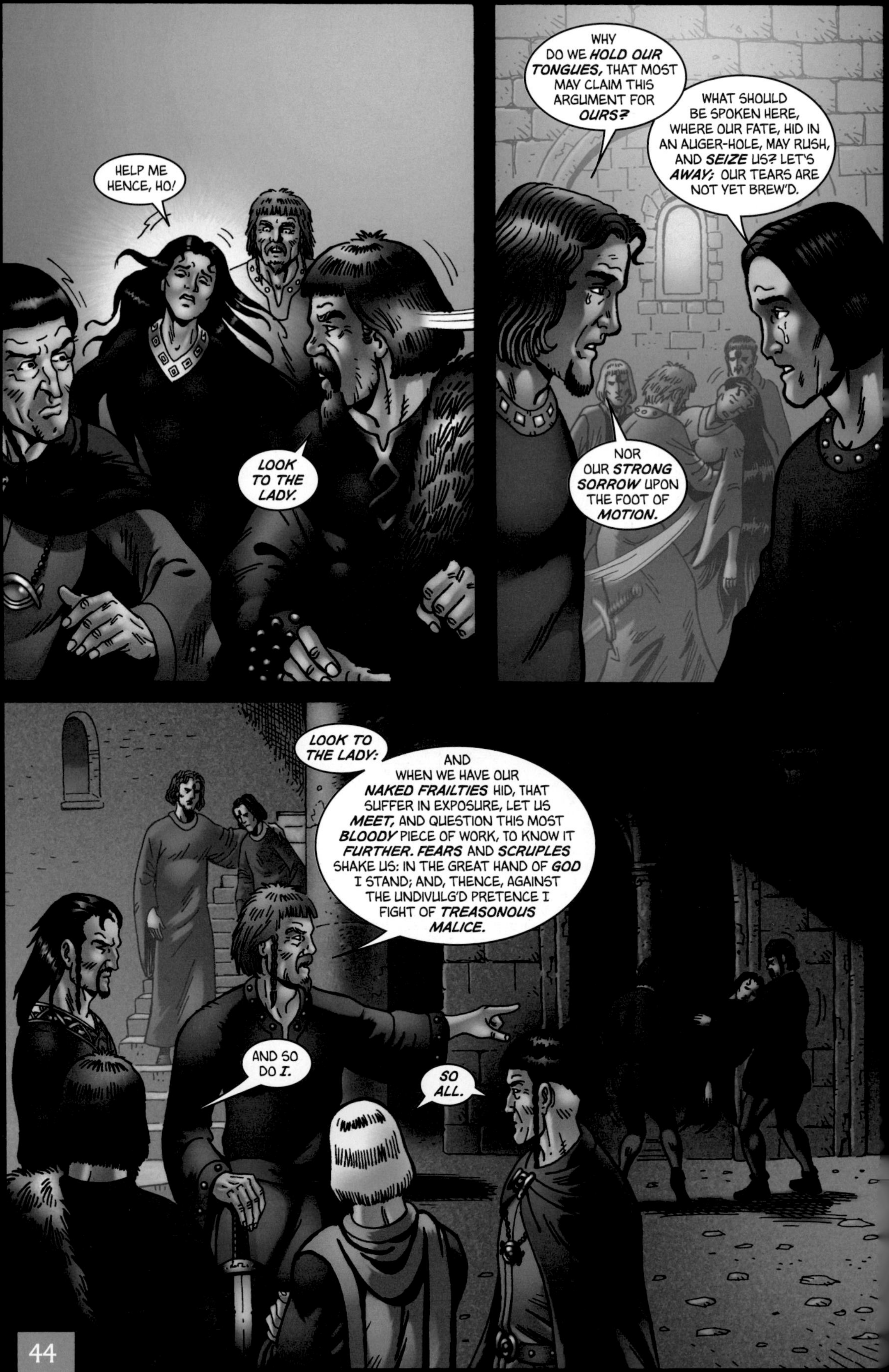
HELP ME HENCE, HO!
LOOK TO THE LADY.
WHY DO WE HOLD OUR TONGUES, THAT MOST MAY CLAIM THIS ARGUMENT FOR OURS?
WHAT SHOULD BE SPOKEN HERE, WHERE OUR FATE, HID IN AN AUGER-HOLE, MAY RUSH, AND SEIZE US? LET'S AWAY; OUR TEARS ARE NOT YET BREW'D.
NOR OUR STRONG SORROW UPON THE FOOT OF MOTION.
LOOK TO THE LADY:
AND WHEN WE HAVE OUR NAKED FRAILTIES HID, THAT SUFFER IN EXPOSURE, LET US MEET, AND QUESTION THIS MOST BLOODY PIECE OF WORK, TO KNOW IT FURTHER. FEARS AND SCRUPLES SHAKE US: IN THE GREAT HAND OF GOD I STAND; AND, THENCE, AGAINST THE UNDIVULG'D PRETENCE I FIGHT OF TREASONOUS MALICE.
AND SO DO I.
SO ALL.

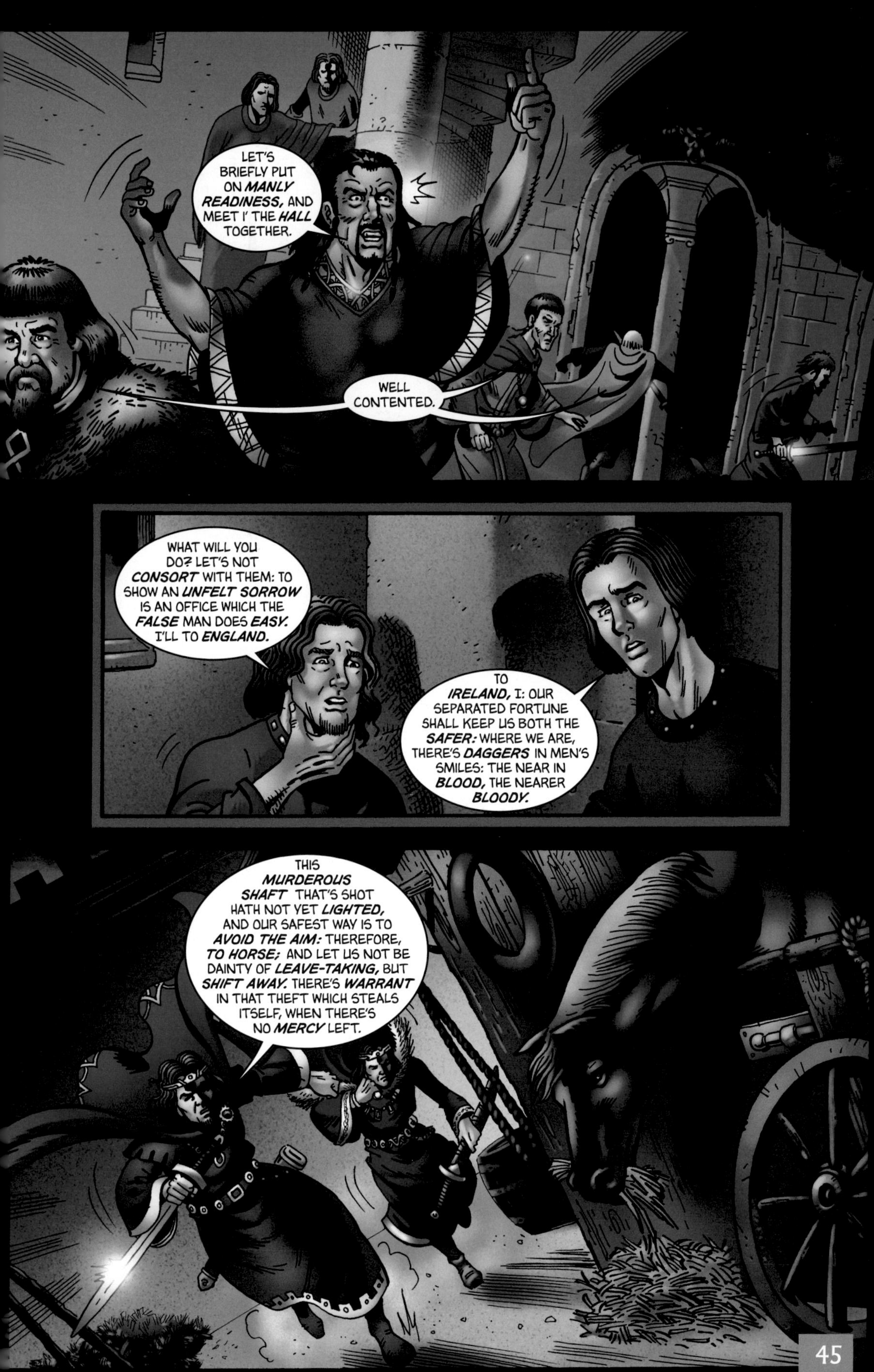
LET'S BRIEFLY PUT ON MANLY READINESS, AND MEET I' THE HALL TOGETHER.
WELL CONTENTED.
WHAT WILL YOU DO? LET'S NOT CONSORT WITH THEM: TO SHOW AN UNFELT SORROW IS AN OFFICE WHICH THE FALSE MAN DOES EASY. I'LL TO ENGLAND.
TO IRELAND, I: OUR SEPARATED FORTUNE SHALL KEEP US BOTH THE SAFER: WHERE WE ARE, THERE'S DAGGERS IN MEN'S SMILES: THE NEAR IN BLOOD, THE NEARER BLOODY.
THIS MURDEROUS SHAFT THAT'S SHOT HATH NOT YET LIGHTED, AND OUR SAFEST WAY IS TO AVOID THE AIM: THEREFORE, TO HORSE; AND LET US NOT BE DAINTY OF LEAVE-TAKING, BUT SHIFT AWAY. THERE'S WARRANT IN THAT THEFT WHICH STEALS ITSELF, WHEN THERE'S NO MERCY LEFT.

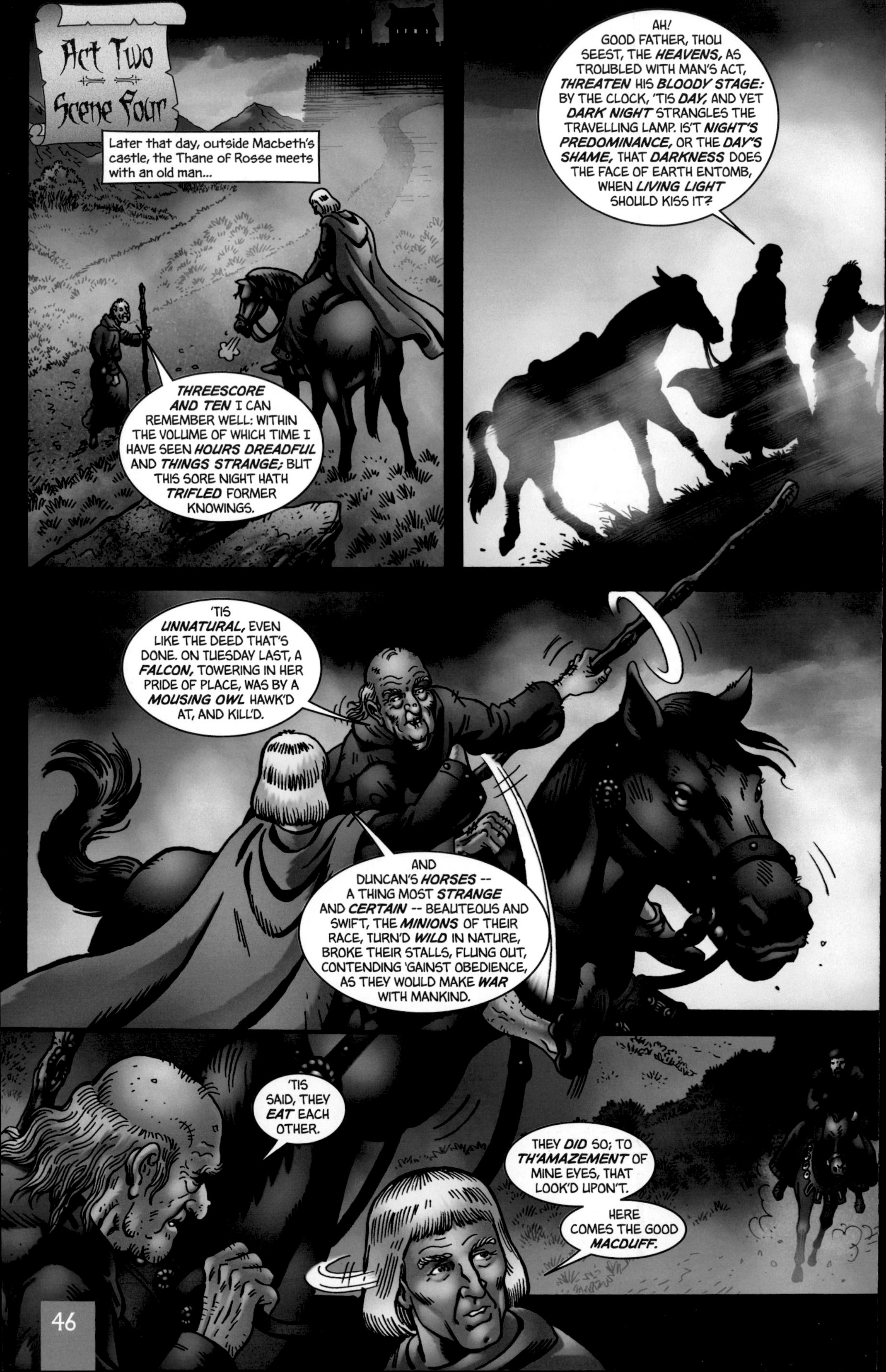

Act Two
Scene Four
Later that day, outside Macbeth's castle, the Thane of Rosse meets with an old man...
THREESCORE AND TEN I CAN REMEMBER WELL: WITHIN THE VOLUME OF WHICH TIME I HAVE SEEN HOURS DREADFUL AND THINGS STRANGE; BUT THIS SORE NIGHT HATH TRIFLED FORMER KNOWINGS.
AH! GOOD FATHER, THOU SEEST, THE HEAVENS, AS TROUBLED WITH MAN'S ACT, THREATEN HIS BLOODY STAGE: BY THE CLOCK, 'TIS DAY, AND YET DARK NIGHT STRANGLES THE TRAVELLING LAMP. IS'T NIGHT'S PREDOMINANCE, OR THE DAY'S SHAME, THAT DARKNESS DOES THE FACE OF EARTH ENTOMB, WHEN LIVING LIGHT SHOULD KISS IT?
'TIS UNNATURAL, EVEN LIKE THE DEED THAT'S DONE. ON TUESDAY LAST, A FALCON, TOWERING IN HER PRIDE OF PLACE, WAS BY A MOUSING OWL HAWK'D AT, AND KILL'D.
AND DUNCAN'S HORSES -- A THING MOST STRANGE AND CERTAIN -- BEAUTEOUS AND SWIFT, THE MINIONS OF THEIR RACE, TURN'D WILD IN NATURE, BROKE THEIR STALLS, FLUNG OUT, CONTENDING 'GAINST OBEDIENCE, AS THEY WOULD MAKE WAR WITH MANKIND.
'TIS SAID, THEY EAT EACH OTHER.
THEY DID SO; TO TH'AMAZEMENT OF MINE EYES, THAT LOOK'D UPON'T.
HERE COMES THE GOOD MACDUFF.

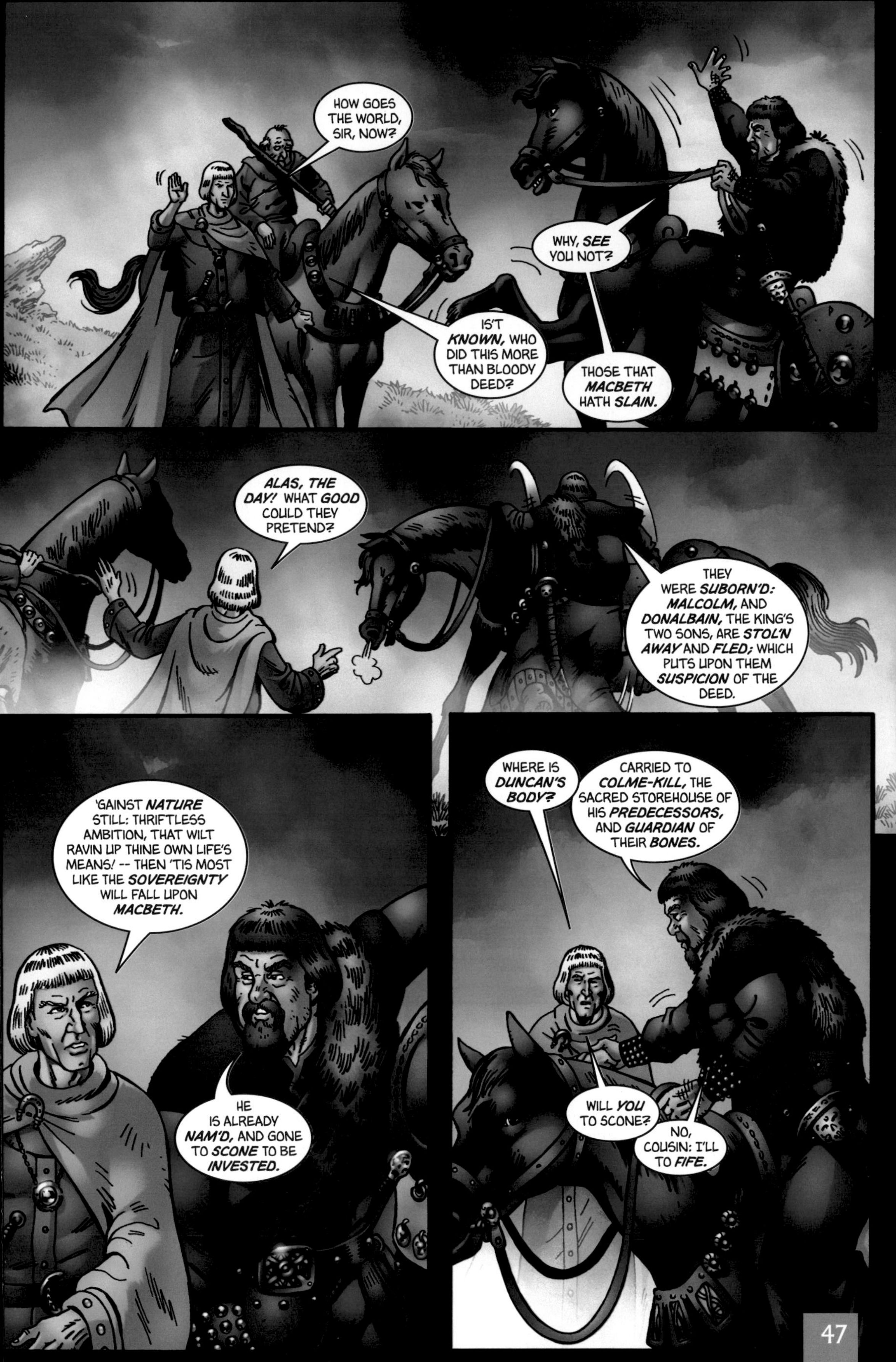
HOW GOES THE WORLD, SIR, NOW?
WHY, SEE YOU NOT?
IS'T KNOWN, WHO DID THIS MORE THAN BLOODY DEED?
THOSE THAT MACBETH HATH SLAIN.
ALAS, THE DAY! WHAT GOOD COULD THEY PRETEND?
THEY WERE SUBORN'D: MALCOLM, AND DONALBAIN, THE KING'S TWO SONS, ARE STOL'N AWAY AND FLED; WHICH PUTS UPON THEM SUSPICION OF THE DEED.
'GAINST NATURE STILL: THRIFTLESS AMBITION, THAT WILT RAVIN UP THINE OWN LIFE'S MEANS! -- THEN 'TIS MOST LIKE THE SOVEREIGNTY WILL FALL UPON MACBETH.
HE IS ALREADY NAM'D, AND GONE TO SCONE TO BE INVESTED.
WHERE IS DUNCAN'S BODY?
CARRIED TO COLME-KILL, THE SACRED STOREHOUSE OF HIS PREDECESSORS, AND GUARDIAN OF THEIR BONES.
WILL YOU TO SCONE?
NO, COUSIN: I'LL TO FIFE.

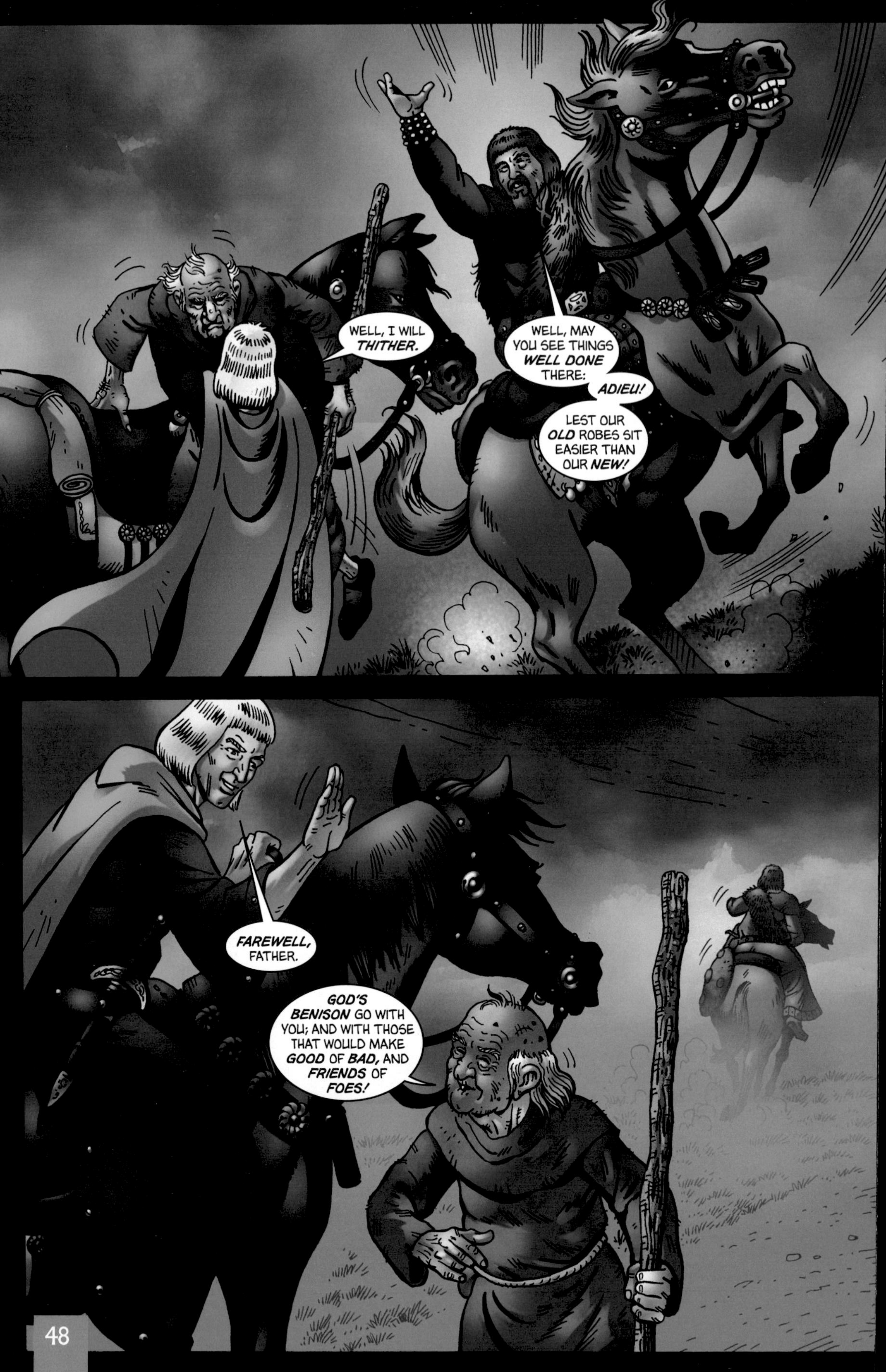
WELL, I WILL THITHER.
WELL, MAY YOU SEE THINGS WELL DONE THERE:
ADIEU!
LEST OUR OLD ROBES SIT EASIER THAN OUR NEW!
FAREWELL, FATHER.
GOD'S BENISON GO WITH YOU; AND WITH THOSE THAT WOULD MAKE GOOD OF BAD, AND FRIENDS OF FOES!

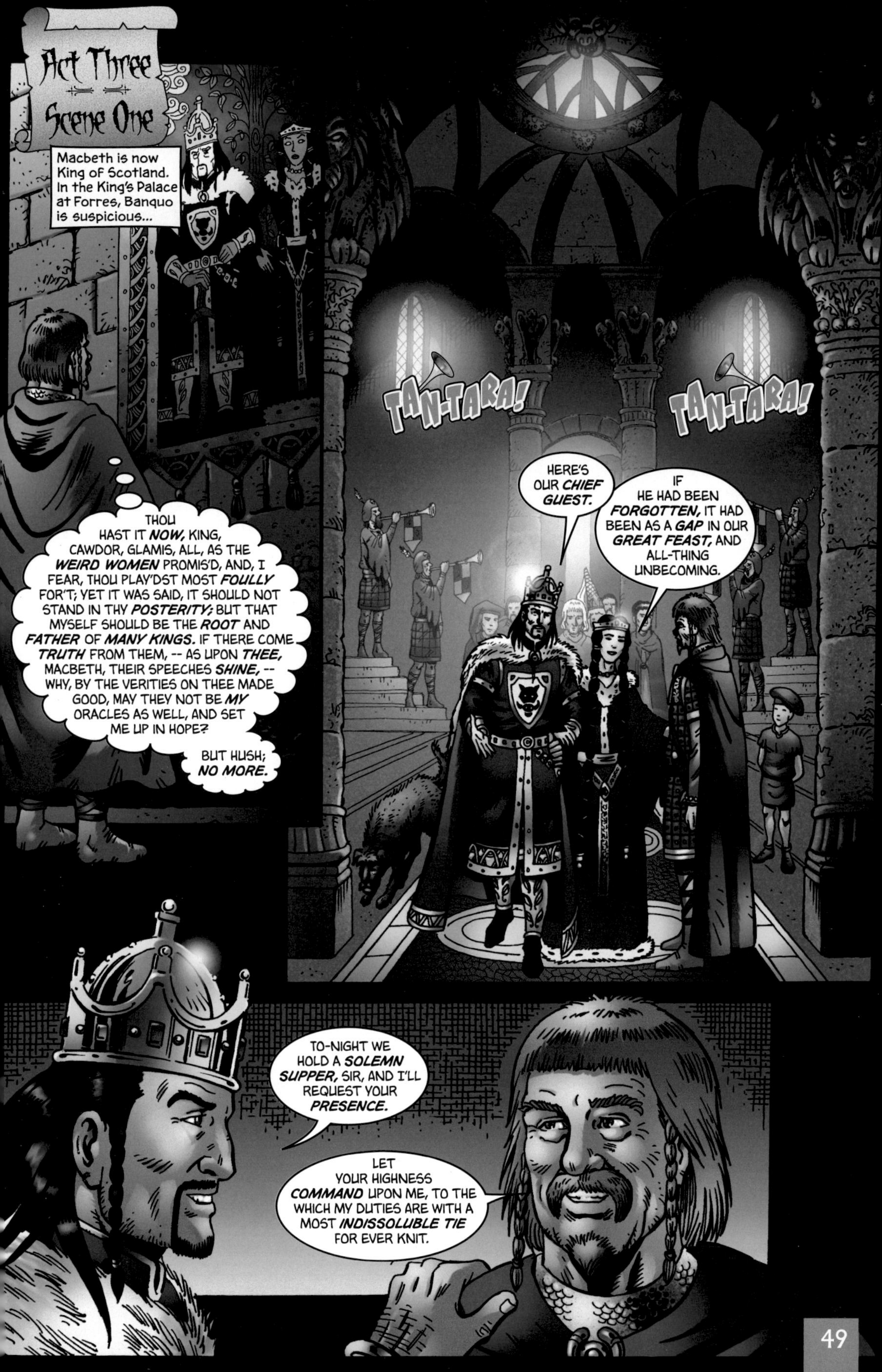
Act Three
Scene One
Macbeth is now King of Scotland. In the King's Palace at Forres, Banquo is suspicious...
THOU HAST IT NOW, KING, CAWDOR, GLAMIS, ALL, AS THE WEIRD WOMEN PROMIS'D, AND, I FEAR, THOU PLAY'DST MOST FOULLY FOR'T; YET IT WAS SAID, IT SHOULD NOT STAND IN THY POSTERITY; BUT THAT MYSELF SHOULD BE THE ROOT AND FATHER OF MANY KINGS. IF THERE COME TRUTH FROM THEM, -- AS UPON THEE, MACBETH, THEIR SPEECHES SHINE, -- WHY, BY THE VERITIES ON THEE MADE GOOD, MAY THEY NOT BE MY ORACLES AS WELL, AND SET ME UP IN HOPE?
BUT HUSH; NO MORE.
TAN-TARA!
TAN-TARA!
HERE'S OUR CHIEF GUEST.
IF HE HAD BEEN FORGOTTEN, IT HAD BEEN AS A GAP IN OUR GREAT FEAST, AND ALL-THING UNBECOMING.
TO-NIGHT WE HOLD A SOLEMN SUPPER, SIR, AND I'LL REQUEST YOUR PRESENCE.
LET YOUR HIGHNESS COMMAND UPON ME, TO THE WHICH MY DUTIES ARE WITH A MOST INDISSOLUBLE TIE FOR EVER KNIT.

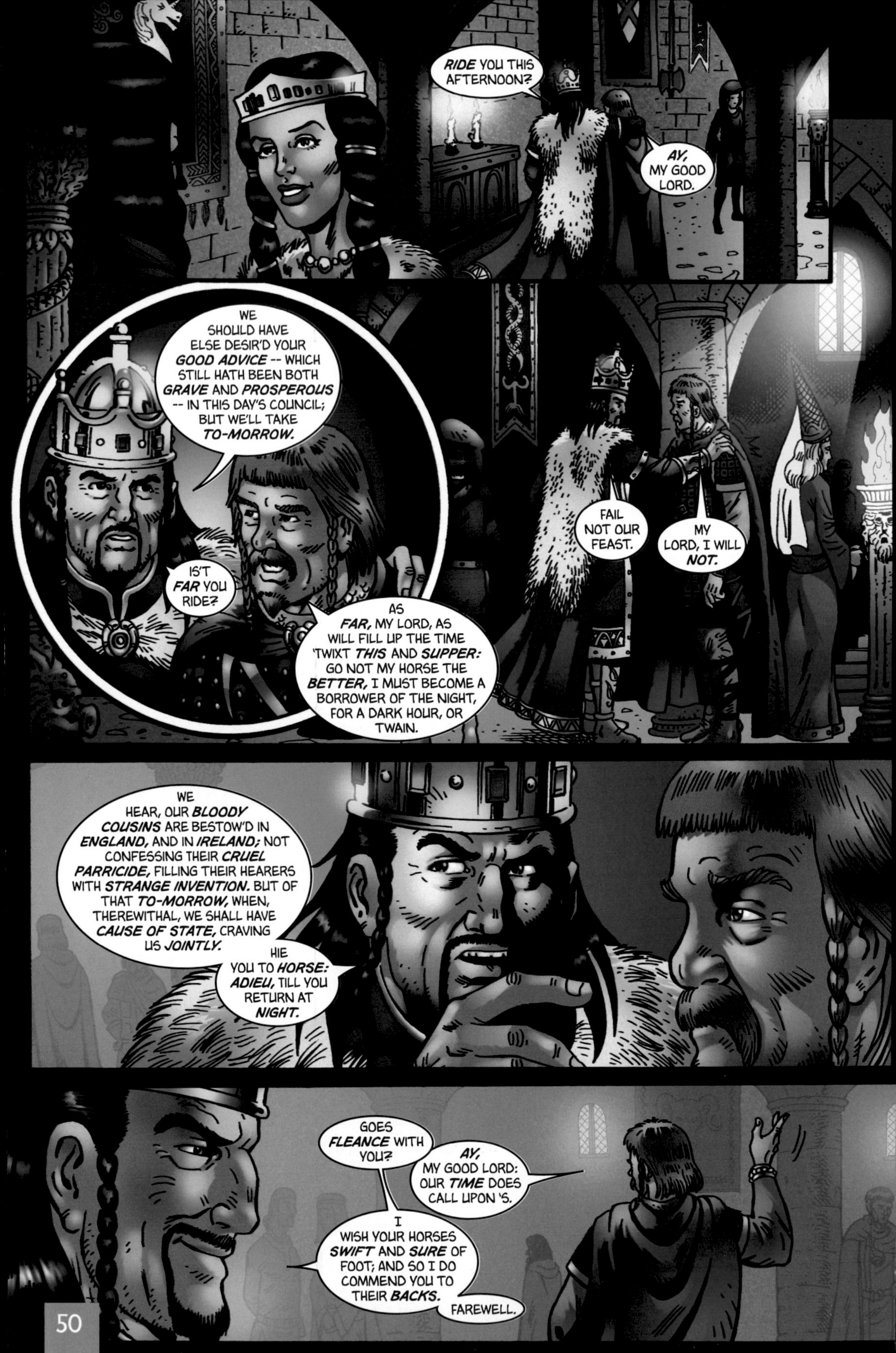
RIDE YOU THIS AFTERNOON?
AY, MY GOOD LORD.
WE SHOULD HAVE ELSE DESIR'D YOUR GOOD ADVICE -- WHICH STILL HATH BEEN BOTH GRAVE AND PROSPEROUS -- IN THIS DAY'S COUNCIL; BUT WE'LL TAKE TO-MORROW.
IS'T FAR YOU RIDE?
AS FAR, MY LORD, AS WILL FILL UP THE TIME 'TWIXT THIS AND SUPPER: GO NOT MY HORSE THE BETTER, I MUST BECOME A BORROWER OF THE NIGHT, FOR A DARK HOUR, OR TWAIN.
FAIL NOT OUR FEAST.
MY LORD, I WILL NOT.
WE HEAR, OUR BLOODY COUSINS ARE BESTOW'D IN ENGLAND, AND IN IRELAND; NOT CONFESSING THEIR CRUEL PARRICIDE, FILLING THEIR HEARERS WITH STRANGE INVENTION. BUT OF THAT TO-MORROW, WHEN, THEREWITHAL, WE SHALL HAVE CAUSE OF STATE, CRAVING US JOINTLY.
HIE YOU TO HORSE: ADIEU, TILL YOU RETURN AT NIGHT.
GOES FLEANCE WITH YOU?
AY, MY GOOD LORD: OUR TIME DOES CALL UPON 'S.
I WISH YOUR HORSES SWIFT AND SURE OF FOOT; AND SO I DO COMMEND YOU TO THEIR BACKS.
FAREWELL.

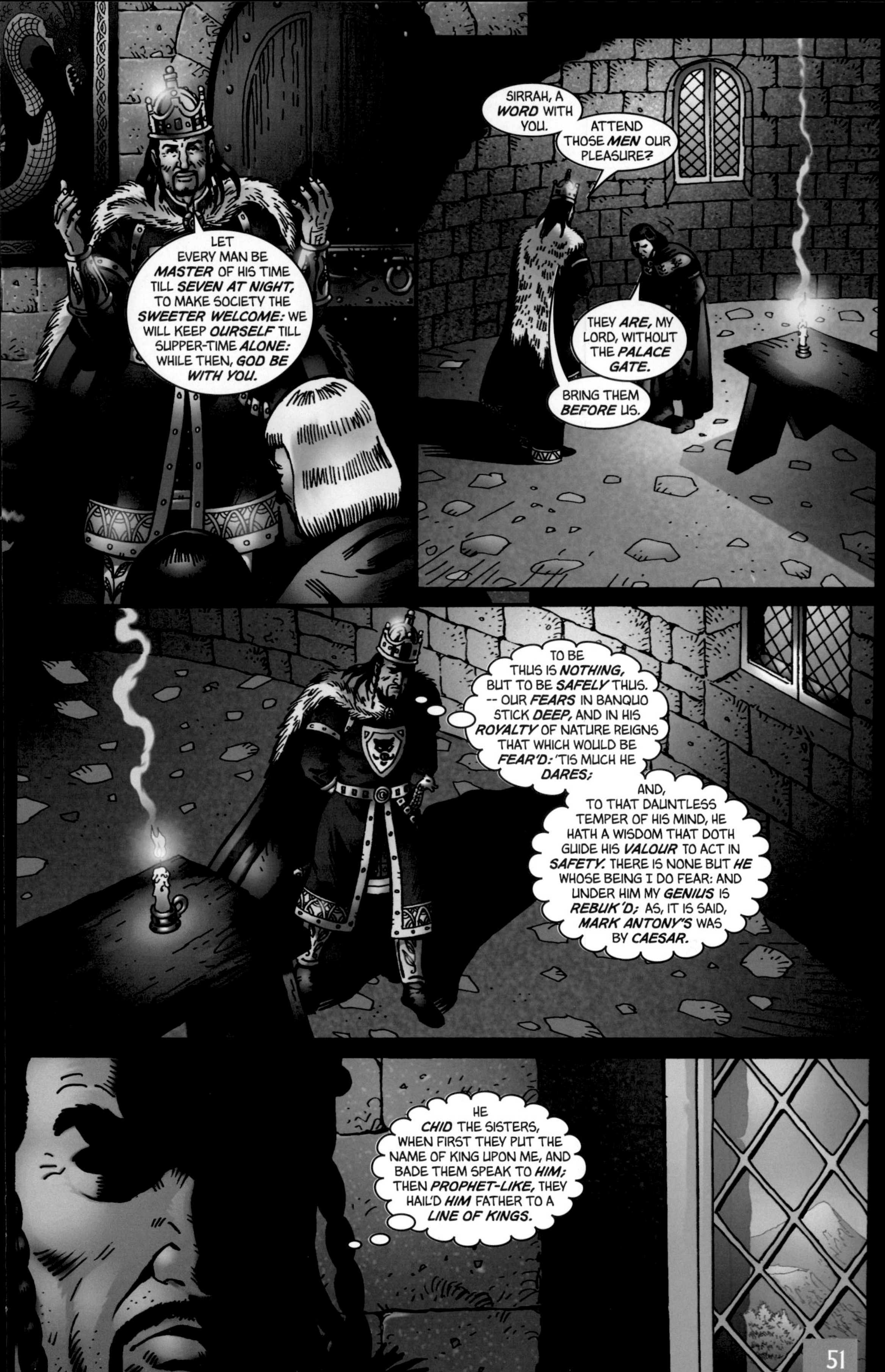
LET EVERY MAN BE MASTER OF HIS TIME TILL SEVEN AT NIGHT, TO MAKE SOCIETY THE SWEETER WELCOME: WE WILL KEEP OURSELF TILL SUPPER-TIME ALONE: WHILE THEN, GOD BE WITH YOU.
SIRRAH, A WORD WITH YOU.
ATTEND THOSE MEN OUR PLEASURE?
THEY ARE, MY LORD, WITHOUT THE PALACE GATE.
BRING THEM BEFORE US.
TO BE THUS IS NOTHING, BUT TO BE SAFELY THUS. -- OUR FEARS IN BANQUO STICK DEEP, AND IN HIS ROYALTY OF NATURE REIGNS THAT WHICH WOULD BE FEAR'D: 'TIS MUCH HE DARES;
AND, TO THAT DAUNTLESS TEMPER OF HIS MIND, HE HATH A WISDOM THAT DOTH GUIDE HIS VALOUR TO ACT IN SAFETY. THERE IS NONE BUT HE WHOSE BEING I DO FEAR: AND UNDER HIM MY GENIUS IS REBUK'D; AS, IT IS SAID, MARK ANTONY'S WAS BY CAESAR.
HE CHID THE SISTERS, WHEN FIRST THEY PUT THE NAME OF KING UPON ME, AND BADE THEM SPEAK TO HIM; THEN PROPHET-LIKE, THEY HAIL'D HIM FATHER TO A LINE OF KINGS.

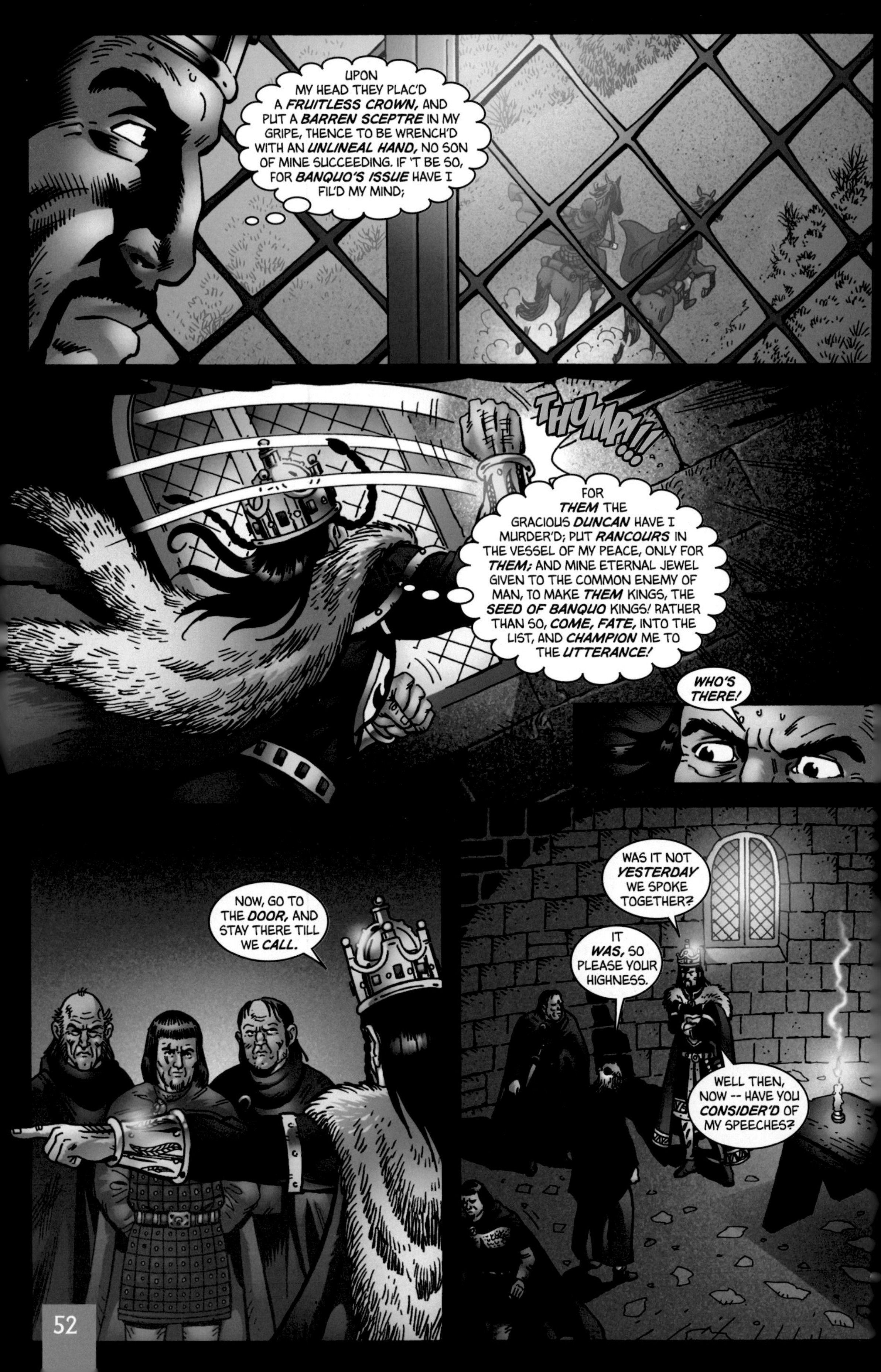
UPON MY HEAD THEY PLAC'D A FRUITLESS CROWN, AND PUT A BARREN SCEPTRE IN MY GRIPE, THENCE TO BE WRENCH'D WITH AN UNLINEAL HAND, NO SON OF MINE SUCCEEDING. IF 'T BE SO, FOR BANQUO'S ISSUE HAVE I FIL'D MY MIND;
THUMP!!!
FOR THEM THE GRACIOUS DUNCAN HAVE I MURDER'D; PUT RANCOURS IN THE VESSEL OF MY PEACE, ONLY FOR THEM; AND MINE ETERNAL JEWEL GIVEN TO THE COMMON ENEMY OF MAN, TO MAKE THEM KINGS, THE SEED OF BANQUO KINGS! RATHER THAN SO, COME, FATE, INTO THE LIST, AND CHAMPION ME TO THE UTTERANCE!
WHO'S THERE!
NOW, GO TO THE DOOR, AND STAY THERE TILL WE CALL.
WAS IT NOT YESTERDAY WE SPOKE TOGETHER?
IT WAS, SO PLEASE YOUR HIGHNESS.
WELL THEN, NOW -- HAVE YOU CONSIDER'D OF MY SPEECHES?

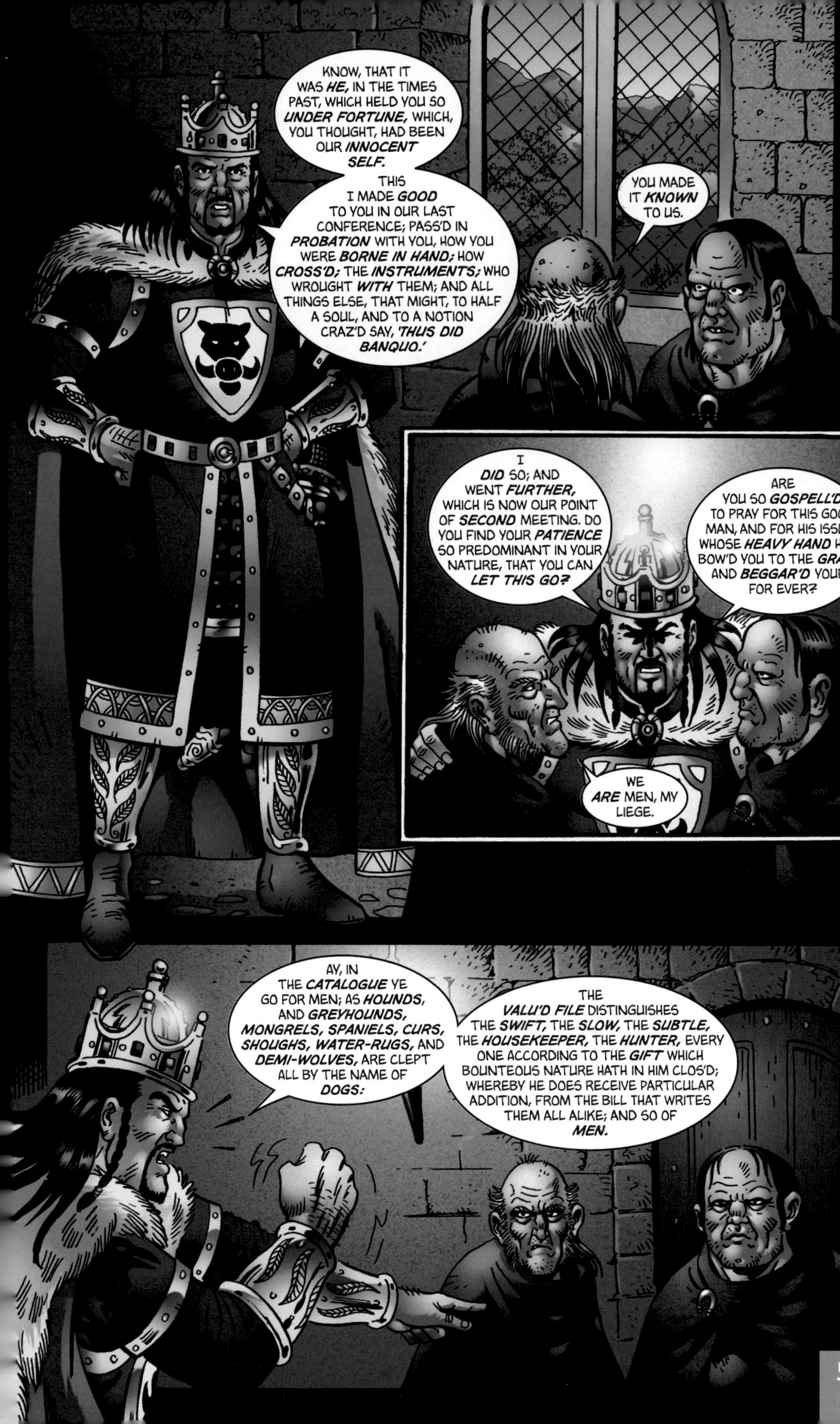
KNOW, THAT IT WAS HE, IN THE TIMES PAST, WHICH HELD YOU SO UNDER FORTUNE, WHICH, YOU THOUGHT, HAD BEEN OUR INNOCENT SELF.
THIS I MADE GOOD TO YOU IN OUR LAST CONFERENCE; PASS'D IN PROBATION WITH YOU, HOW YOU WERE BORNE IN HAND; HOW CROSS'D; THE INSTRUMENTS; WHO WROUGHT WITH THEM; AND ALL THINGS ELSE, THAT MIGHT, TO HALF A SOUL, AND TO A NOTION CRAZ'D SAY, 'THUS DID BANQUO.'
YOU MADE IT KNOWN TO US.
I DID SO; AND WENT FURTHER, WHICH IS NOW OUR POINT OF SECOND MEETING. DO YOU FIND YOUR PATIENCE SO PREDOMINANT IN YOUR NATURE, THAT YOU CAN LET THIS GO?
ARE YOU SO GOSPELL'D TO PRAY FOR THIS GOOD MAN, AND FOR HIS ISSUE, WHOSE HEAVY HAND HATH BOW'D YOU TO THE GRAVE, AND BEGGAR'D YOURS FOR EVER?
WE ARE MEN, MY LIEGE.
AY, IN THE CATALOGUE YE GO FOR MEN; AS HOUNDS, AND GREYHOUNDS, MONGRELS, SPANIELS, CURS, SHOUGHS, WATER-RUGS, AND DEMI-WOLVES, ARE CLEPT ALL BY THE NAME OF DOGS:
THE VALU'D FILE DISTINGUISHES THE SWIFT, THE SLOW, THE SUBTLE, THE HOUSEKEEPER, THE HUNTER, EVERY ONE ACCORDING TO THE GIFT WHICH BOUNTEOUS NATURE HATH IN HIM CLOS'D; WHEREBY HE DOES RECEIVE PARTICULAR ADDITION, FROM THE BILL THAT WRITES THEM ALL ALIKE; AND SO OF MEN.

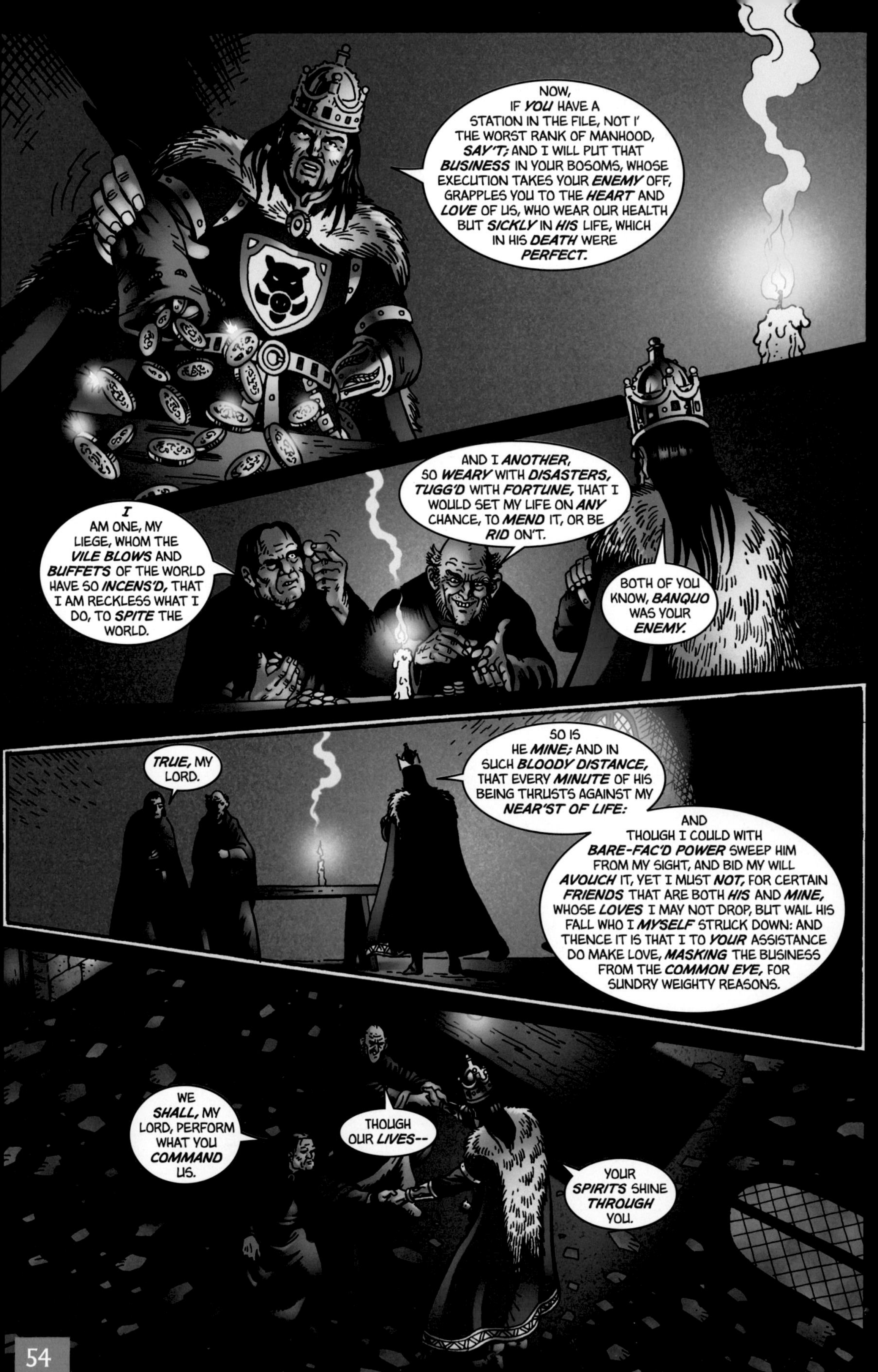
NOW, IF *YOU* HAVE A STATION IN THE FILE, NOT I' THE WORST RANK OF MANHOOD, *SAY'T;* AND I WILL PUT THAT *BUSINESS* IN YOUR BOSOMS, WHOSE EXECUTION TAKES YOUR *ENEMY* OFF, GRAPPLES YOU TO THE *HEART* AND *LOVE* OF US, WHO WEAR OUR HEALTH BUT *SICKLY* IN *HIS* LIFE, WHICH IN HIS *DEATH* WERE *PERFECT.*
I AM ONE, MY LIEGE, WHOM THE *VILE BLOWS* AND *BUFFETS* OF THE WORLD HAVE SO *INCENS'D,* THAT I AM RECKLESS WHAT I DO, TO *SPITE* THE WORLD.
AND I *ANOTHER,* SO *WEARY* WITH *DISASTERS, TUGG'D* WITH *FORTUNE,* THAT I WOULD SET MY LIFE ON *ANY* CHANCE, TO *MEND* IT, OR BE *RID* ON'T.
BOTH OF YOU KNOW, *BANQUO* WAS YOUR *ENEMY.*
TRUE, MY LORD.
SO IS HE *MINE;* AND IN SUCH *BLOODY DISTANCE,* THAT EVERY *MINUTE* OF HIS BEING THRUSTS AGAINST MY *NEAR'ST OF LIFE:*
AND THOUGH I COULD WITH *BARE-FAC'D POWER* SWEEP HIM FROM MY SIGHT, AND BID MY WILL *AVOUCH* IT, YET I MUST *NOT,* FOR CERTAIN *FRIENDS* THAT ARE BOTH *HIS* AND *MINE,* WHOSE *LOVES* I MAY NOT DROP, BUT WAIL HIS FALL WHO I *MYSELF* STRUCK DOWN: AND THENCE IT IS THAT I TO *YOUR* ASSISTANCE DO MAKE LOVE, *MASKING* THE BUSINESS FROM THE *COMMON EYE,* FOR SUNDRY WEIGHTY REASONS.
WE *SHALL,* MY LORD, PERFORM WHAT YOU *COMMAND* US.
THOUGH OUR *LIVES*--
YOUR *SPIRITS* SHINE *THROUGH* YOU.

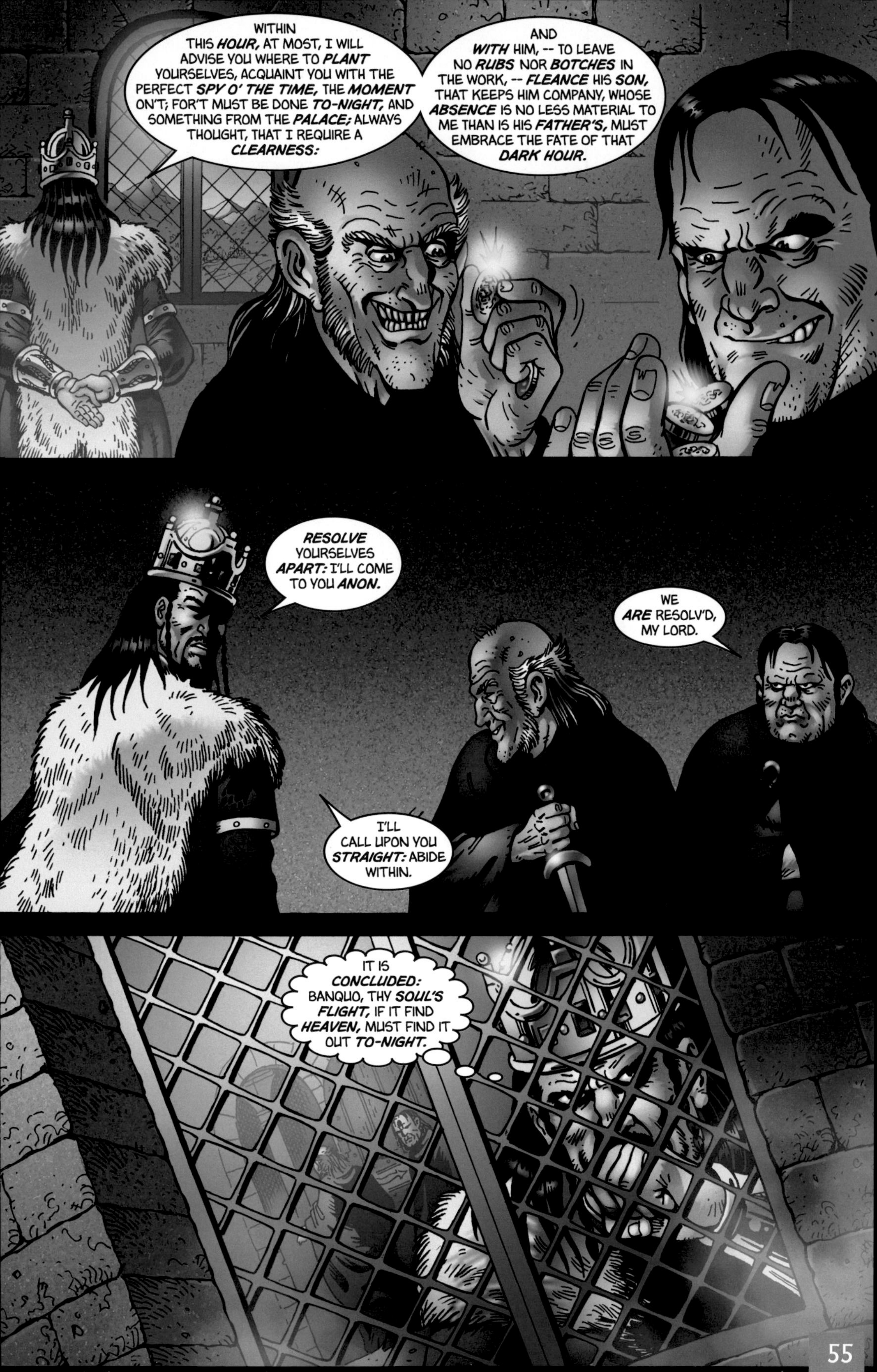
WITHIN THIS HOUR, AT MOST, I WILL ADVISE YOU WHERE TO PLANT YOURSELVES, ACQUAINT YOU WITH THE PERFECT SPY O' THE TIME, THE MOMENT ON'T; FOR'T MUST BE DONE TO-NIGHT, AND SOMETHING FROM THE PALACE; ALWAYS THOUGHT, THAT I REQUIRE A CLEARNESS:
AND WITH HIM, -- TO LEAVE NO RUBS NOR BOTCHES IN THE WORK, -- FLEANCE HIS SON, THAT KEEPS HIM COMPANY, WHOSE ABSENCE IS NO LESS MATERIAL TO ME THAN IS HIS FATHER'S, MUST EMBRACE THE FATE OF THAT DARK HOUR.
RESOLVE YOURSELVES APART: I'LL COME TO YOU ANON.
WE ARE RESOLV'D, MY LORD.
I'LL CALL UPON YOU STRAIGHT: ABIDE WITHIN.
IT IS CONCLUDED: BANQUO, THY SOUL'S FLIGHT, IF IT FIND HEAVEN, MUST FIND IT OUT TO-NIGHT.

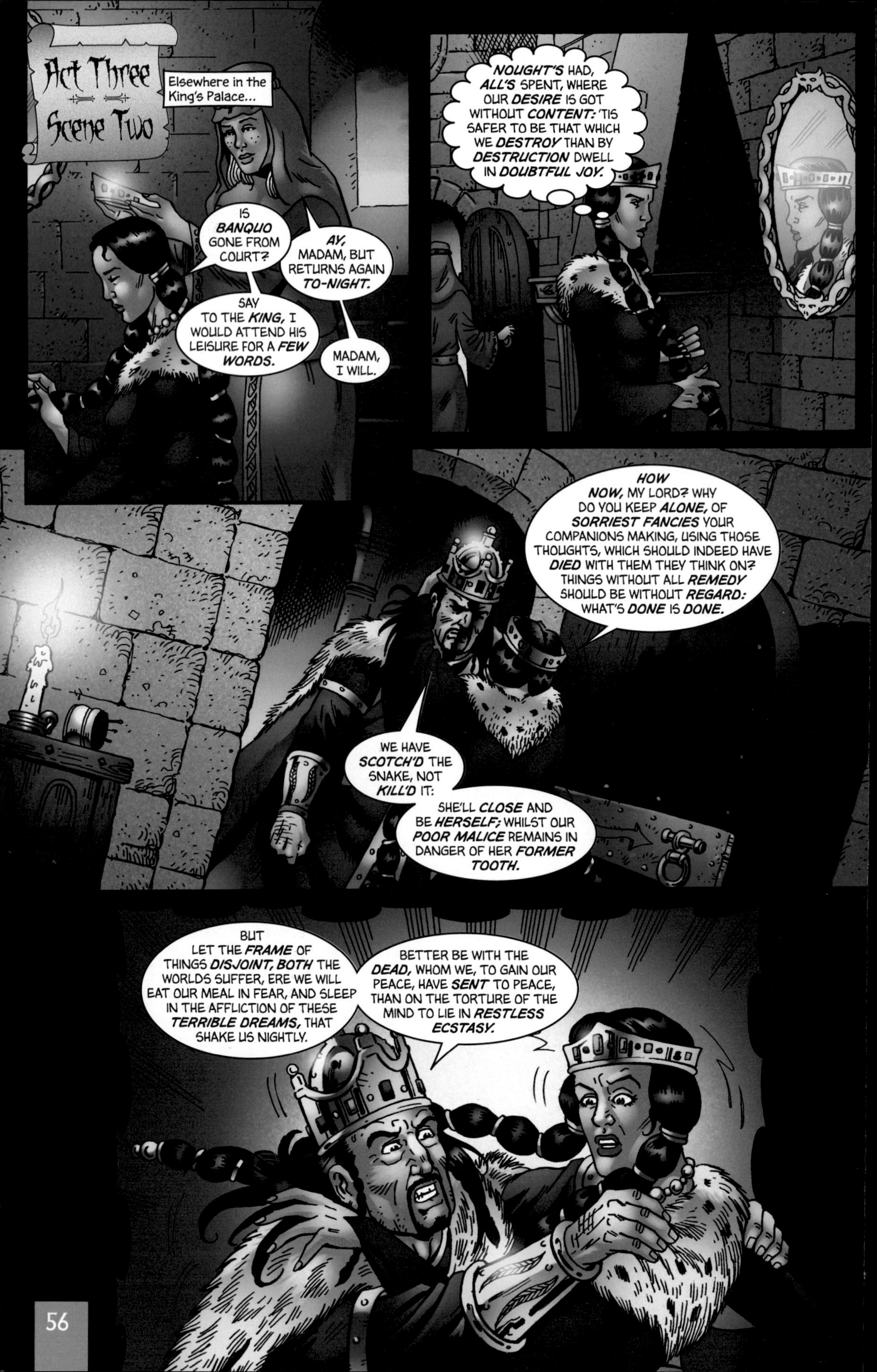
Act Three
Scene Two
Elsewhere in the King's Palace...
IS BANQUO GONE FROM COURT?
AY, MADAM, BUT RETURNS AGAIN TO-NIGHT.
SAY TO THE KING, I WOULD ATTEND HIS LEISURE FOR A FEW WORDS.
MADAM, I WILL.
NOUGHT'S HAD, ALL'S SPENT, WHERE OUR DESIRE IS GOT WITHOUT CONTENT: 'TIS SAFER TO BE THAT WHICH WE DESTROY THAN BY DESTRUCTION DWELL IN DOUBTFUL JOY.
HOW NOW, MY LORD? WHY DO YOU KEEP ALONE, OF SORRIEST FANCIES YOUR COMPANIONS MAKING, USING THOSE THOUGHTS, WHICH SHOULD INDEED HAVE DIED WITH THEM THEY THINK ON? THINGS WITHOUT ALL REMEDY SHOULD BE WITHOUT REGARD: WHAT'S DONE IS DONE.
WE HAVE SCOTCH'D THE SNAKE, NOT KILL'D IT:
SHE'LL CLOSE AND BE HERSELF; WHILST OUR POOR MALICE REMAINS IN DANGER OF HER FORMER TOOTH.
BUT LET THE FRAME OF THINGS DISJOINT, BOTH THE WORLDS SUFFER, ERE WE WILL EAT OUR MEAL IN FEAR, AND SLEEP IN THE AFFLICTION OF THESE TERRIBLE DREAMS, THAT SHAKE US NIGHTLY.
BETTER BE WITH THE DEAD, WHOM WE, TO GAIN OUR PEACE, HAVE SENT TO PEACE, THAN ON THE TORTURE OF THE MIND TO LIE IN RESTLESS ECSTASY.

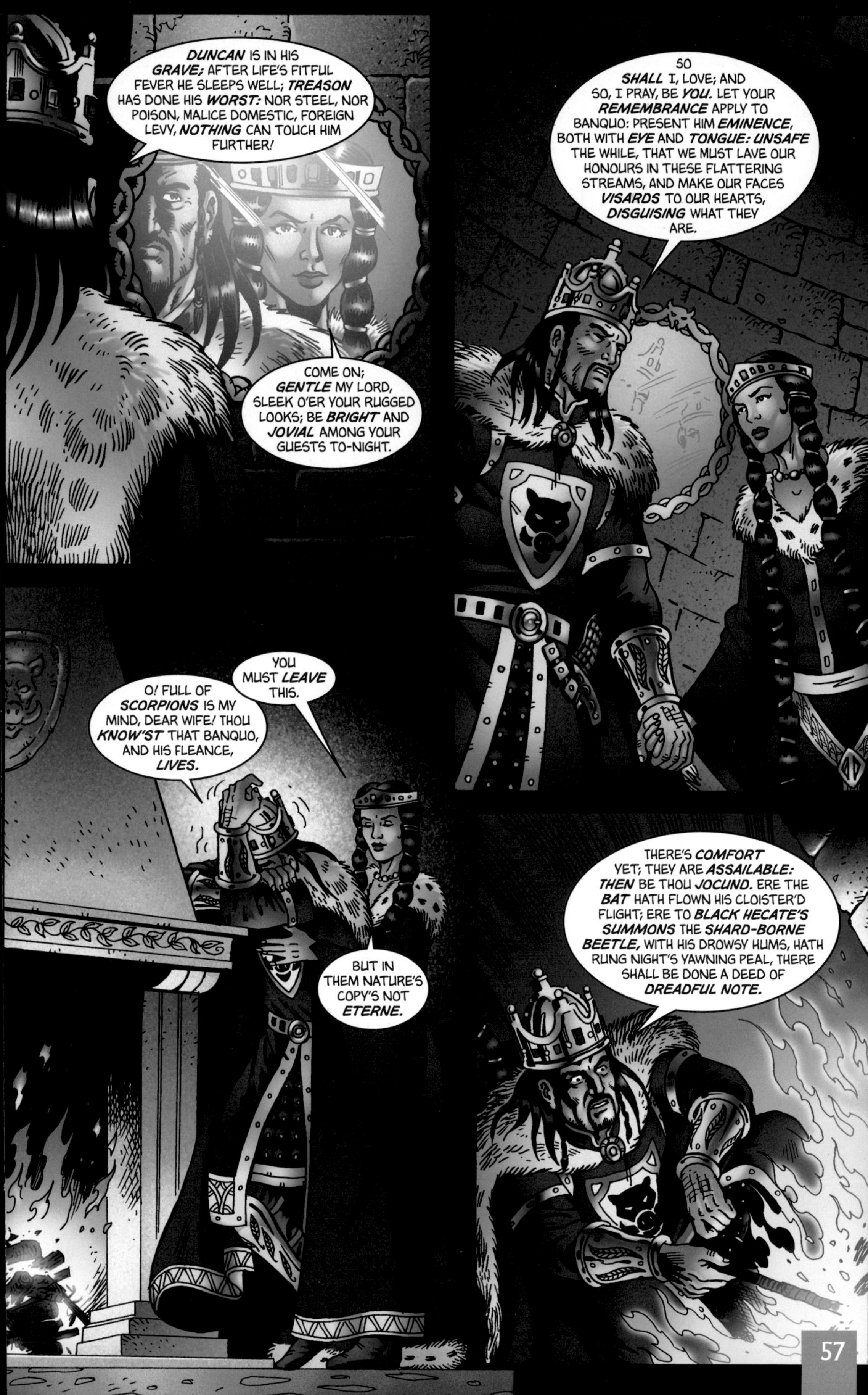
DUNCAN IS IN HIS GRAVE; AFTER LIFE'S FITFUL FEVER HE SLEEPS WELL; TREASON HAS DONE HIS WORST: NOR STEEL, NOR POISON, MALICE DOMESTIC, FOREIGN LEVY, NOTHING CAN TOUCH HIM FURTHER!
COME ON; GENTLE MY LORD, SLEEK O'ER YOUR RUGGED LOOKS; BE BRIGHT AND JOVIAL AMONG YOUR GUESTS TO-NIGHT.
SO SHALL I, LOVE; AND SO, I PRAY, BE YOU. LET YOUR REMEMBRANCE APPLY TO BANQUO: PRESENT HIM EMINENCE, BOTH WITH EYE AND TONGUE: UNSAFE THE WHILE, THAT WE MUST LAVE OUR HONOURS IN THESE FLATTERING STREAMS, AND MAKE OUR FACES VISARDS TO OUR HEARTS, DISGUISING WHAT THEY ARE.
YOU MUST LEAVE THIS.
O! FULL OF SCORPIONS IS MY MIND, DEAR WIFE! THOU KNOW'ST THAT BANQUO, AND HIS FLEANCE, LIVES.
BUT IN THEM NATURE'S COPY'S NOT ETERNE.
THERE'S COMFORT YET; THEY ARE ASSAILABLE: THEN BE THOU JOCUND. ERE THE BAT HATH FLOWN HIS CLOISTER'D FLIGHT; ERE TO BLACK HECATE'S SUMMONS THE SHARD-BORNE BEETLE, WITH HIS DROWSY HUMS, HATH RUNG NIGHT'S YAWNING PEAL, THERE SHALL BE DONE A DEED OF DREADFUL NOTE.

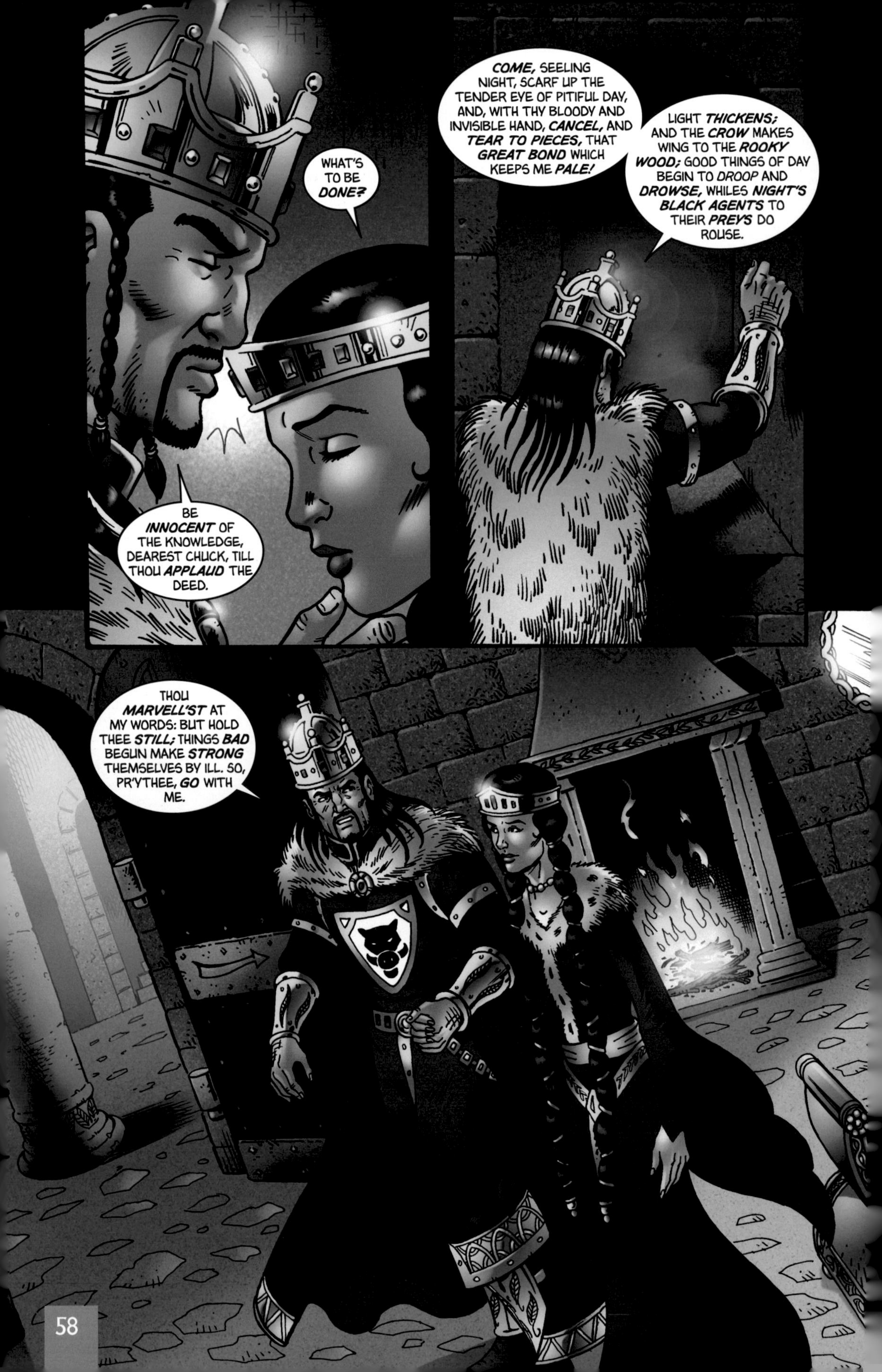
WHAT'S TO BE DONE?
COME, SEELING NIGHT, SCARF UP THE TENDER EYE OF PITIFUL DAY, AND, WITH THY BLOODY AND INVISIBLE HAND, CANCEL, AND TEAR TO PIECES, THAT GREAT BOND WHICH KEEPS ME PALE!
LIGHT THICKENS; AND THE CROW MAKES WING TO THE ROOKY WOOD; GOOD THINGS OF DAY BEGIN TO DROOP AND DROWSE, WHILES NIGHT'S BLACK AGENTS TO THEIR PREYS DO ROUSE.
BE INNOCENT OF THE KNOWLEDGE, DEAREST CHUCK, TILL THOU APPLAUD THE DEED.
THOU MARVELL'ST AT MY WORDS: BUT HOLD THEE STILL; THINGS BAD BEGUN MAKE STRONG THEMSELVES BY ILL. SO, PR'YTHEE, GO WITH ME.

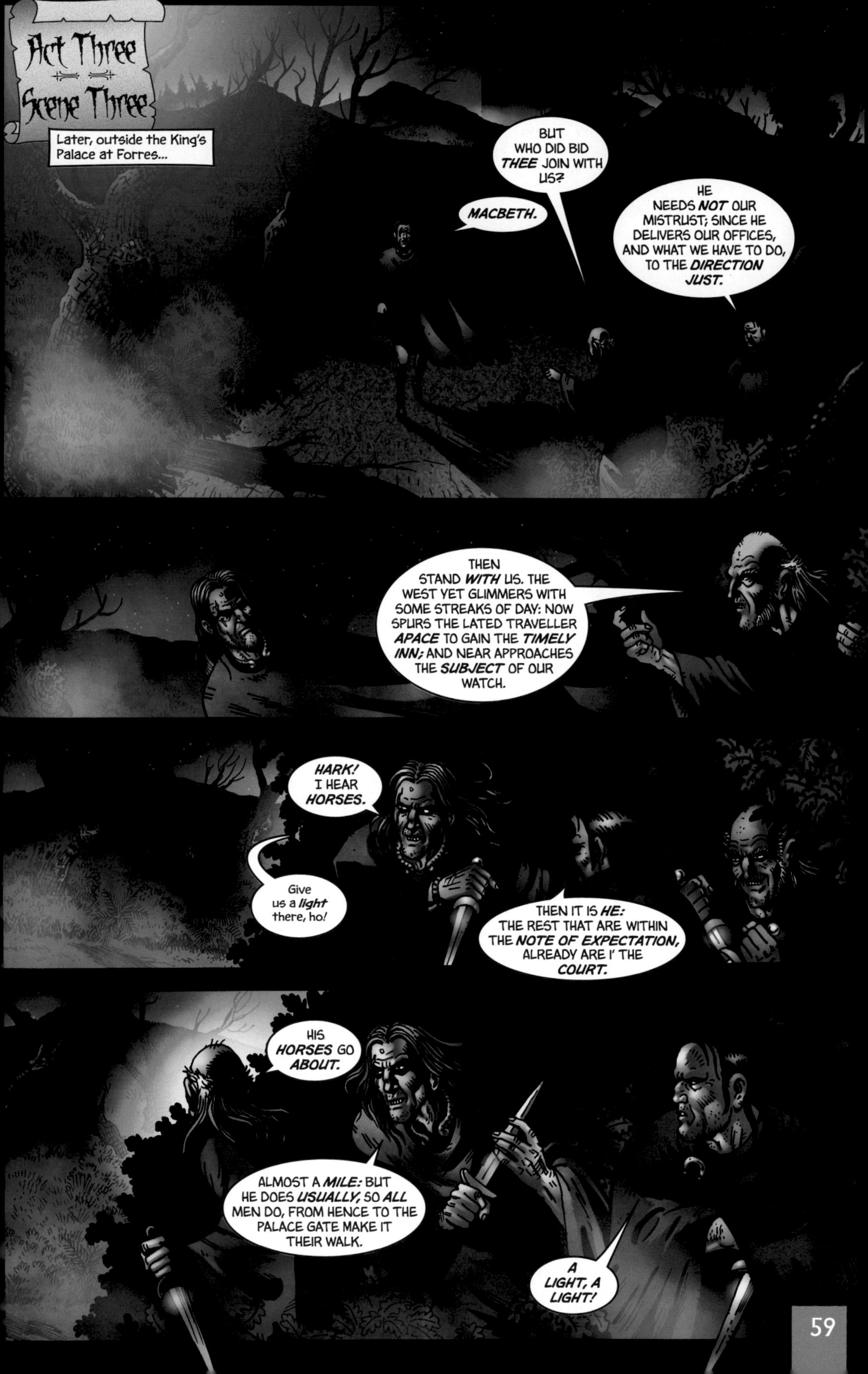
Act Three
Scene Three
Later, outside the King's Palace at Forres...
BUT WHO DID BID THEE JOIN WITH US?
MACBETH.
HE NEEDS NOT OUR MISTRUST; SINCE HE DELIVERS OUR OFFICES, AND WHAT WE HAVE TO DO, TO THE DIRECTION JUST.
THEN STAND WITH US. THE WEST YET GLIMMERS WITH SOME STREAKS OF DAY: NOW SPURS THE LATED TRAVELLER APACE TO GAIN THE TIMELY INN; AND NEAR APPROACHES THE SUBJECT OF OUR WATCH.
HARK! I HEAR HORSES.
Give us a light there, ho!
THEN IT IS HE: THE REST THAT ARE WITHIN THE NOTE OF EXPECTATION, ALREADY ARE I' THE COURT.
HIS HORSES GO ABOUT.
ALMOST A MILE: BUT HE DOES USUALLY, SO ALL MEN DO, FROM HENCE TO THE PALACE GATE MAKE IT THEIR WALK.
A LIGHT, A LIGHT!

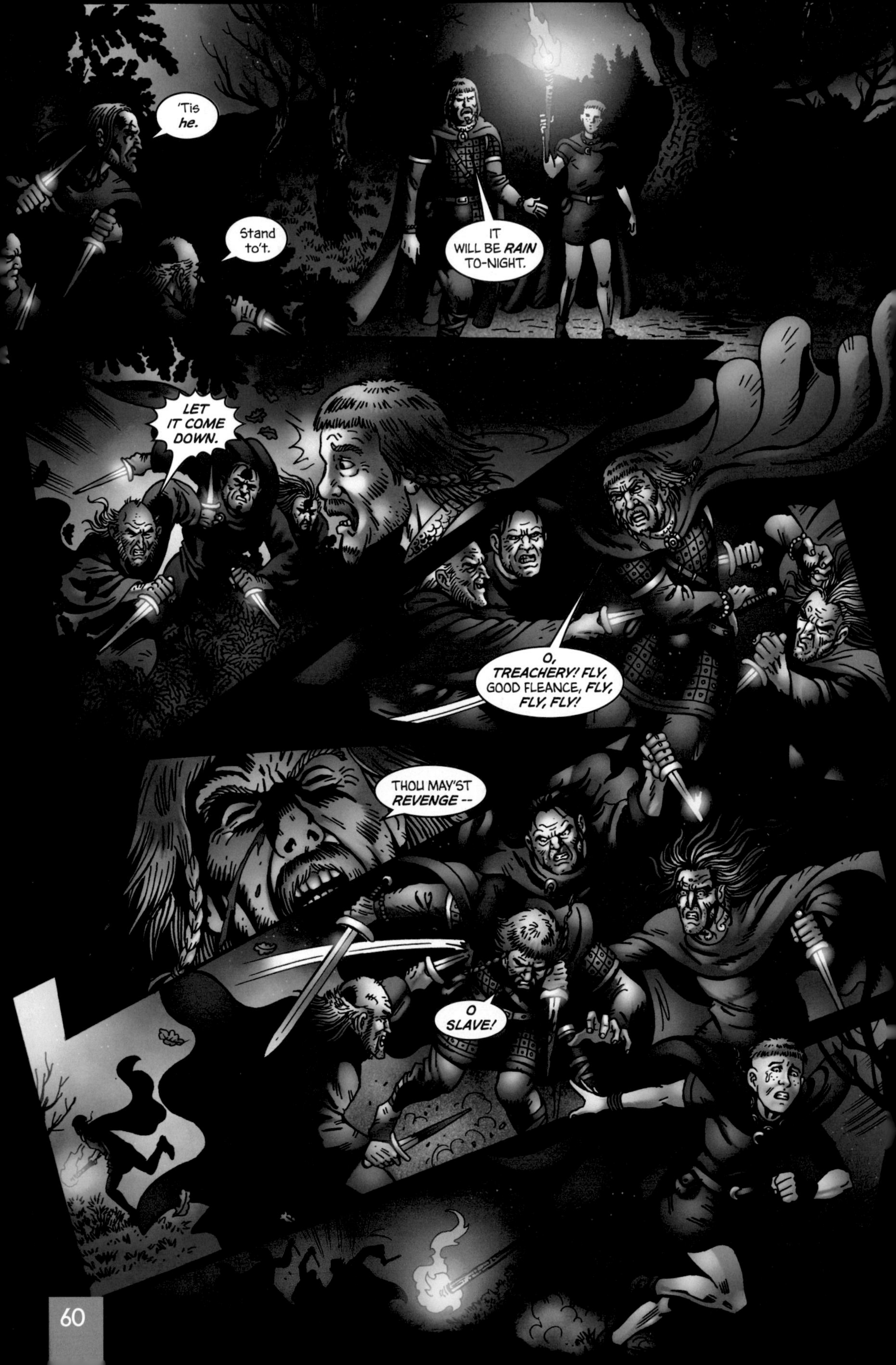
'Tis *he.*
Stand to't.
IT WILL BE *RAIN* TO-NIGHT.
LET IT COME DOWN.
O, TREACHERY! FLY, GOOD FLEANCE, *FLY, FLY, FLY!*
THOU MAY'ST *REVENGE --*
O SLAVE!

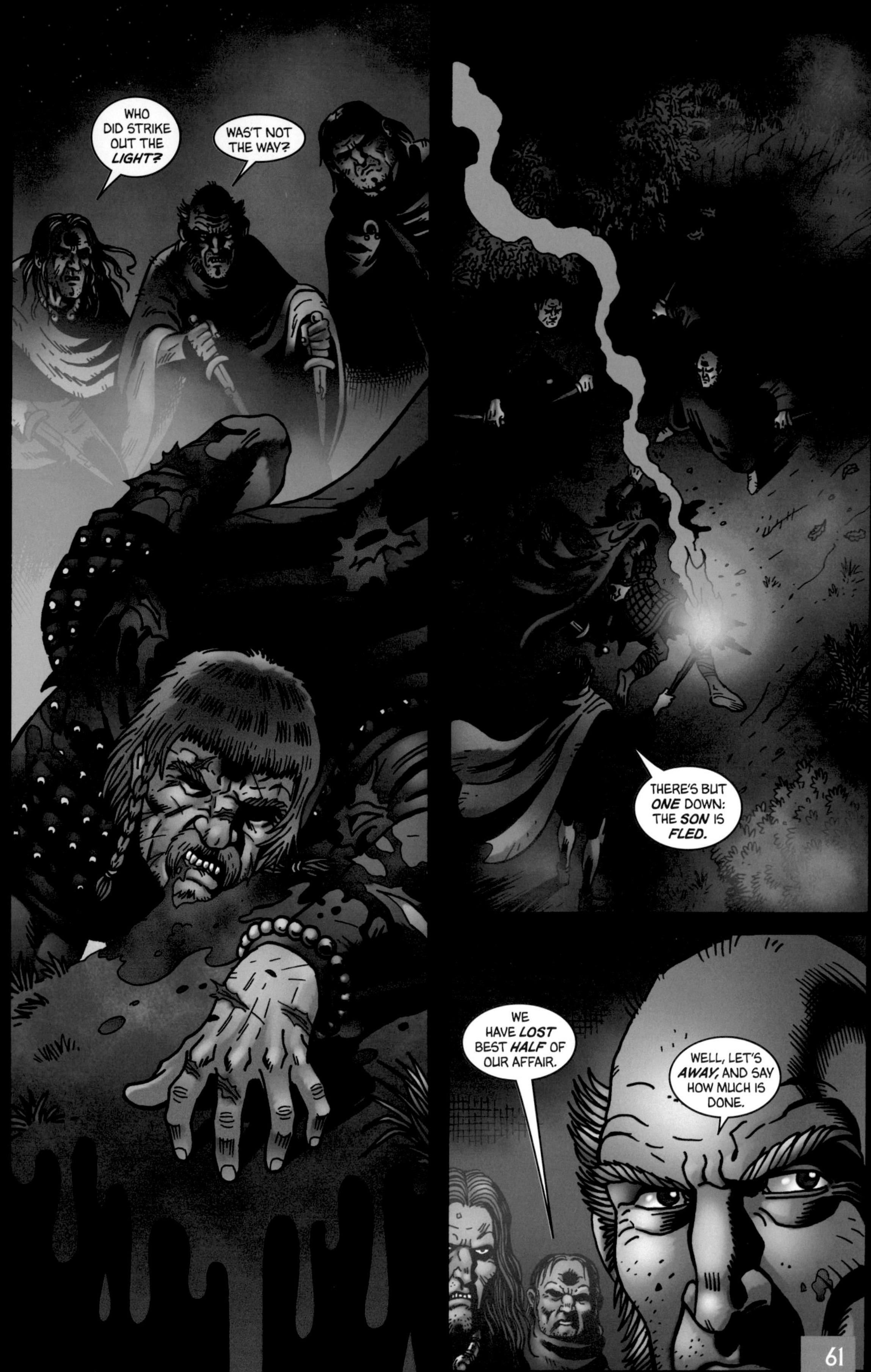
WHO DID STRIKE OUT THE LIGHT?
WAS'T NOT THE WAY?
THERE'S BUT ONE DOWN: THE SON IS FLED.
WE HAVE LOST BEST HALF OF OUR AFFAIR.
WELL, LET'S AWAY, AND SAY HOW MUCH IS DONE.

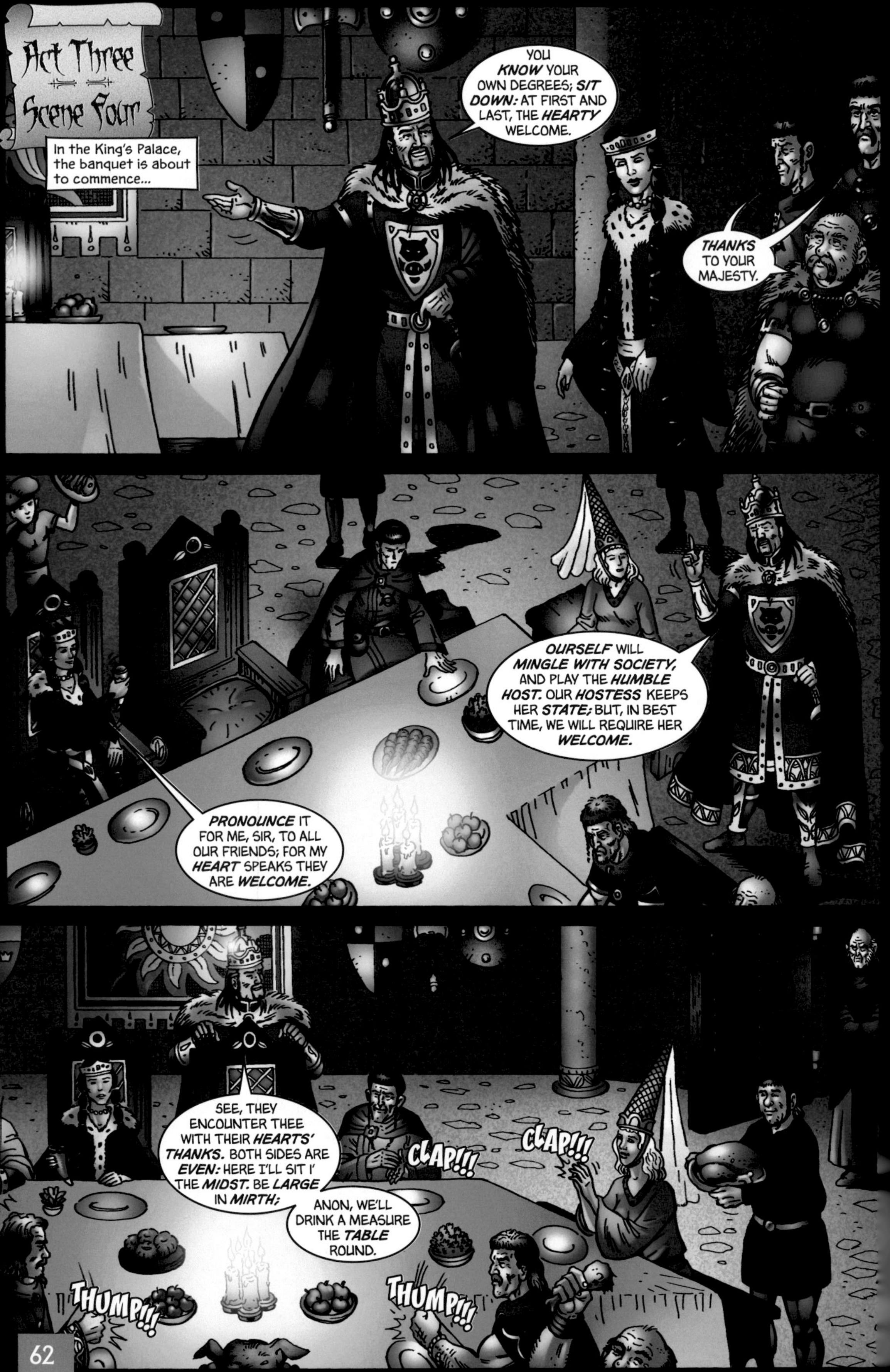
Act Three
Scene Four
In the King's Palace, the banquet is about to commence...
YOU KNOW YOUR OWN DEGREES; SIT DOWN: AT FIRST AND LAST, THE HEARTY WELCOME.
THANKS TO YOUR MAJESTY.
OURSELF WILL MINGLE WITH SOCIETY, AND PLAY THE HUMBLE HOST. OUR HOSTESS KEEPS HER STATE; BUT, IN BEST TIME, WE WILL REQUIRE HER WELCOME.
PRONOUNCE IT FOR ME, SIR, TO ALL OUR FRIENDS; FOR MY HEART SPEAKS THEY ARE WELCOME.
SEE, THEY ENCOUNTER THEE WITH THEIR HEARTS' THANKS. BOTH SIDES ARE EVEN: HERE I'LL SIT I' THE MIDST. BE LARGE IN MIRTH;
ANON, WE'LL DRINK A MEASURE THE TABLE ROUND.
CLAP!!!
CLAP!!!
THUMP!!!
THUMP!!!

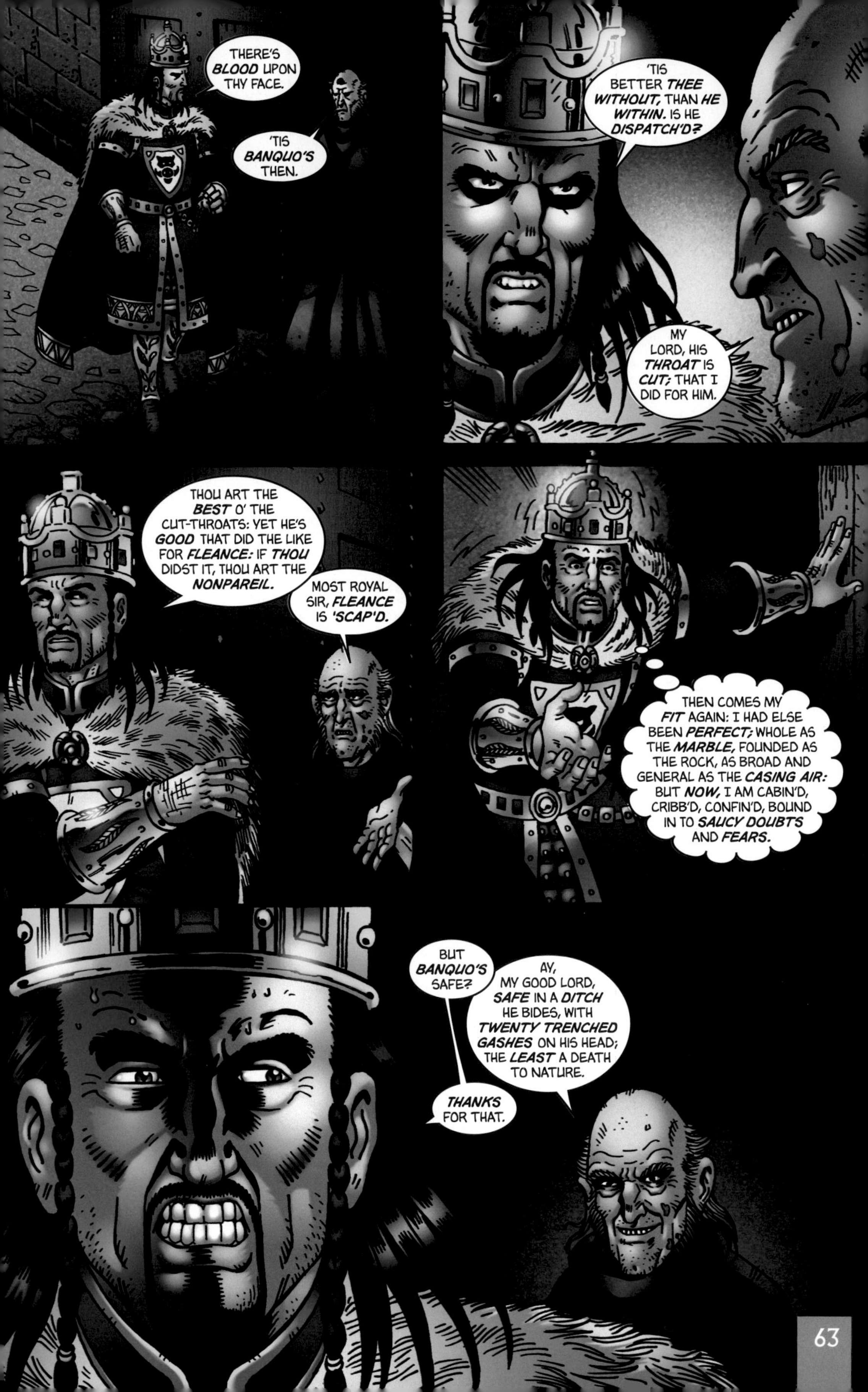
THERE'S BLOOD UPON THY FACE.
'TIS BANQUO'S THEN.
'TIS BETTER THEE WITHOUT, THAN HE WITHIN. IS HE DISPATCH'D?
MY LORD, HIS THROAT IS CUT; THAT I DID FOR HIM.
THOU ART THE BEST O' THE CUT-THROATS: YET HE'S GOOD THAT DID THE LIKE FOR FLEANCE: IF THOU DIDST IT, THOU ART THE NONPAREIL.
MOST ROYAL SIR, FLEANCE IS 'SCAP'D.
THEN COMES MY FIT AGAIN: I HAD ELSE BEEN PERFECT; WHOLE AS THE MARBLE, FOUNDED AS THE ROCK, AS BROAD AND GENERAL AS THE CASING AIR: BUT NOW, I AM CABIN'D, CRIBB'D, CONFIN'D, BOUND IN TO SAUCY DOUBTS AND FEARS.
BUT BANQUO'S SAFE?
AY, MY GOOD LORD, SAFE IN A DITCH HE BIDES, WITH TWENTY TRENCHED GASHES ON HIS HEAD; THE LEAST A DEATH TO NATURE.
THANKS FOR THAT.

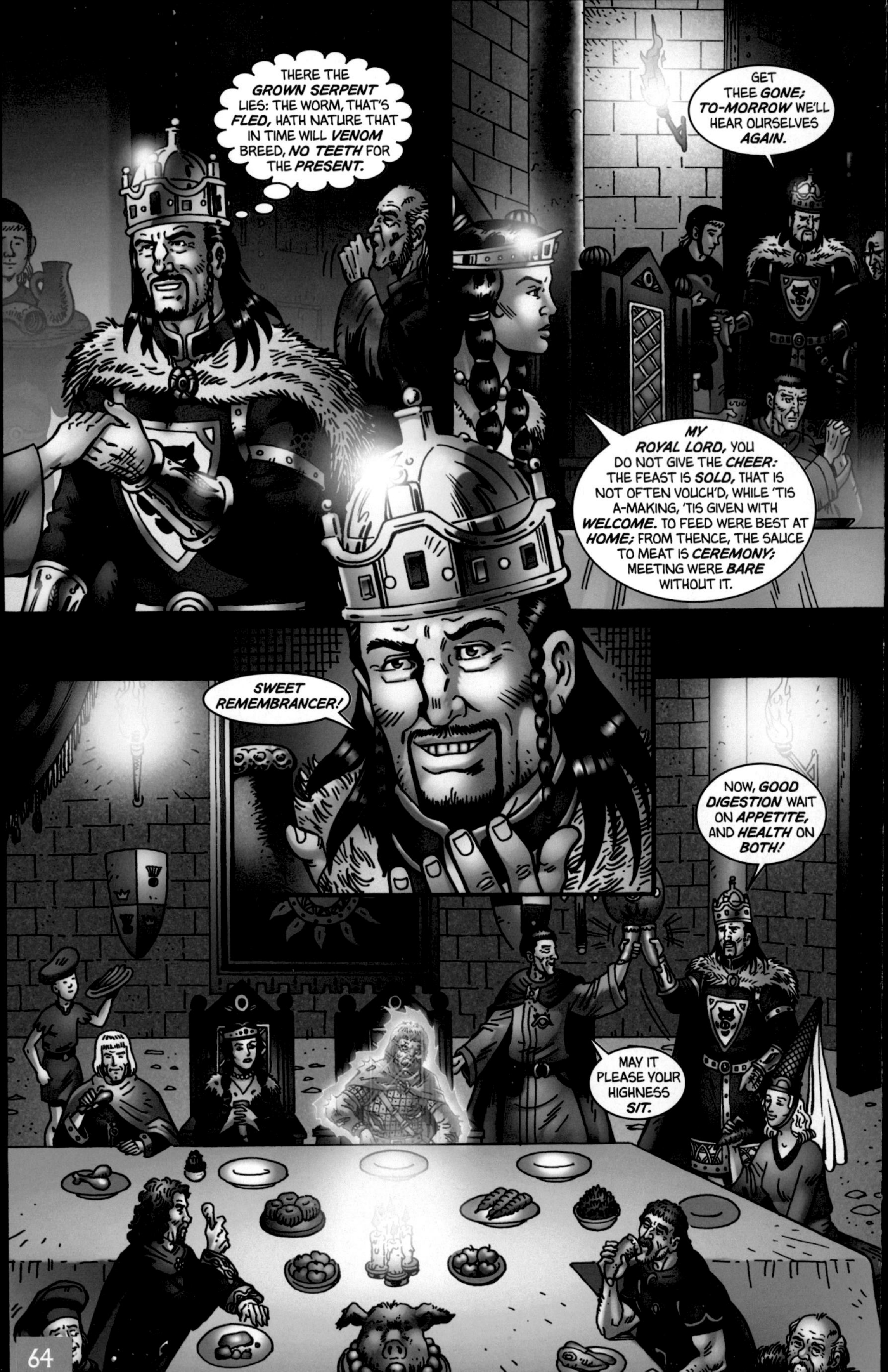
THERE THE GROWN SERPENT LIES: THE WORM, THAT'S FLED, HATH NATURE THAT IN TIME WILL VENOM BREED, NO TEETH FOR THE PRESENT.
GET THEE GONE; TO-MORROW WE'LL HEAR OURSELVES AGAIN.
MY ROYAL LORD, YOU DO NOT GIVE THE CHEER: THE FEAST IS SOLD, THAT IS NOT OFTEN VOUCH'D, WHILE 'TIS A-MAKING, 'TIS GIVEN WITH WELCOME. TO FEED WERE BEST AT HOME; FROM THENCE, THE SAUCE TO MEAT IS CEREMONY: MEETING WERE BARE WITHOUT IT.
SWEET REMEMBRANCER!
NOW, GOOD DIGESTION WAIT ON APPETITE, AND HEALTH ON BOTH!
MAY IT PLEASE YOUR HIGHNESS SIT.

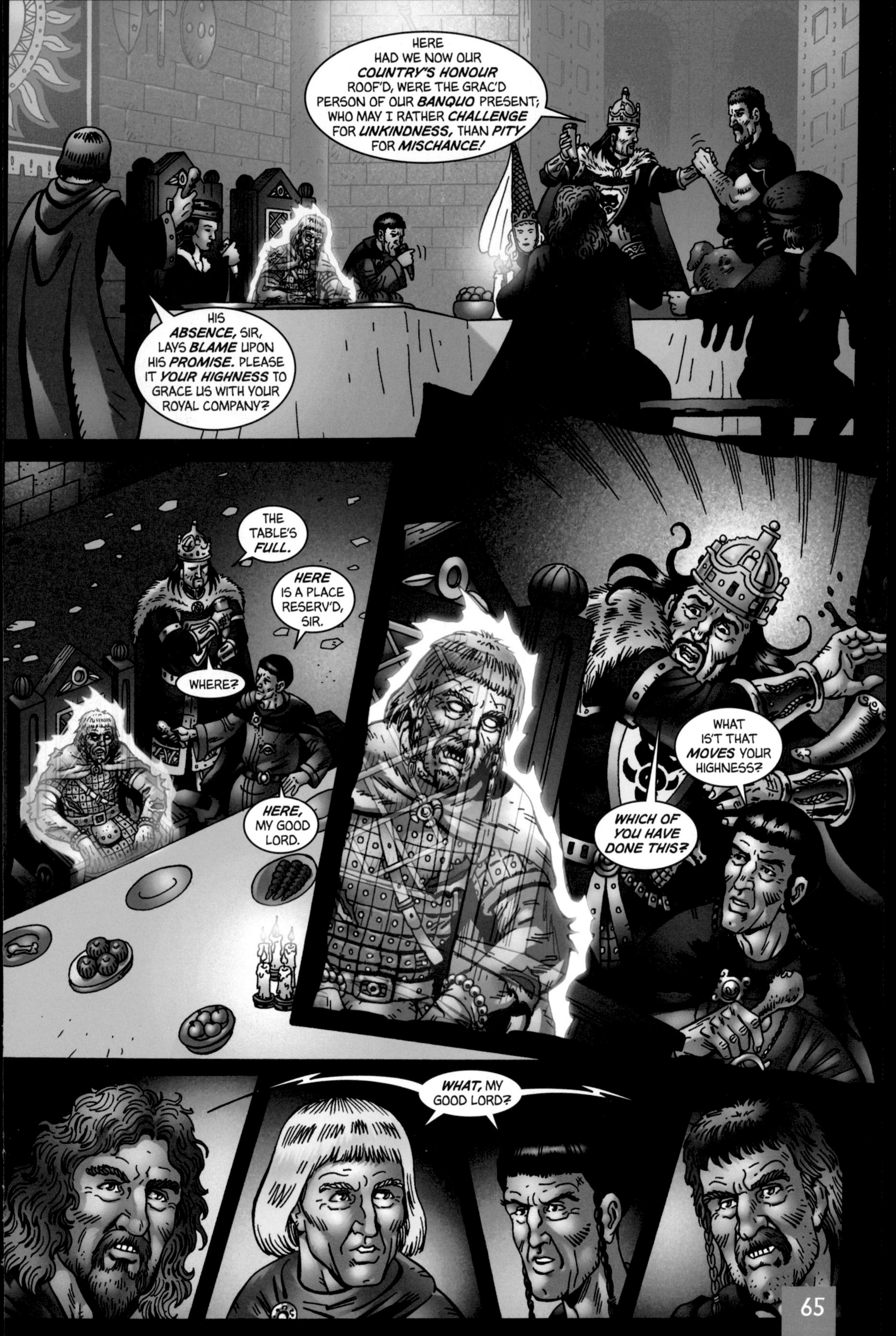

HERE HAD WE NOW OUR COUNTRY'S HONOUR ROOF'D, WERE THE GRAC'D PERSON OF OUR BANQUO PRESENT; WHO MAY I RATHER CHALLENGE FOR UNKINDNESS, THAN PITY FOR MISCHANCE!
HIS ABSENCE, SIR, LAYS BLAME UPON HIS PROMISE. PLEASE IT YOUR HIGHNESS TO GRACE US WITH YOUR ROYAL COMPANY?
THE TABLE'S FULL.
HERE IS A PLACE RESERV'D, SIR.
WHERE?
HERE, MY GOOD LORD.
WHAT IS'T THAT MOVES YOUR HIGHNESS?
WHICH OF YOU HAVE DONE THIS?
WHAT, MY GOOD LORD?

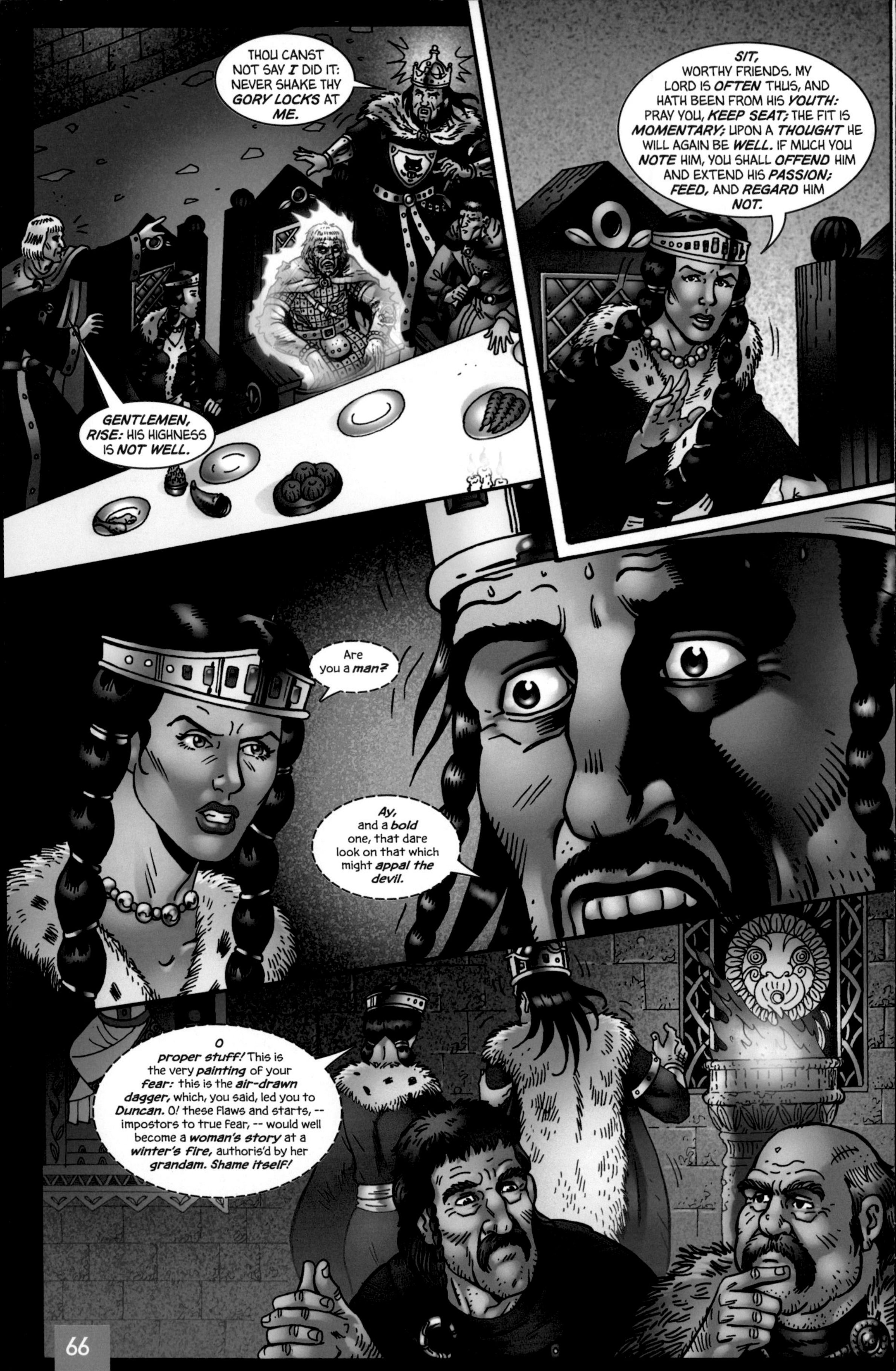
THOU CANST NOT SAY *I* DID IT: NEVER SHAKE THY *GORY LOCKS* AT *ME.*
GENTLEMEN, RISE: HIS HIGHNESS IS *NOT WELL.*
SIT, WORTHY FRIENDS. MY LORD IS *OFTEN* THUS, AND HATH BEEN FROM HIS *YOUTH:* PRAY YOU, *KEEP SEAT;* THE FIT IS *MOMENTARY;* UPON A *THOUGHT* HE WILL AGAIN BE *WELL.* IF MUCH YOU *NOTE* HIM, YOU SHALL *OFFEND* HIM AND EXTEND HIS *PASSION; FEED,* AND *REGARD* HIM *NOT.*
Are you a *man?*
Ay, and a *bold* one, that dare look on that which might *appal the devil.*
O proper stuff! This is the very *painting* of your *fear:* this is the *air-drawn dagger,* which, you said, led you to *Duncan.* O! these flaws and starts, -- impostors to true fear, -- would well become a *woman's story* at a *winter's fire,* authoris'd by her *grandam. Shame itself!*

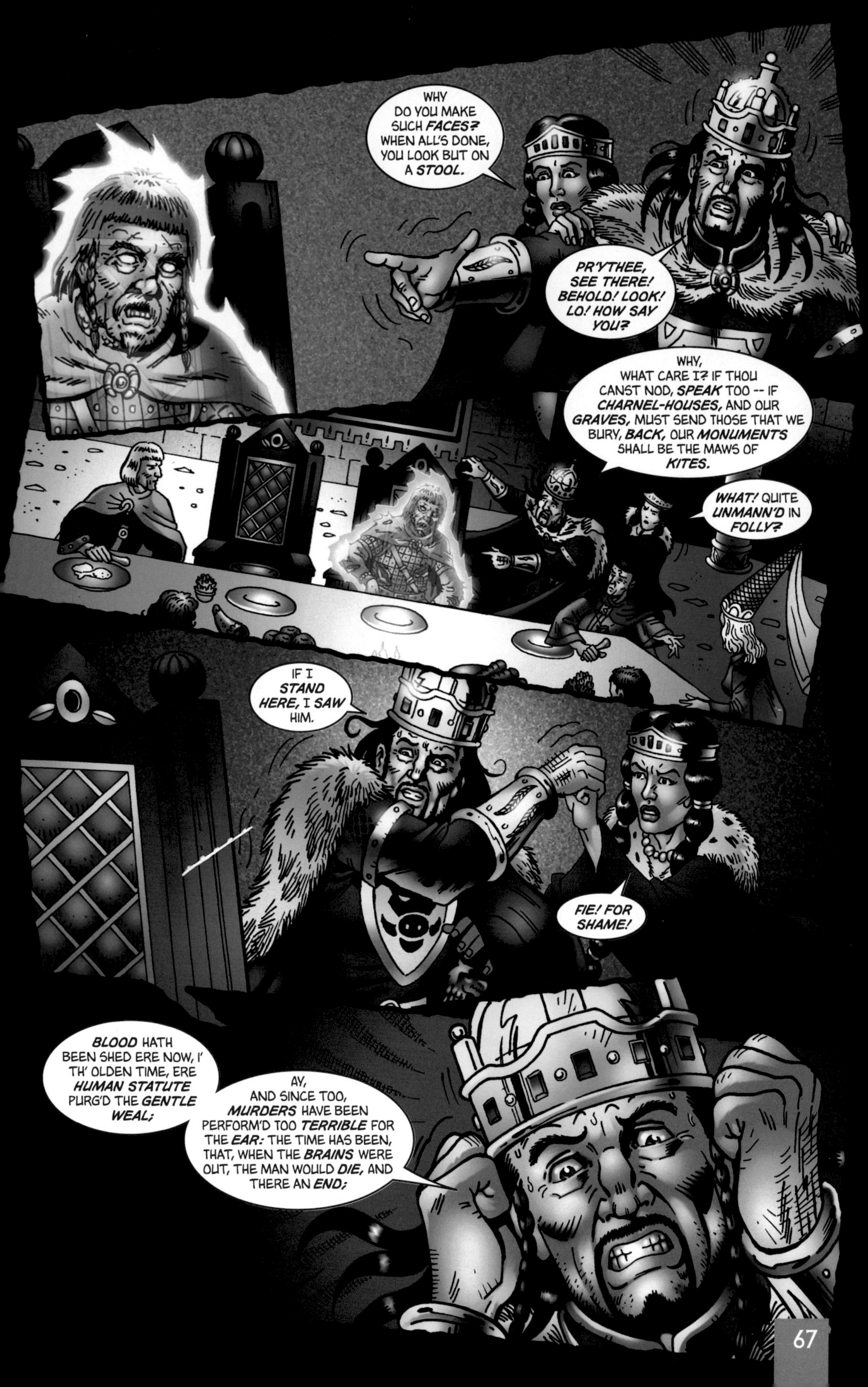
WHY DO YOU MAKE SUCH FACES? WHEN ALL'S DONE, YOU LOOK BUT ON A STOOL.
PR'YTHEE, SEE THERE! BEHOLD! LOOK! LO! HOW SAY YOU?
WHY, WHAT CARE I? IF THOU CANST NOD, SPEAK TOO -- IF CHARNEL-HOUSES, AND OUR GRAVES, MUST SEND THOSE THAT WE BURY, BACK, OUR MONUMENTS SHALL BE THE MAWS OF KITES.
WHAT! QUITE UNMANN'D IN FOLLY?
IF I STAND HERE, I SAW HIM.
FIE! FOR SHAME!
BLOOD HATH BEEN SHED ERE NOW, I' TH' OLDEN TIME, ERE HUMAN STATUTE PURG'D THE GENTLE WEAL;
AY, AND SINCE TOO, MURDERS HAVE BEEN PERFORM'D TOO TERRIBLE FOR THE EAR: THE TIME HAS BEEN, THAT, WHEN THE BRAINS WERE OUT, THE MAN WOULD DIE, AND THERE AN END;

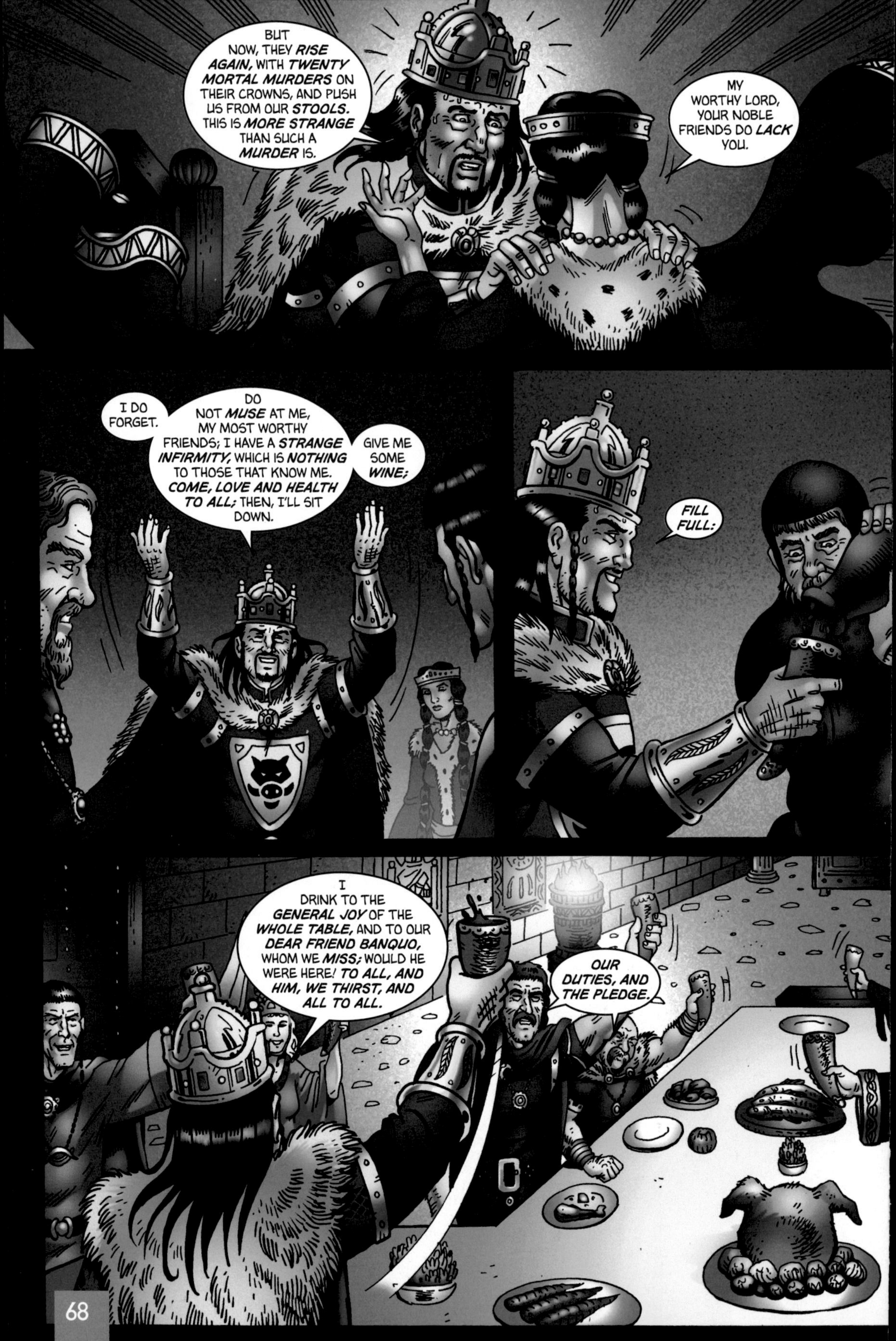

BUT NOW, THEY RISE AGAIN, WITH TWENTY MORTAL MURDERS ON THEIR CROWNS, AND PUSH US FROM OUR STOOLS. THIS IS MORE STRANGE THAN SUCH A MURDER IS.
MY WORTHY LORD, YOUR NOBLE FRIENDS DO LACK YOU.
I DO FORGET.
DO NOT MUSE AT ME, MY MOST WORTHY FRIENDS; I HAVE A STRANGE INFIRMITY, WHICH IS NOTHING TO THOSE THAT KNOW ME. COME, LOVE AND HEALTH TO ALL; THEN, I'LL SIT DOWN.
GIVE ME SOME WINE;
FILL FULL:
I DRINK TO THE GENERAL JOY OF THE WHOLE TABLE, AND TO OUR DEAR FRIEND BANQUO, WHOM WE MISS; WOULD HE WERE HERE! TO ALL, AND HIM, WE THIRST, AND ALL TO ALL.
OUR DUTIES, AND THE PLEDGE.

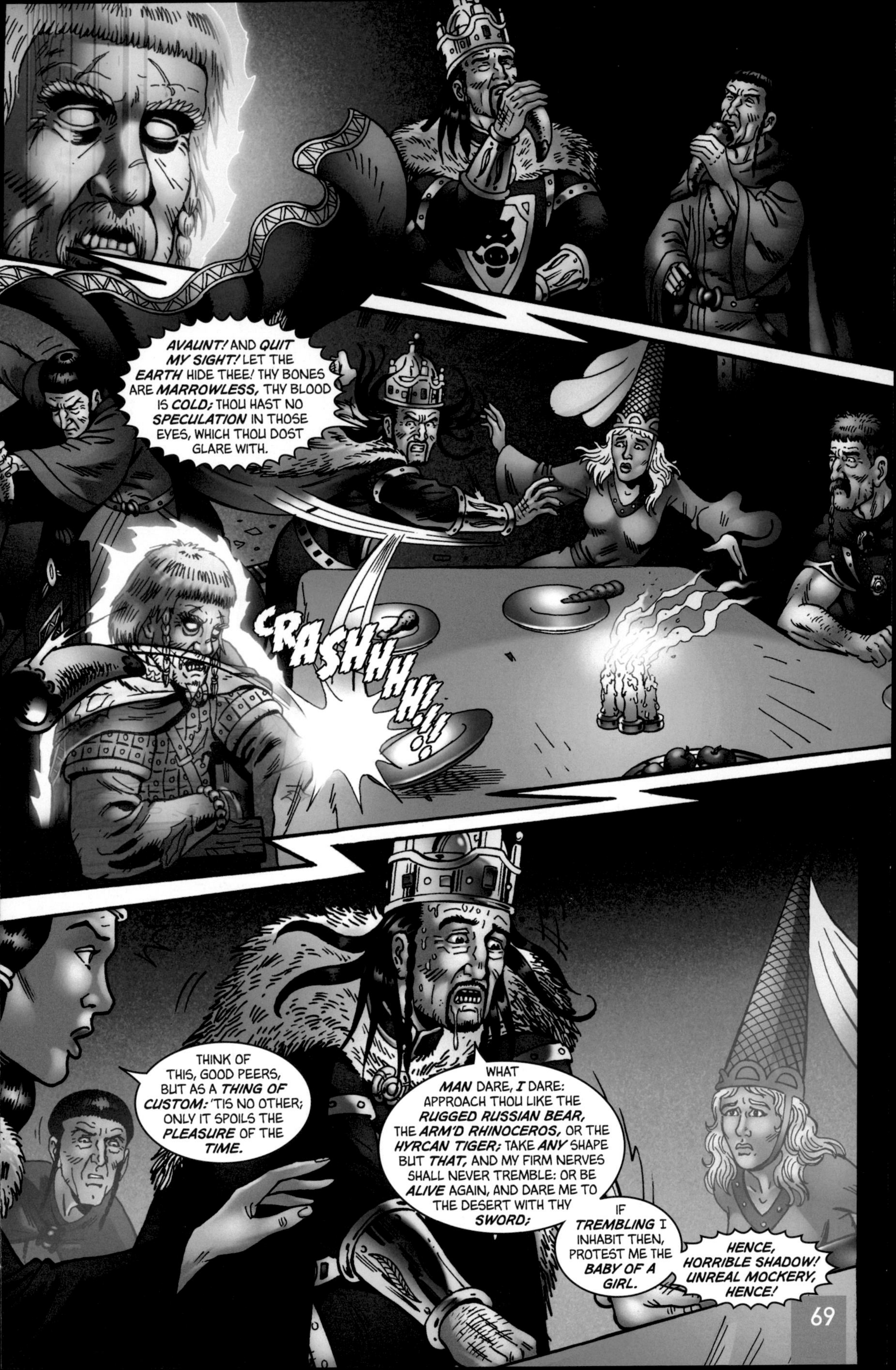
AVAUNT! AND QUIT MY SIGHT! LET THE EARTH HIDE THEE! THY BONES ARE MARROWLESS, THY BLOOD IS COLD; THOU HAST NO SPECULATION IN THOSE EYES, WHICH THOU DOST GLARE WITH.
CRASHHHH!!!!
THINK OF THIS, GOOD PEERS, BUT AS A THING OF CUSTOM: 'TIS NO OTHER; ONLY IT SPOILS THE PLEASURE OF THE TIME.
WHAT MAN DARE, I DARE: APPROACH THOU LIKE THE RUGGED RUSSIAN BEAR, THE ARM'D RHINOCEROS, OR THE HYRCAN TIGER; TAKE ANY SHAPE BUT THAT, AND MY FIRM NERVES SHALL NEVER TREMBLE: OR BE ALIVE AGAIN, AND DARE ME TO THE DESERT WITH THY SWORD;
IF TREMBLING I INHABIT THEN, PROTEST ME THE BABY OF A GIRL.
HENCE, HORRIBLE SHADOW! UNREAL MOCKERY, HENCE!

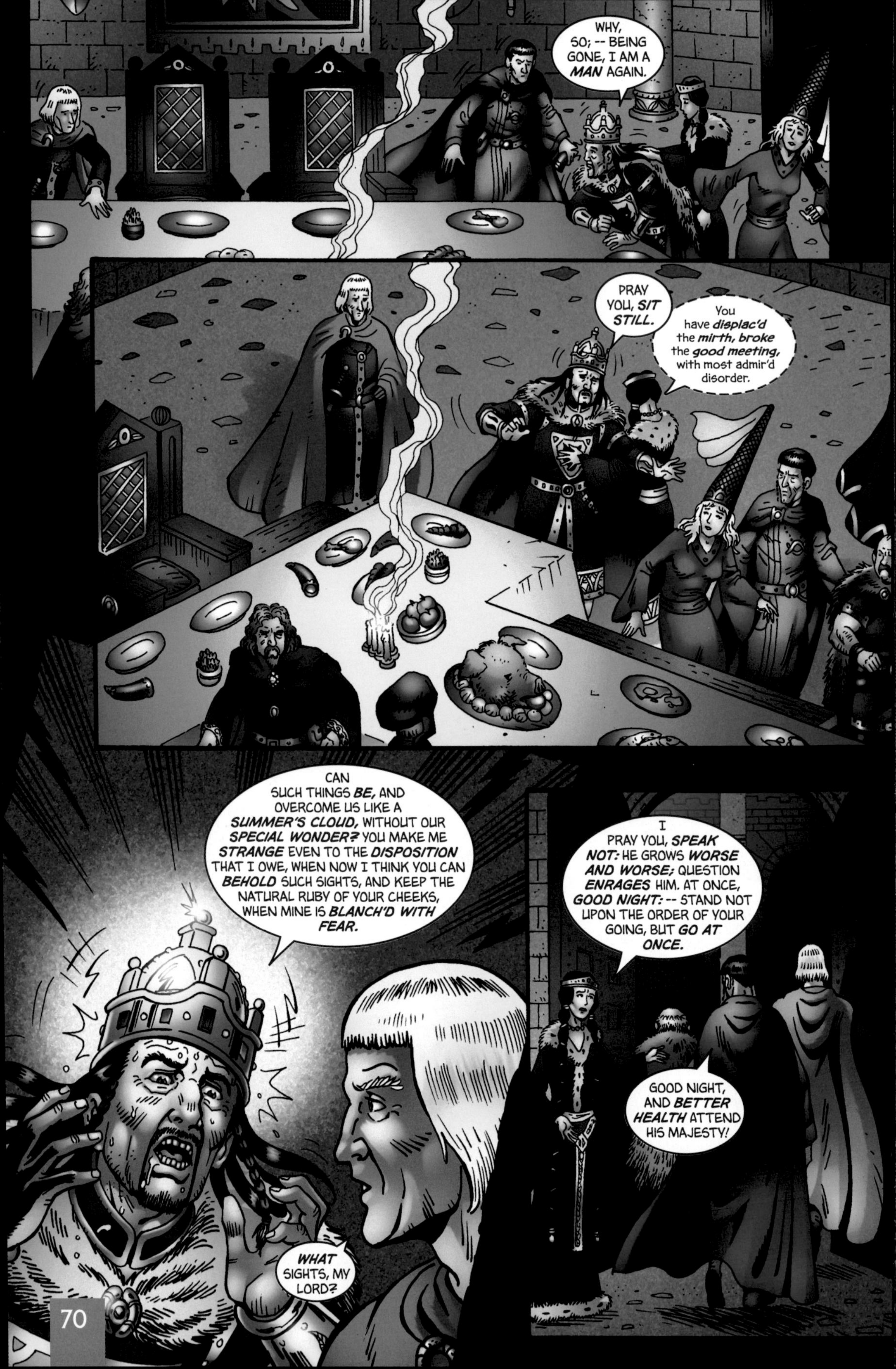
WHY, SO; -- BEING GONE, I AM A MAN AGAIN.
PRAY YOU, SIT STILL.
You have displac'd the mirth, broke the good meeting, with most admir'd disorder.
CAN SUCH THINGS BE, AND OVERCOME US LIKE A SUMMER'S CLOUD, WITHOUT OUR SPECIAL WONDER? YOU MAKE ME STRANGE EVEN TO THE DISPOSITION THAT I OWE, WHEN NOW I THINK YOU CAN BEHOLD SUCH SIGHTS, AND KEEP THE NATURAL RUBY OF YOUR CHEEKS, WHEN MINE IS BLANCH'D WITH FEAR.
WHAT SIGHTS, MY LORD?
I PRAY YOU, SPEAK NOT: HE GROWS WORSE AND WORSE; QUESTION ENRAGES HIM. AT ONCE, GOOD NIGHT: -- STAND NOT UPON THE ORDER OF YOUR GOING, BUT GO AT ONCE.
GOOD NIGHT, AND BETTER HEALTH ATTEND HIS MAJESTY!

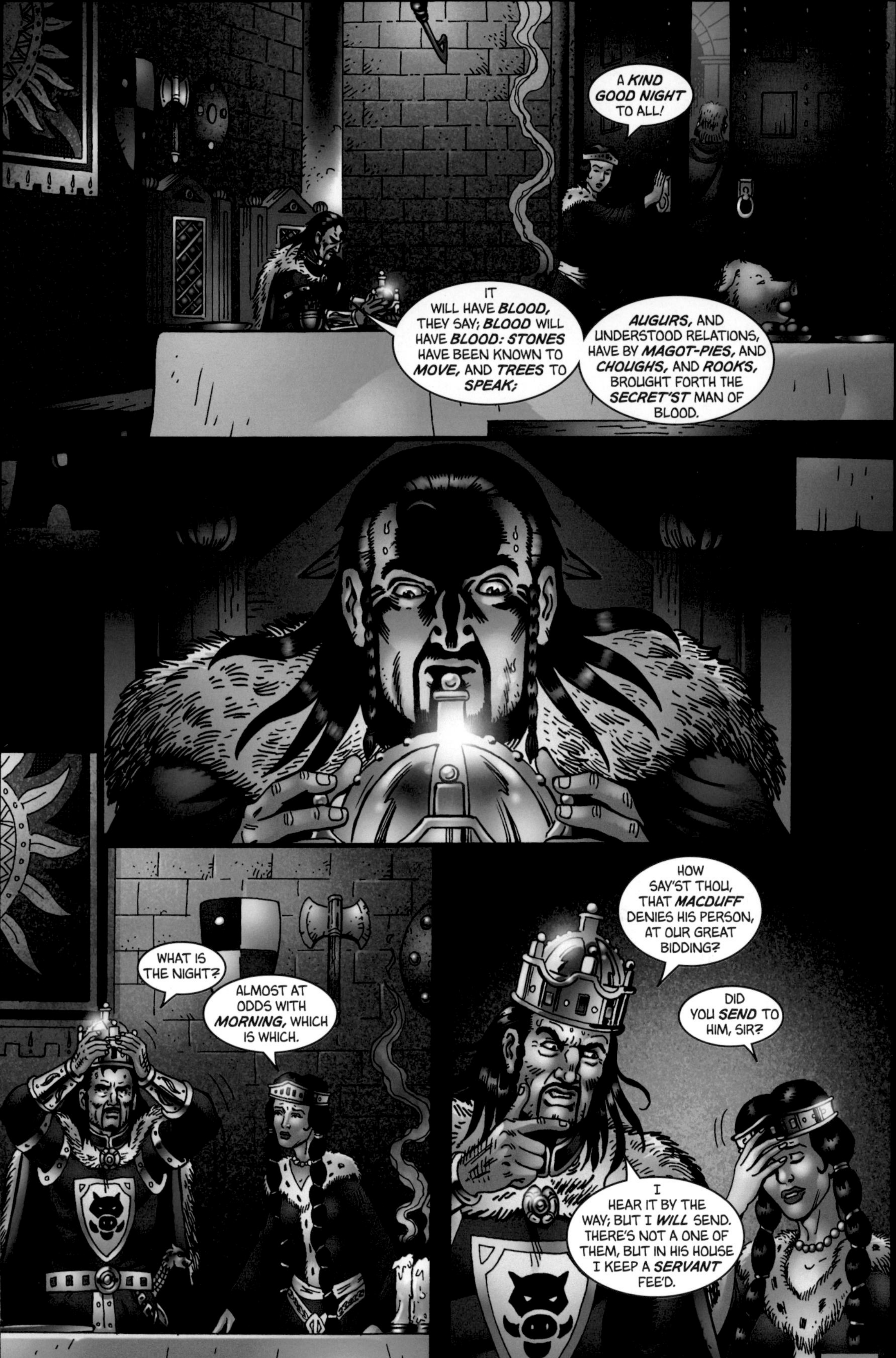
A KIND GOOD NIGHT TO ALL!
IT WILL HAVE BLOOD, THEY SAY; BLOOD WILL HAVE BLOOD: STONES HAVE BEEN KNOWN TO MOVE, AND TREES TO SPEAK;
AUGURS, AND UNDERSTOOD RELATIONS, HAVE BY MAGOT-PIES, AND CHOUGHS, AND ROOKS, BROUGHT FORTH THE SECRET'ST MAN OF BLOOD.
WHAT IS THE NIGHT?
ALMOST AT ODDS WITH MORNING, WHICH IS WHICH.
HOW SAY'ST THOU, THAT MACDUFF DENIES HIS PERSON, AT OUR GREAT BIDDING?
DID YOU SEND TO HIM, SIR?
I HEAR IT BY THE WAY; BUT I WILL SEND. THERE'S NOT A ONE OF THEM, BUT IN HIS HOUSE I KEEP A SERVANT FEE'D.

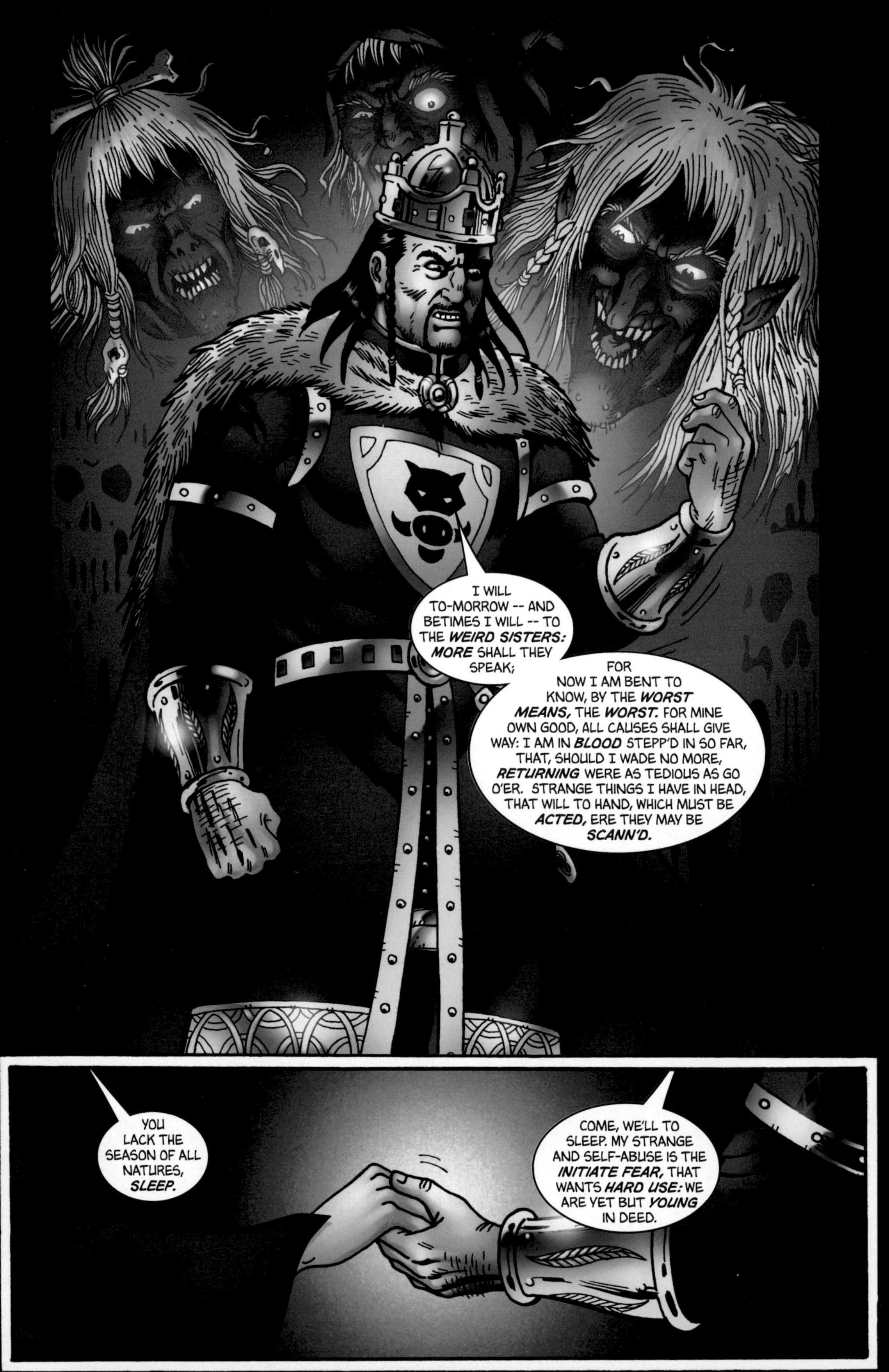
I WILL TO-MORROW -- AND BETIMES I WILL -- TO THE WEIRD SISTERS: MORE SHALL THEY SPEAK;
FOR NOW I AM BENT TO KNOW, BY THE WORST MEANS, THE WORST. FOR MINE OWN GOOD, ALL CAUSES SHALL GIVE WAY: I AM IN BLOOD STEPP'D IN SO FAR, THAT, SHOULD I WADE NO MORE, RETURNING WERE AS TEDIOUS AS GO O'ER. STRANGE THINGS I HAVE IN HEAD, THAT WILL TO HAND, WHICH MUST BE ACTED, ERE THEY MAY BE SCANN'D.
YOU LACK THE SEASON OF ALL NATURES, SLEEP.
COME, WE'LL TO SLEEP. MY STRANGE AND SELF-ABUSE IS THE INITIATE FEAR, THAT WANTS HARD USE: WE ARE YET BUT YOUNG IN DEED.

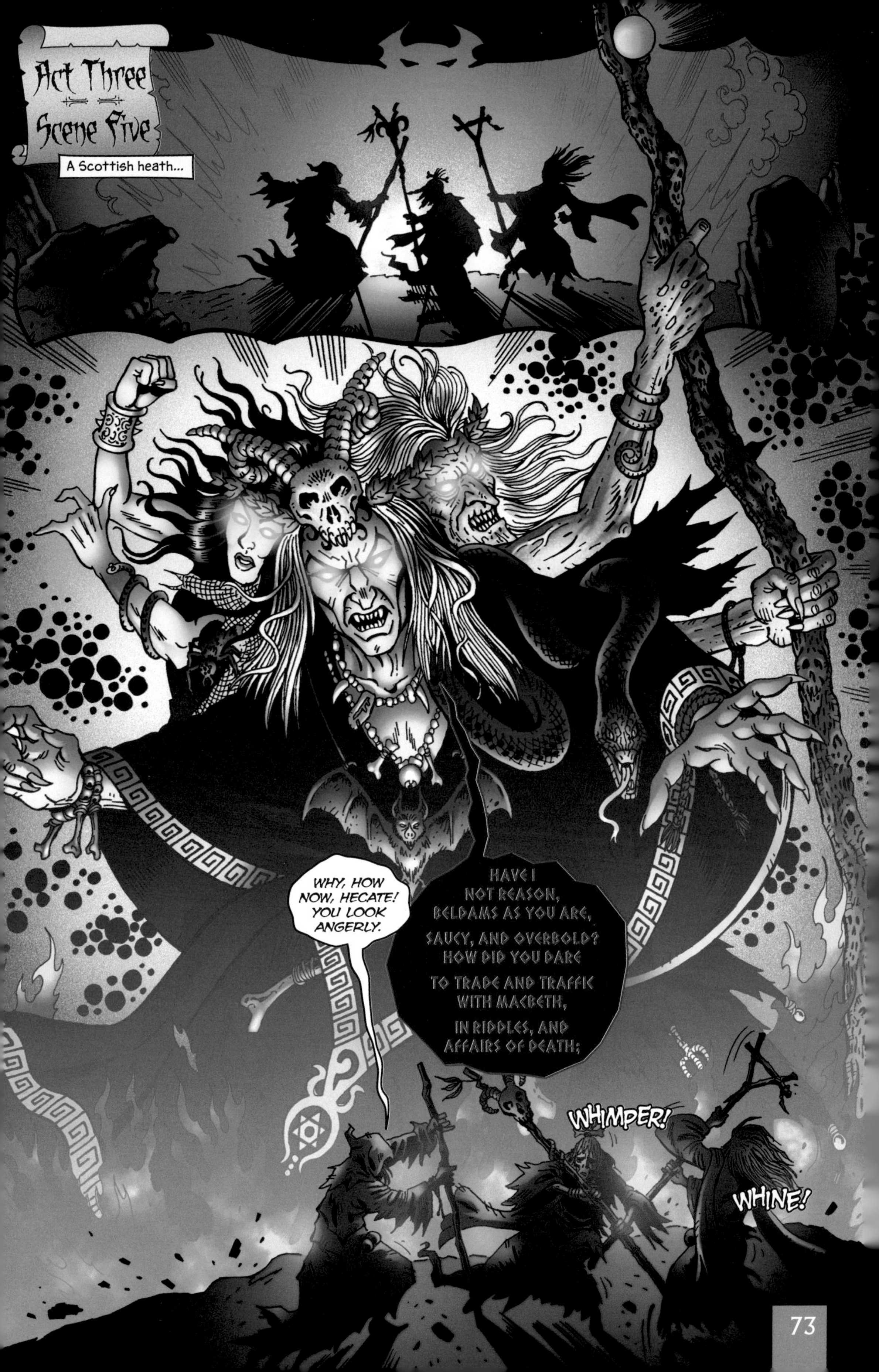

Act Three
Scene Five
A Scottish heath...
WHY, HOW NOW, HECATE! YOU LOOK ANGERLY.
HAVE I NOT REASON, BELDAMS AS YOU ARE,
SAUCY, AND OVERBOLD? HOW DID YOU DARE
TO TRADE AND TRAFFIC WITH MACBETH,
IN RIDDLES, AND AFFAIRS OF DEATH;
WHIMPER!
WHINE!

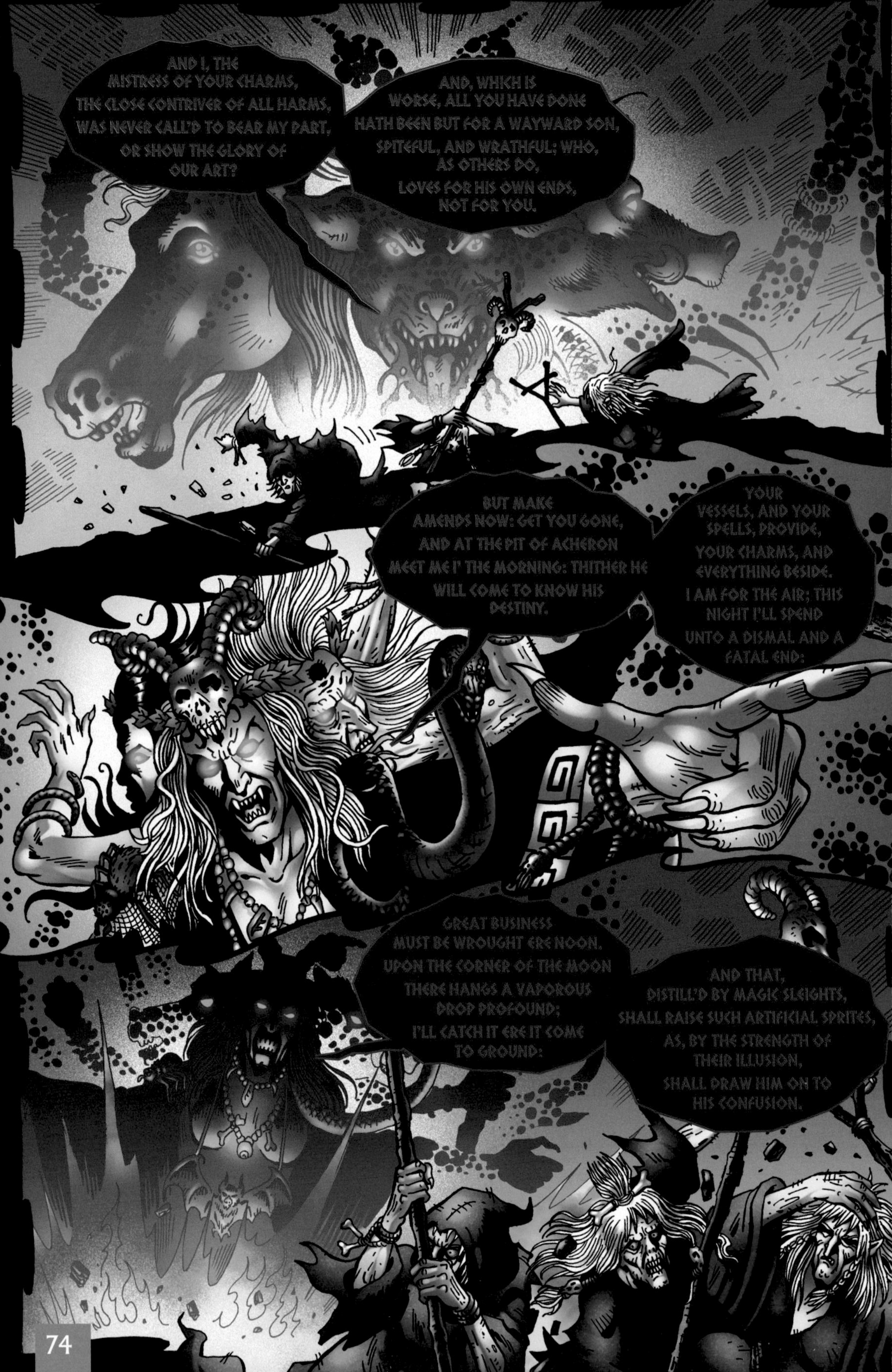
AND I, THE MISTRESS OF YOUR CHARMS, THE CLOSE CONTRIVER OF ALL HARMS, WAS NEVER CALL'D TO BEAR MY PART, OR SHOW THE GLORY OF OUR ART?
AND, WHICH IS WORSE, ALL YOU HAVE DONE HATH BEEN BUT FOR A WAYWARD SON, SPITEFUL, AND WRATHFUL; WHO, AS OTHERS DO, LOVES FOR HIS OWN ENDS, NOT FOR YOU.
BUT MAKE AMENDS NOW: GET YOU GONE, AND AT THE PIT OF ACHERON MEET ME I' THE MORNING: THITHER HE WILL COME TO KNOW HIS DESTINY.
YOUR VESSELS, AND YOUR SPELLS, PROVIDE, YOUR CHARMS, AND EVERYTHING BESIDE. I AM FOR THE AIR; THIS NIGHT I'LL SPEND UNTO A DISMAL AND A FATAL END:
GREAT BUSINESS MUST BE WROUGHT ERE NOON. UPON THE CORNER OF THE MOON THERE HANGS A VAPOROUS DROP PROFOUND; I'LL CATCH IT ERE IT COME TO GROUND:
AND THAT, DISTILL'D BY MAGIC SLEIGHTS, SHALL RAISE SUCH ARTIFICIAL SPRITES, AS, BY THE STRENGTH OF THEIR ILLUSION, SHALL DRAW HIM ON TO HIS CONFUSION.

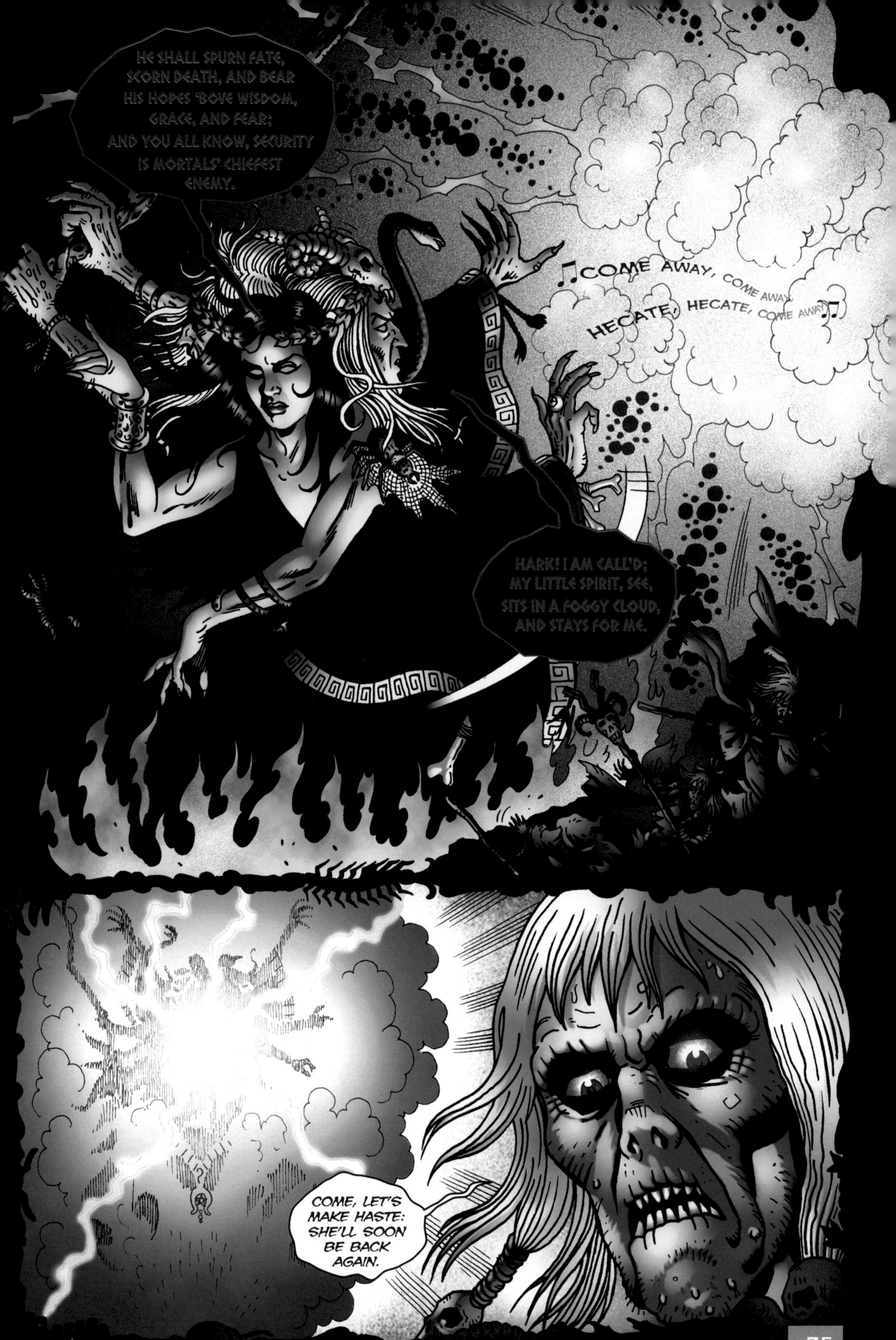
HE SHALL SPURN FATE, SCORN DEATH, AND BEAR HIS HOPES 'BOVE WISDOM, GRACE, AND FEAR; AND YOU ALL KNOW, SECURITY IS MORTALS' CHIEFEST ENEMY.
COME AWAY, COME AWAY, HECATE, HECATE, COME AWAY
HARK! I AM CALL'D; MY LITTLE SPIRIT, SEE, SITS IN A FOGGY CLOUD, AND STAYS FOR ME.
COME, LET'S MAKE HASTE: SHE'LL SOON BE BACK AGAIN.

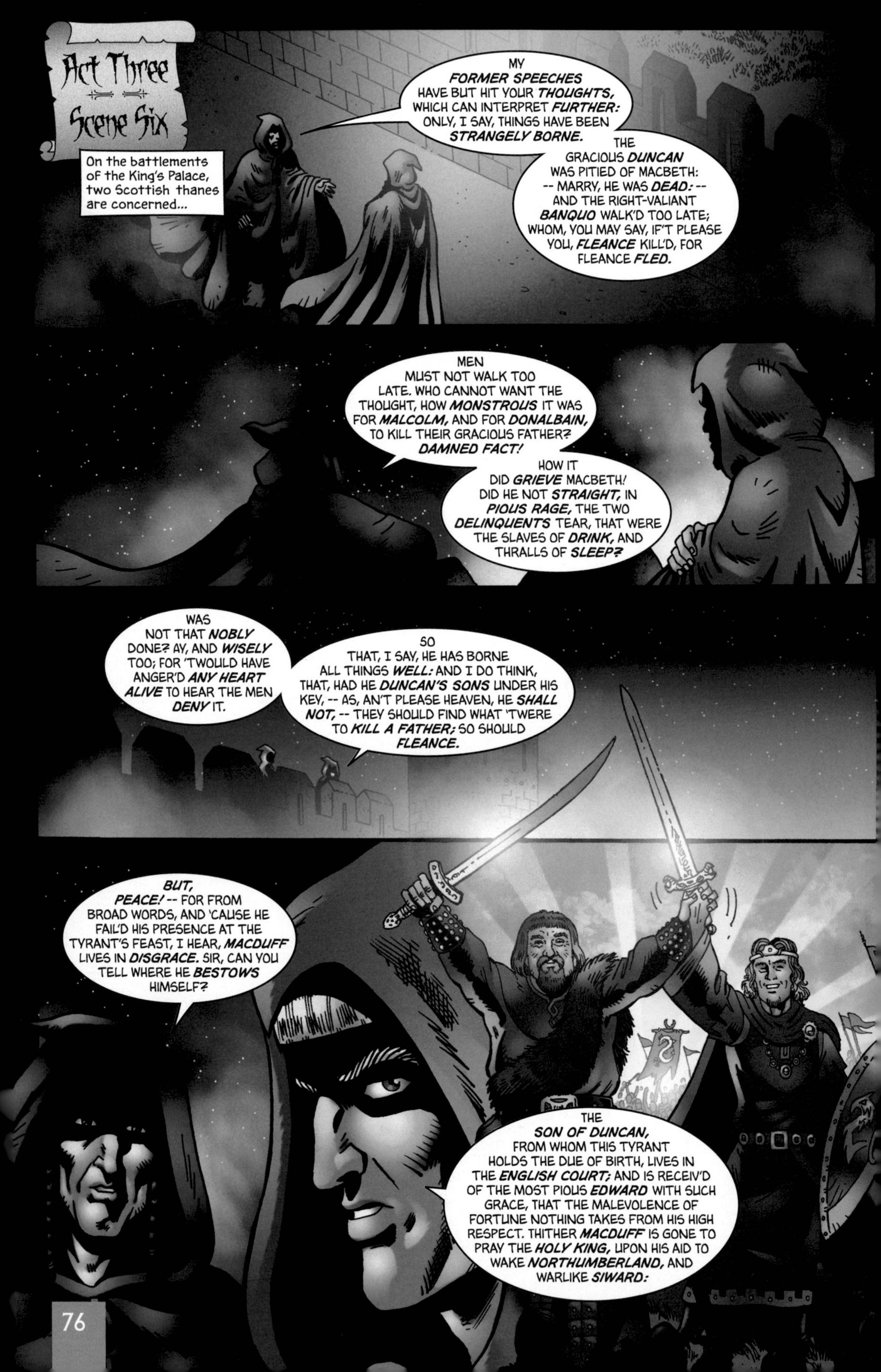
Act Three
Scene Six
On the battlements of the King's Palace, two Scottish thanes are concerned...
MY FORMER SPEECHES HAVE BUT HIT YOUR THOUGHTS, WHICH CAN INTERPRET FURTHER: ONLY, I SAY, THINGS HAVE BEEN STRANGELY BORNE.
THE GRACIOUS DUNCAN WAS PITIED OF MACBETH: -- MARRY, HE WAS DEAD: -- AND THE RIGHT-VALIANT BANQUO WALK'D TOO LATE; WHOM, YOU MAY SAY, IF'T PLEASE YOU, FLEANCE KILL'D, FOR FLEANCE FLED.
MEN MUST NOT WALK TOO LATE. WHO CANNOT WANT THE THOUGHT, HOW MONSTROUS IT WAS FOR MALCOLM, AND FOR DONALBAIN, TO KILL THEIR GRACIOUS FATHER? DAMNED FACT!
HOW IT DID GRIEVE MACBETH! DID HE NOT STRAIGHT, IN PIOUS RAGE, THE TWO DELINQUENTS TEAR, THAT WERE THE SLAVES OF DRINK, AND THRALLS OF SLEEP?
WAS NOT THAT NOBLY DONE? AY, AND WISELY TOO; FOR 'TWOULD HAVE ANGER'D ANY HEART ALIVE TO HEAR THE MEN DENY IT.
SO THAT, I SAY, HE HAS BORNE ALL THINGS WELL: AND I DO THINK, THAT, HAD HE DUNCAN'S SONS UNDER HIS KEY, -- AS, AN'T PLEASE HEAVEN, HE SHALL NOT, -- THEY SHOULD FIND WHAT 'TWERE TO KILL A FATHER; SO SHOULD FLEANCE.
BUT, PEACE! -- FOR FROM BROAD WORDS, AND 'CAUSE HE FAIL'D HIS PRESENCE AT THE TYRANT'S FEAST, I HEAR, MACDUFF LIVES IN DISGRACE. SIR, CAN YOU TELL WHERE HE BESTOWS HIMSELF?
THE SON OF DUNCAN, FROM WHOM THIS TYRANT HOLDS THE DUE OF BIRTH, LIVES IN THE ENGLISH COURT; AND IS RECEIV'D OF THE MOST PIOUS EDWARD WITH SUCH GRACE, THAT THE MALEVOLENCE OF FORTUNE NOTHING TAKES FROM HIS HIGH RESPECT. THITHER MACDUFF IS GONE TO PRAY THE HOLY KING, UPON HIS AID TO WAKE NORTHUMBERLAND, AND WARLIKE SIWARD:

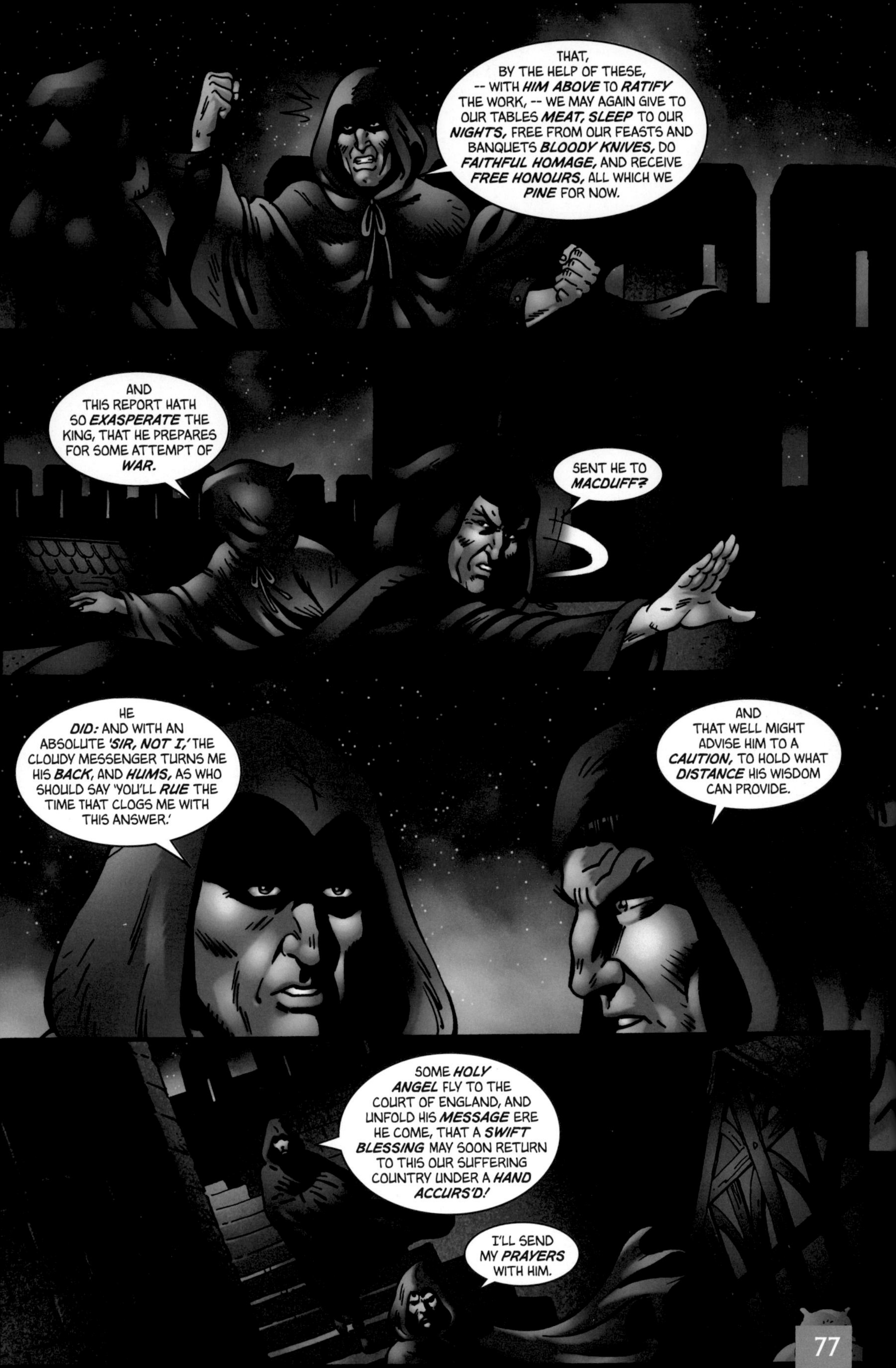
THAT, BY THE HELP OF THESE, -- WITH HIM ABOVE TO RATIFY THE WORK, -- WE MAY AGAIN GIVE TO OUR TABLES MEAT, SLEEP TO OUR NIGHTS, FREE FROM OUR FEASTS AND BANQUETS BLOODY KNIVES, DO FAITHFUL HOMAGE, AND RECEIVE FREE HONOURS, ALL WHICH WE PINE FOR NOW.
AND THIS REPORT HATH SO EXASPERATE THE KING, THAT HE PREPARES FOR SOME ATTEMPT OF WAR.
SENT HE TO MACDUFF?
HE DID: AND WITH AN ABSOLUTE 'SIR, NOT I,' THE CLOUDY MESSENGER TURNS ME HIS BACK, AND HUMS, AS WHO SHOULD SAY 'YOU'LL RUE THE TIME THAT CLOGS ME WITH THIS ANSWER.'
AND THAT WELL MIGHT ADVISE HIM TO A CAUTION, TO HOLD WHAT DISTANCE HIS WISDOM CAN PROVIDE.
SOME HOLY ANGEL FLY TO THE COURT OF ENGLAND, AND UNFOLD HIS MESSAGE ERE HE COME, THAT A SWIFT BLESSING MAY SOON RETURN TO THIS OUR SUFFERING COUNTRY UNDER A HAND ACCURS'D!
I'LL SEND MY PRAYERS WITH HIM.

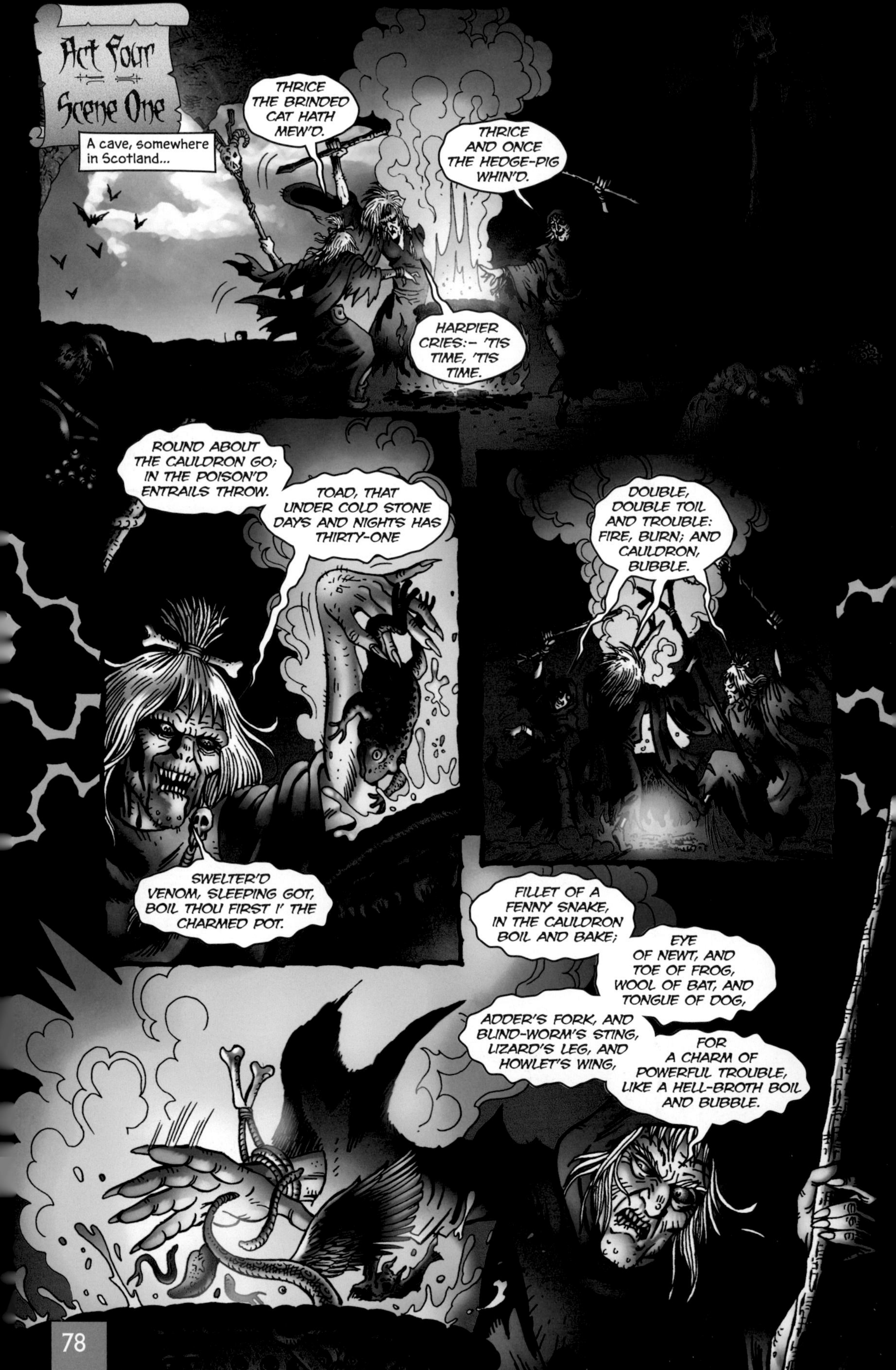
Act Four
Scene One
A cave, somewhere in Scotland...
THRICE THE BRINDED CAT HATH MEW'D.
THRICE AND ONCE THE HEDGE-PIG WHIN'D.
HARPIER CRIES:– 'TIS TIME, 'TIS TIME.
ROUND ABOUT THE CAULDRON GO; IN THE POISON'D ENTRAILS THROW.
TOAD, THAT UNDER COLD STONE DAYS AND NIGHTS HAS THIRTY-ONE
SWELTER'D VENOM, SLEEPING GOT, BOIL THOU FIRST I' THE CHARMED POT.
DOUBLE, DOUBLE TOIL AND TROUBLE: FIRE, BURN; AND CAULDRON, BUBBLE.
FILLET OF A FENNY SNAKE, IN THE CAULDRON BOIL AND BAKE;
EYE OF NEWT, AND TOE OF FROG, WOOL OF BAT, AND TONGUE OF DOG,
ADDER'S FORK, AND BLIND-WORM'S STING, LIZARD'S LEG, AND HOWLET'S WING,
FOR A CHARM OF POWERFUL TROUBLE, LIKE A HELL-BROTH BOIL AND BUBBLE.

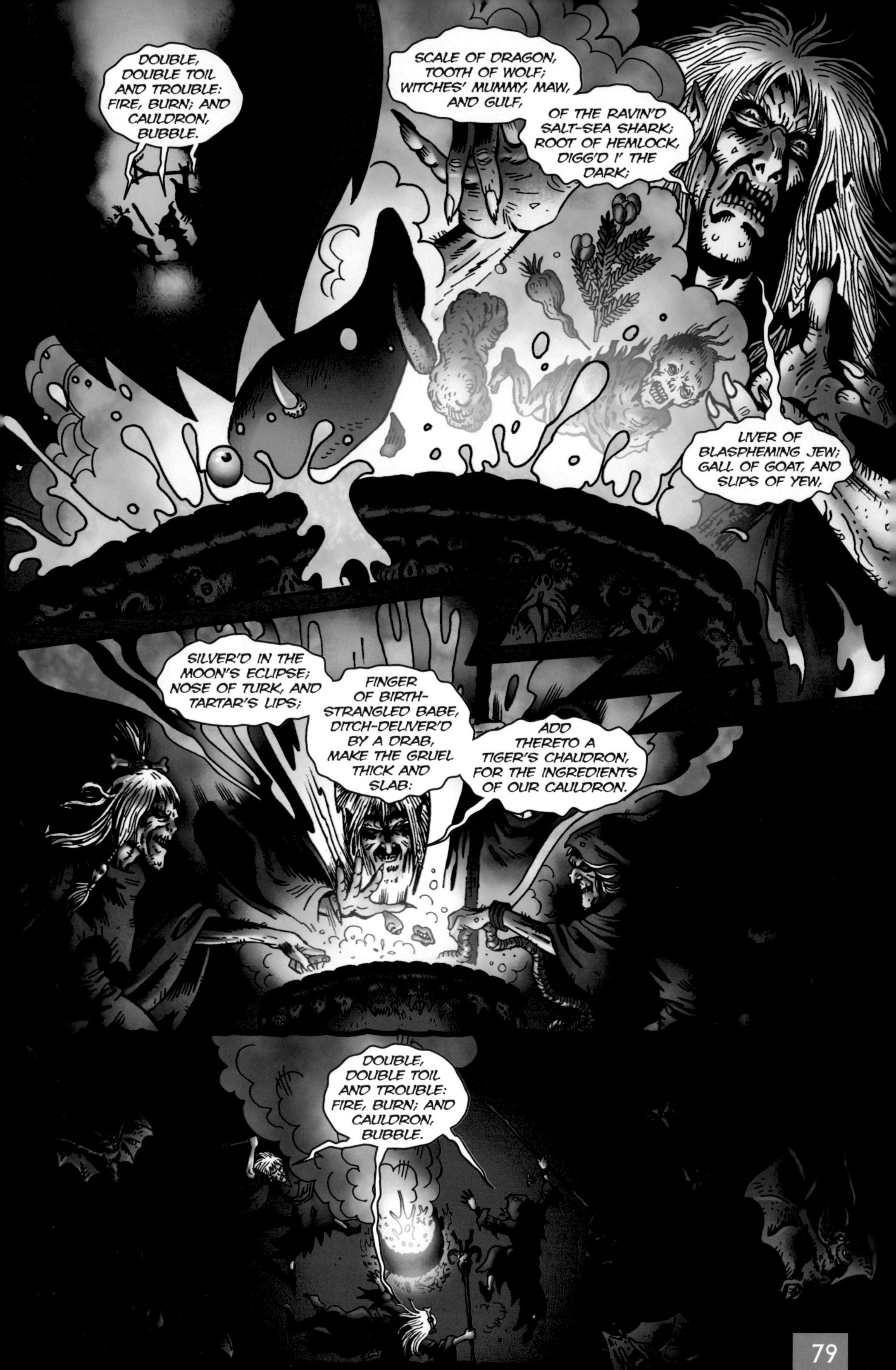
DOUBLE, DOUBLE TOIL AND TROUBLE: FIRE, BURN; AND CAULDRON, BUBBLE.
SCALE OF DRAGON, TOOTH OF WOLF; WITCHES' MUMMY, MAW, AND GULF,
OF THE RAVIN'D SALT-SEA SHARK; ROOT OF HEMLOCK, DIGG'D I' THE DARK;
LIVER OF BLASPHEMING JEW; GALL OF GOAT, AND SLIPS OF YEW,
SILVER'D IN THE MOON'S ECLIPSE; NOSE OF TURK, AND TARTAR'S LIPS;
FINGER OF BIRTH-STRANGLED BABE, DITCH-DELIVER'D BY A DRAB, MAKE THE GRUEL THICK AND SLAB:
ADD THERETO A TIGER'S CHAUDRON, FOR THE INGREDIENTS OF OUR CAULDRON.
DOUBLE, DOUBLE TOIL AND TROUBLE: FIRE, BURN; AND CAULDRON, BUBBLE.

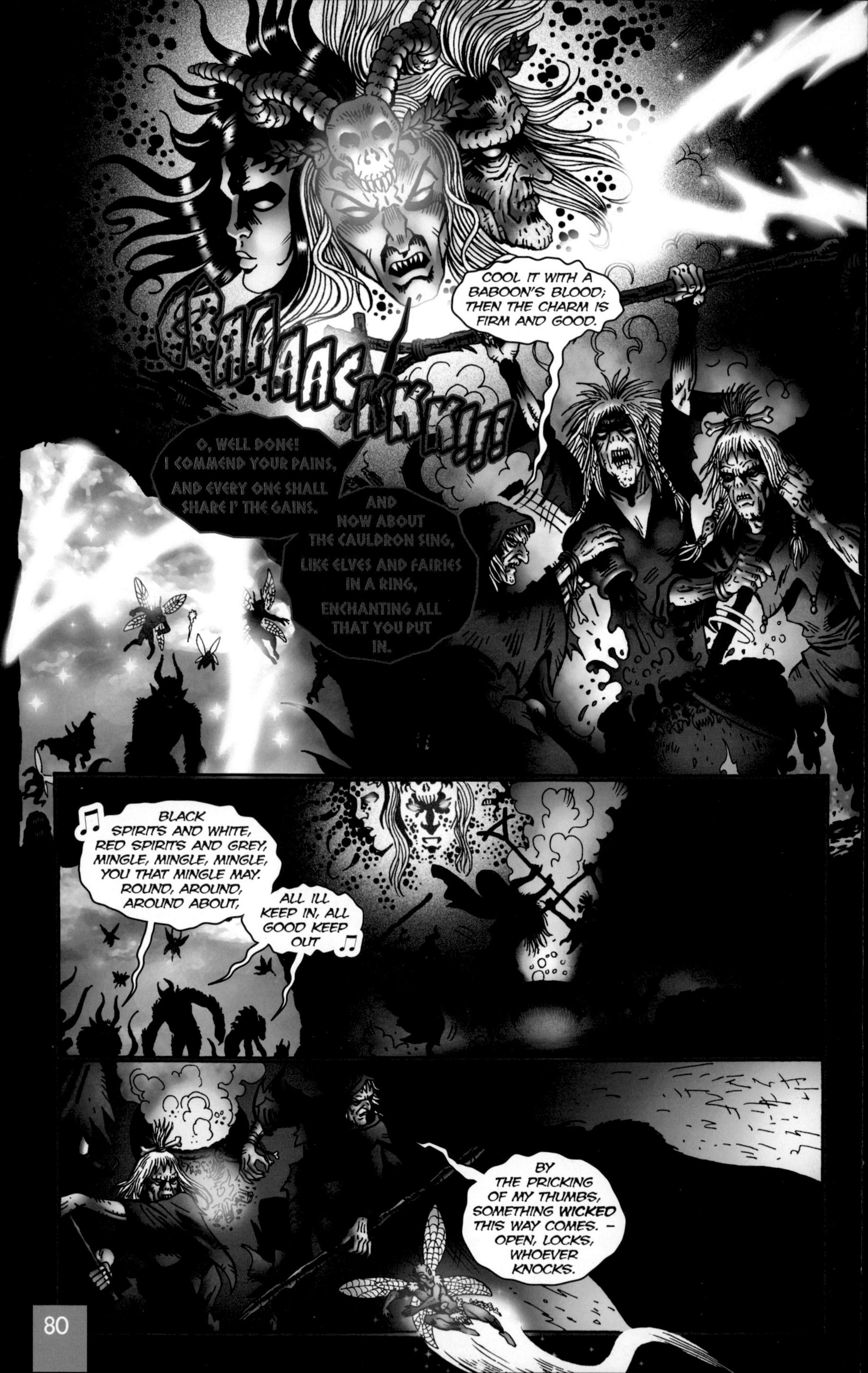
KRAAAACKKKK!!!
COOL IT WITH A BABOON'S BLOOD; THEN THE CHARM IS FIRM AND GOOD.
O, WELL DONE! I COMMEND YOUR PAINS, AND EVERY ONE SHALL SHARE I' THE GAINS.
AND NOW ABOUT THE CAULDRON SING, LIKE ELVES AND FAIRIES IN A RING, ENCHANTING ALL THAT YOU PUT IN.
BLACK SPIRITS AND WHITE, RED SPIRITS AND GREY, MINGLE, MINGLE, MINGLE, YOU THAT MINGLE MAY. ROUND, AROUND, AROUND ABOUT,
ALL ILL KEEP IN, ALL GOOD KEEP OUT
BY THE PRICKING OF MY THUMBS, SOMETHING WICKED THIS WAY COMES. – OPEN, LOCKS, WHOEVER KNOCKS.

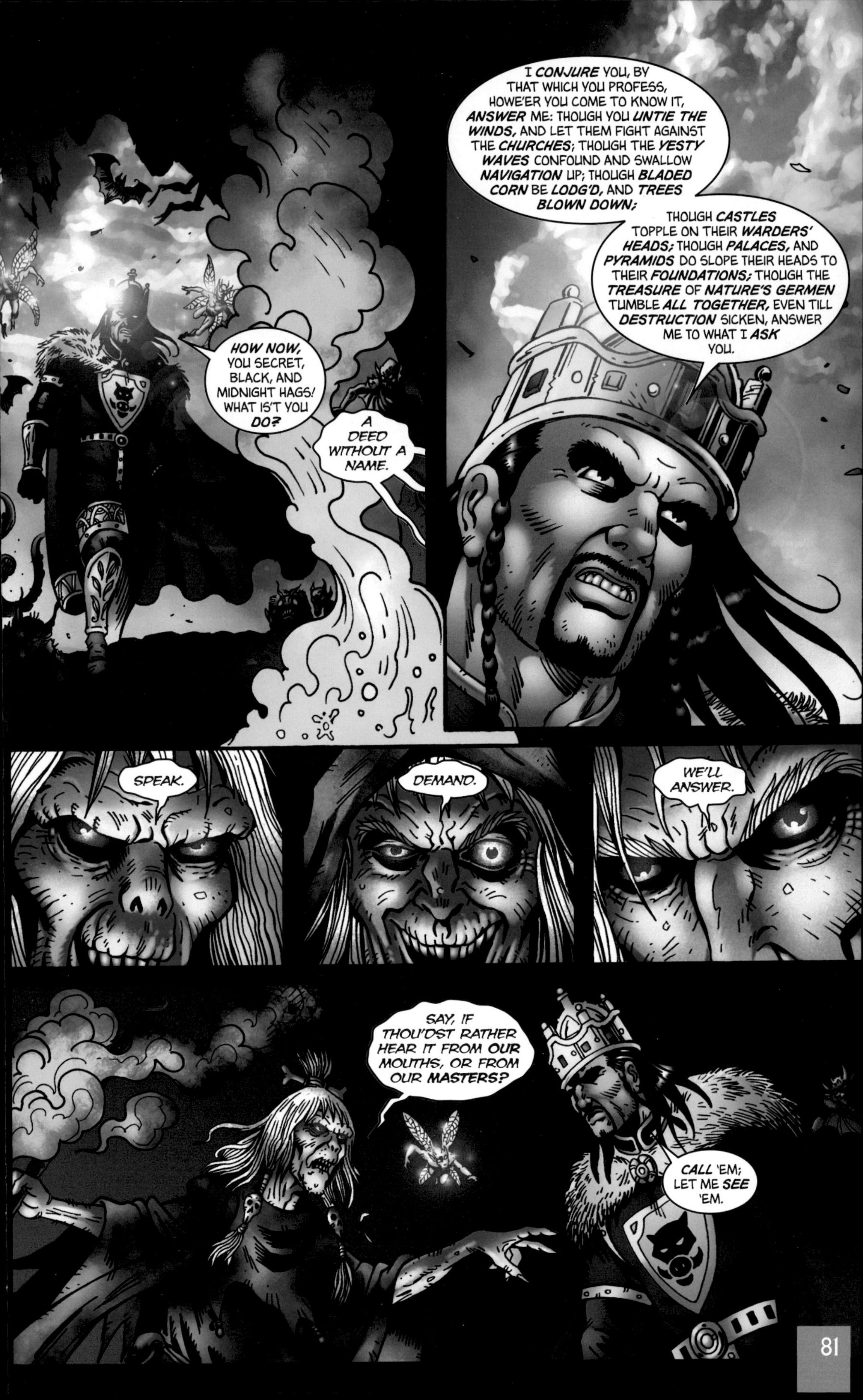
HOW NOW, YOU SECRET, BLACK, AND MIDNIGHT HAGS! WHAT IS'T YOU DO?
A DEED WITHOUT A NAME.
I CONJURE YOU, BY THAT WHICH YOU PROFESS, HOWE'ER YOU COME TO KNOW IT, ANSWER ME: THOUGH YOU UNTIE THE WINDS, AND LET THEM FIGHT AGAINST THE CHURCHES; THOUGH THE YESTY WAVES CONFOUND AND SWALLOW NAVIGATION UP; THOUGH BLADED CORN BE LODG'D, AND TREES BLOWN DOWN;
THOUGH CASTLES TOPPLE ON THEIR WARDERS' HEADS; THOUGH PALACES, AND PYRAMIDS DO SLOPE THEIR HEADS TO THEIR FOUNDATIONS; THOUGH THE TREASURE OF NATURE'S GERMEN TUMBLE ALL TOGETHER, EVEN TILL DESTRUCTION SICKEN, ANSWER ME TO WHAT I ASK YOU.
SPEAK.
DEMAND.
WE'LL ANSWER.
SAY, IF THOU'DST RATHER HEAR IT FROM OUR MOUTHS, OR FROM OUR MASTERS?
CALL 'EM; LET ME SEE 'EM.

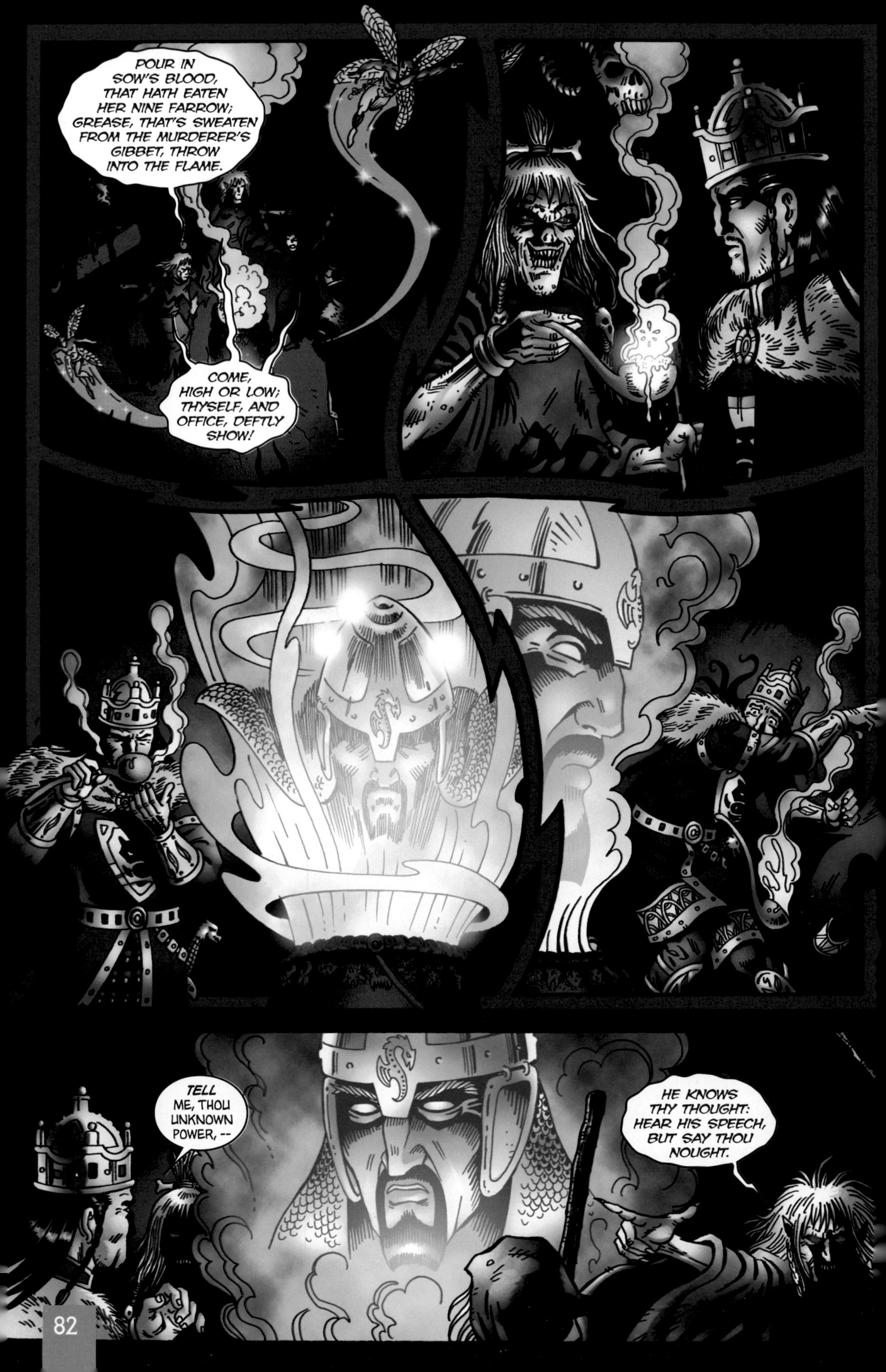
POUR IN SOW'S BLOOD, THAT HATH EATEN HER NINE FARROW; GREASE, THAT'S SWEATEN FROM THE MURDERER'S GIBBET, THROW INTO THE FLAME.
COME, HIGH OR LOW; THYSELF, AND OFFICE, DEFTLY SHOW!
TELL ME, THOU UNKNOWN POWER, --
HE KNOWS THY THOUGHT: HEAR HIS SPEECH, BUT SAY THOU NOUGHT.

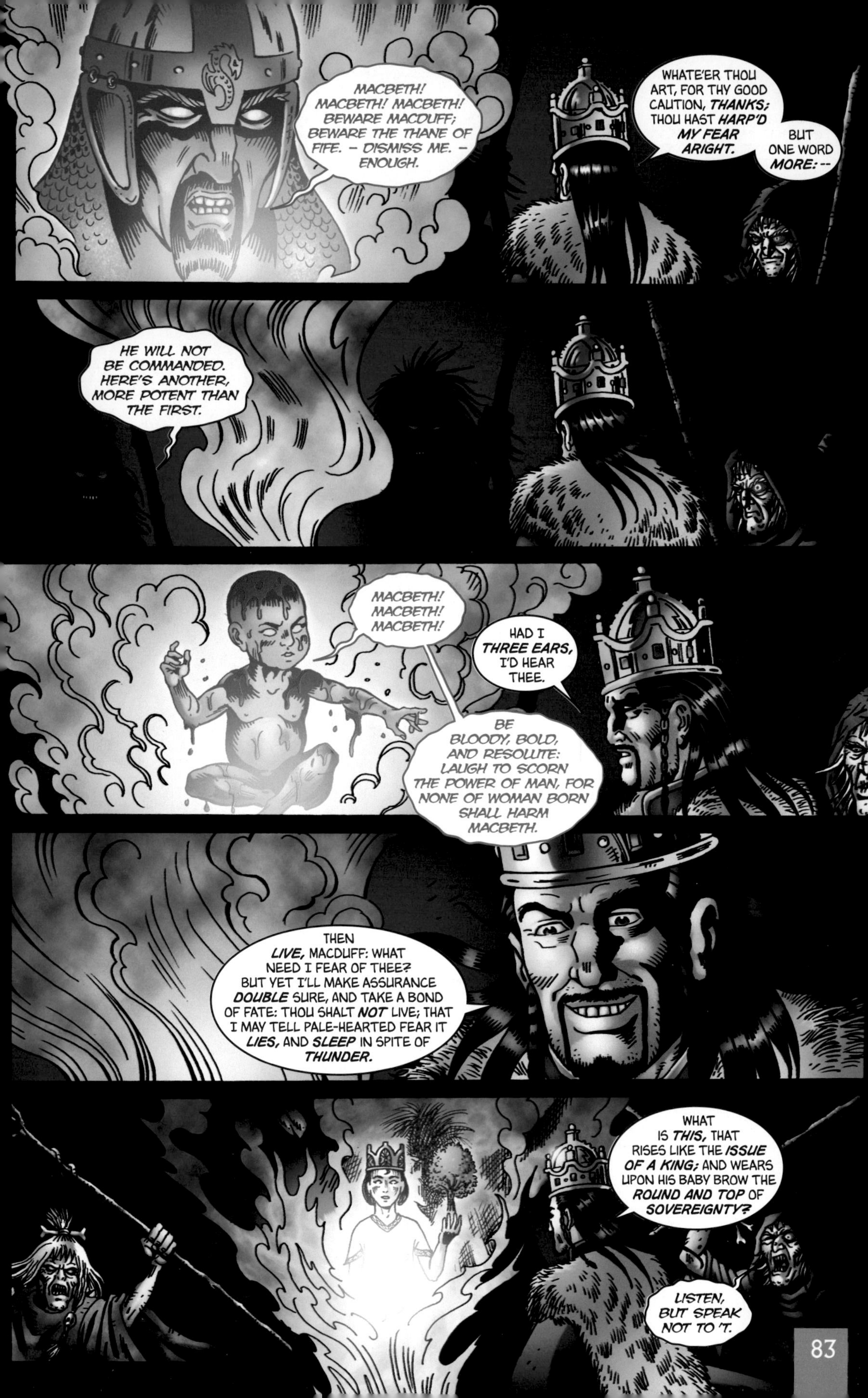
MACBETH! MACBETH! MACBETH! BEWARE MACDUFF; BEWARE THE THANE OF FIFE. – DISMISS ME. – ENOUGH.
WHATE'ER THOU ART, FOR THY GOOD CAUTION, THANKS; THOU HAST HARP'D MY FEAR ARIGHT.
BUT ONE WORD MORE: --
HE WILL NOT BE COMMANDED. HERE'S ANOTHER, MORE POTENT THAN THE FIRST.
MACBETH! MACBETH! MACBETH!
HAD I THREE EARS, I'D HEAR THEE.
BE BLOODY, BOLD, AND RESOLUTE: LAUGH TO SCORN THE POWER OF MAN, FOR NONE OF WOMAN BORN SHALL HARM MACBETH.
THEN LIVE, MACDUFF: WHAT NEED I FEAR OF THEE? BUT YET I'LL MAKE ASSURANCE DOUBLE SURE, AND TAKE A BOND OF FATE: THOU SHALT NOT LIVE; THAT I MAY TELL PALE-HEARTED FEAR IT LIES, AND SLEEP IN SPITE OF THUNDER.
WHAT IS THIS, THAT RISES LIKE THE ISSUE OF A KING; AND WEARS UPON HIS BABY BROW THE ROUND AND TOP OF SOVEREIGNTY?
LISTEN, BUT SPEAK NOT TO 'T.

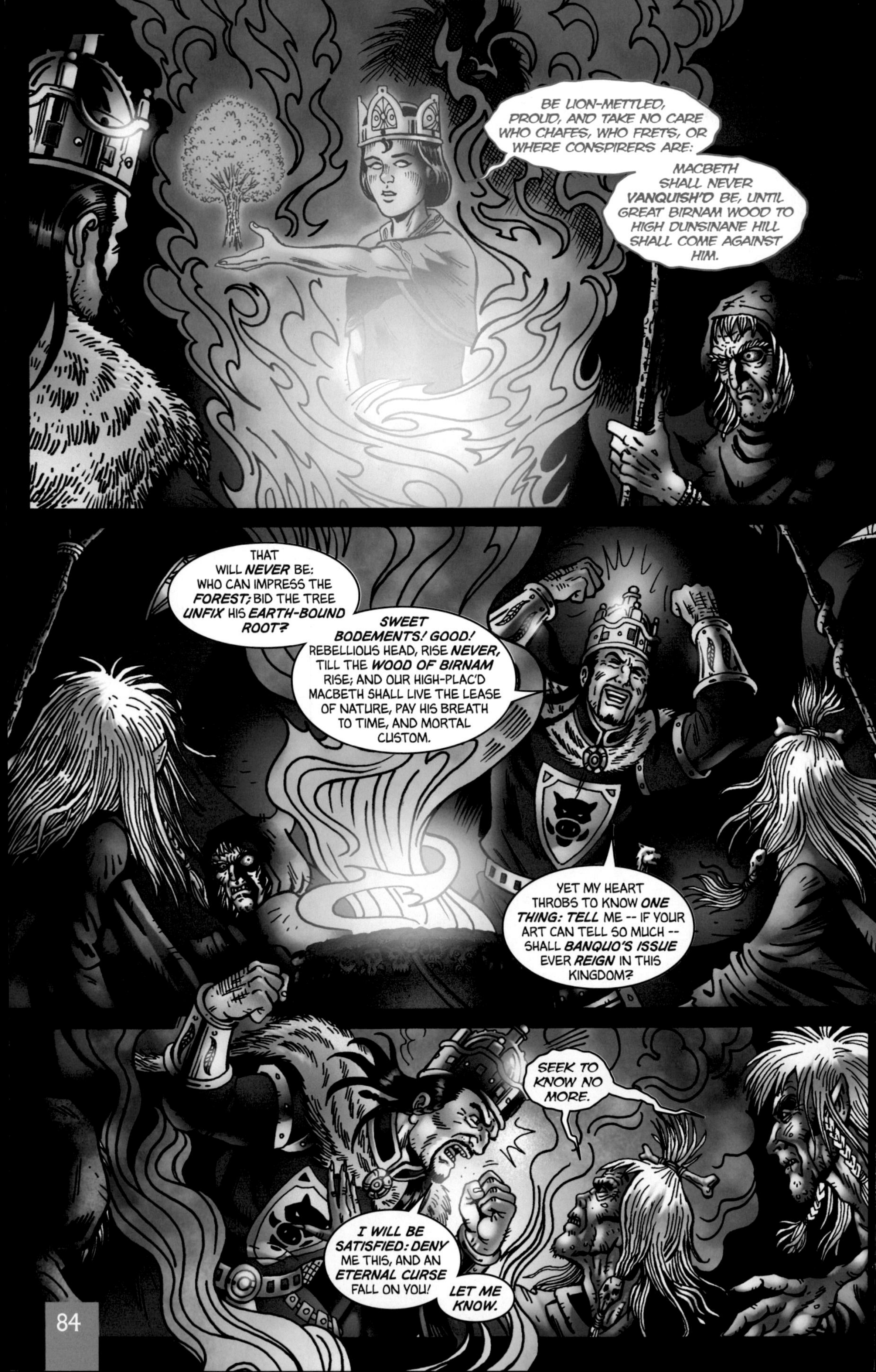
BE LION-METTLED, PROUD, AND TAKE NO CARE WHO CHAFES, WHO FRETS, OR WHERE CONSPIRERS ARE:
MACBETH SHALL NEVER VANQUISH'D BE, UNTIL GREAT BIRNAM WOOD TO HIGH DUNSINANE HILL SHALL COME AGAINST HIM.
THAT WILL NEVER BE: WHO CAN IMPRESS THE FOREST; BID THE TREE UNFIX HIS EARTH-BOUND ROOT?
SWEET BODEMENTS! GOOD! REBELLIOUS HEAD, RISE NEVER, TILL THE WOOD OF BIRNAM RISE; AND OUR HIGH-PLAC'D MACBETH SHALL LIVE THE LEASE OF NATURE, PAY HIS BREATH TO TIME, AND MORTAL CUSTOM.
YET MY HEART THROBS TO KNOW ONE THING: TELL ME -- IF YOUR ART CAN TELL SO MUCH -- SHALL BANQUO'S ISSUE EVER REIGN IN THIS KINGDOM?
SEEK TO KNOW NO MORE.
I WILL BE SATISFIED: DENY ME THIS, AND AN ETERNAL CURSE FALL ON YOU!
LET ME KNOW.

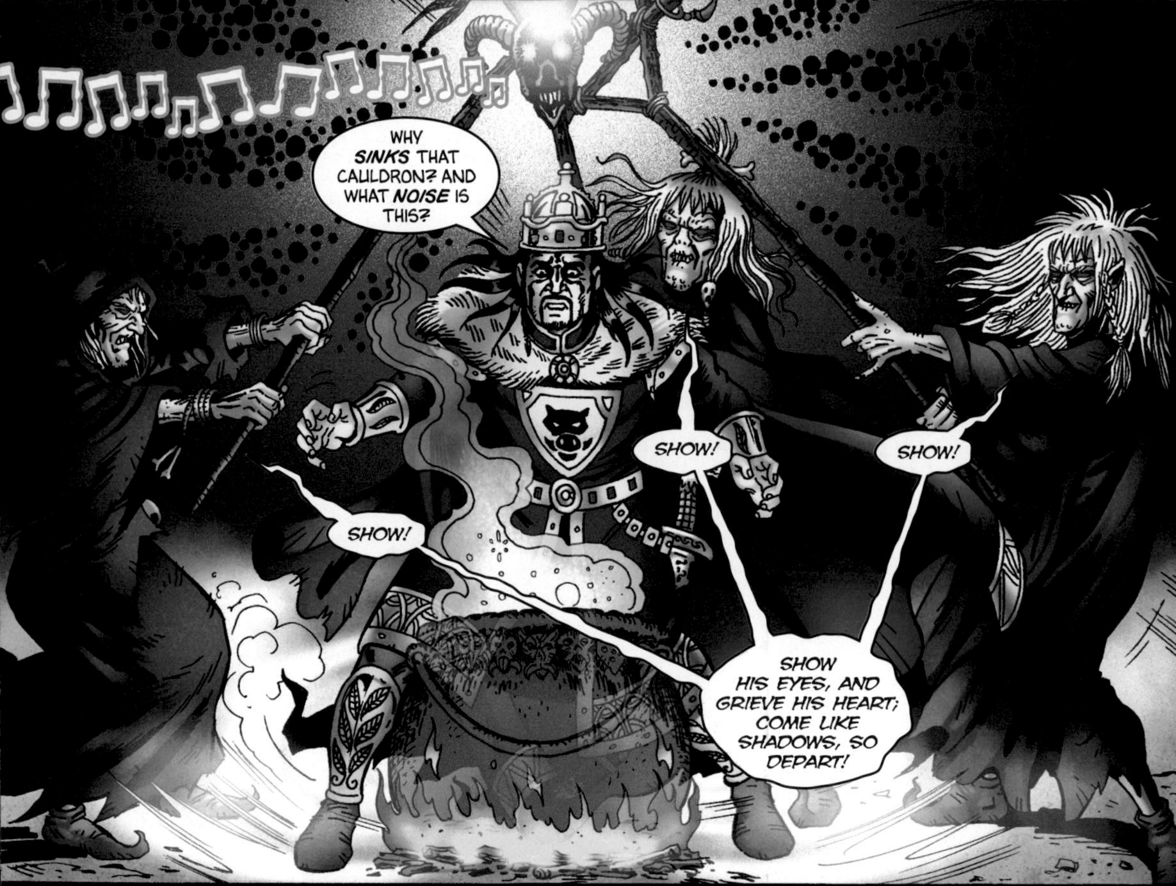
WHY SINKS THAT CAULDRON? AND WHAT NOISE IS THIS?
SHOW!
SHOW!
SHOW!
SHOW HIS EYES, AND GRIEVE HIS HEART; COME LIKE SHADOWS, SO DEPART!

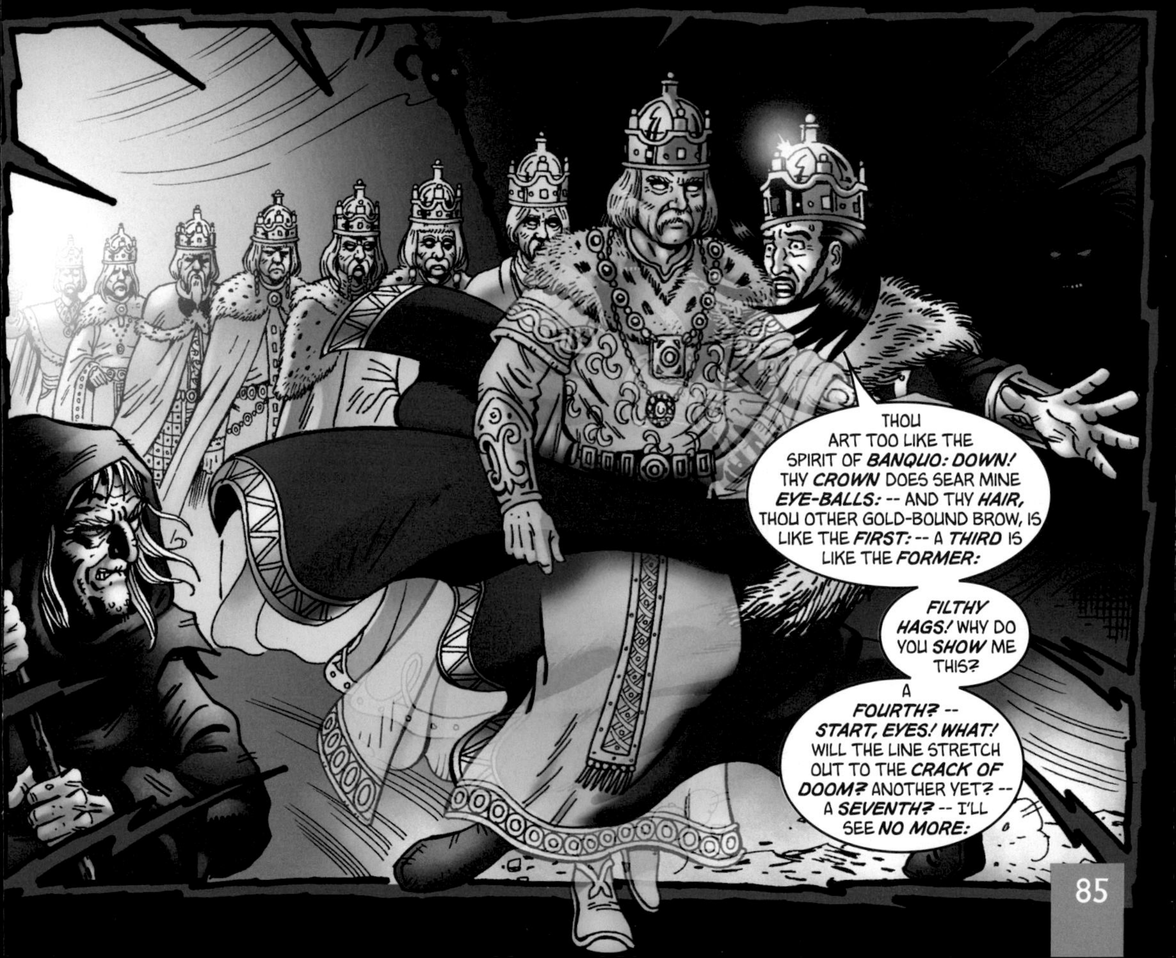
THOU ART TOO LIKE THE SPIRIT OF BANQUO: DOWN! THY CROWN DOES SEAR MINE EYE-BALLS: -- AND THY HAIR, THOU OTHER GOLD-BOUND BROW, IS LIKE THE FIRST: -- A THIRD IS LIKE THE FORMER:
FILTHY HAGS! WHY DO YOU SHOW ME THIS?
A FOURTH? -- START, EYES! WHAT! WILL THE LINE STRETCH OUT TO THE CRACK OF DOOM? ANOTHER YET? -- A SEVENTH? -- I'LL SEE NO MORE:

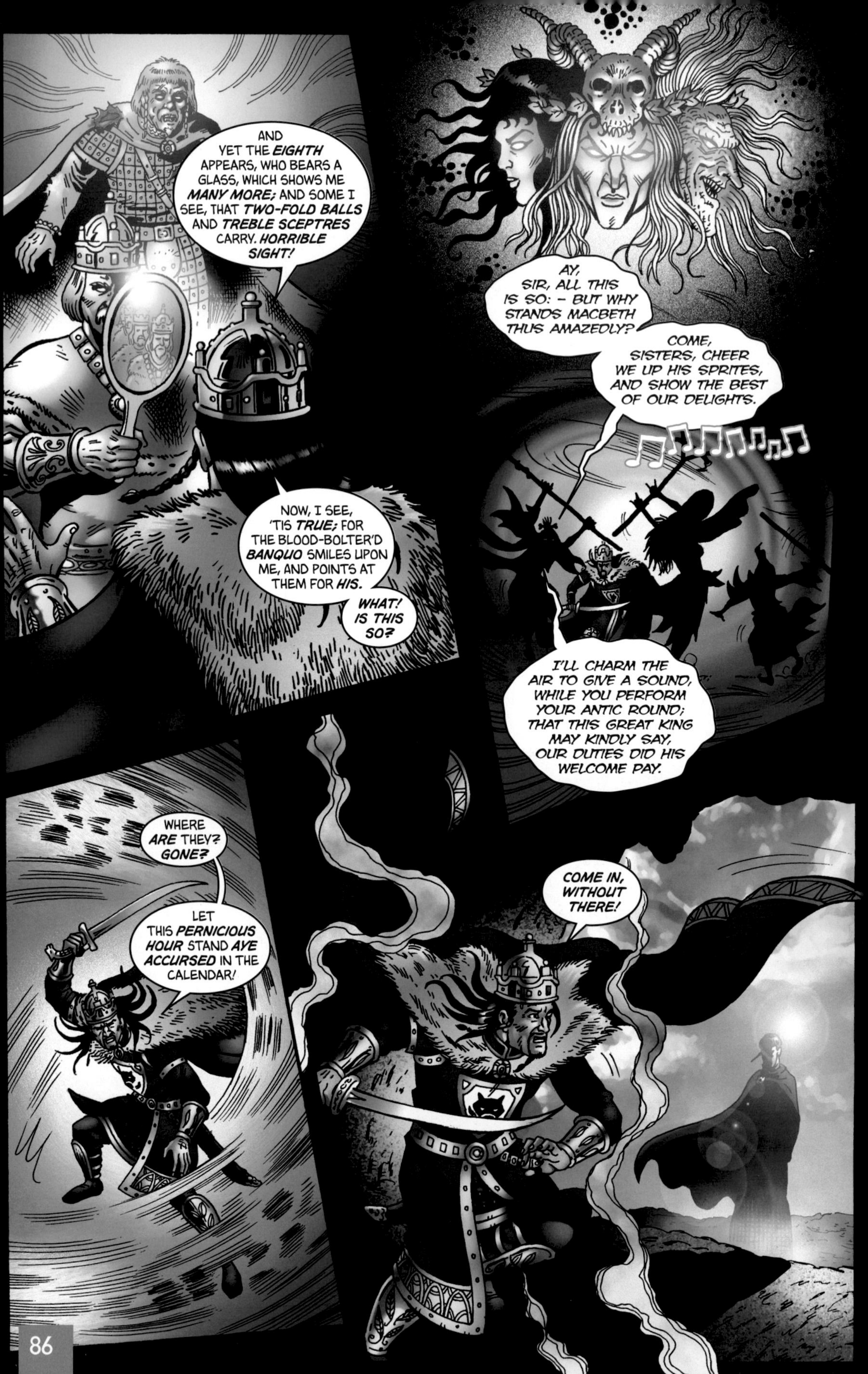
AND YET THE EIGHTH APPEARS, WHO BEARS A GLASS, WHICH SHOWS ME MANY MORE; AND SOME I SEE, THAT TWO-FOLD BALLS AND TREBLE SCEPTRES CARRY. HORRIBLE SIGHT!
NOW, I SEE, 'TIS TRUE; FOR THE BLOOD-BOLTER'D BANQUO SMILES UPON ME, AND POINTS AT THEM FOR HIS.
WHAT! IS THIS SO?
AY, SIR, ALL THIS IS SO: - BUT WHY STANDS MACBETH THUS AMAZEDLY?
COME, SISTERS, CHEER WE UP HIS SPRITES, AND SHOW THE BEST OF OUR DELIGHTS.
I'LL CHARM THE AIR TO GIVE A SOUND, WHILE YOU PERFORM YOUR ANTIC ROUND; THAT THIS GREAT KING MAY KINDLY SAY, OUR DUTIES DID HIS WELCOME PAY.
WHERE ARE THEY? GONE?
LET THIS PERNICIOUS HOUR STAND AYE ACCURSED IN THE CALENDAR!
COME IN, WITHOUT THERE!

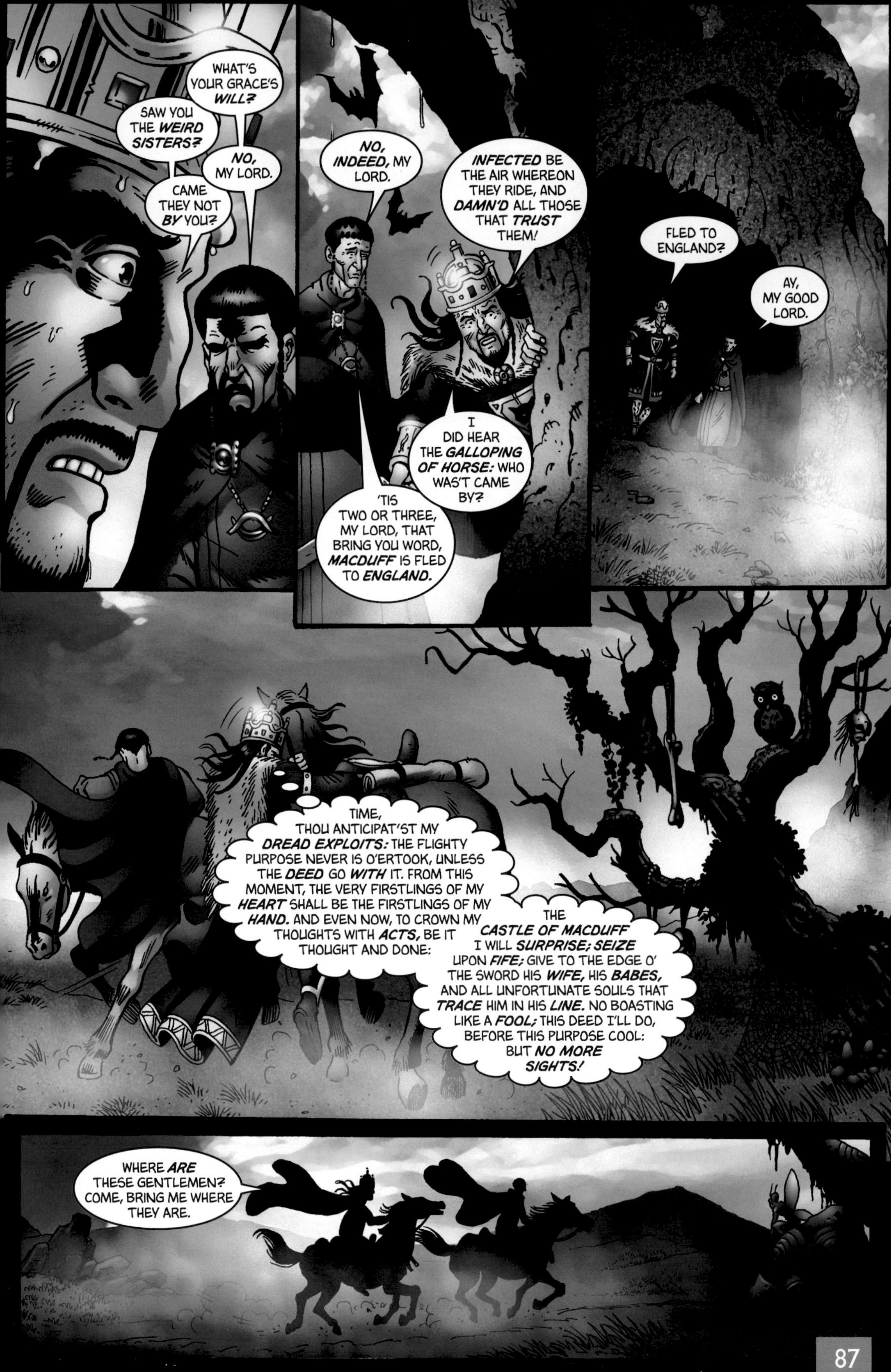
SAW YOU THE WEIRD SISTERS?
WHAT'S YOUR GRACE'S WILL?
NO, MY LORD.
CAME THEY NOT BY YOU?
NO, INDEED, MY LORD.
INFECTED BE THE AIR WHEREON THEY RIDE, AND DAMN'D ALL THOSE THAT TRUST THEM!
I DID HEAR THE GALLOPING OF HORSE: WHO WAS'T CAME BY?
'TIS TWO OR THREE, MY LORD, THAT BRING YOU WORD, MACDUFF IS FLED TO ENGLAND.
FLED TO ENGLAND?
AY, MY GOOD LORD.
TIME, THOU ANTICIPAT'ST MY DREAD EXPLOITS: THE FLIGHTY PURPOSE NEVER IS O'ERTOOK, UNLESS THE DEED GO WITH IT. FROM THIS MOMENT, THE VERY FIRSTLINGS OF MY HEART SHALL BE THE FIRSTLINGS OF MY HAND. AND EVEN NOW, TO CROWN MY THOUGHTS WITH ACTS, BE IT THOUGHT AND DONE:
THE CASTLE OF MACDUFF I WILL SURPRISE; SEIZE UPON FIFE; GIVE TO THE EDGE O' THE SWORD HIS WIFE, HIS BABES, AND ALL UNFORTUNATE SOULS THAT TRACE HIM IN HIS LINE. NO BOASTING LIKE A FOOL; THIS DEED I'LL DO, BEFORE THIS PURPOSE COOL: BUT NO MORE SIGHTS!
WHERE ARE THESE GENTLEMEN? COME, BRING ME WHERE THEY ARE.

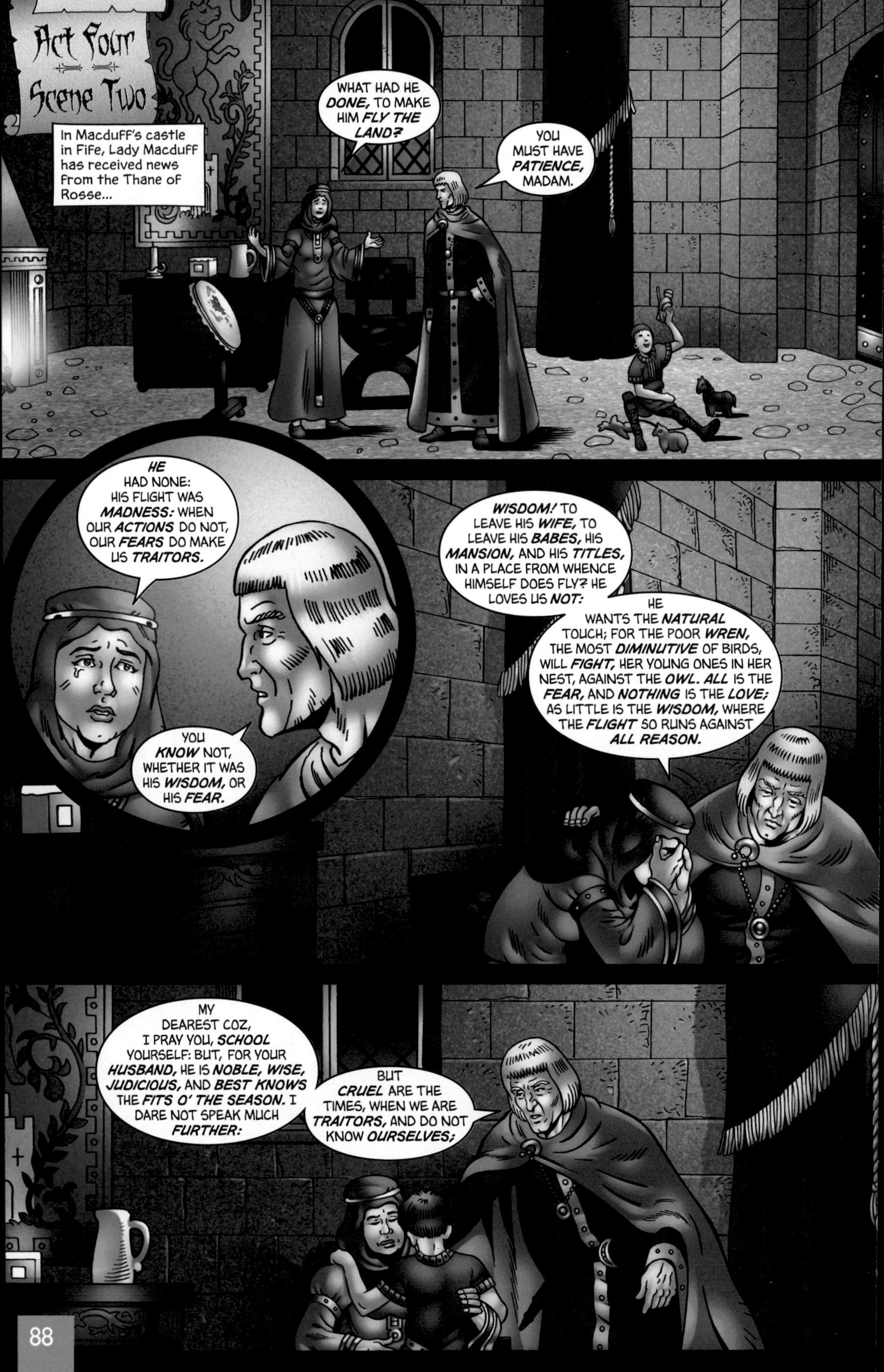
Act Four
Scene Two
In Macduff's castle in Fife, Lady Macduff has received news from the Thane of Rosse...
WHAT HAD HE DONE, TO MAKE HIM FLY THE LAND?
YOU MUST HAVE PATIENCE, MADAM.
HE HAD NONE: HIS FLIGHT WAS MADNESS: WHEN OUR ACTIONS DO NOT, OUR FEARS DO MAKE US TRAITORS.
YOU KNOW NOT, WHETHER IT WAS HIS WISDOM, OR HIS FEAR.
WISDOM! TO LEAVE HIS WIFE, TO LEAVE HIS BABES, HIS MANSION, AND HIS TITLES, IN A PLACE FROM WHENCE HIMSELF DOES FLY? HE LOVES US NOT:
HE WANTS THE NATURAL TOUCH; FOR THE POOR WREN, THE MOST DIMINUTIVE OF BIRDS, WILL FIGHT, HER YOUNG ONES IN HER NEST, AGAINST THE OWL. ALL IS THE FEAR, AND NOTHING IS THE LOVE; AS LITTLE IS THE WISDOM, WHERE THE FLIGHT SO RUNS AGAINST ALL REASON.
MY DEAREST COZ, I PRAY YOU, SCHOOL YOURSELF: BUT, FOR YOUR HUSBAND, HE IS NOBLE, WISE, JUDICIOUS, AND BEST KNOWS THE FITS O' THE SEASON. I DARE NOT SPEAK MUCH FURTHER:
BUT CRUEL ARE THE TIMES, WHEN WE ARE TRAITORS, AND DO NOT KNOW OURSELVES;

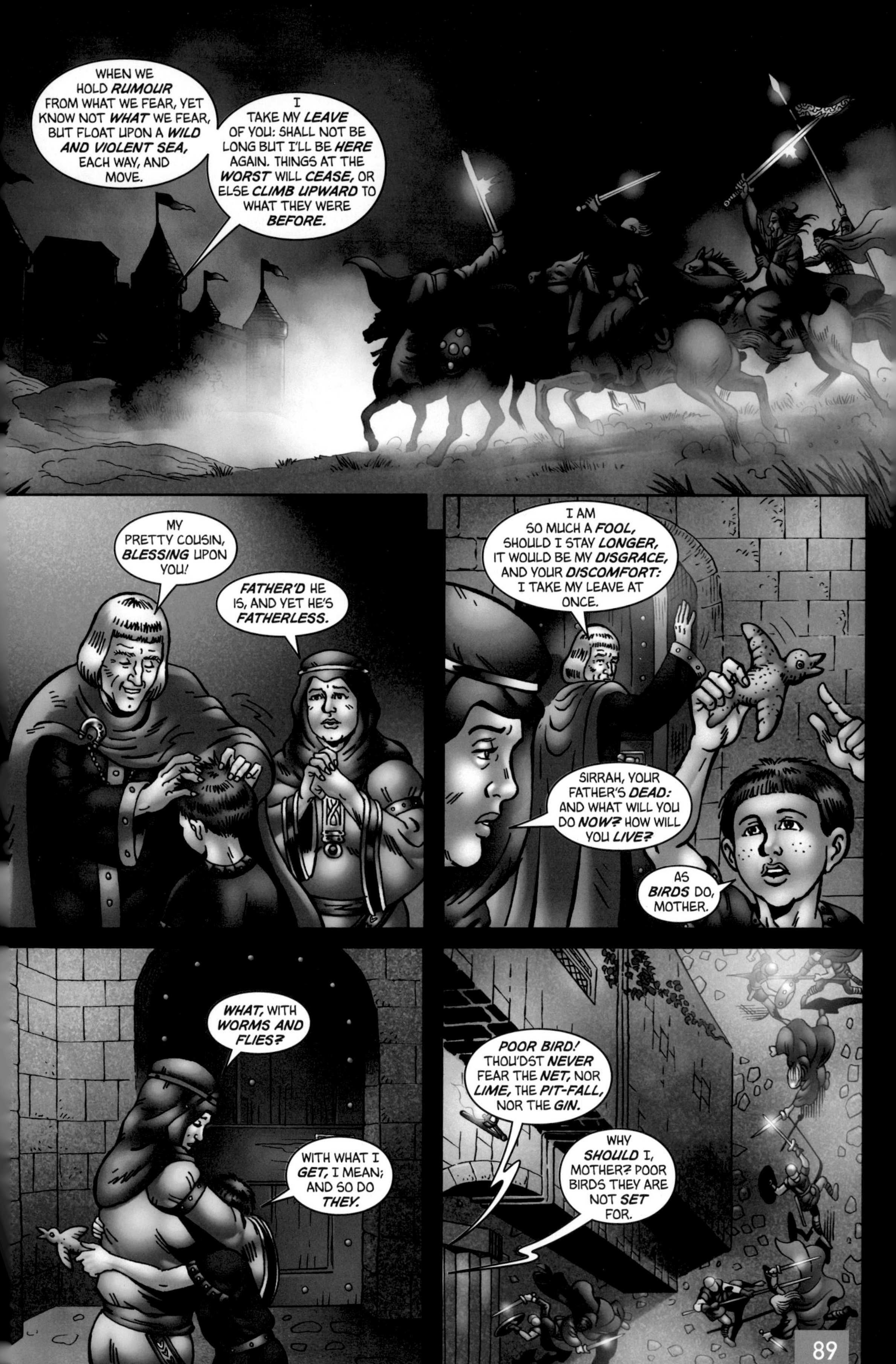

WHEN WE HOLD RUMOUR FROM WHAT WE FEAR, YET KNOW NOT WHAT WE FEAR, BUT FLOAT UPON A WILD AND VIOLENT SEA, EACH WAY, AND MOVE.
I TAKE MY LEAVE OF YOU: SHALL NOT BE LONG BUT I'LL BE HERE AGAIN. THINGS AT THE WORST WILL CEASE, OR ELSE CLIMB UPWARD TO WHAT THEY WERE BEFORE.
MY PRETTY COUSIN, BLESSING UPON YOU!
FATHER'D HE IS, AND YET HE'S FATHERLESS.
I AM SO MUCH A FOOL, SHOULD I STAY LONGER, IT WOULD BE MY DISGRACE, AND YOUR DISCOMFORT: I TAKE MY LEAVE AT ONCE.
SIRRAH, YOUR FATHER'S DEAD: AND WHAT WILL YOU DO NOW? HOW WILL YOU LIVE?
AS BIRDS DO, MOTHER.
WHAT, WITH WORMS AND FLIES?
WITH WHAT I GET, I MEAN; AND SO DO THEY.
POOR BIRD! THOU'DST NEVER FEAR THE NET, NOR LIME, THE PIT-FALL, NOR THE GIN.
WHY SHOULD I, MOTHER? POOR BIRDS THEY ARE NOT SET FOR.

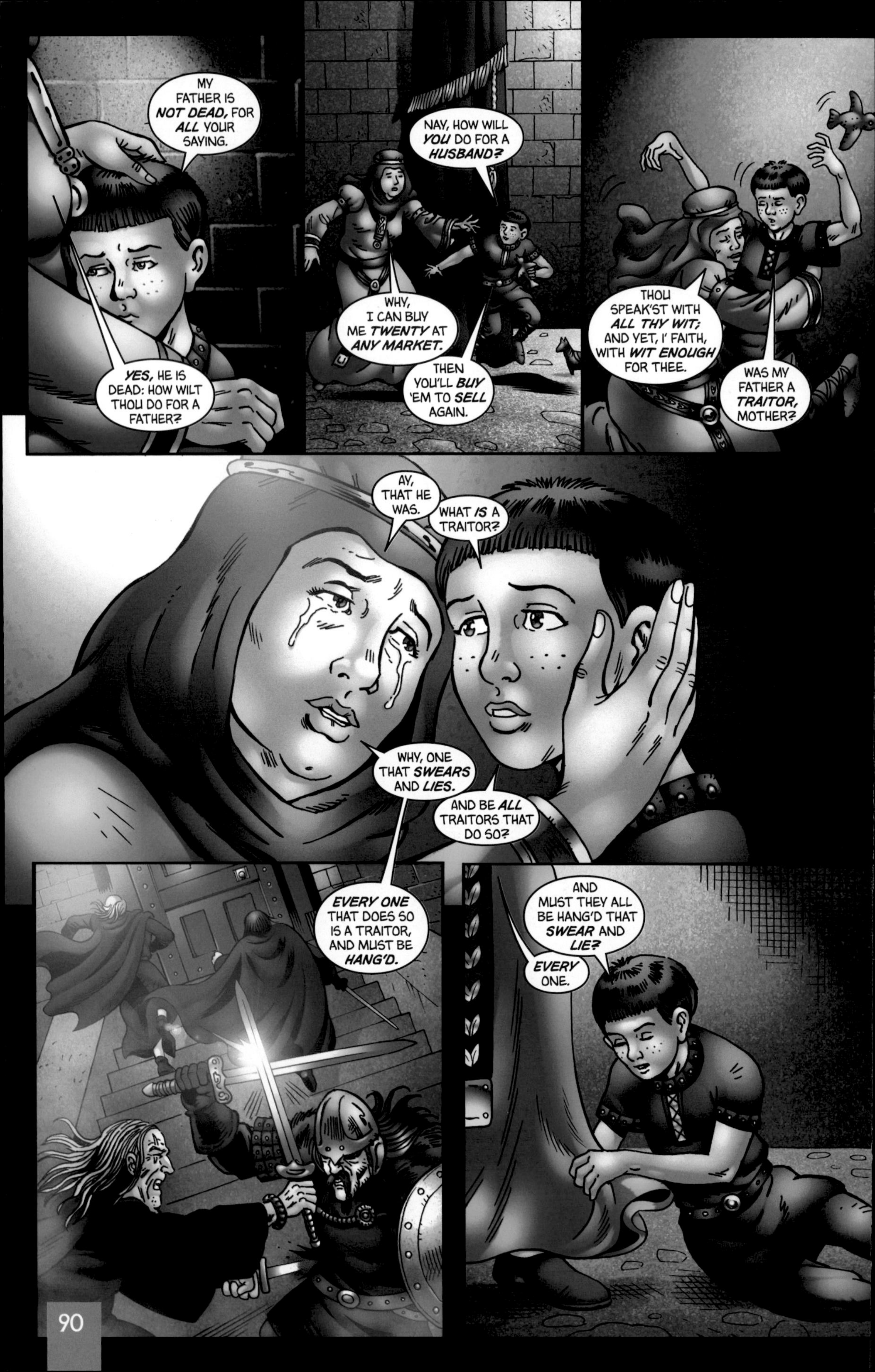
MY FATHER IS NOT DEAD, FOR ALL YOUR SAYING.
YES, HE IS DEAD: HOW WILT THOU DO FOR A FATHER?
NAY, HOW WILL YOU DO FOR A HUSBAND?
WHY, I CAN BUY ME TWENTY AT ANY MARKET.
THEN YOU'LL BUY 'EM TO SELL AGAIN.
THOU SPEAK'ST WITH ALL THY WIT; AND YET, I' FAITH, WITH WIT ENOUGH FOR THEE.
WAS MY FATHER A TRAITOR, MOTHER?
AY, THAT HE WAS.
WHAT IS A TRAITOR?
WHY, ONE THAT SWEARS AND LIES.
AND BE ALL TRAITORS THAT DO SO?
EVERY ONE THAT DOES SO IS A TRAITOR, AND MUST BE HANG'D.
AND MUST THEY ALL BE HANG'D THAT SWEAR AND LIE?
EVERY ONE.

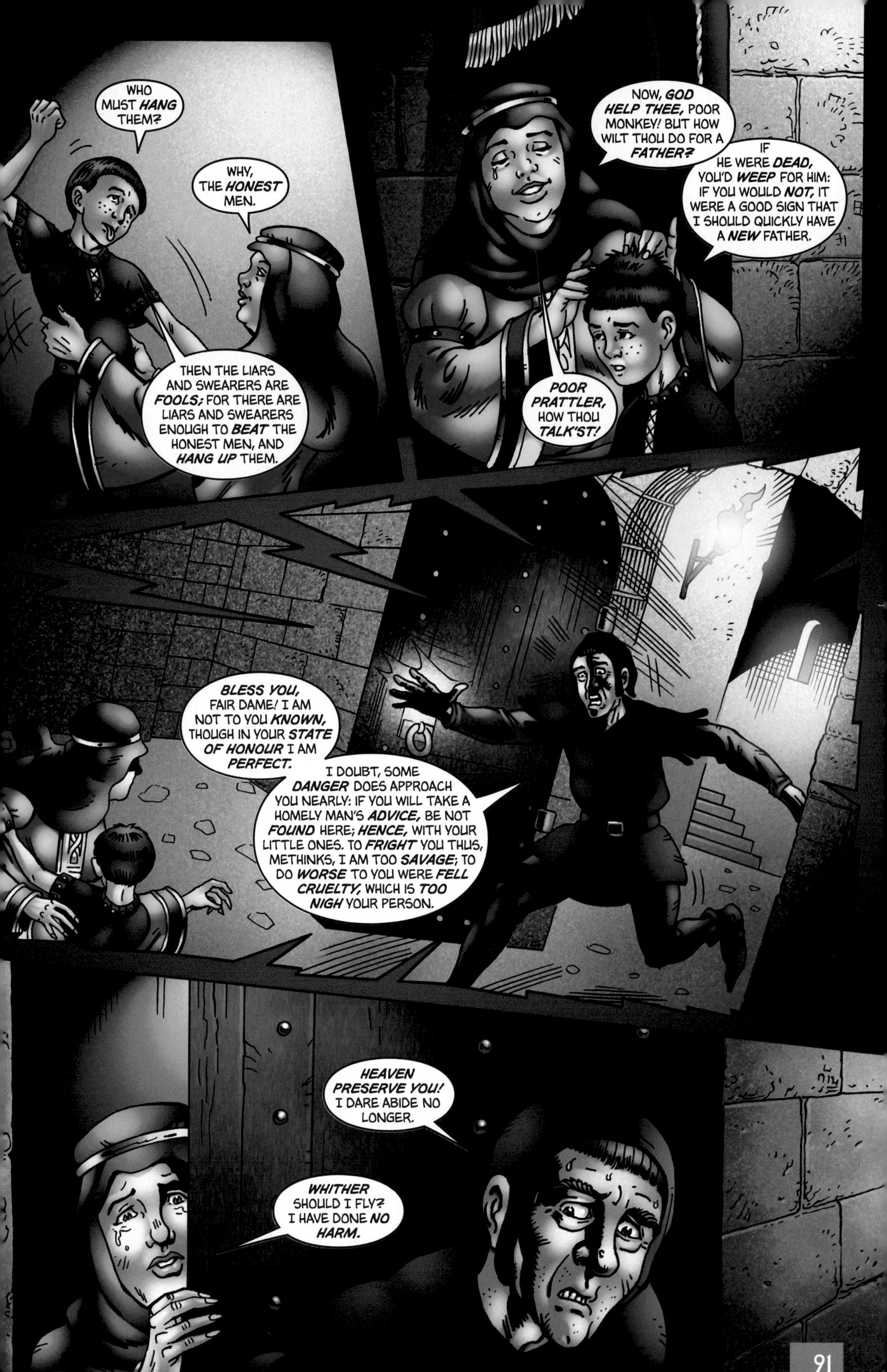
WHO MUST HANG THEM?
WHY, THE HONEST MEN.
THEN THE LIARS AND SWEARERS ARE FOOLS; FOR THERE ARE LIARS AND SWEARERS ENOUGH TO BEAT THE HONEST MEN, AND HANG UP THEM.
NOW, GOD HELP THEE, POOR MONKEY! BUT HOW WILT THOU DO FOR A FATHER?
IF HE WERE DEAD, YOU'D WEEP FOR HIM: IF YOU WOULD NOT, IT WERE A GOOD SIGN THAT I SHOULD QUICKLY HAVE A NEW FATHER.
POOR PRATTLER, HOW THOU TALK'ST!
BLESS YOU, FAIR DAME! I AM NOT TO YOU KNOWN, THOUGH IN YOUR STATE OF HONOUR I AM PERFECT.
I DOUBT, SOME DANGER DOES APPROACH YOU NEARLY: IF YOU WILL TAKE A HOMELY MAN'S ADVICE, BE NOT FOUND HERE; HENCE, WITH YOUR LITTLE ONES. TO FRIGHT YOU THUS, METHINKS, I AM TOO SAVAGE; TO DO WORSE TO YOU WERE FELL CRUELTY, WHICH IS TOO NIGH YOUR PERSON.
HEAVEN PRESERVE YOU! I DARE ABIDE NO LONGER.
WHITHER SHOULD I FLY? I HAVE DONE NO HARM.

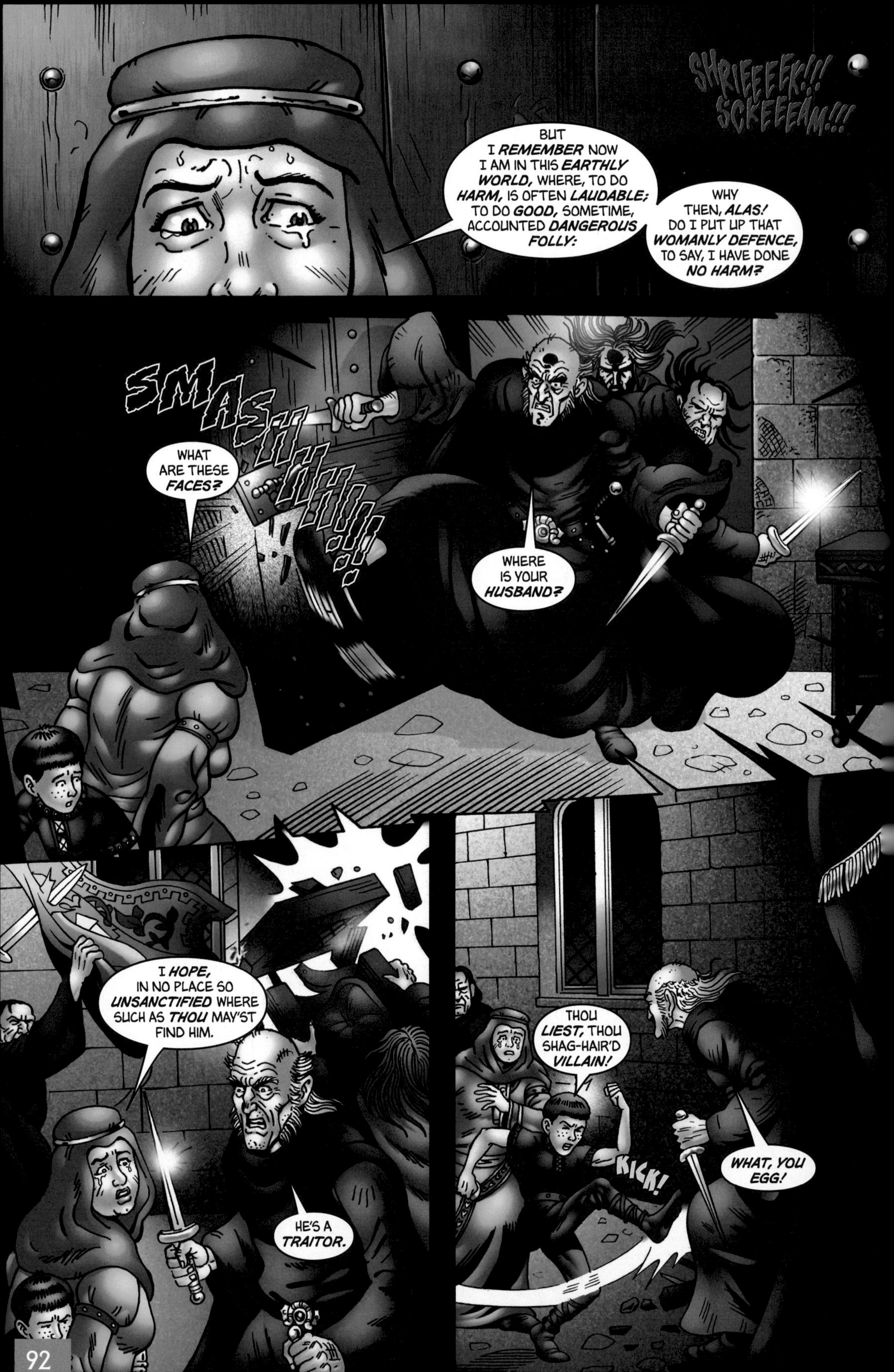
SHRIEEEEK!!!
SCREEEAM!!!
BUT I REMEMBER NOW I AM IN THIS EARTHLY WORLD, WHERE, TO DO HARM, IS OFTEN LAUDABLE; TO DO GOOD, SOMETIME, ACCOUNTED DANGEROUS FOLLY:
WHY THEN, ALAS! DO I PUT UP THAT WOMANLY DEFENCE, TO SAY, I HAVE DONE NO HARM?
SMASHHHH!!!
WHAT ARE THESE FACES?
WHERE IS YOUR HUSBAND?
I HOPE, IN NO PLACE SO UNSANCTIFIED WHERE SUCH AS THOU MAY'ST FIND HIM.
HE'S A TRAITOR.
THOU LIEST, THOU SHAG-HAIR'D VILLAIN!
KICK!
WHAT, YOU EGG!

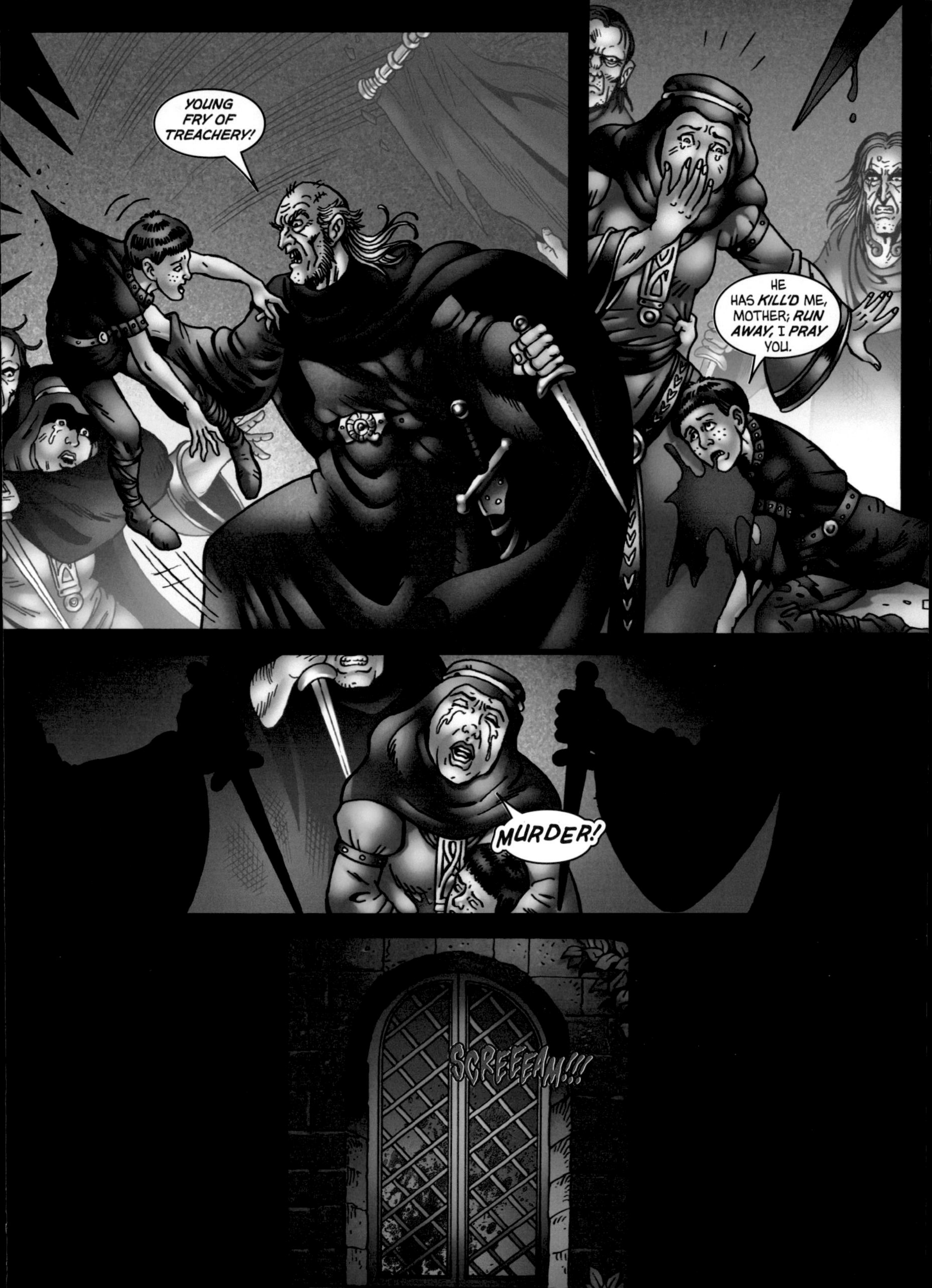
YOUNG FRY OF TREACHERY!
HE HAS KILL'D ME, MOTHER; RUN AWAY, I PRAY YOU.
MURDER!
SCREEEAM!!!

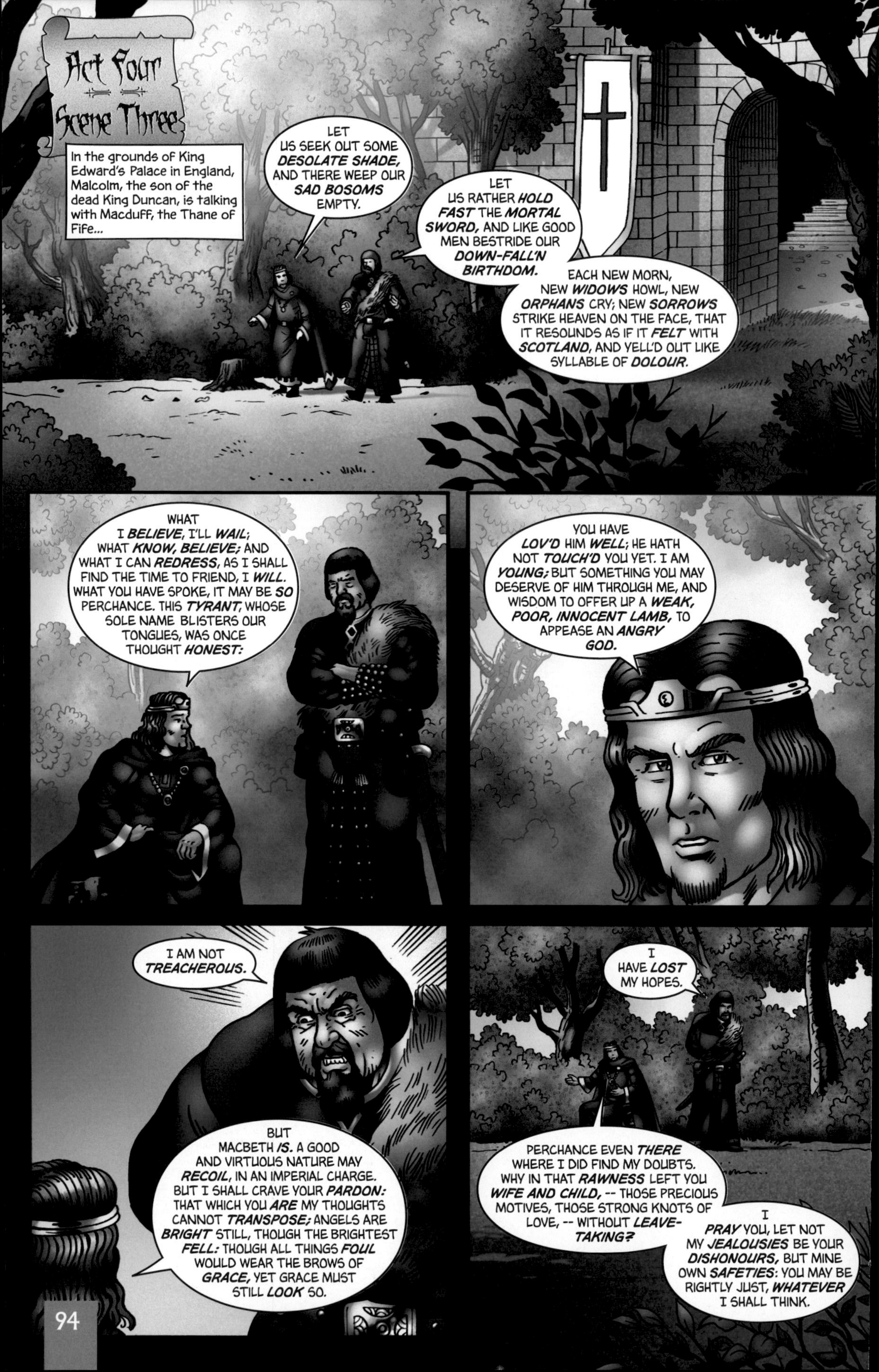
Act Four
Scene Three
In the grounds of King Edward's Palace in England, Malcolm, the son of the dead King Duncan, is talking with Macduff, the Thane of Fife...
LET US SEEK OUT SOME DESOLATE SHADE, AND THERE WEEP OUR SAD BOSOMS EMPTY.
LET US RATHER HOLD FAST THE MORTAL SWORD, AND LIKE GOOD MEN BESTRIDE OUR DOWN-FALL'N BIRTHDOM.
EACH NEW MORN, NEW WIDOWS HOWL, NEW ORPHANS CRY; NEW SORROWS STRIKE HEAVEN ON THE FACE, THAT IT RESOUNDS AS IF IT FELT WITH SCOTLAND, AND YELL'D OUT LIKE SYLLABLE OF DOLOUR.
WHAT I BELIEVE, I'LL WAIL; WHAT KNOW, BELIEVE; AND WHAT I CAN REDRESS, AS I SHALL FIND THE TIME TO FRIEND, I WILL. WHAT YOU HAVE SPOKE, IT MAY BE SO PERCHANCE. THIS TYRANT, WHOSE SOLE NAME BLISTERS OUR TONGUES, WAS ONCE THOUGHT HONEST:
YOU HAVE LOV'D HIM WELL; HE HATH NOT TOUCH'D YOU YET. I AM YOUNG; BUT SOMETHING YOU MAY DESERVE OF HIM THROUGH ME, AND WISDOM TO OFFER UP A WEAK, POOR, INNOCENT LAMB, TO APPEASE AN ANGRY GOD.
I AM NOT TREACHEROUS.
BUT MACBETH IS. A GOOD AND VIRTUOUS NATURE MAY RECOIL, IN AN IMPERIAL CHARGE. BUT I SHALL CRAVE YOUR PARDON: THAT WHICH YOU ARE MY THOUGHTS CANNOT TRANSPOSE; ANGELS ARE BRIGHT STILL, THOUGH THE BRIGHTEST FELL: THOUGH ALL THINGS FOUL WOULD WEAR THE BROWS OF GRACE, YET GRACE MUST STILL LOOK SO.
I HAVE LOST MY HOPES.
PERCHANCE EVEN THERE WHERE I DID FIND MY DOUBTS. WHY IN THAT RAWNESS LEFT YOU WIFE AND CHILD, -- THOSE PRECIOUS MOTIVES, THOSE STRONG KNOTS OF LOVE, -- WITHOUT LEAVE-TAKING?
I PRAY YOU, LET NOT MY JEALOUSIES BE YOUR DISHONOURS, BUT MINE OWN SAFETIES: YOU MAY BE RIGHTLY JUST, WHATEVER I SHALL THINK.

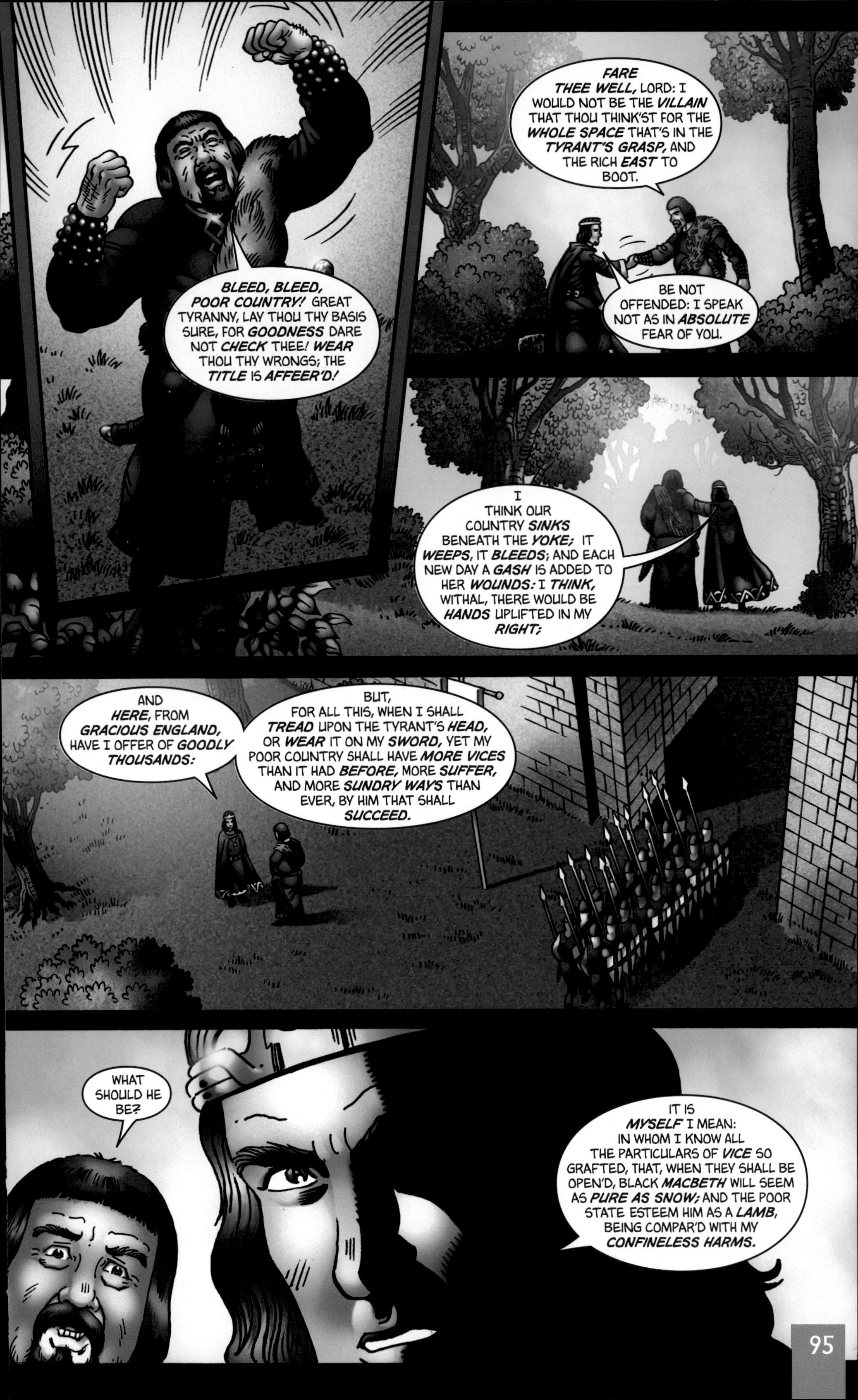
BLEED, BLEED, POOR COUNTRY! GREAT TYRANNY, LAY THOU THY BASIS SURE, FOR GOODNESS DARE NOT CHECK THEE! WEAR THOU THY WRONGS; THE TITLE IS AFFEER'D!
FARE THEE WELL, LORD: I WOULD NOT BE THE VILLAIN THAT THOU THINK'ST FOR THE WHOLE SPACE THAT'S IN THE TYRANT'S GRASP, AND THE RICH EAST TO BOOT.
BE NOT OFFENDED: I SPEAK NOT AS IN ABSOLUTE FEAR OF YOU.
I THINK OUR COUNTRY SINKS BENEATH THE YOKE; IT WEEPS, IT BLEEDS; AND EACH NEW DAY A GASH IS ADDED TO HER WOUNDS: I THINK, WITHAL, THERE WOULD BE HANDS UPLIFTED IN MY RIGHT;
AND HERE, FROM GRACIOUS ENGLAND, HAVE I OFFER OF GOODLY THOUSANDS:
BUT, FOR ALL THIS, WHEN I SHALL TREAD UPON THE TYRANT'S HEAD, OR WEAR IT ON MY SWORD, YET MY POOR COUNTRY SHALL HAVE MORE VICES THAN IT HAD BEFORE, MORE SUFFER, AND MORE SUNDRY WAYS THAN EVER, BY HIM THAT SHALL SUCCEED.
WHAT SHOULD HE BE?
IT IS MYSELF I MEAN: IN WHOM I KNOW ALL THE PARTICULARS OF VICE SO GRAFTED, THAT, WHEN THEY SHALL BE OPEN'D, BLACK MACBETH WILL SEEM AS PURE AS SNOW; AND THE POOR STATE ESTEEM HIM AS A LAMB, BEING COMPAR'D WITH MY CONFINELESS HARMS.

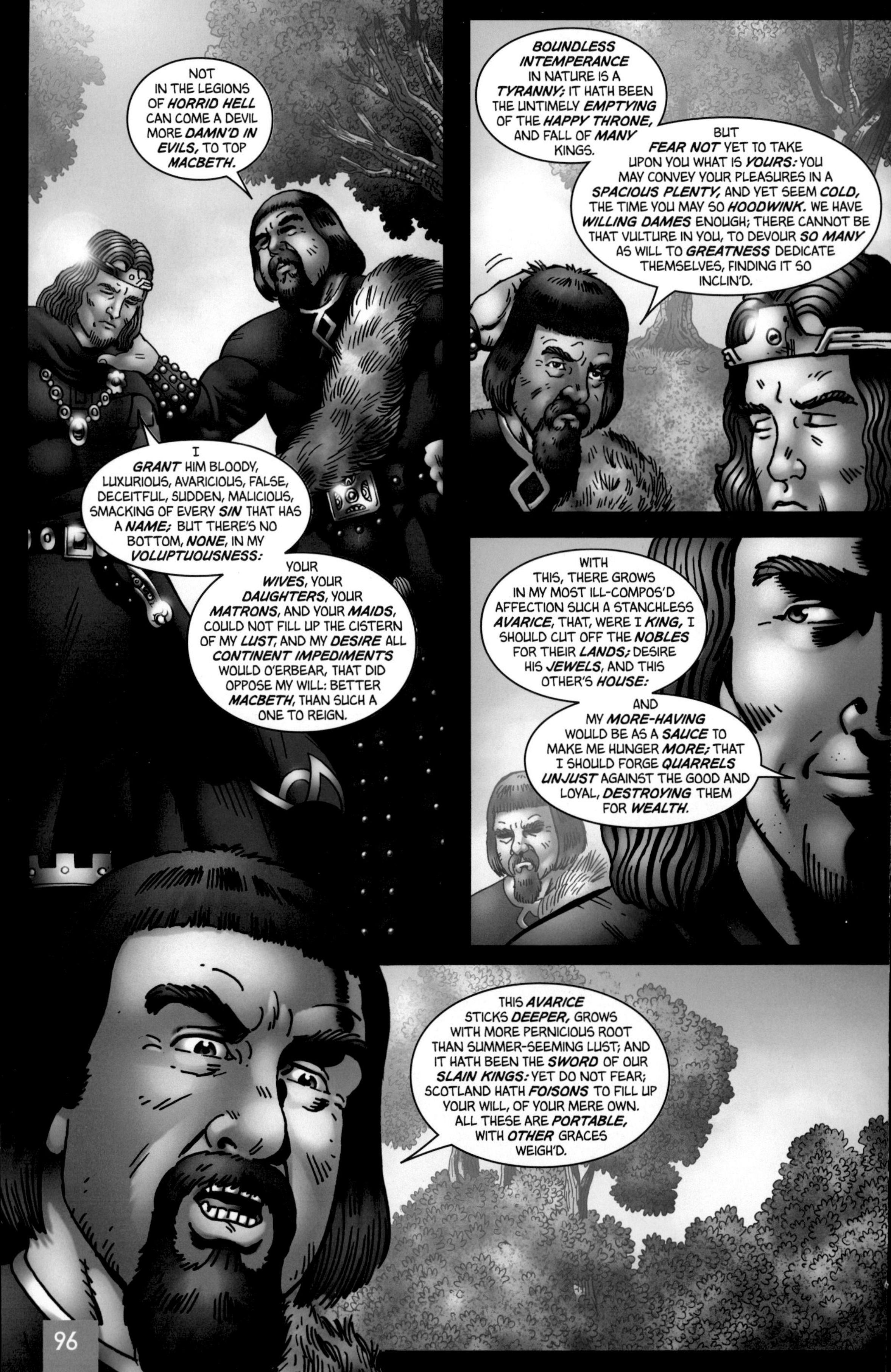
NOT IN THE LEGIONS OF HORRID HELL CAN COME A DEVIL MORE DAMN'D IN EVILS, TO TOP MACBETH.
I GRANT HIM BLOODY, LUXURIOUS, AVARICIOUS, FALSE, DECEITFUL, SUDDEN, MALICIOUS, SMACKING OF EVERY SIN THAT HAS A NAME; BUT THERE'S NO BOTTOM, NONE, IN MY VOLUPTUOUSNESS:
YOUR WIVES, YOUR DAUGHTERS, YOUR MATRONS, AND YOUR MAIDS, COULD NOT FILL UP THE CISTERN OF MY LUST; AND MY DESIRE ALL CONTINENT IMPEDIMENTS WOULD O'ERBEAR, THAT DID OPPOSE MY WILL: BETTER MACBETH, THAN SUCH A ONE TO REIGN.
BOUNDLESS INTEMPERANCE IN NATURE IS A TYRANNY; IT HATH BEEN THE UNTIMELY EMPTYING OF THE HAPPY THRONE, AND FALL OF MANY KINGS.
BUT FEAR NOT YET TO TAKE UPON YOU WHAT IS YOURS: YOU MAY CONVEY YOUR PLEASURES IN A SPACIOUS PLENTY, AND YET SEEM COLD, THE TIME YOU MAY SO HOODWINK. WE HAVE WILLING DAMES ENOUGH; THERE CANNOT BE THAT VULTURE IN YOU, TO DEVOUR SO MANY AS WILL TO GREATNESS DEDICATE THEMSELVES, FINDING IT SO INCLIN'D.
WITH THIS, THERE GROWS IN MY MOST ILL-COMPOS'D AFFECTION SUCH A STANCHLESS AVARICE, THAT, WERE I KING, I SHOULD CUT OFF THE NOBLES FOR THEIR LANDS; DESIRE HIS JEWELS, AND THIS OTHER'S HOUSE:
AND MY MORE-HAVING WOULD BE AS A SAUCE TO MAKE ME HUNGER MORE; THAT I SHOULD FORGE QUARRELS UNJUST AGAINST THE GOOD AND LOYAL, DESTROYING THEM FOR WEALTH.
THIS AVARICE STICKS DEEPER, GROWS WITH MORE PERNICIOUS ROOT THAN SUMMER-SEEMING LUST; AND IT HATH BEEN THE SWORD OF OUR SLAIN KINGS: YET DO NOT FEAR; SCOTLAND HATH FOISONS TO FILL UP YOUR WILL, OF YOUR MERE OWN. ALL THESE ARE PORTABLE, WITH OTHER GRACES WEIGH'D.

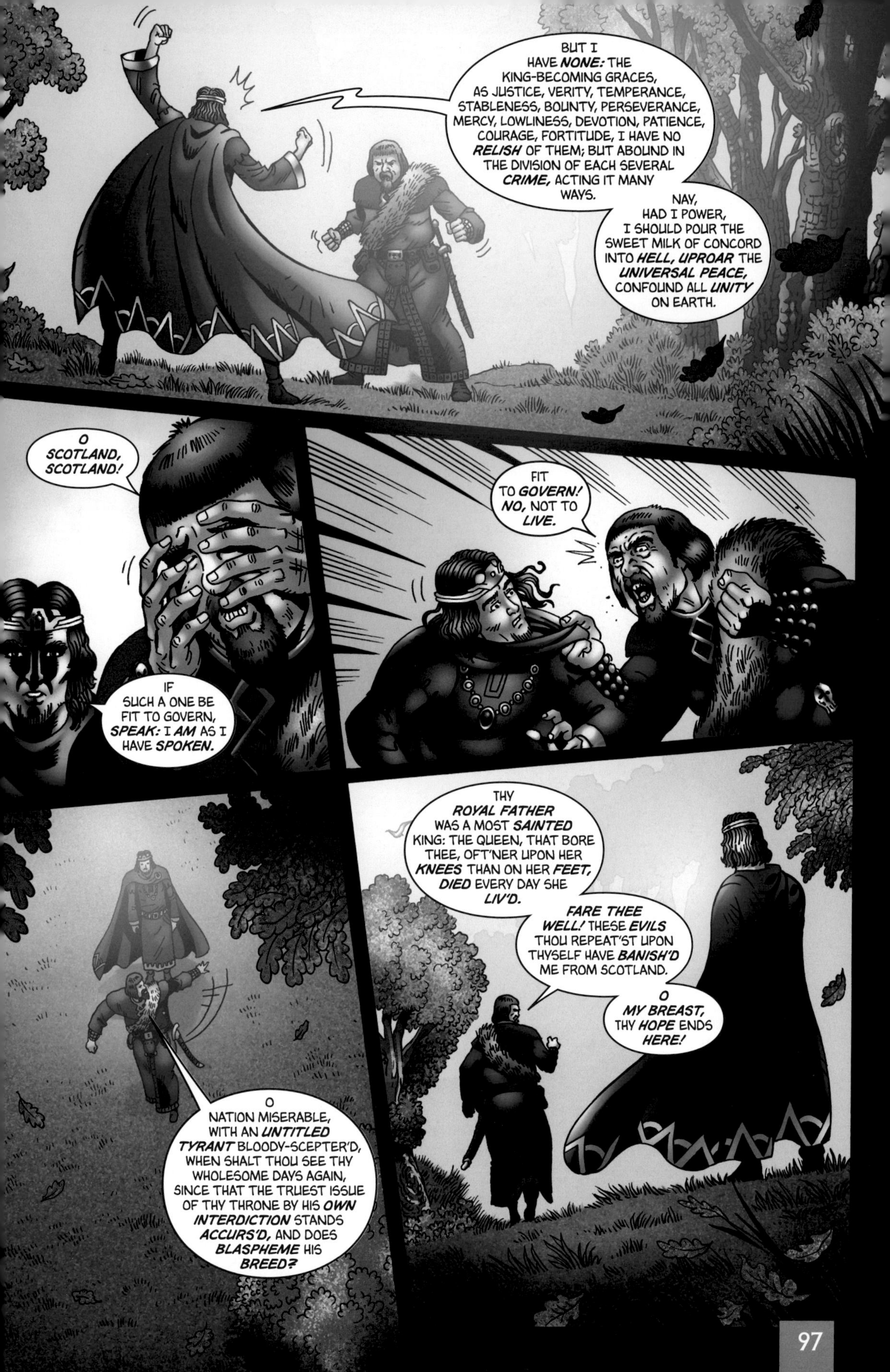
BUT I HAVE NONE: THE KING-BECOMING GRACES, AS JUSTICE, VERITY, TEMPERANCE, STABLENESS, BOUNTY, PERSEVERANCE, MERCY, LOWLINESS, DEVOTION, PATIENCE, COURAGE, FORTITUDE, I HAVE NO RELISH OF THEM; BUT ABOUND IN THE DIVISION OF EACH SEVERAL CRIME, ACTING IT MANY WAYS.
NAY, HAD I POWER, I SHOULD POUR THE SWEET MILK OF CONCORD INTO HELL, UPROAR THE UNIVERSAL PEACE, CONFOUND ALL UNITY ON EARTH.
O SCOTLAND, SCOTLAND!
IF SUCH A ONE BE FIT TO GOVERN, SPEAK: I AM AS I HAVE SPOKEN.
FIT TO GOVERN! NO, NOT TO LIVE.
O NATION MISERABLE, WITH AN UNTITLED TYRANT BLOODY-SCEPTER'D, WHEN SHALT THOU SEE THY WHOLESOME DAYS AGAIN, SINCE THAT THE TRUEST ISSUE OF THY THRONE BY HIS OWN INTERDICTION STANDS ACCURS'D, AND DOES BLASPHEME HIS BREED?
THY ROYAL FATHER WAS A MOST SAINTED KING: THE QUEEN, THAT BORE THEE, OFT'NER UPON HER KNEES THAN ON HER FEET, DIED EVERY DAY SHE LIV'D.
FARE THEE WELL! THESE EVILS THOU REPEAT'ST UPON THYSELF HAVE BANISH'D ME FROM SCOTLAND.
O MY BREAST, THY HOPE ENDS HERE!

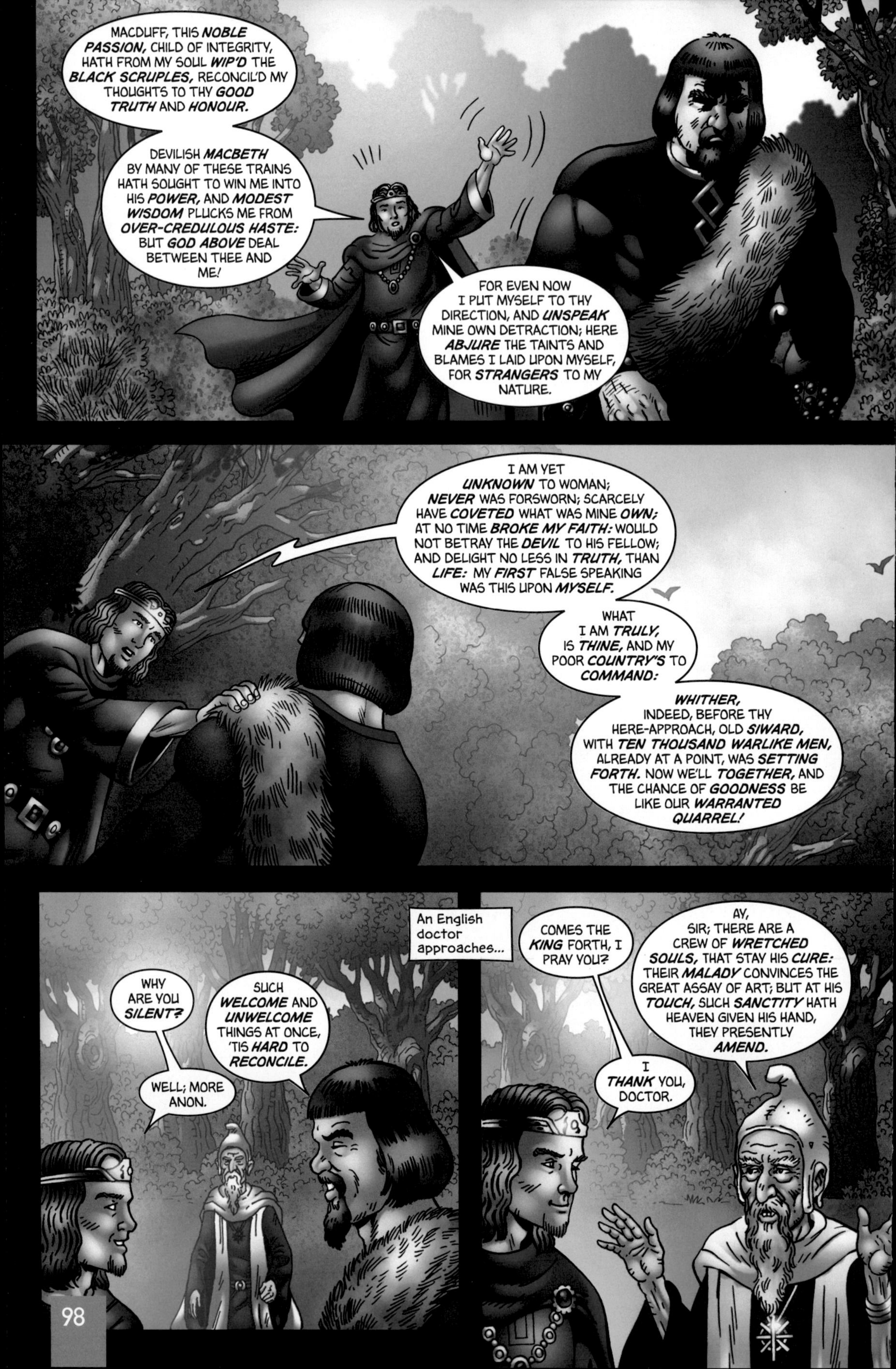
MACDUFF, THIS NOBLE PASSION, CHILD OF INTEGRITY, HATH FROM MY SOUL WIP'D THE BLACK SCRUPLES, RECONCIL'D MY THOUGHTS TO THY GOOD TRUTH AND HONOUR.
DEVILISH MACBETH BY MANY OF THESE TRAINS HATH SOUGHT TO WIN ME INTO HIS POWER, AND MODEST WISDOM PLUCKS ME FROM OVER-CREDULOUS HASTE: BUT GOD ABOVE DEAL BETWEEN THEE AND ME!
FOR EVEN NOW I PUT MYSELF TO THY DIRECTION, AND UNSPEAK MINE OWN DETRACTION; HERE ABJURE THE TAINTS AND BLAMES I LAID UPON MYSELF, FOR STRANGERS TO MY NATURE.
I AM YET UNKNOWN TO WOMAN; NEVER WAS FORSWORN; SCARCELY HAVE COVETED WHAT WAS MINE OWN; AT NO TIME BROKE MY FAITH: WOULD NOT BETRAY THE DEVIL TO HIS FELLOW; AND DELIGHT NO LESS IN TRUTH, THAN LIFE: MY FIRST FALSE SPEAKING WAS THIS UPON MYSELF.
WHAT I AM TRULY, IS THINE, AND MY POOR COUNTRY'S TO COMMAND:
WHITHER, INDEED, BEFORE THY HERE-APPROACH, OLD SIWARD, WITH TEN THOUSAND WARLIKE MEN, ALREADY AT A POINT, WAS SETTING FORTH. NOW WE'LL TOGETHER, AND THE CHANCE OF GOODNESS BE LIKE OUR WARRANTED QUARREL!
WHY ARE YOU SILENT?
SUCH WELCOME AND UNWELCOME THINGS AT ONCE, 'TIS HARD TO RECONCILE.
WELL; MORE ANON.
An English doctor approaches...
COMES THE KING FORTH, I PRAY YOU?
AY, SIR; THERE ARE A CREW OF WRETCHED SOULS, THAT STAY HIS CURE: THEIR MALADY CONVINCES THE GREAT ASSAY OF ART; BUT AT HIS TOUCH, SUCH SANCTITY HATH HEAVEN GIVEN HIS HAND, THEY PRESENTLY AMEND.
I THANK YOU, DOCTOR.

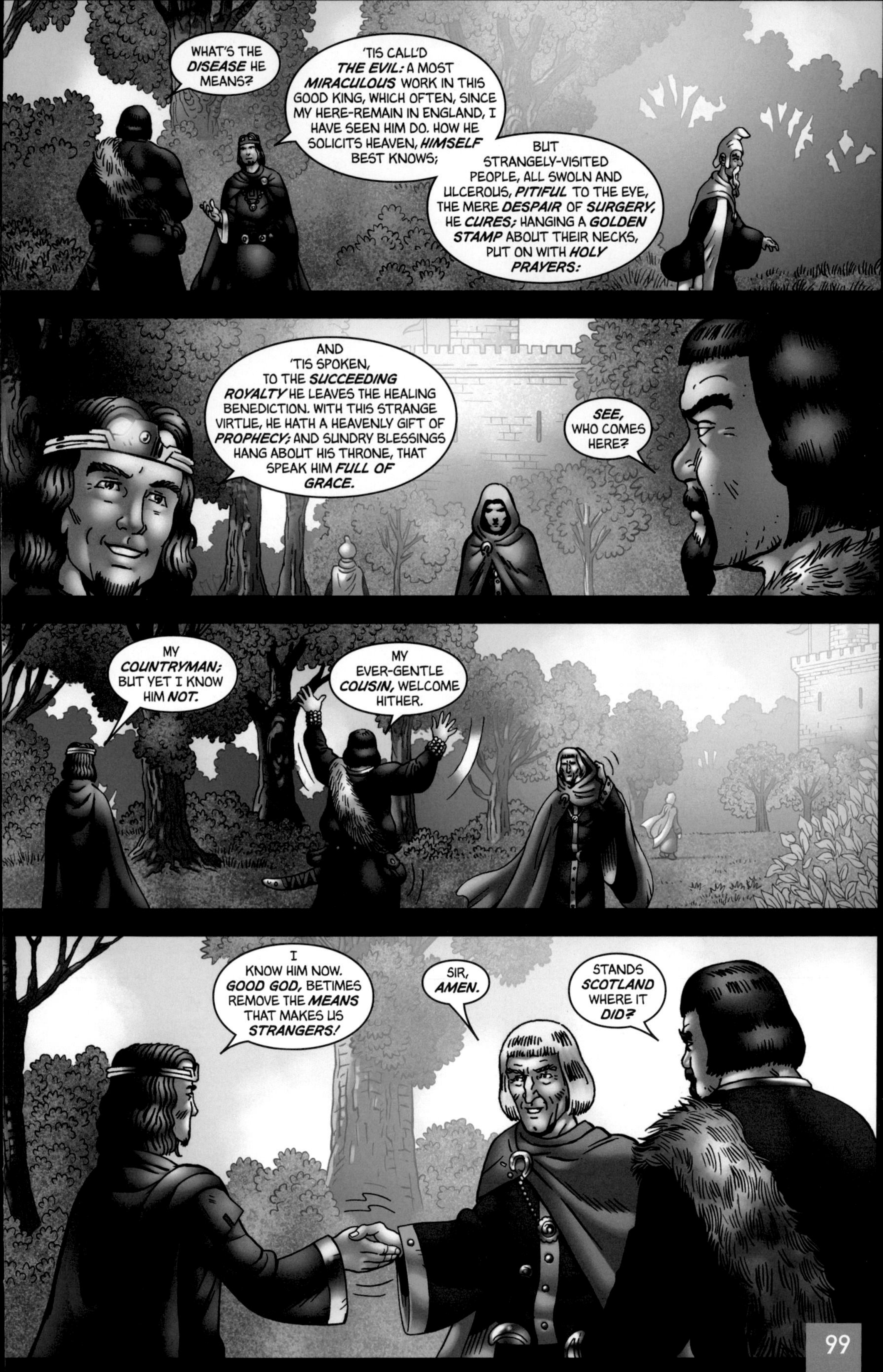
WHAT'S THE DISEASE HE MEANS?
'TIS CALL'D THE EVIL: A MOST MIRACULOUS WORK IN THIS GOOD KING, WHICH OFTEN, SINCE MY HERE-REMAIN IN ENGLAND, I HAVE SEEN HIM DO. HOW HE SOLICITS HEAVEN, HIMSELF BEST KNOWS;
BUT STRANGELY-VISITED PEOPLE, ALL SWOLN AND ULCEROUS, PITIFUL TO THE EYE, THE MERE DESPAIR OF SURGERY, HE CURES; HANGING A GOLDEN STAMP ABOUT THEIR NECKS, PUT ON WITH HOLY PRAYERS:
AND 'TIS SPOKEN, TO THE SUCCEEDING ROYALTY HE LEAVES THE HEALING BENEDICTION. WITH THIS STRANGE VIRTUE, HE HATH A HEAVENLY GIFT OF PROPHECY; AND SUNDRY BLESSINGS HANG ABOUT HIS THRONE, THAT SPEAK HIM FULL OF GRACE.
SEE, WHO COMES HERE?
MY COUNTRYMAN; BUT YET I KNOW HIM NOT.
MY EVER-GENTLE COUSIN, WELCOME HITHER.
I KNOW HIM NOW. GOOD GOD, BETIMES REMOVE THE MEANS THAT MAKES US STRANGERS!
SIR, AMEN.
STANDS SCOTLAND WHERE IT DID?

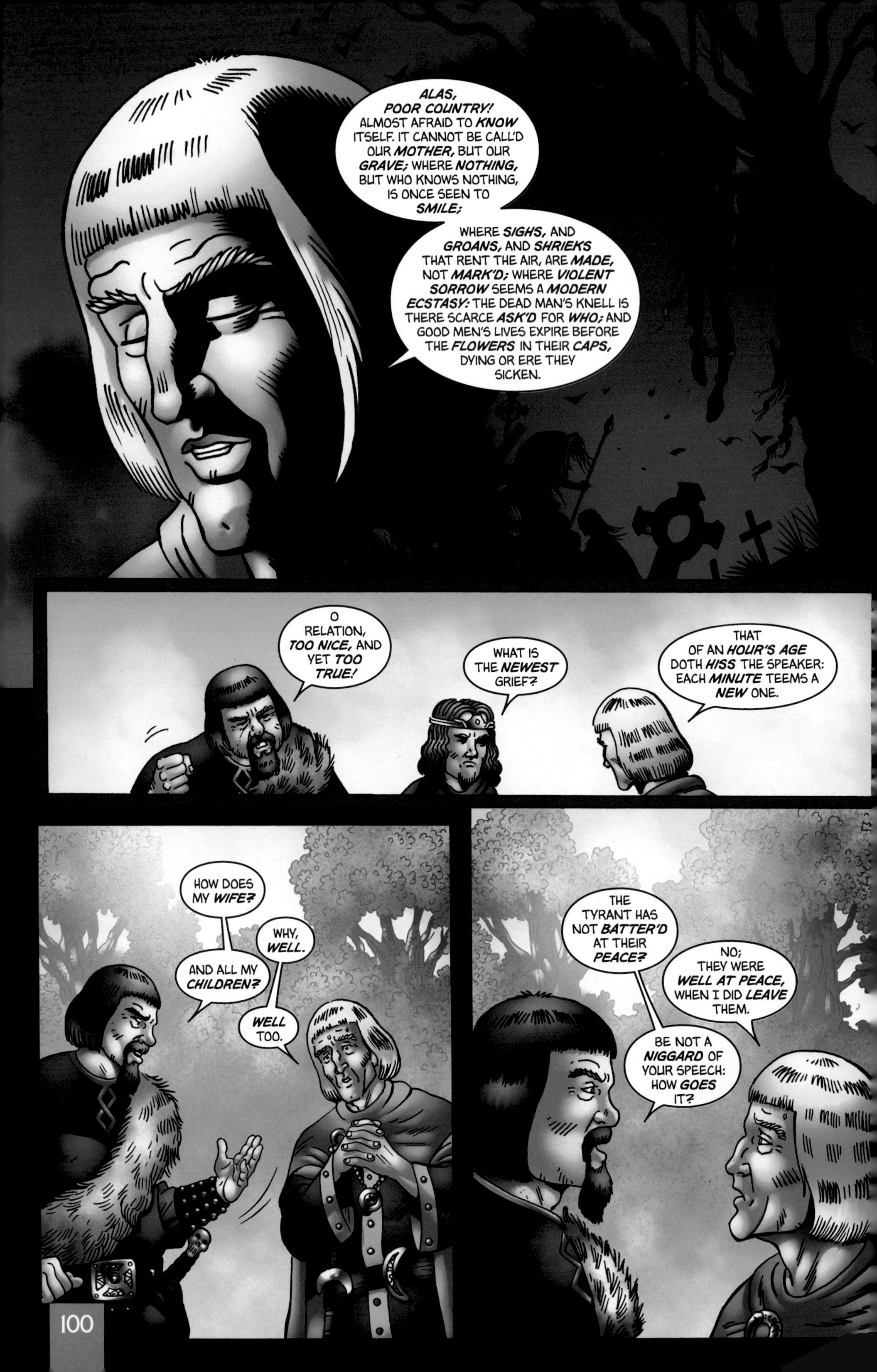

ALAS, POOR COUNTRY! ALMOST AFRAID TO KNOW ITSELF. IT CANNOT BE CALL'D OUR MOTHER, BUT OUR GRAVE; WHERE NOTHING, BUT WHO KNOWS NOTHING, IS ONCE SEEN TO SMILE;
WHERE SIGHS, AND GROANS, AND SHRIEKS THAT RENT THE AIR, ARE MADE, NOT MARK'D; WHERE VIOLENT SORROW SEEMS A MODERN ECSTASY: THE DEAD MAN'S KNELL IS THERE SCARCE ASK'D FOR WHO; AND GOOD MEN'S LIVES EXPIRE BEFORE THE FLOWERS IN THEIR CAPS, DYING OR ERE THEY SICKEN.
O RELATION, TOO NICE, AND YET TOO TRUE!
WHAT IS THE NEWEST GRIEF?
THAT OF AN HOUR'S AGE DOTH HISS THE SPEAKER: EACH MINUTE TEEMS A NEW ONE.
HOW DOES MY WIFE?
WHY, WELL.
AND ALL MY CHILDREN?
WELL TOO.
THE TYRANT HAS NOT BATTER'D AT THEIR PEACE?
NO; THEY WERE WELL AT PEACE, WHEN I DID LEAVE THEM.
BE NOT A NIGGARD OF YOUR SPEECH: HOW GOES IT?

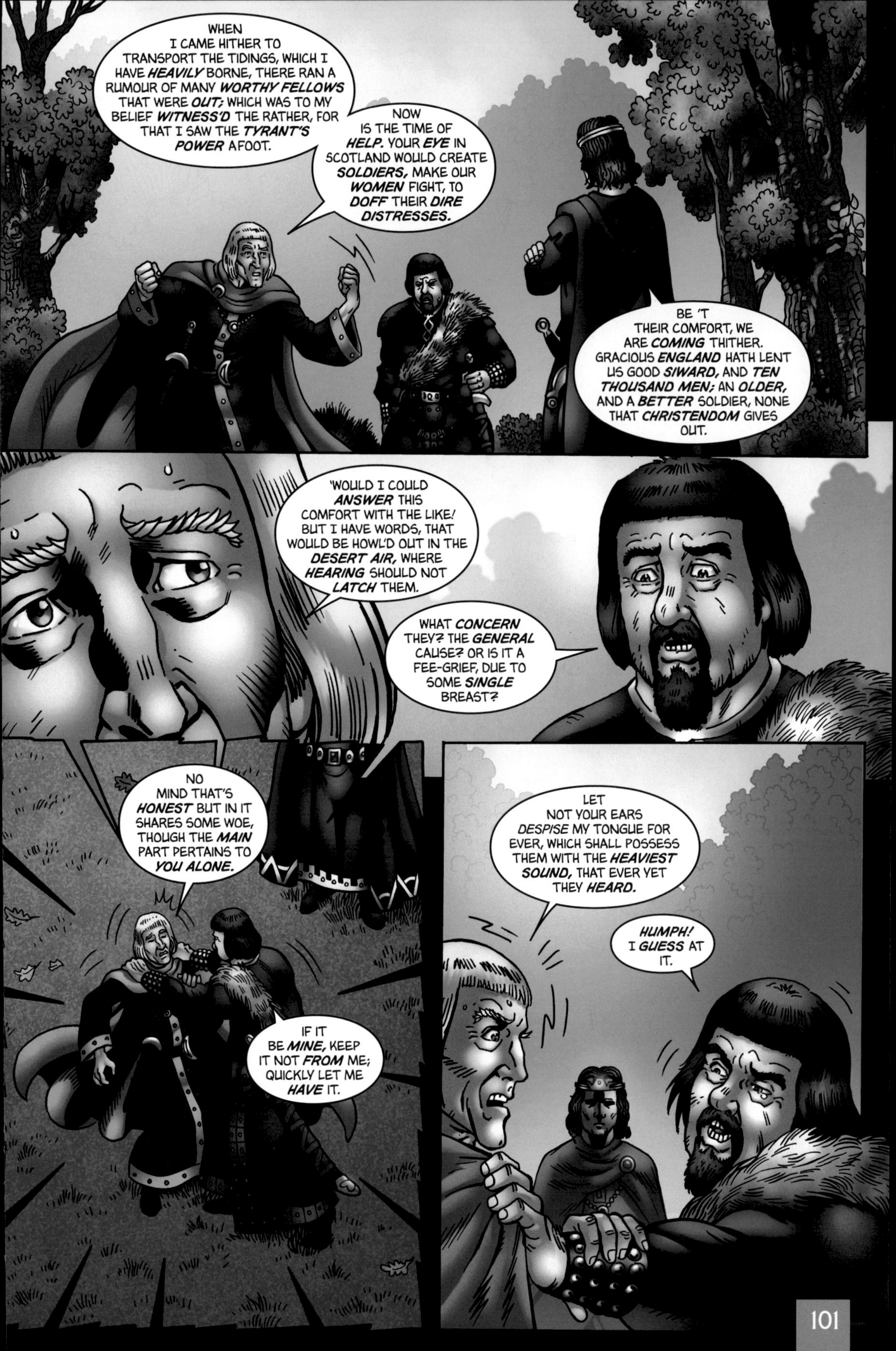
WHEN I CAME HITHER TO TRANSPORT THE TIDINGS, WHICH I HAVE HEAVILY BORNE, THERE RAN A RUMOUR OF MANY WORTHY FELLOWS THAT WERE OUT; WHICH WAS TO MY BELIEF WITNESS'D THE RATHER, FOR THAT I SAW THE TYRANT'S POWER AFOOT.
NOW IS THE TIME OF HELP. YOUR EYE IN SCOTLAND WOULD CREATE SOLDIERS, MAKE OUR WOMEN FIGHT, TO DOFF THEIR DIRE DISTRESSES.
BE 'T THEIR COMFORT, WE ARE COMING THITHER. GRACIOUS ENGLAND HATH LENT US GOOD SIWARD, AND TEN THOUSAND MEN; AN OLDER, AND A BETTER SOLDIER, NONE THAT CHRISTENDOM GIVES OUT.
'WOULD I COULD ANSWER THIS COMFORT WITH THE LIKE! BUT I HAVE WORDS, THAT WOULD BE HOWL'D OUT IN THE DESERT AIR, WHERE HEARING SHOULD NOT LATCH THEM.
WHAT CONCERN THEY? THE GENERAL CAUSE? OR IS IT A FEE-GRIEF, DUE TO SOME SINGLE BREAST?
NO MIND THAT'S HONEST BUT IN IT SHARES SOME WOE, THOUGH THE MAIN PART PERTAINS TO YOU ALONE.
IF IT BE MINE, KEEP IT NOT FROM ME; QUICKLY LET ME HAVE IT.
LET NOT YOUR EARS DESPISE MY TONGUE FOR EVER, WHICH SHALL POSSESS THEM WITH THE HEAVIEST SOUND, THAT EVER YET THEY HEARD.
HUMPH! I GUESS AT IT.

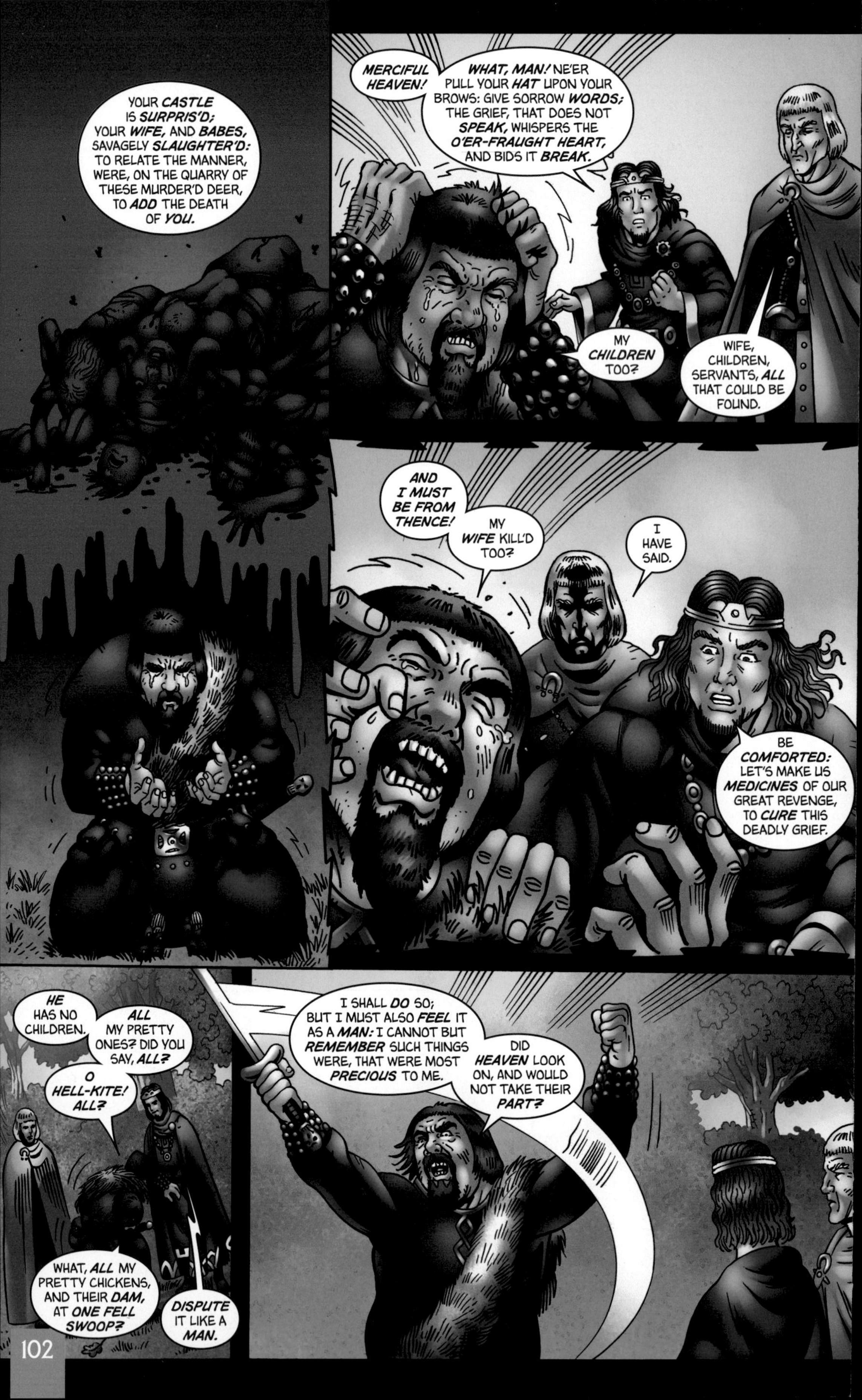
YOUR CASTLE IS SURPRIS'D; YOUR WIFE, AND BABES, SAVAGELY SLAUGHTER'D: TO RELATE THE MANNER, WERE, ON THE QUARRY OF THESE MURDER'D DEER, TO ADD THE DEATH OF YOU.
MERCIFUL HEAVEN!
WHAT, MAN! NE'ER PULL YOUR HAT UPON YOUR BROWS: GIVE SORROW WORDS; THE GRIEF, THAT DOES NOT SPEAK, WHISPERS THE O'ER-FRAUGHT HEART, AND BIDS IT BREAK.
MY CHILDREN TOO?
WIFE, CHILDREN, SERVANTS, ALL THAT COULD BE FOUND.
AND I MUST BE FROM THENCE!
MY WIFE KILL'D TOO?
I HAVE SAID.
BE COMFORTED: LET'S MAKE US MEDICINES OF OUR GREAT REVENGE, TO CURE THIS DEADLY GRIEF.
HE HAS NO CHILDREN.
ALL MY PRETTY ONES? DID YOU SAY, ALL?
O HELL-KITE! ALL?
WHAT, ALL MY PRETTY CHICKENS, AND THEIR DAM, AT ONE FELL SWOOP?
DISPUTE IT LIKE A MAN.
I SHALL DO SO; BUT I MUST ALSO FEEL IT AS A MAN: I CANNOT BUT REMEMBER SUCH THINGS WERE, THAT WERE MOST PRECIOUS TO ME.
DID HEAVEN LOOK ON, AND WOULD NOT TAKE THEIR PART?

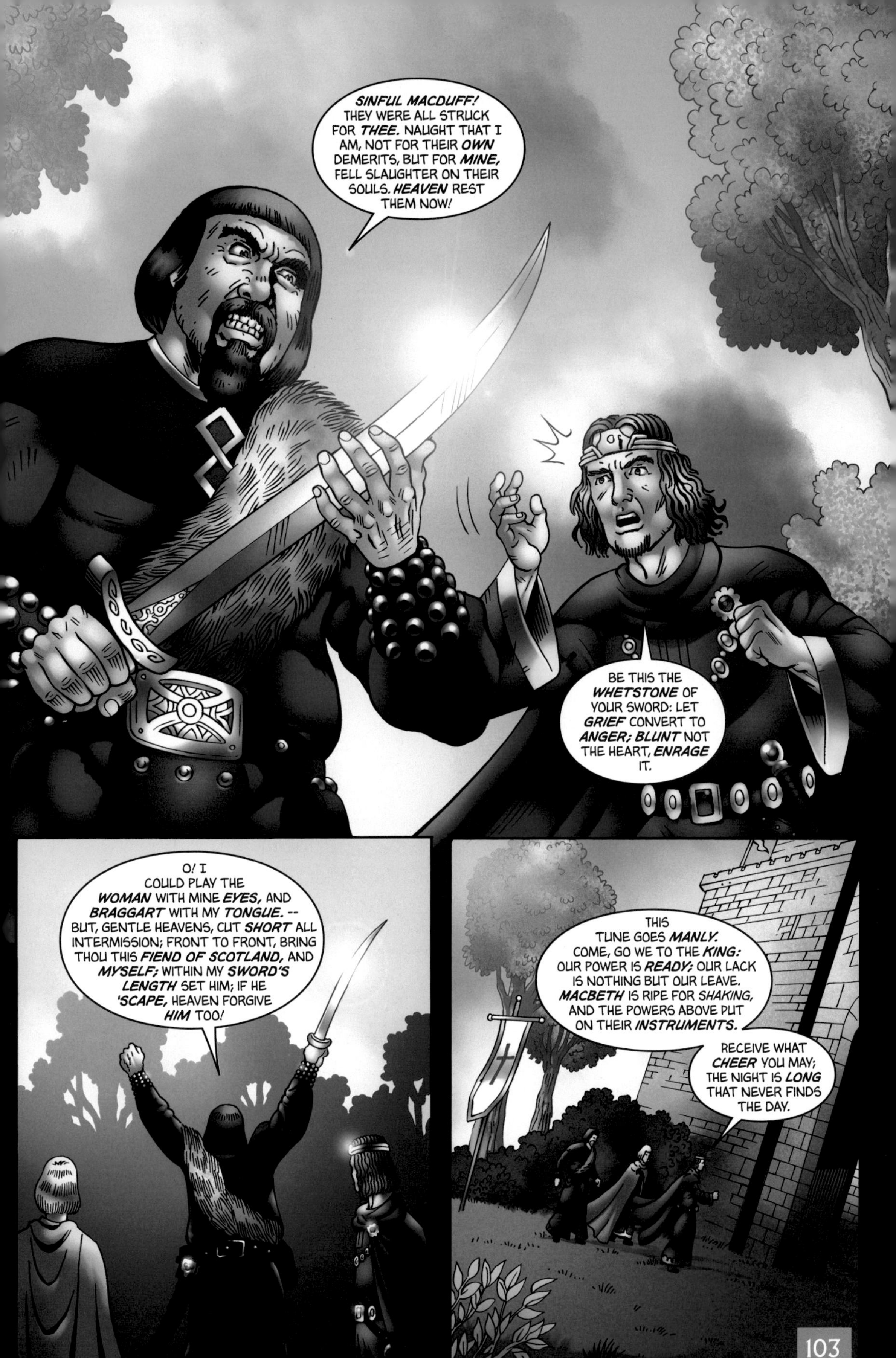
SINFUL MACDUFF! THEY WERE ALL STRUCK FOR THEE. NAUGHT THAT I AM, NOT FOR THEIR OWN DEMERITS, BUT FOR MINE, FELL SLAUGHTER ON THEIR SOULS. HEAVEN REST THEM NOW!
BE THIS THE WHETSTONE OF YOUR SWORD: LET GRIEF CONVERT TO ANGER; BLUNT NOT THE HEART, ENRAGE IT.
O! I COULD PLAY THE WOMAN WITH MINE EYES, AND BRAGGART WITH MY TONGUE. -- BUT, GENTLE HEAVENS, CUT SHORT ALL INTERMISSION; FRONT TO FRONT, BRING THOU THIS FIEND OF SCOTLAND, AND MYSELF; WITHIN MY SWORD'S LENGTH SET HIM; IF HE 'SCAPE, HEAVEN FORGIVE HIM TOO!
THIS TUNE GOES MANLY. COME, GO WE TO THE KING: OUR POWER IS READY; OUR LACK IS NOTHING BUT OUR LEAVE. MACBETH IS RIPE FOR SHAKING, AND THE POWERS ABOVE PUT ON THEIR INSTRUMENTS.
RECEIVE WHAT CHEER YOU MAY; THE NIGHT IS LONG THAT NEVER FINDS THE DAY.

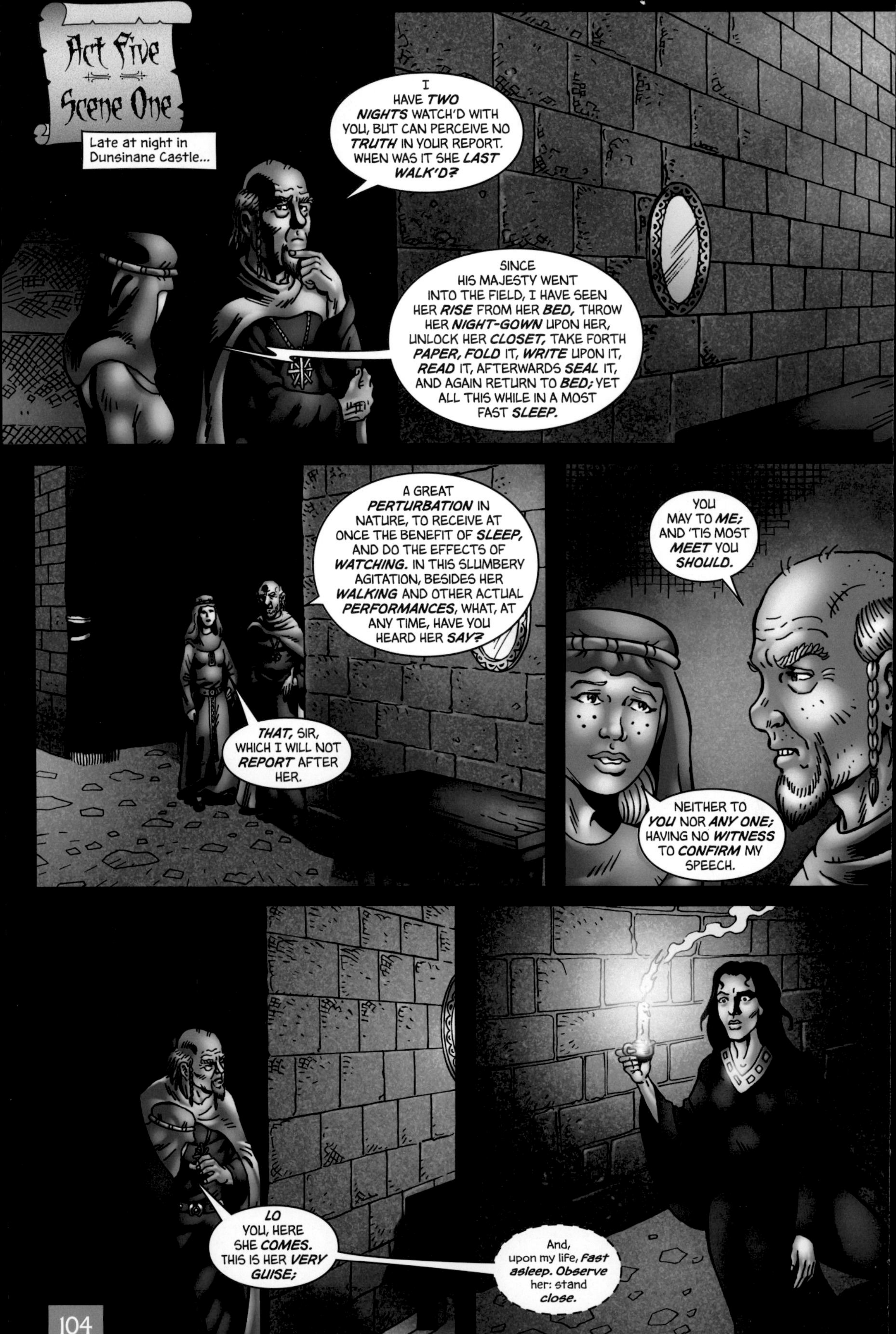
Act Five
Scene One
Late at night in Dunsinane Castle...
I HAVE TWO NIGHTS WATCH'D WITH YOU, BUT CAN PERCEIVE NO TRUTH IN YOUR REPORT. WHEN WAS IT SHE LAST WALK'D?
SINCE HIS MAJESTY WENT INTO THE FIELD, I HAVE SEEN HER RISE FROM HER BED, THROW HER NIGHT-GOWN UPON HER, UNLOCK HER CLOSET, TAKE FORTH PAPER, FOLD IT, WRITE UPON IT, READ IT, AFTERWARDS SEAL IT, AND AGAIN RETURN TO BED; YET ALL THIS WHILE IN A MOST FAST SLEEP.
A GREAT PERTURBATION IN NATURE, TO RECEIVE AT ONCE THE BENEFIT OF SLEEP, AND DO THE EFFECTS OF WATCHING. IN THIS SLUMBERY AGITATION, BESIDES HER WALKING AND OTHER ACTUAL PERFORMANCES, WHAT, AT ANY TIME, HAVE YOU HEARD HER SAY?
THAT, SIR, WHICH I WILL NOT REPORT AFTER HER.
YOU MAY TO ME; AND 'TIS MOST MEET YOU SHOULD.
NEITHER TO YOU NOR ANY ONE; HAVING NO WITNESS TO CONFIRM MY SPEECH.
LO YOU, HERE SHE COMES. THIS IS HER VERY GUISE;
And, upon my life, fast asleep. Observe her: stand close.

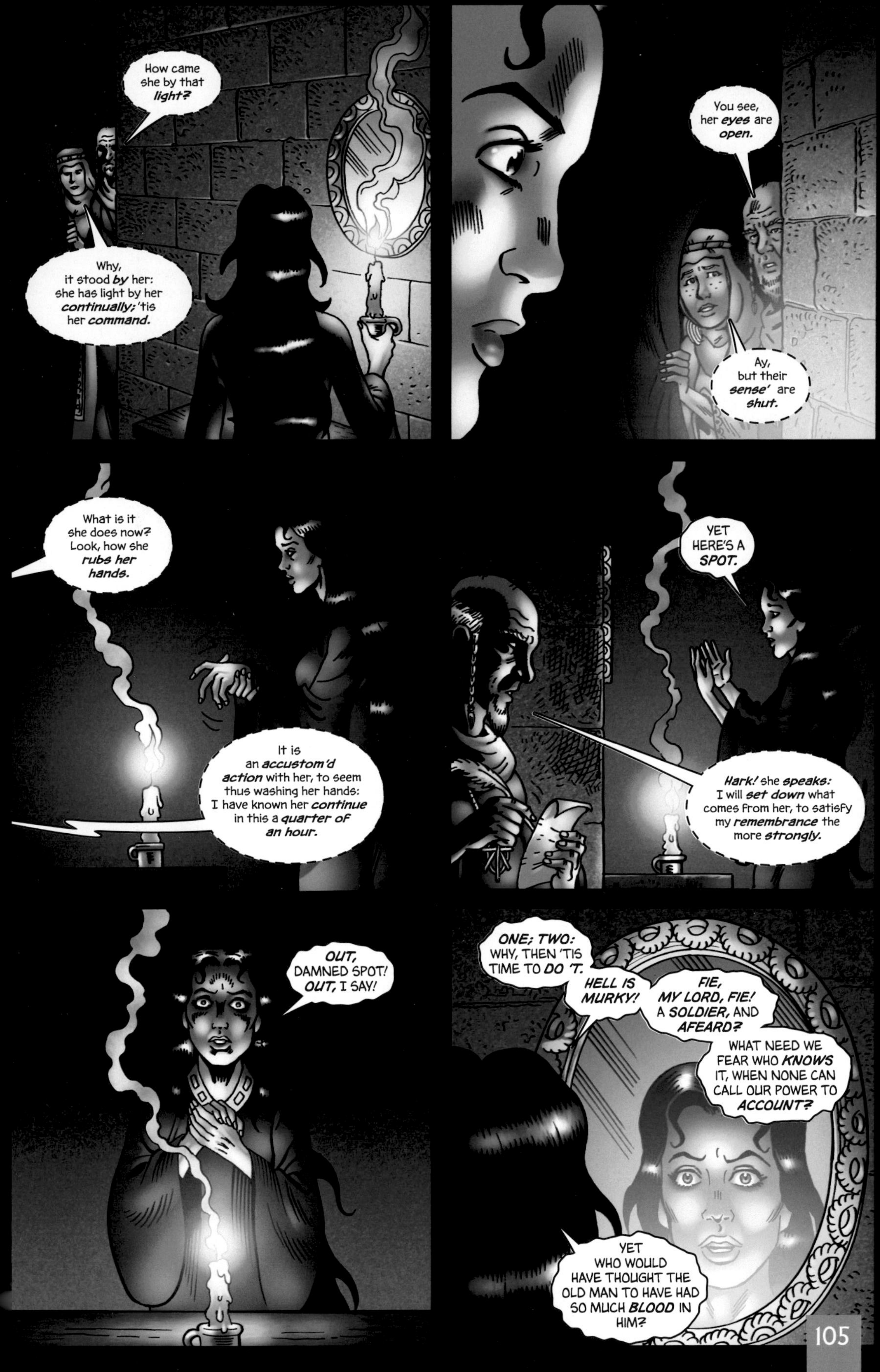
How came she by that light?
Why, it stood by her: she has light by her continually; 'tis her command.
You see, her eyes are open.
Ay, but their sense' are shut.
What is it she does now? Look, how she rubs her hands.
It is an accustom'd action with her, to seem thus washing her hands: I have known her continue in this a quarter of an hour.
YET HERE'S A SPOT.
Hark! she speaks: I will set down what comes from her, to satisfy my remembrance the more strongly.
OUT, DAMNED SPOT! OUT, I SAY!
ONE; TWO: WHY, THEN 'TIS TIME TO DO 'T.
HELL IS MURKY!
FIE, MY LORD, FIE! A SOLDIER, AND AFEARD?
WHAT NEED WE FEAR WHO KNOWS IT, WHEN NONE CAN CALL OUR POWER TO ACCOUNT?
YET WHO WOULD HAVE THOUGHT THE OLD MAN TO HAVE HAD SO MUCH BLOOD IN HIM?

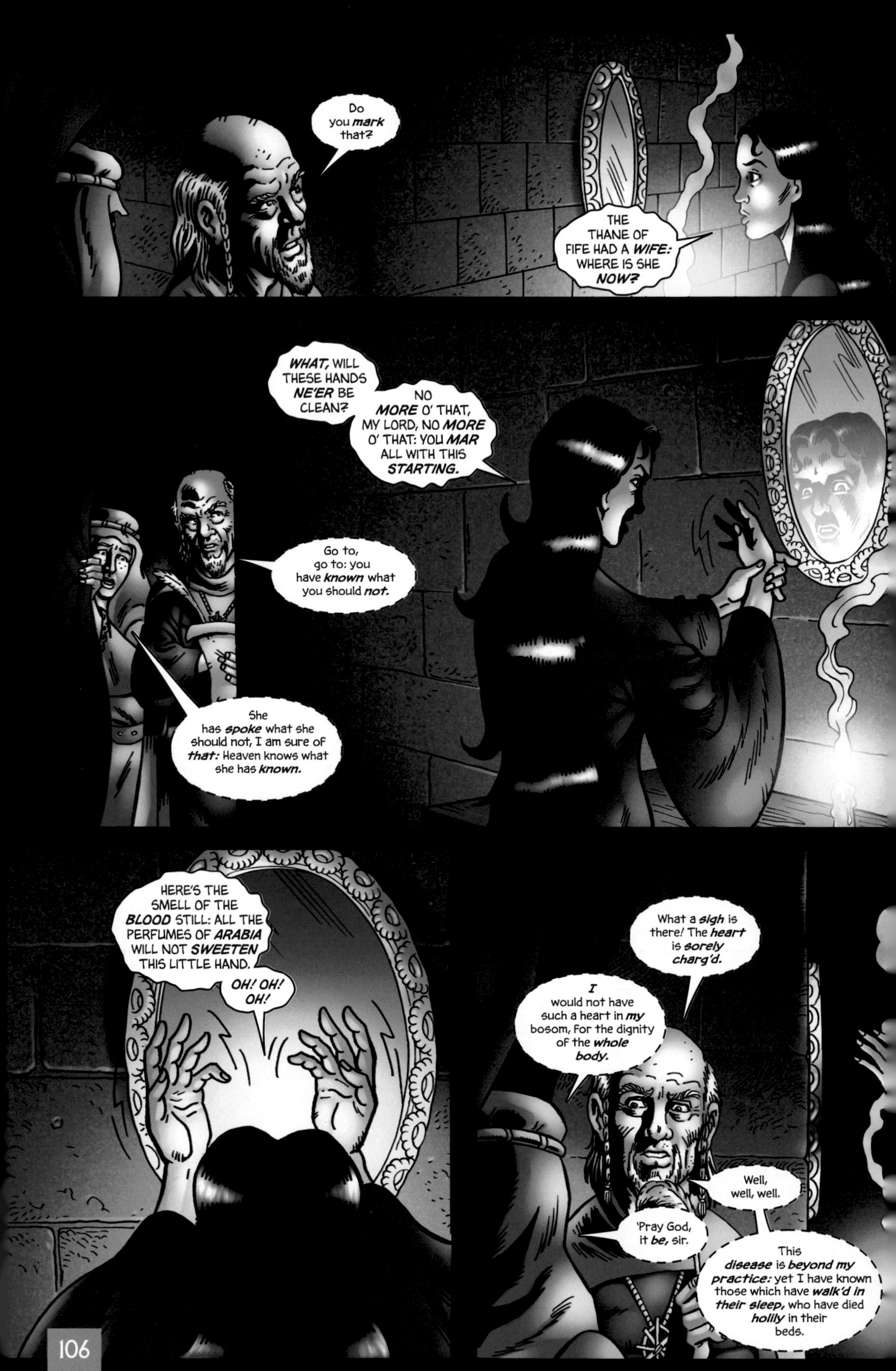
Do you *mark* that?
THE THANE OF FIFE HAD A *WIFE:* WHERE IS SHE *NOW?*
WHAT, WILL THESE HANDS *NE'ER* BE CLEAN?
NO *MORE* O' THAT, MY LORD, NO *MORE* O' THAT: YOU *MAR* ALL WITH THIS *STARTING.*
Go to, go to: you have *known* what you should *not.*
She has *spoke* what she should not, I am sure of *that:* Heaven knows what she has *known.*
HERE'S THE SMELL OF THE *BLOOD* STILL: ALL THE PERFUMES OF *ARABIA* WILL NOT *SWEETEN* THIS LITTLE HAND.
OH! OH! OH!
What a *sigh* is there! The *heart* is *sorely charg'd.*
I would not have such a heart in *my* bosom, for the dignity of the *whole body.*
Well, well, well.
'Pray God, it *be,* sir.
This *disease* is *beyond my practice:* yet I have known those which have *walk'd in their sleep,* who have died *holily* in their beds.

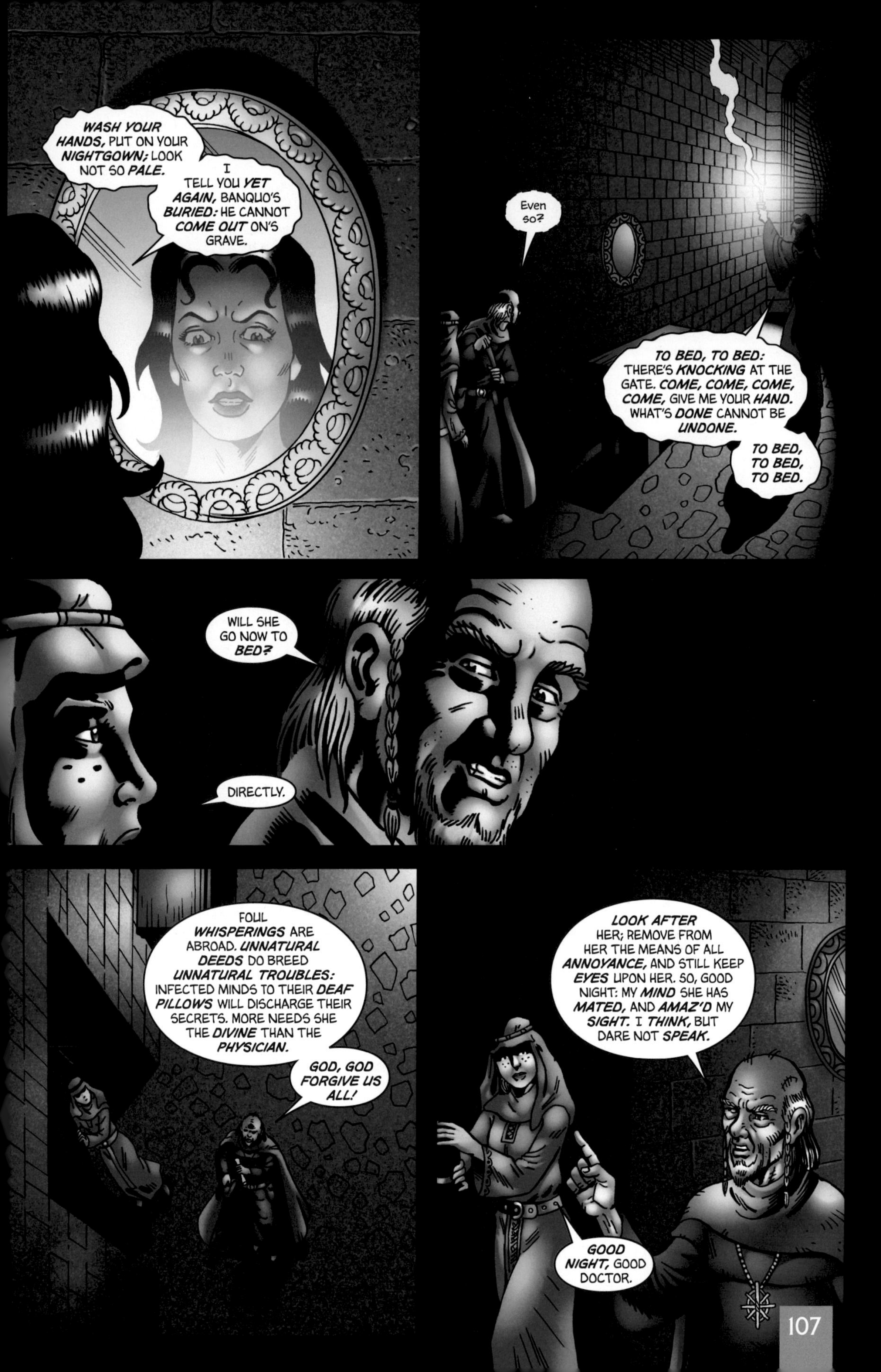
WASH YOUR HANDS, PUT ON YOUR NIGHTGOWN; LOOK NOT SO PALE.
I TELL YOU YET AGAIN, BANQUO'S BURIED: HE CANNOT COME OUT ON'S GRAVE.
Even so?
TO BED, TO BED: THERE'S KNOCKING AT THE GATE. COME, COME, COME, COME, GIVE ME YOUR HAND. WHAT'S DONE CANNOT BE UNDONE.
TO BED, TO BED, TO BED.
WILL SHE GO NOW TO BED?
DIRECTLY.
FOUL WHISPERINGS ARE ABROAD. UNNATURAL DEEDS DO BREED UNNATURAL TROUBLES: INFECTED MINDS TO THEIR DEAF PILLOWS WILL DISCHARGE THEIR SECRETS. MORE NEEDS SHE THE DIVINE THAN THE PHYSICIAN.
GOD, GOD FORGIVE US ALL!
LOOK AFTER HER; REMOVE FROM HER THE MEANS OF ALL ANNOYANCE, AND STILL KEEP EYES UPON HER. SO, GOOD NIGHT: MY MIND SHE HAS MATED, AND AMAZ'D MY SIGHT. I THINK, BUT DARE NOT SPEAK.
GOOD NIGHT, GOOD DOCTOR.

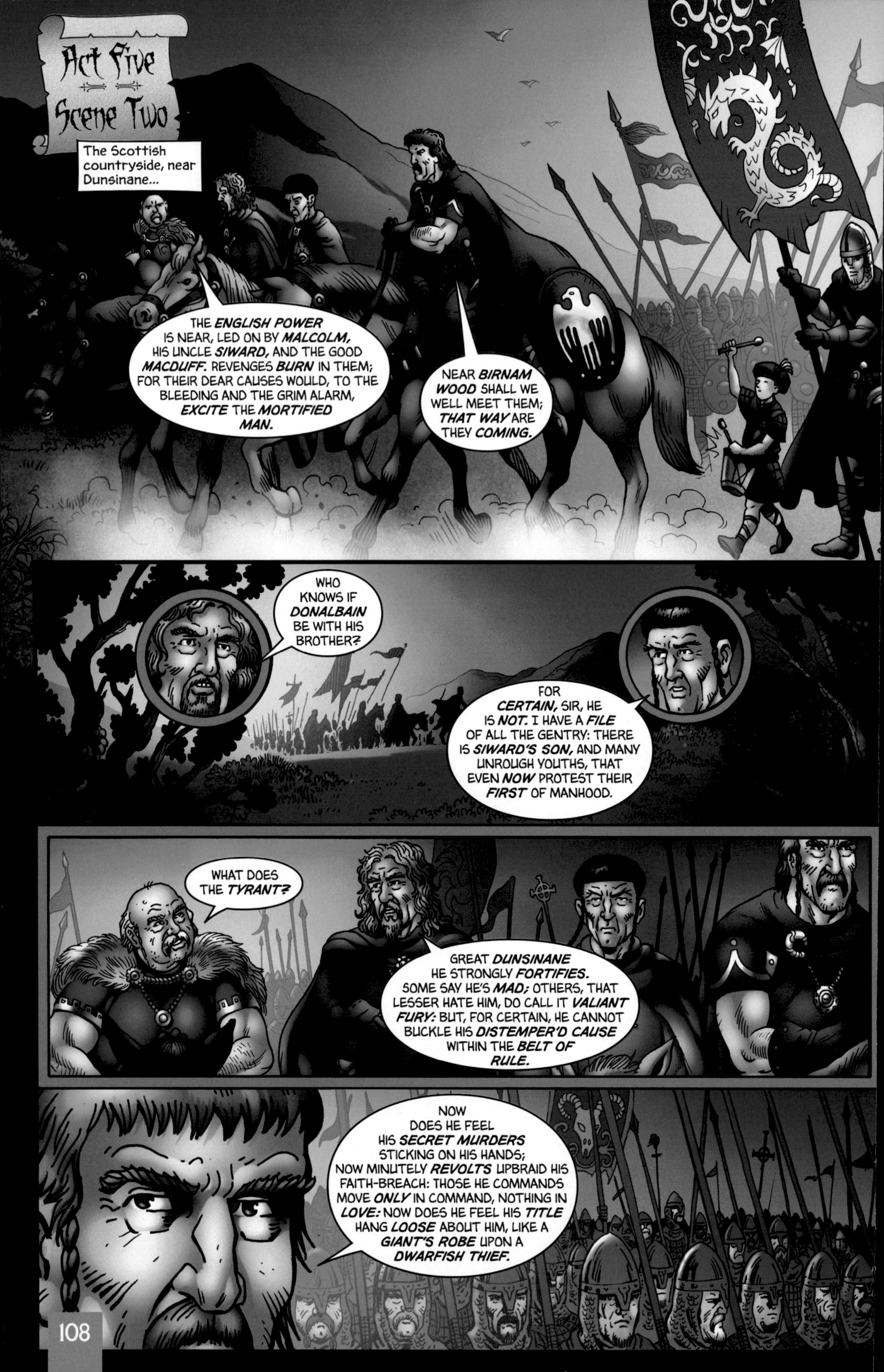
Act Five
Scene Two
The Scottish countryside, near Dunsinane...
THE ENGLISH POWER IS NEAR, LED ON BY MALCOLM, HIS UNCLE SIWARD, AND THE GOOD MACDUFF. REVENGES BURN IN THEM; FOR THEIR DEAR CAUSES WOULD, TO THE BLEEDING AND THE GRIM ALARM, EXCITE THE MORTIFIED MAN.
NEAR BIRNAM WOOD SHALL WE WELL MEET THEM; THAT WAY ARE THEY COMING.
WHO KNOWS IF DONALBAIN BE WITH HIS BROTHER?
FOR CERTAIN, SIR, HE IS NOT. I HAVE A FILE OF ALL THE GENTRY: THERE IS SIWARD'S SON, AND MANY UNROUGH YOUTHS, THAT EVEN NOW PROTEST THEIR FIRST OF MANHOOD.
WHAT DOES THE TYRANT?
GREAT DUNSINANE HE STRONGLY FORTIFIES. SOME SAY HE'S MAD; OTHERS, THAT LESSER HATE HIM, DO CALL IT VALIANT FURY: BUT, FOR CERTAIN, HE CANNOT BUCKLE HIS DISTEMPER'D CAUSE WITHIN THE BELT OF RULE.
NOW DOES HE FEEL HIS SECRET MURDERS STICKING ON HIS HANDS; NOW MINUTELY REVOLTS UPBRAID HIS FAITH-BREACH: THOSE HE COMMANDS MOVE ONLY IN COMMAND, NOTHING IN LOVE: NOW DOES HE FEEL HIS TITLE HANG LOOSE ABOUT HIM, LIKE A GIANT'S ROBE UPON A DWARFISH THIEF.

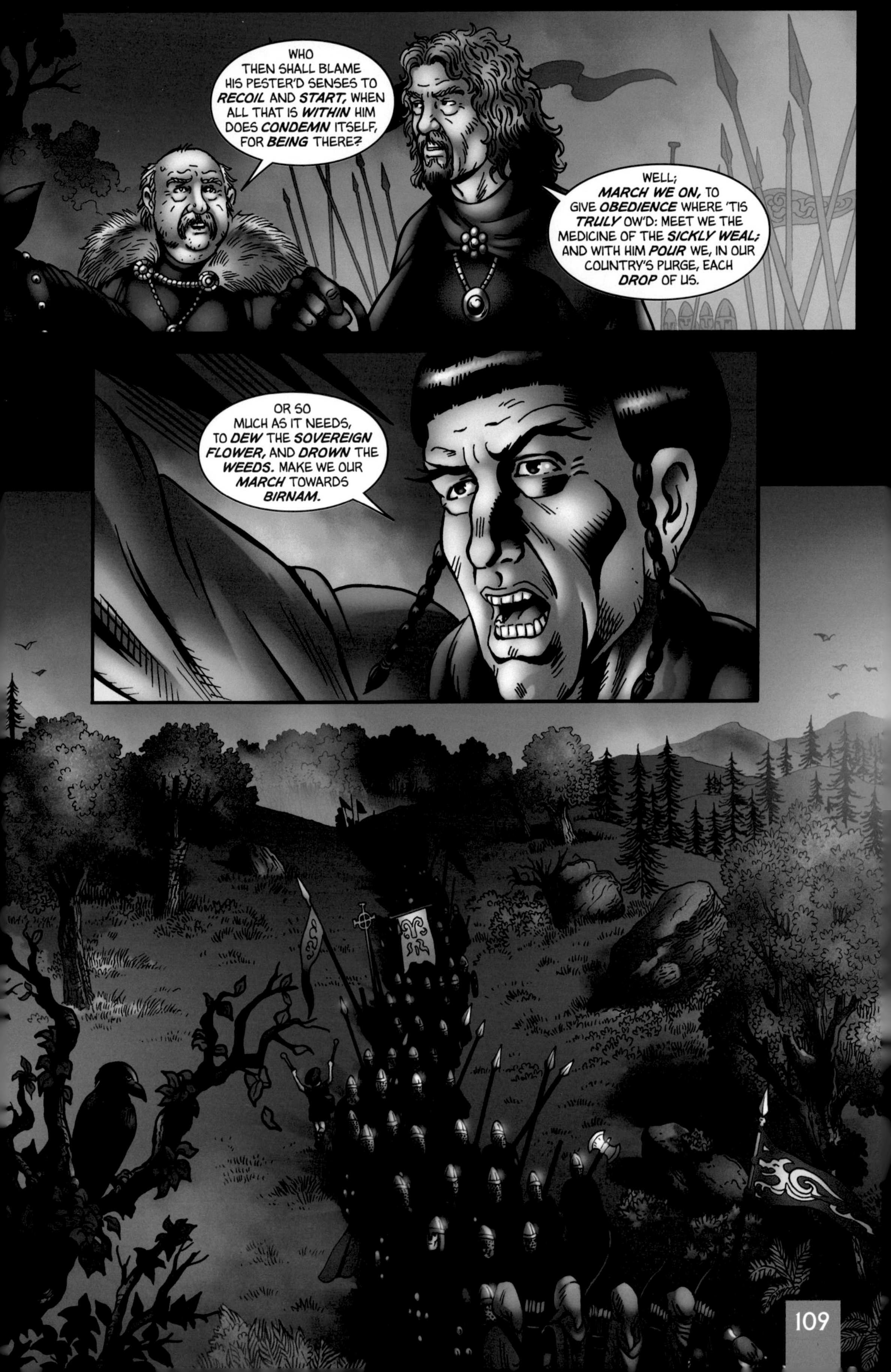
WHO THEN SHALL BLAME HIS PESTER'D SENSES TO RECOIL AND START, WHEN ALL THAT IS WITHIN HIM DOES CONDEMN ITSELF, FOR BEING THERE?
WELL; MARCH WE ON, TO GIVE OBEDIENCE WHERE 'TIS TRULY OW'D: MEET WE THE MEDICINE OF THE SICKLY WEAL; AND WITH HIM POUR WE, IN OUR COUNTRY'S PURGE, EACH DROP OF US.
OR SO MUCH AS IT NEEDS, TO DEW THE SOVEREIGN FLOWER, AND DROWN THE WEEDS. MAKE WE OUR MARCH TOWARDS BIRNAM.

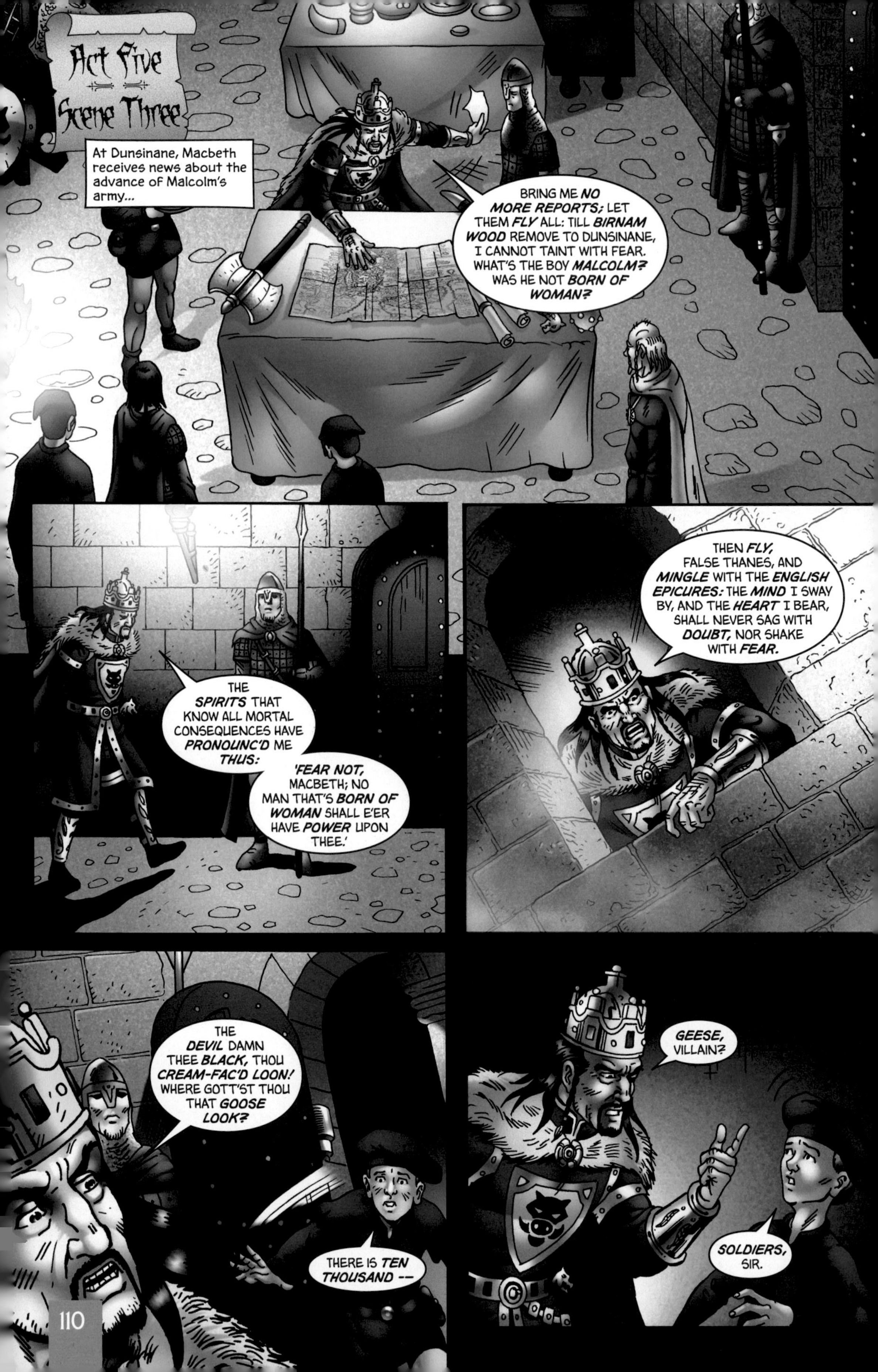
Act Five
Scene Three
At Dunsinane, Macbeth receives news about the advance of Malcolm's army...
BRING ME NO MORE REPORTS; LET THEM FLY ALL: TILL BIRNAM WOOD REMOVE TO DUNSINANE, I CANNOT TAINT WITH FEAR. WHAT'S THE BOY MALCOLM? WAS HE NOT BORN OF WOMAN?
THE SPIRITS THAT KNOW ALL MORTAL CONSEQUENCES HAVE PRONOUNC'D ME THUS:
'FEAR NOT, MACBETH; NO MAN THAT'S BORN OF WOMAN SHALL E'ER HAVE POWER UPON THEE.'
THEN FLY, FALSE THANES, AND MINGLE WITH THE ENGLISH EPICURES: THE MIND I SWAY BY, AND THE HEART I BEAR, SHALL NEVER SAG WITH DOUBT, NOR SHAKE WITH FEAR.
THE DEVIL DAMN THEE BLACK, THOU CREAM-FAC'D LOON! WHERE GOTT'ST THOU THAT GOOSE LOOK?
THERE IS TEN THOUSAND --
GEESE, VILLAIN?
SOLDIERS, SIR.

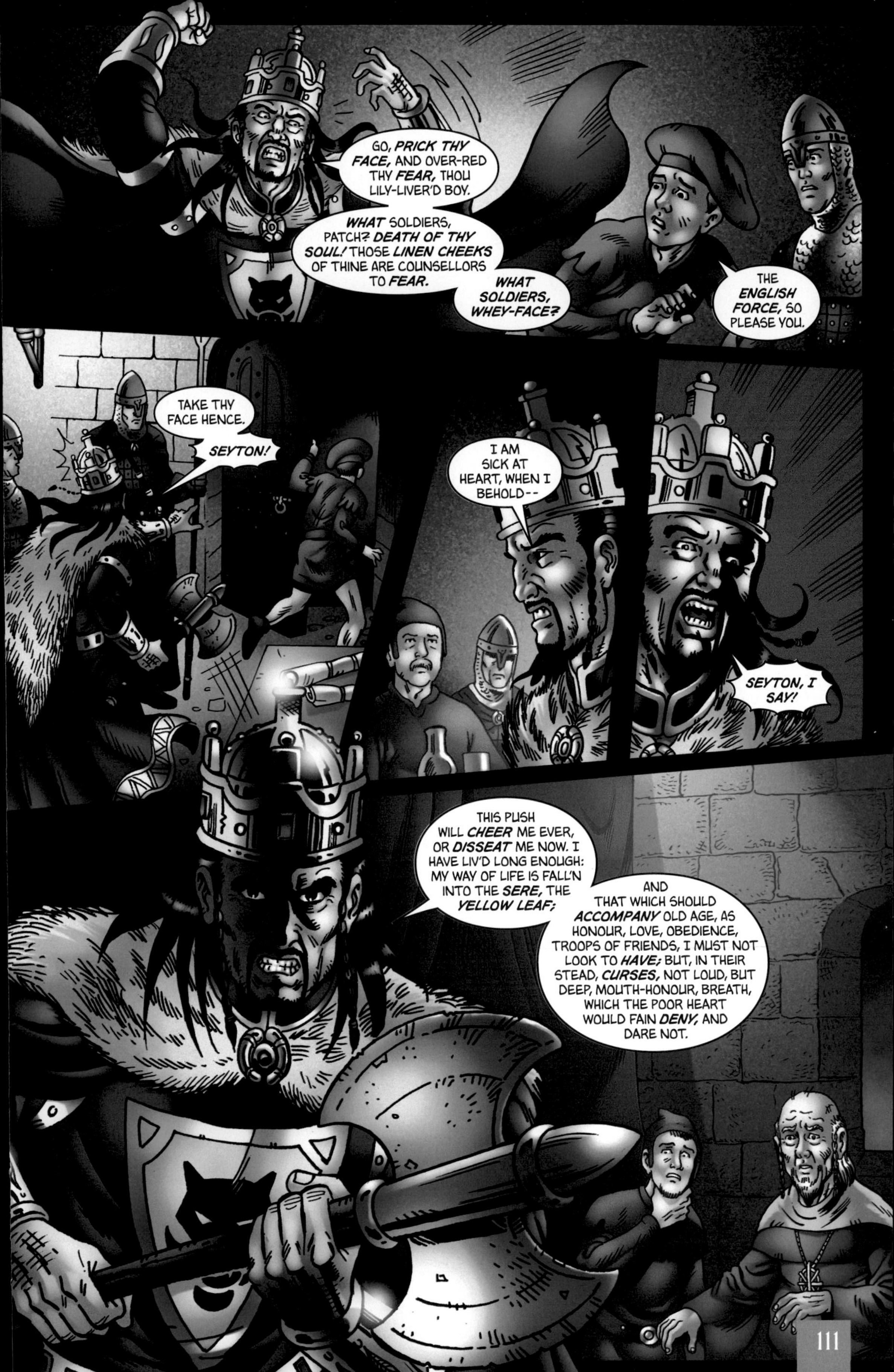
GO, PRICK THY FACE, AND OVER-RED THY FEAR, THOU LILY-LIVER'D BOY.
WHAT SOLDIERS, PATCH? DEATH OF THY SOUL! THOSE LINEN CHEEKS OF THINE ARE COUNSELLORS TO FEAR.
WHAT SOLDIERS, WHEY-FACE?
THE ENGLISH FORCE, SO PLEASE YOU.
TAKE THY FACE HENCE.
SEYTON!
I AM SICK AT HEART, WHEN I BEHOLD--
SEYTON, I SAY!
THIS PUSH WILL CHEER ME EVER, OR DISSEAT ME NOW. I HAVE LIV'D LONG ENOUGH: MY WAY OF LIFE IS FALL'N INTO THE SERE, THE YELLOW LEAF;
AND THAT WHICH SHOULD ACCOMPANY OLD AGE, AS HONOUR, LOVE, OBEDIENCE, TROOPS OF FRIENDS, I MUST NOT LOOK TO HAVE; BUT, IN THEIR STEAD, CURSES, NOT LOUD, BUT DEEP, MOUTH-HONOUR, BREATH, WHICH THE POOR HEART WOULD FAIN DENY, AND DARE NOT.

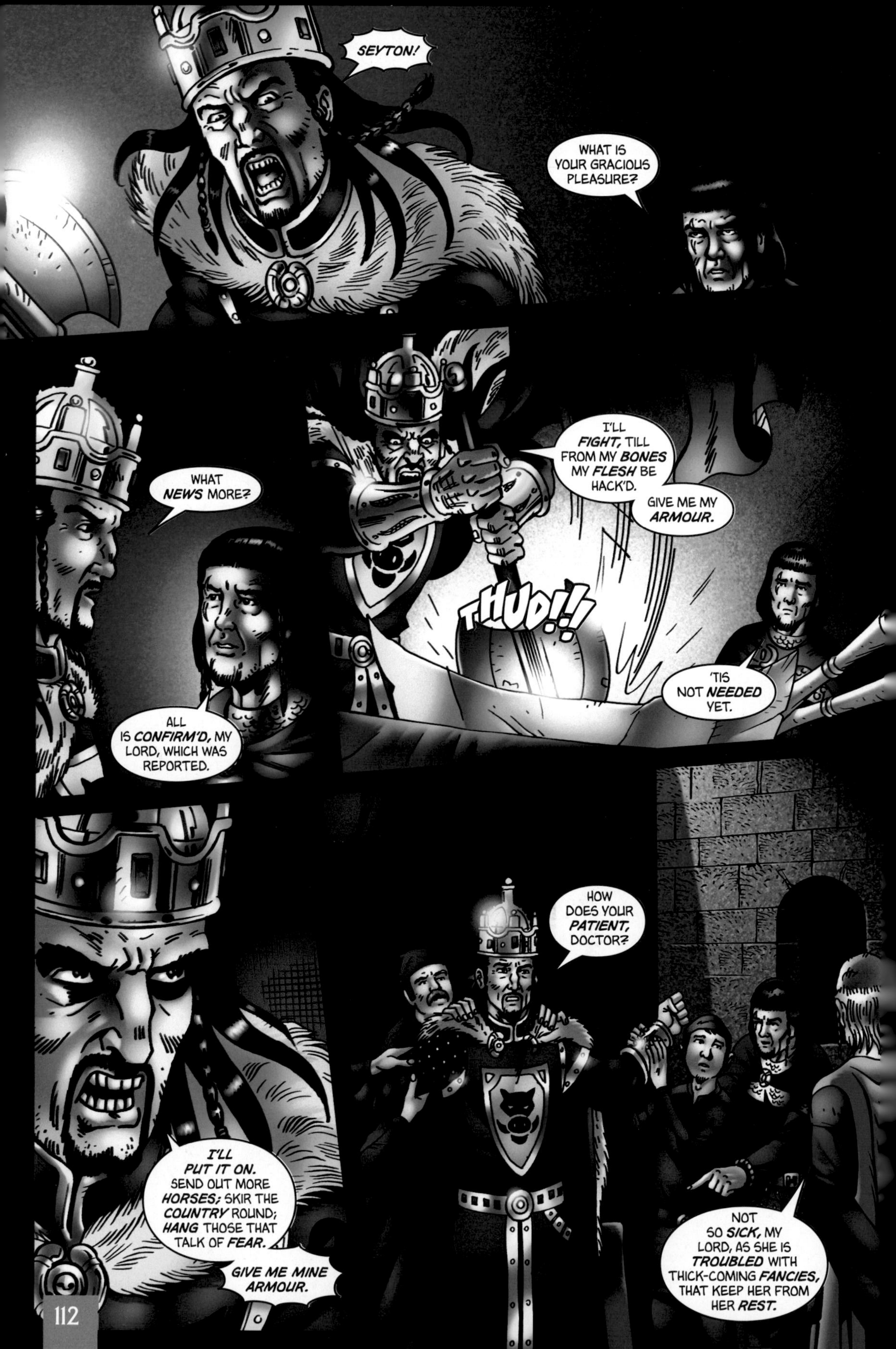
SEYTON!
WHAT IS YOUR GRACIOUS PLEASURE?
WHAT NEWS MORE?
ALL IS CONFIRM'D, MY LORD, WHICH WAS REPORTED.
I'LL FIGHT, TILL FROM MY BONES MY FLESH BE HACK'D.
GIVE ME MY ARMOUR.
THUD!!
'TIS NOT NEEDED YET.
I'LL PUT IT ON. SEND OUT MORE HORSES; SKIR THE COUNTRY ROUND; HANG THOSE THAT TALK OF FEAR.
GIVE ME MINE ARMOUR.
HOW DOES YOUR PATIENT, DOCTOR?
NOT SO SICK, MY LORD, AS SHE IS TROUBLED WITH THICK-COMING FANCIES, THAT KEEP HER FROM HER REST.

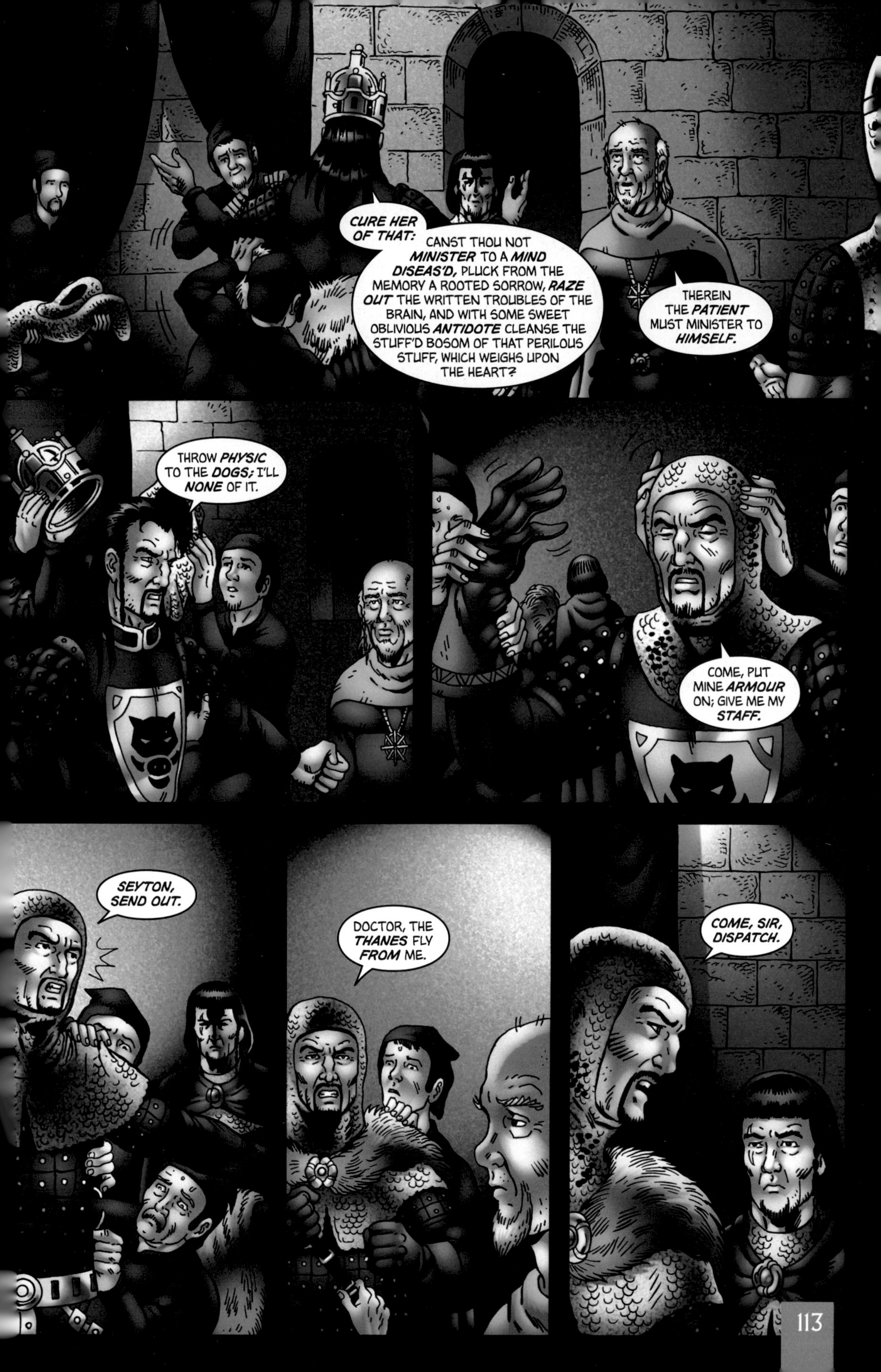
CURE HER OF THAT:
CANST THOU NOT MINISTER TO A MIND DISEAS'D, PLUCK FROM THE MEMORY A ROOTED SORROW, RAZE OUT THE WRITTEN TROUBLES OF THE BRAIN, AND WITH SOME SWEET OBLIVIOUS ANTIDOTE CLEANSE THE STUFF'D BOSOM OF THAT PERILOUS STUFF, WHICH WEIGHS UPON THE HEART?
THEREIN THE PATIENT MUST MINISTER TO HIMSELF.
THROW PHYSIC TO THE DOGS; I'LL NONE OF IT.
COME, PUT MINE ARMOUR ON; GIVE ME MY STAFF.
SEYTON, SEND OUT.
DOCTOR, THE THANES FLY FROM ME.
COME, SIR, DISPATCH.

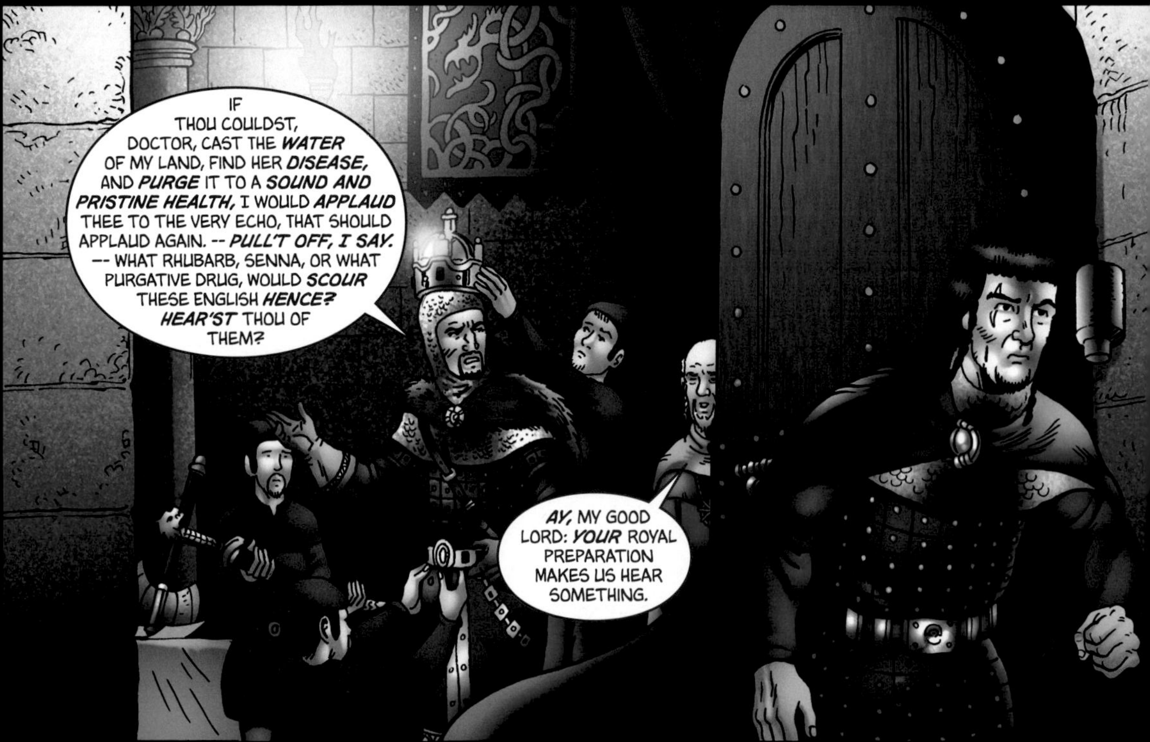
IF THOU COULDST, DOCTOR, CAST THE WATER OF MY LAND, FIND HER DISEASE, AND PURGE IT TO A SOUND AND PRISTINE HEALTH, I WOULD APPLAUD THEE TO THE VERY ECHO, THAT SHOULD APPLAUD AGAIN. -- PULL'T OFF, I SAY. -- WHAT RHUBARB, SENNA, OR WHAT PURGATIVE DRUG, WOULD SCOUR THESE ENGLISH HENCE? HEAR'ST THOU OF THEM?
AY, MY GOOD LORD: YOUR ROYAL PREPARATION MAKES US HEAR SOMETHING.

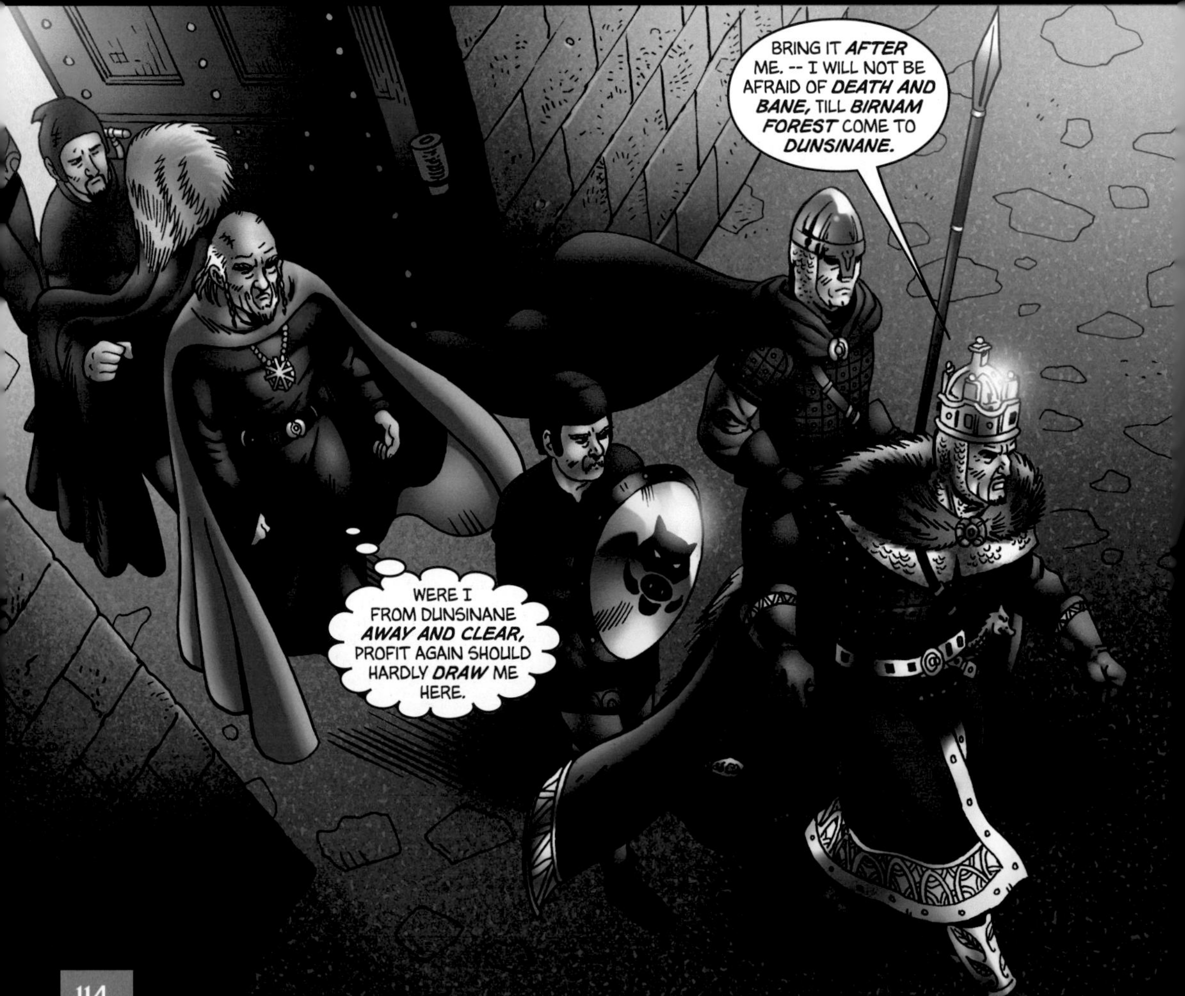
BRING IT AFTER ME. -- I WILL NOT BE AFRAID OF DEATH AND BANE, TILL BIRNAM FOREST COME TO DUNSINANE.
WERE I FROM DUNSINANE AWAY AND CLEAR, PROFIT AGAIN SHOULD HARDLY DRAW ME HERE.

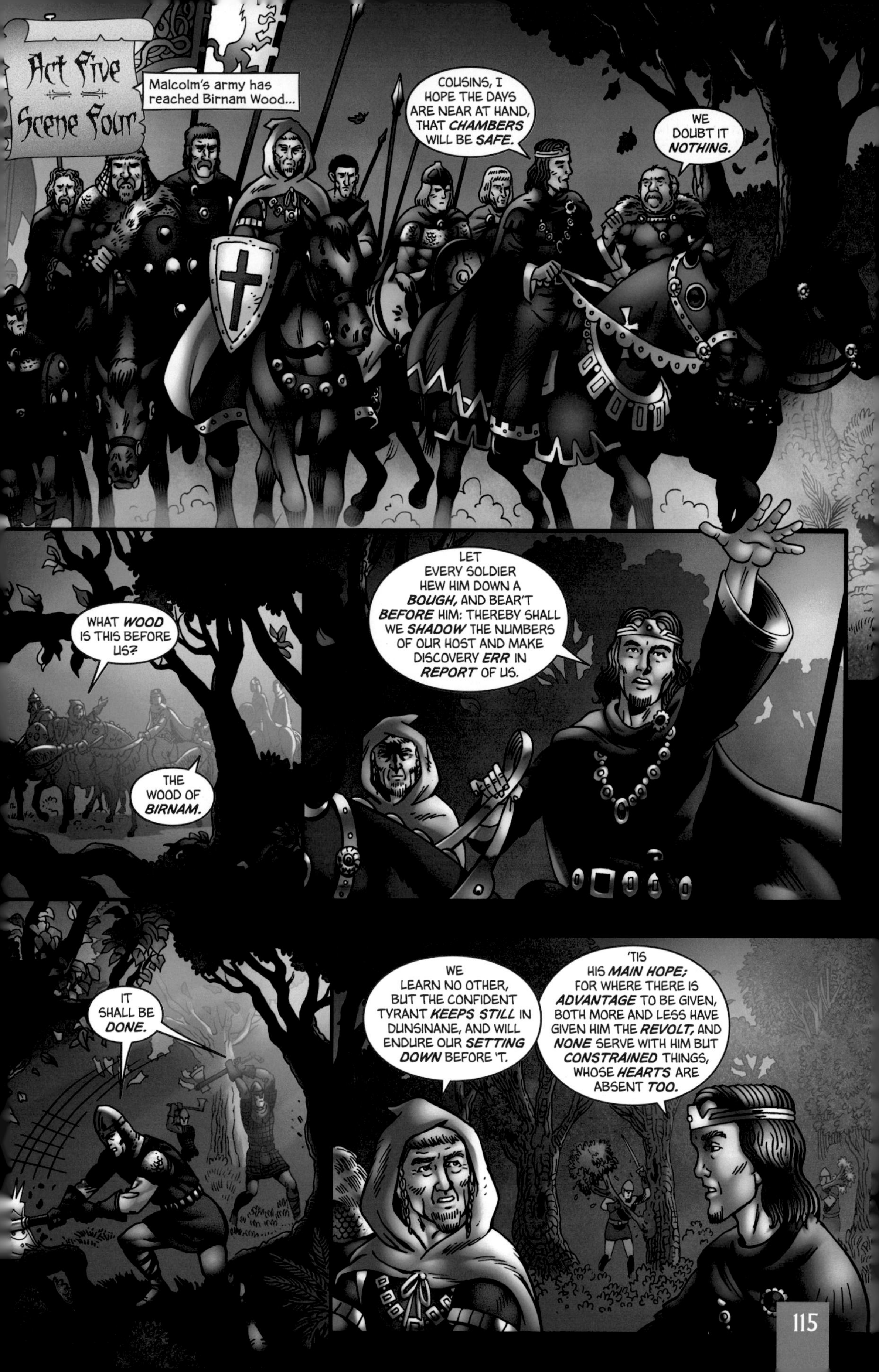
Act Five
Scene Four
Malcolm's army has reached Birnam Wood...
COUSINS, I HOPE THE DAYS ARE NEAR AT HAND, THAT CHAMBERS WILL BE SAFE.
WE DOUBT IT NOTHING.
WHAT WOOD IS THIS BEFORE US?
THE WOOD OF BIRNAM.
LET EVERY SOLDIER HEW HIM DOWN A BOUGH, AND BEAR'T BEFORE HIM: THEREBY SHALL WE SHADOW THE NUMBERS OF OUR HOST AND MAKE DISCOVERY ERR IN REPORT OF US.
IT SHALL BE DONE.
WE LEARN NO OTHER, BUT THE CONFIDENT TYRANT KEEPS STILL IN DUNSINANE, AND WILL ENDURE OUR SETTING DOWN BEFORE 'T.
'TIS HIS MAIN HOPE; FOR WHERE THERE IS ADVANTAGE TO BE GIVEN, BOTH MORE AND LESS HAVE GIVEN HIM THE REVOLT, AND NONE SERVE WITH HIM BUT CONSTRAINED THINGS, WHOSE HEARTS ARE ABSENT TOO.

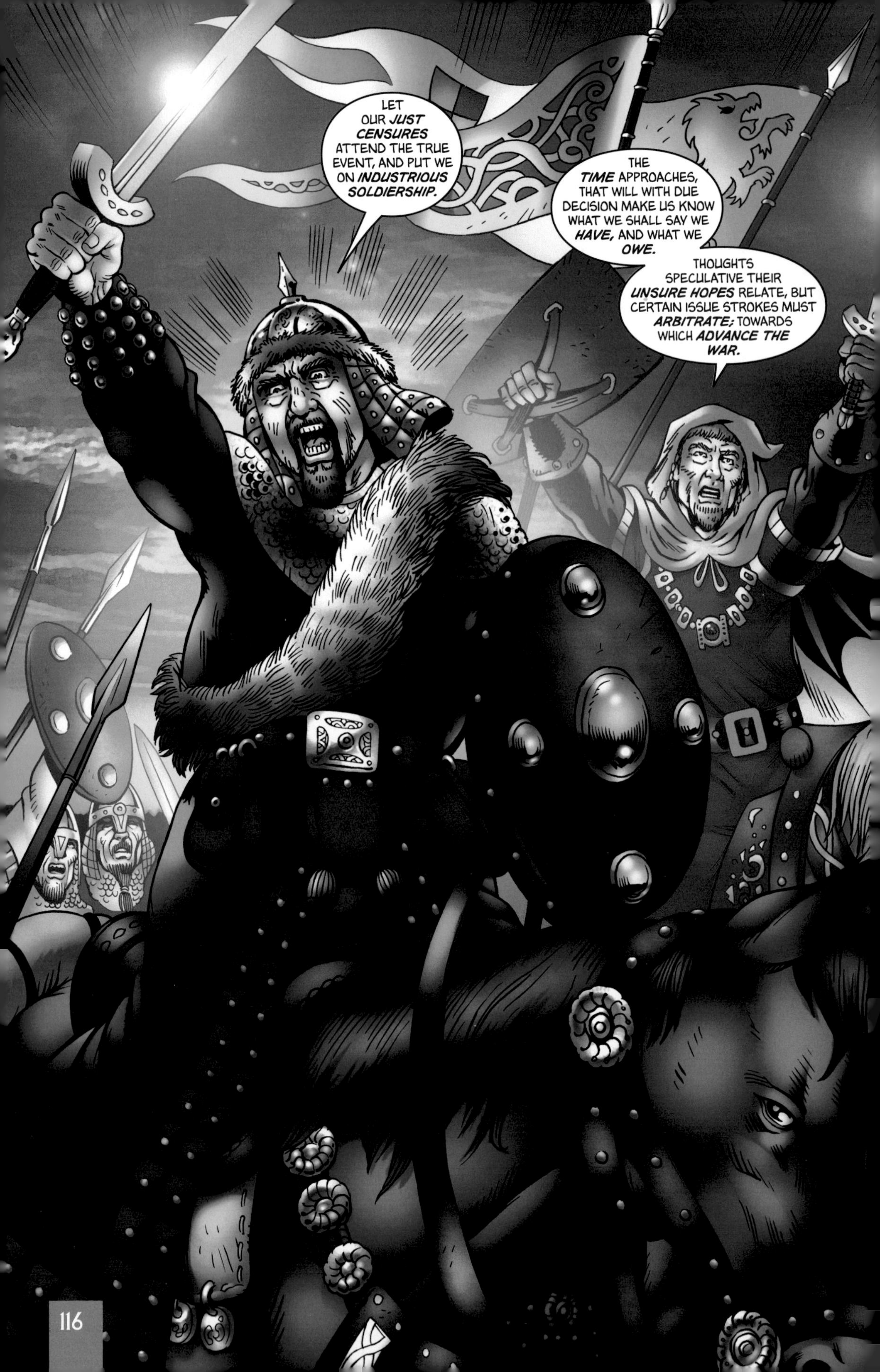
LET OUR ***JUST CENSURES*** ATTEND THE TRUE EVENT, AND PUT WE ON ***INDUSTRIOUS SOLDIERSHIP.***
THE ***TIME*** APPROACHES, THAT WILL WITH DUE DECISION MAKE US KNOW WHAT WE SHALL SAY WE ***HAVE,*** AND WHAT WE ***OWE.***
THOUGHTS SPECULATIVE THEIR ***UNSURE HOPES*** RELATE, BUT CERTAIN ISSUE STROKES MUST ***ARBITRATE;*** TOWARDS WHICH ***ADVANCE THE WAR.***

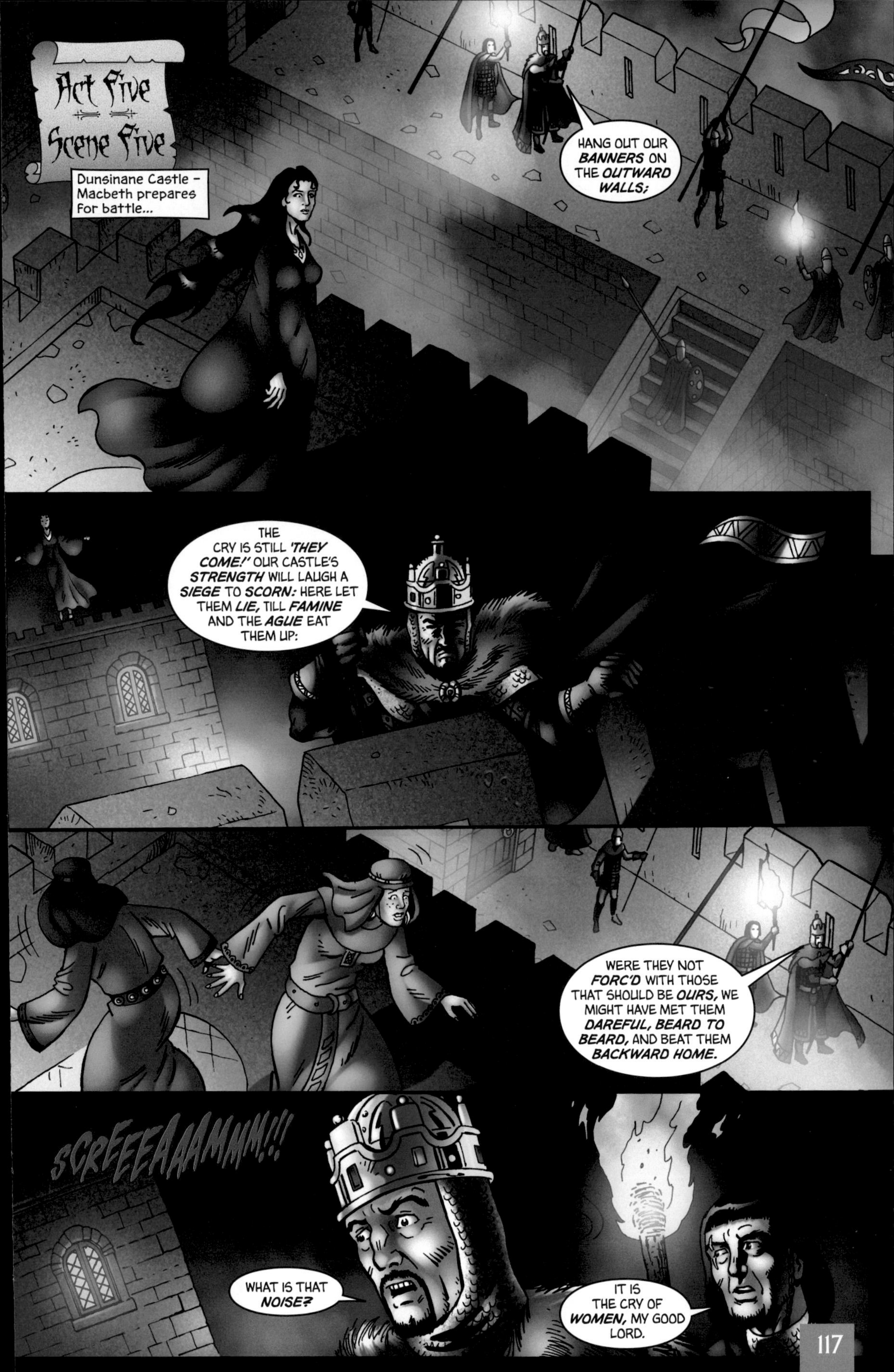
Act Five
Scene Five
Dunsinane Castle – Macbeth prepares for battle...
HANG OUT OUR BANNERS ON THE OUTWARD WALLS;
THE CRY IS STILL 'THEY COME!' OUR CASTLE'S STRENGTH WILL LAUGH A SIEGE TO SCORN: HERE LET THEM LIE, TILL FAMINE AND THE AGUE EAT THEM UP:
WERE THEY NOT FORC'D WITH THOSE THAT SHOULD BE OURS, WE MIGHT HAVE MET THEM DAREFUL, BEARD TO BEARD, AND BEAT THEM BACKWARD HOME.
SCREEEAAAMMM!!!
WHAT IS THAT NOISE?
IT IS THE CRY OF WOMEN, MY GOOD LORD.

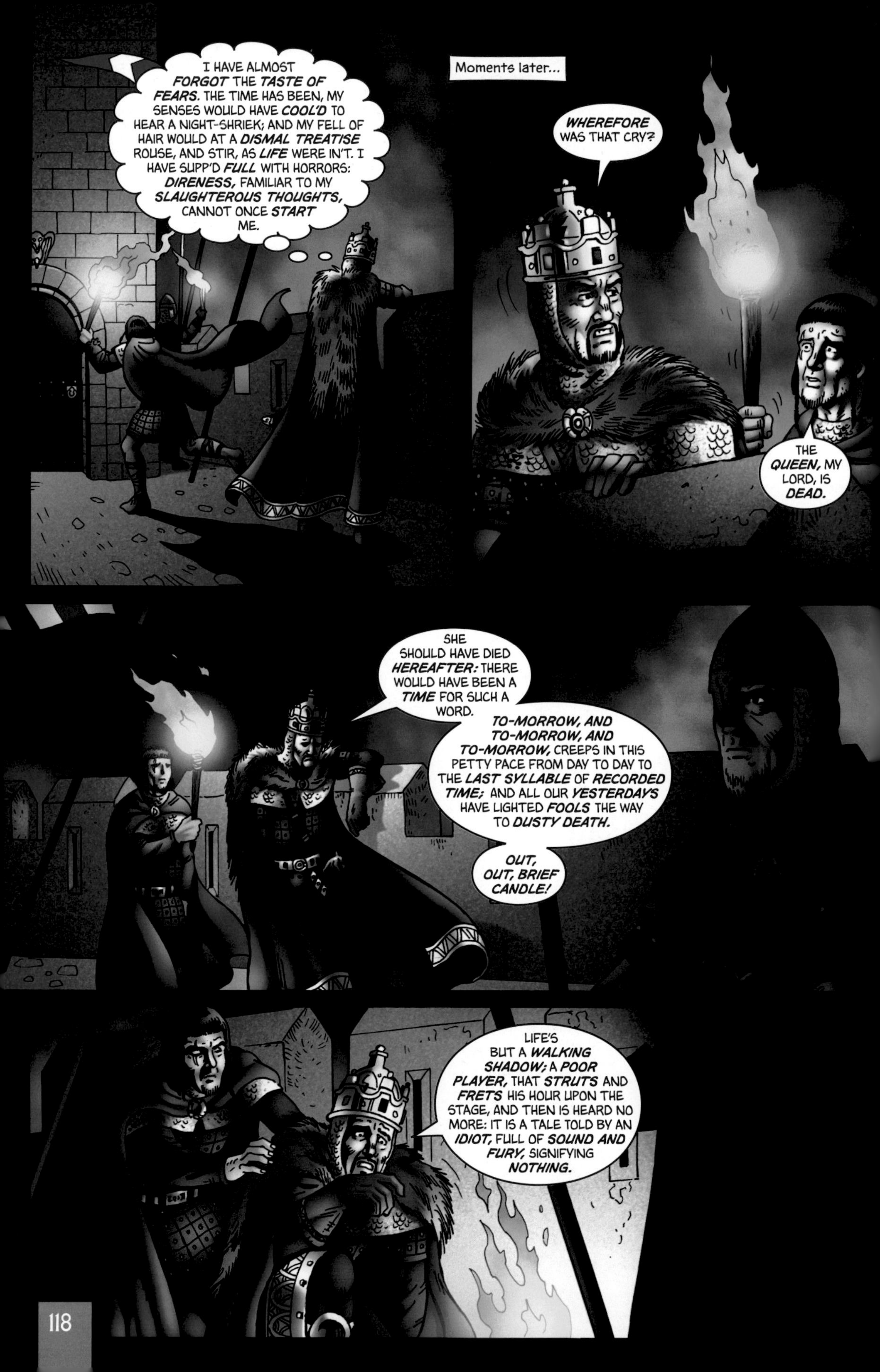
I HAVE ALMOST FORGOT THE TASTE OF FEARS. THE TIME HAS BEEN, MY SENSES WOULD HAVE COOL'D TO HEAR A NIGHT-SHRIEK; AND MY FELL OF HAIR WOULD AT A DISMAL TREATISE ROUSE, AND STIR, AS LIFE WERE IN'T. I HAVE SUPP'D FULL WITH HORRORS: DIRENESS, FAMILIAR TO MY SLAUGHTEROUS THOUGHTS, CANNOT ONCE START ME.
Moments later...
WHEREFORE WAS THAT CRY?
THE QUEEN, MY LORD, IS DEAD.
SHE SHOULD HAVE DIED HEREAFTER: THERE WOULD HAVE BEEN A TIME FOR SUCH A WORD.
TO-MORROW, AND TO-MORROW, AND TO-MORROW, CREEPS IN THIS PETTY PACE FROM DAY TO DAY TO THE LAST SYLLABLE OF RECORDED TIME; AND ALL OUR YESTERDAYS HAVE LIGHTED FOOLS THE WAY TO DUSTY DEATH.
OUT, OUT, BRIEF CANDLE!
LIFE'S BUT A WALKING SHADOW; A POOR PLAYER, THAT STRUTS AND FRETS HIS HOUR UPON THE STAGE, AND THEN IS HEARD NO MORE: IT IS A TALE TOLD BY AN IDIOT, FULL OF SOUND AND FURY, SIGNIFYING NOTHING.

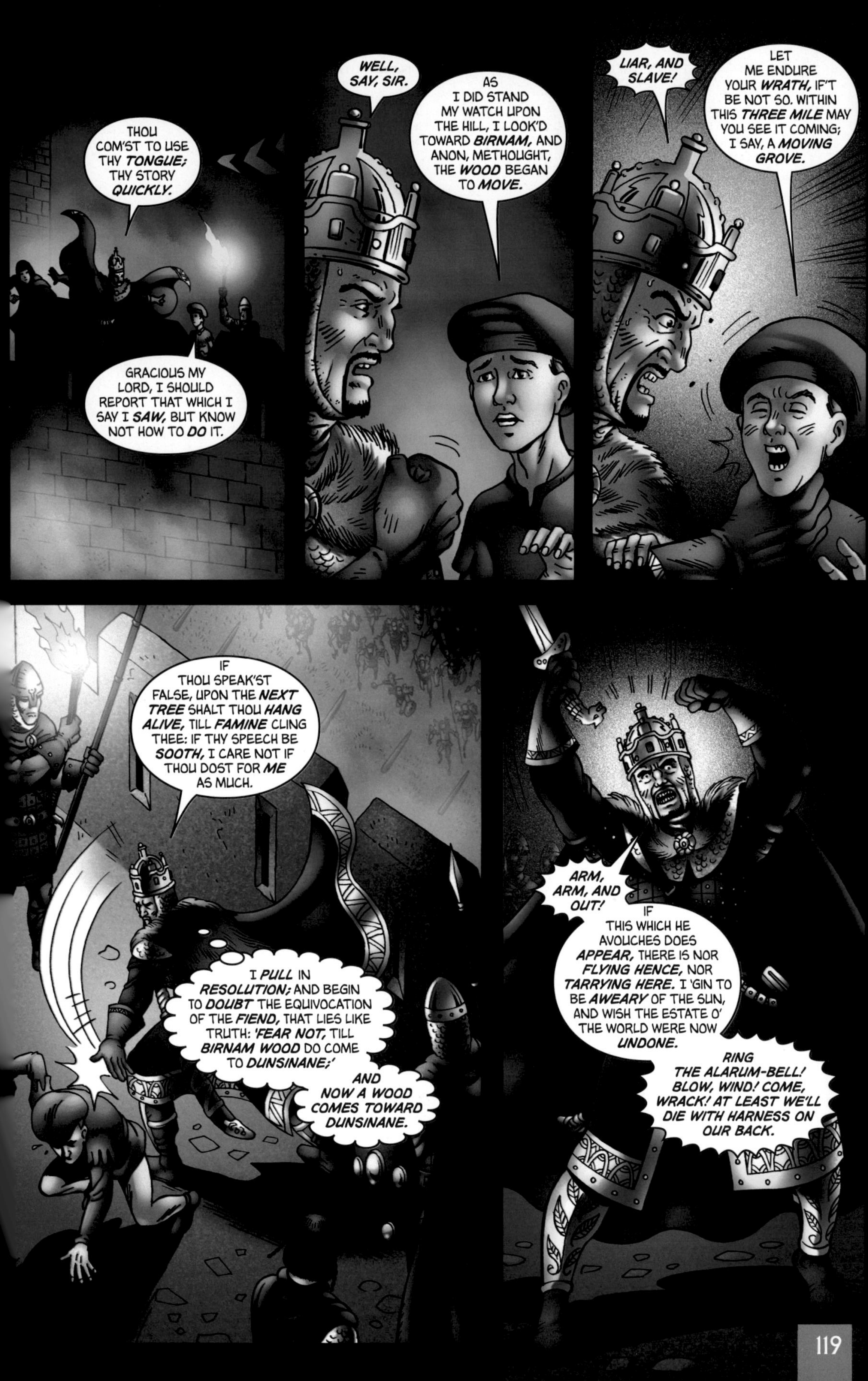
THOU COM'ST TO USE THY TONGUE; THY STORY QUICKLY.
GRACIOUS MY LORD, I SHOULD REPORT THAT WHICH I SAY I SAW, BUT KNOW NOT HOW TO DO IT.
WELL, SAY, SIR.
AS I DID STAND MY WATCH UPON THE HILL, I LOOK'D TOWARD BIRNAM, AND ANON, METHOUGHT, THE WOOD BEGAN TO MOVE.
LIAR, AND SLAVE!
LET ME ENDURE YOUR WRATH, IF'T BE NOT SO. WITHIN THIS THREE MILE MAY YOU SEE IT COMING; I SAY, A MOVING GROVE.
IF THOU SPEAK'ST FALSE, UPON THE NEXT TREE SHALT THOU HANG ALIVE, TILL FAMINE CLING THEE: IF THY SPEECH BE SOOTH, I CARE NOT IF THOU DOST FOR ME AS MUCH.
I PULL IN RESOLUTION; AND BEGIN TO DOUBT THE EQUIVOCATION OF THE FIEND, THAT LIES LIKE TRUTH: 'FEAR NOT, TILL BIRNAM WOOD DO COME TO DUNSINANE;'
AND NOW A WOOD COMES TOWARD DUNSINANE.
ARM, ARM, AND OUT!
IF THIS WHICH HE AVOUCHES DOES APPEAR, THERE IS NOR FLYING HENCE, NOR TARRYING HERE. I 'GIN TO BE AWEARY OF THE SUN, AND WISH THE ESTATE O' THE WORLD WERE NOW UNDONE.
RING THE ALARUM-BELL! BLOW, WIND! COME, WRACK! AT LEAST WE'LL DIE WITH HARNESS ON OUR BACK.

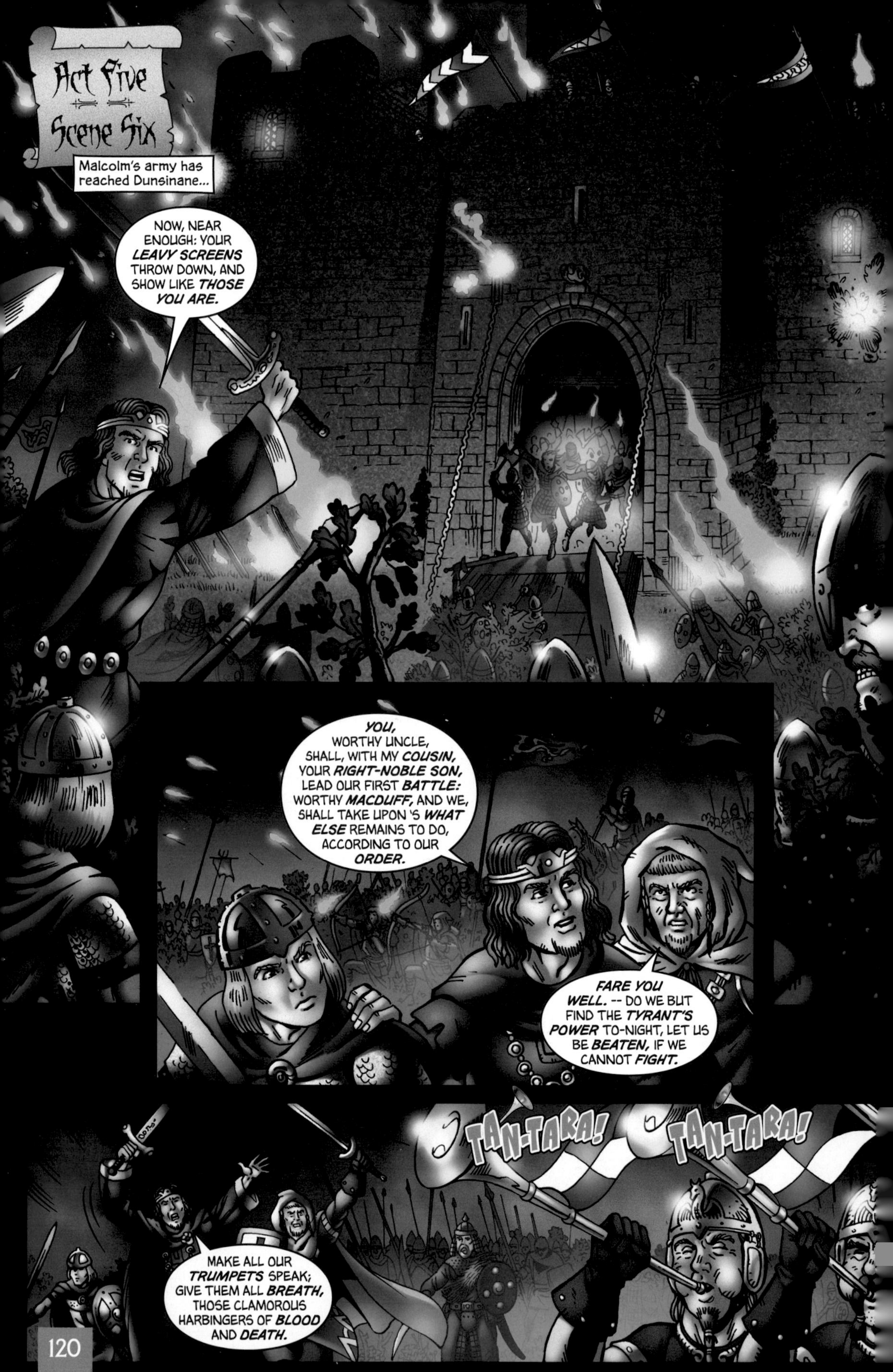
Act Five
Scene Six
Malcolm's army has reached Dunsinane...
NOW, NEAR ENOUGH: YOUR LEAVY SCREENS THROW DOWN, AND SHOW LIKE THOSE YOU ARE.
YOU, WORTHY UNCLE, SHALL, WITH MY COUSIN, YOUR RIGHT-NOBLE SON, LEAD OUR FIRST BATTLE: WORTHY MACDUFF, AND WE, SHALL TAKE UPON 'S WHAT ELSE REMAINS TO DO, ACCORDING TO OUR ORDER.
FARE YOU WELL. -- DO WE BUT FIND THE TYRANT'S POWER TO-NIGHT, LET US BE BEATEN, IF WE CANNOT FIGHT.
TAN-TARA!
TAN-TARA!
MAKE ALL OUR TRUMPETS SPEAK; GIVE THEM ALL BREATH, THOSE CLAMOROUS HARBINGERS OF BLOOD AND DEATH.

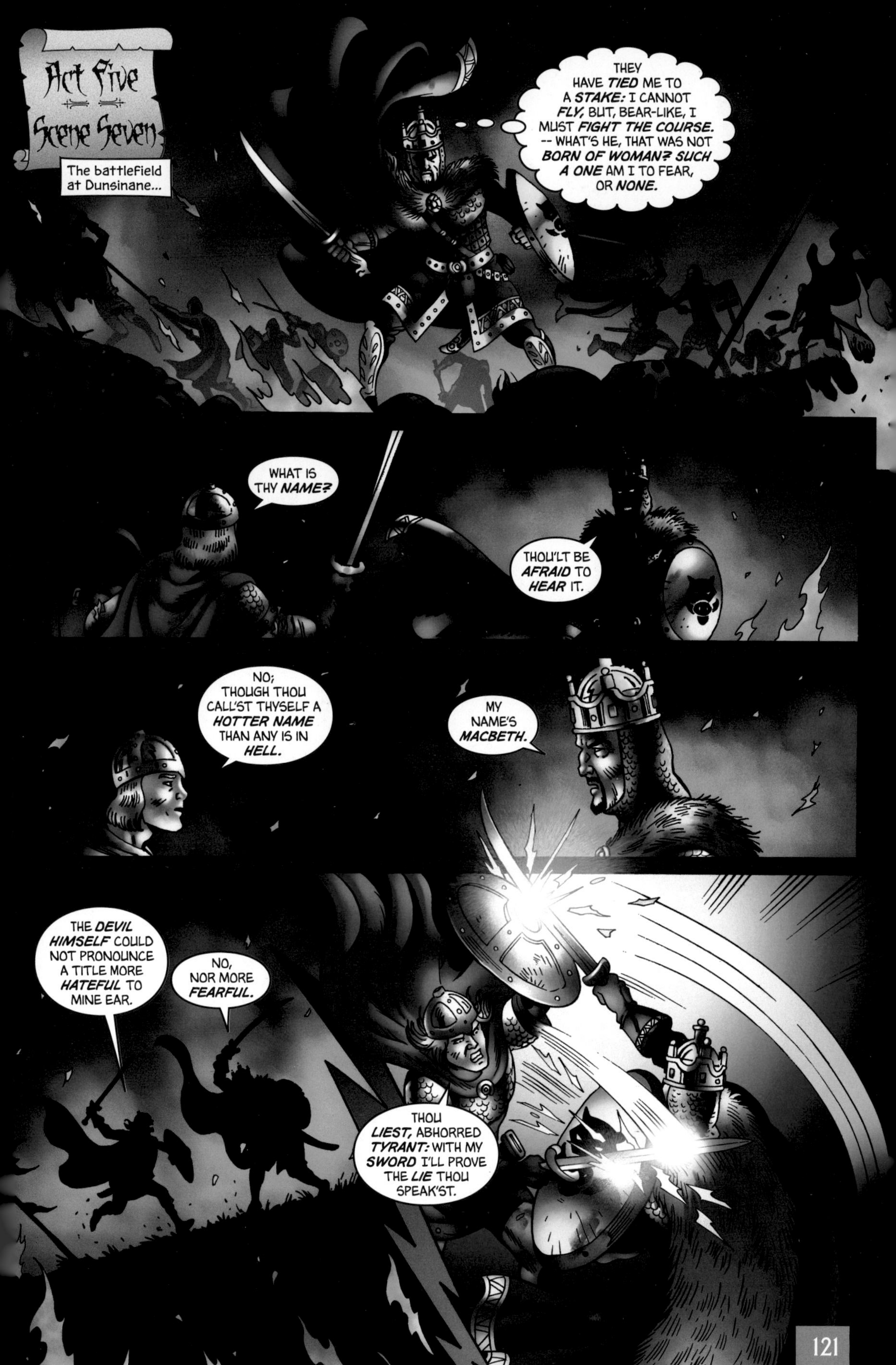
Act Five
Scene Seven
The battlefield at Dunsinane...
THEY HAVE TIED ME TO A STAKE: I CANNOT FLY, BUT, BEAR-LIKE, I MUST FIGHT THE COURSE. -- WHAT'S HE, THAT WAS NOT BORN OF WOMAN? SUCH A ONE AM I TO FEAR, OR NONE.
WHAT IS THY NAME?
THOU'LT BE AFRAID TO HEAR IT.
NO; THOUGH THOU CALL'ST THYSELF A HOTTER NAME THAN ANY IS IN HELL.
MY NAME'S MACBETH.
THE DEVIL HIMSELF COULD NOT PRONOUNCE A TITLE MORE HATEFUL TO MINE EAR.
NO, NOR MORE FEARFUL.
THOU LIEST, ABHORRED TYRANT: WITH MY SWORD I'LL PROVE THE LIE THOU SPEAK'ST.

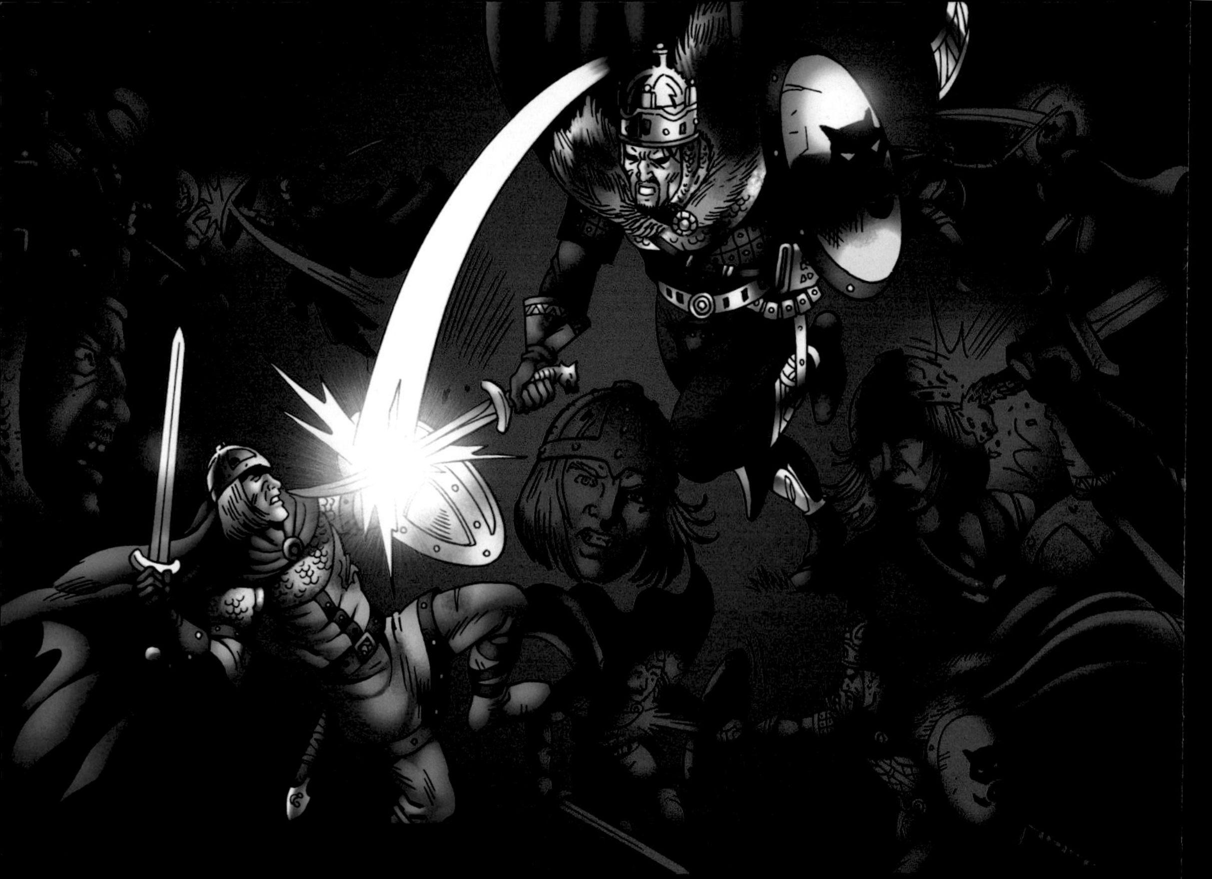

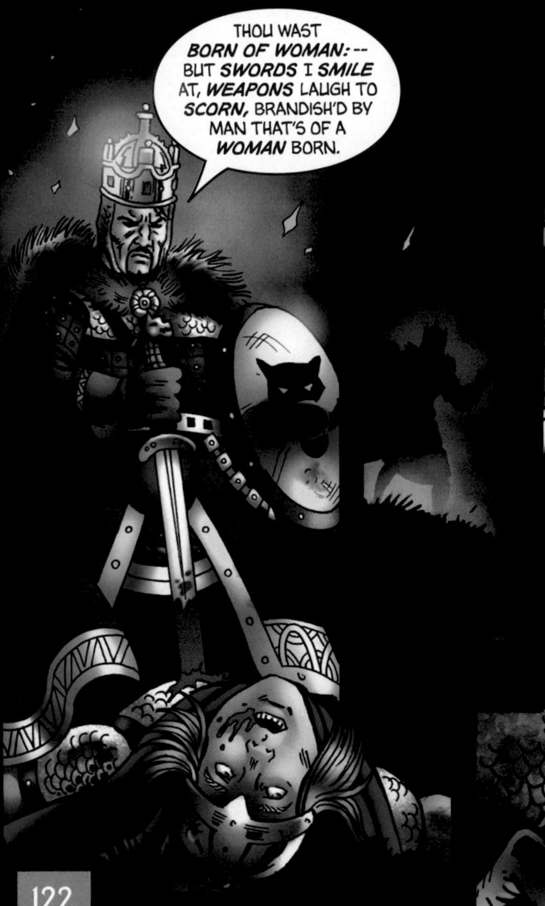
THOU WAST BORN OF WOMAN: -- BUT SWORDS I SMILE AT, WEAPONS LAUGH TO SCORN, BRANDISH'D BY MAN THAT'S OF A WOMAN BORN.

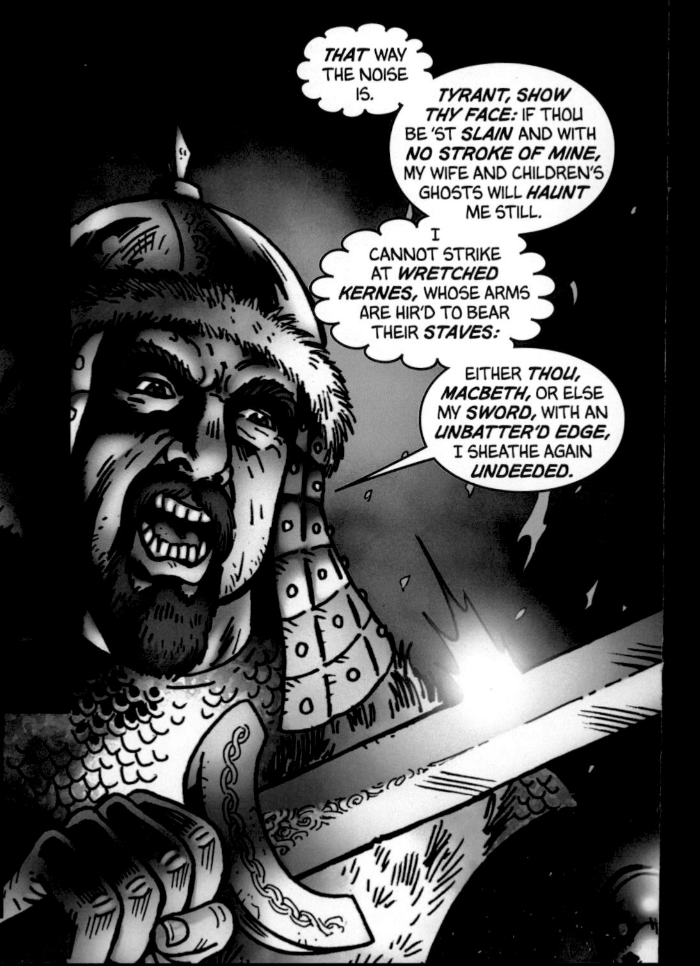
THAT WAY THE NOISE IS.
TYRANT, SHOW THY FACE: IF THOU BE 'ST SLAIN AND WITH NO STROKE OF MINE, MY WIFE AND CHILDREN'S GHOSTS WILL HAUNT ME STILL.
I CANNOT STRIKE AT WRETCHED KERNES, WHOSE ARMS ARE HIR'D TO BEAR THEIR STAVES:
EITHER THOU, MACBETH, OR ELSE MY SWORD, WITH AN UNBATTER'D EDGE, I SHEATHE AGAIN UNDEEDED.

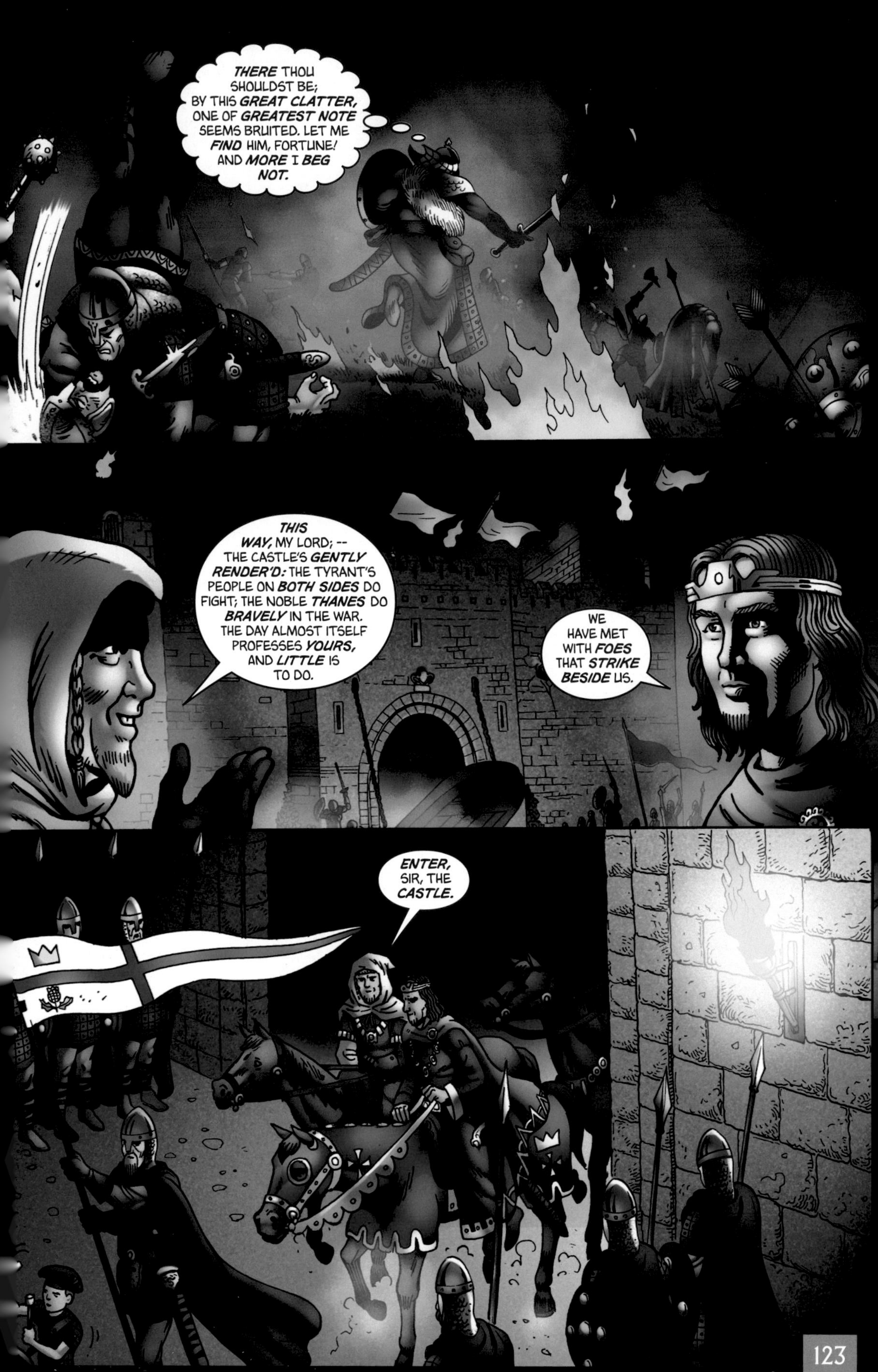
THERE THOU SHOULDST BE; BY THIS GREAT CLATTER, ONE OF GREATEST NOTE SEEMS BRUITED. LET ME FIND HIM, FORTUNE! AND MORE I BEG NOT.
THIS WAY, MY LORD; -- THE CASTLE'S GENTLY RENDER'D: THE TYRANT'S PEOPLE ON BOTH SIDES DO FIGHT; THE NOBLE THANES DO BRAVELY IN THE WAR. THE DAY ALMOST ITSELF PROFESSES YOURS, AND LITTLE IS TO DO.
WE HAVE MET WITH FOES THAT STRIKE BESIDE US.
ENTER, SIR, THE CASTLE.

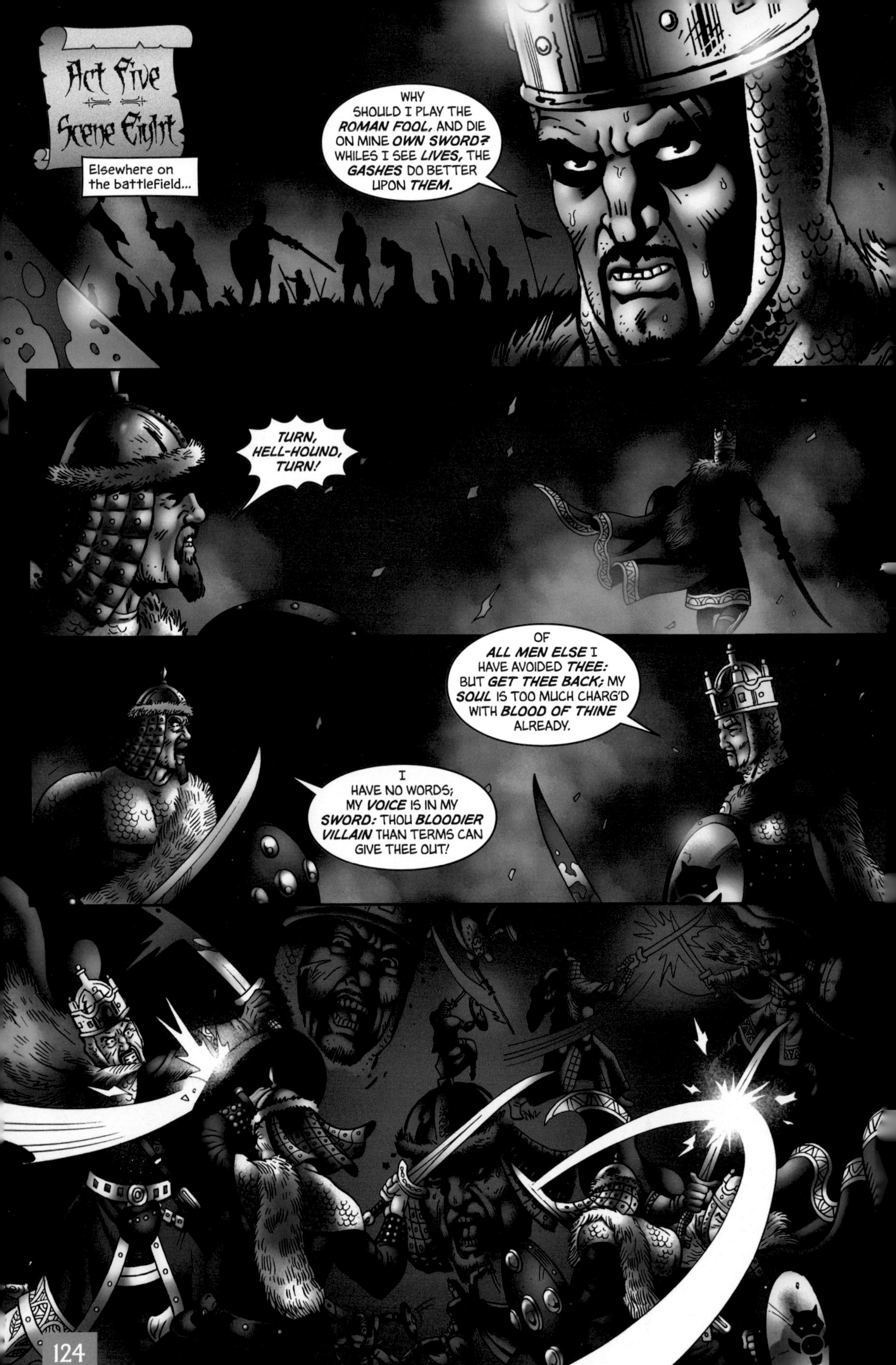
Act Five
Scene Eight
Elsewhere on the battlefield...
WHY SHOULD I PLAY THE ROMAN FOOL, AND DIE ON MINE OWN SWORD? WHILES I SEE LIVES, THE GASHES DO BETTER UPON THEM.
TURN, HELL-HOUND, TURN!
OF ALL MEN ELSE I HAVE AVOIDED THEE: BUT GET THEE BACK; MY SOUL IS TOO MUCH CHARG'D WITH BLOOD OF THINE ALREADY.
I HAVE NO WORDS; MY VOICE IS IN MY SWORD: THOU BLOODIER VILLAIN THAN TERMS CAN GIVE THEE OUT!

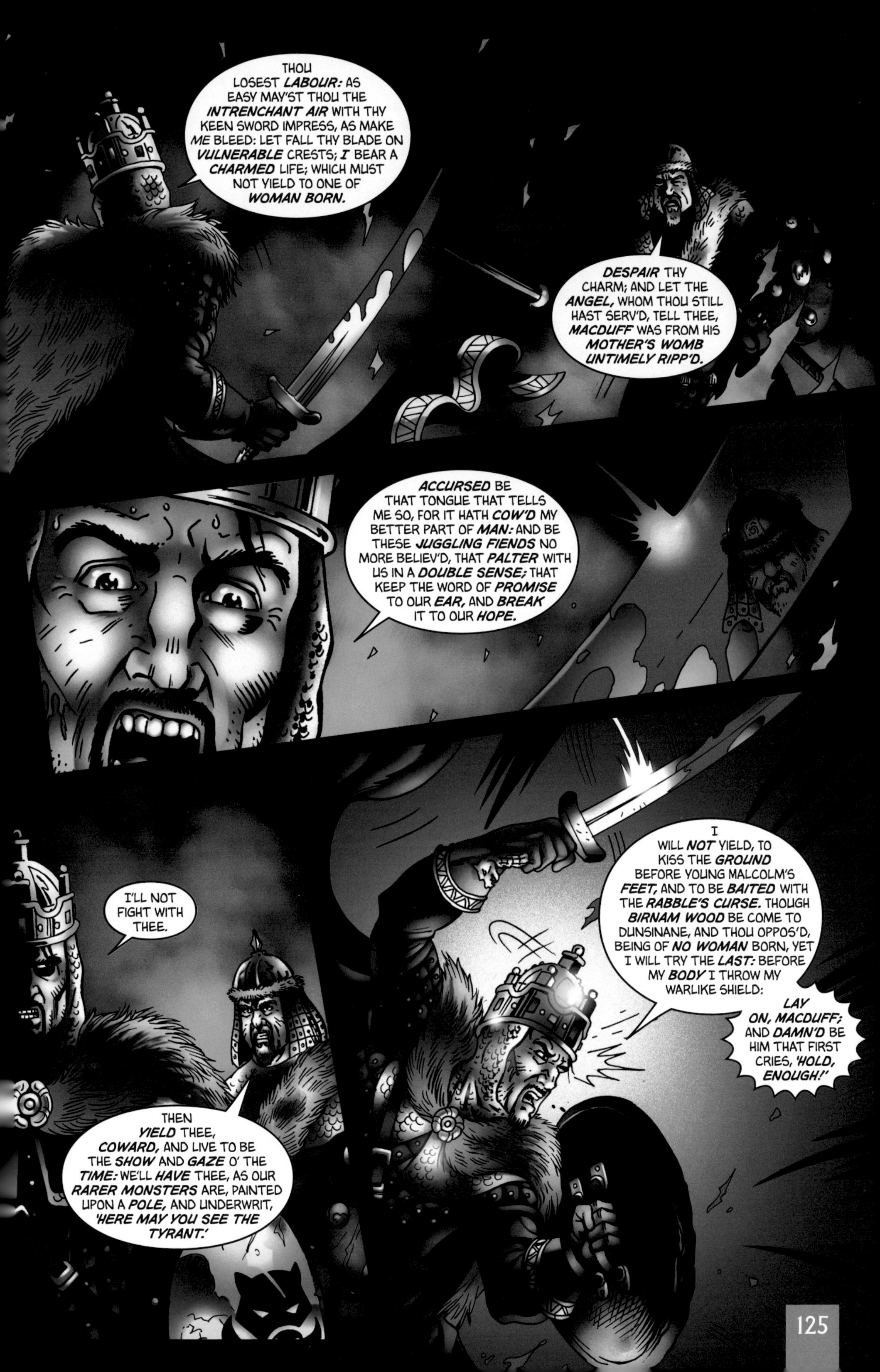

THOU LOSEST LABOUR: AS EASY MAY'ST THOU THE INTRENCHANT AIR WITH THY KEEN SWORD IMPRESS, AS MAKE ME BLEED: LET FALL THY BLADE ON VULNERABLE CRESTS; I BEAR A CHARMED LIFE; WHICH MUST NOT YIELD TO ONE OF WOMAN BORN.
DESPAIR THY CHARM; AND LET THE ANGEL, WHOM THOU STILL HAST SERV'D, TELL THEE, MACDUFF WAS FROM HIS MOTHER'S WOMB UNTIMELY RIPP'D.
ACCURSED BE THAT TONGUE THAT TELLS ME SO, FOR IT HATH COW'D MY BETTER PART OF MAN: AND BE THESE JUGGLING FIENDS NO MORE BELIEV'D, THAT PALTER WITH US IN A DOUBLE SENSE; THAT KEEP THE WORD OF PROMISE TO OUR EAR, AND BREAK IT TO OUR HOPE.
I'LL NOT FIGHT WITH THEE.
THEN YIELD THEE, COWARD, AND LIVE TO BE THE SHOW AND GAZE O' THE TIME: WE'LL HAVE THEE, AS OUR RARER MONSTERS ARE, PAINTED UPON A POLE, AND UNDERWRIT, 'HERE MAY YOU SEE THE TYRANT.'
I WILL NOT YIELD, TO KISS THE GROUND BEFORE YOUNG MALCOLM'S FEET, AND TO BE BAITED WITH THE RABBLE'S CURSE. THOUGH BIRNAM WOOD BE COME TO DUNSINANE, AND THOU OPPOS'D, BEING OF NO WOMAN BORN, YET I WILL TRY THE LAST: BEFORE MY BODY I THROW MY WARLIKE SHIELD:
LAY ON, MACDUFF; AND DAMN'D BE HIM THAT FIRST CRIES, 'HOLD, ENOUGH!'

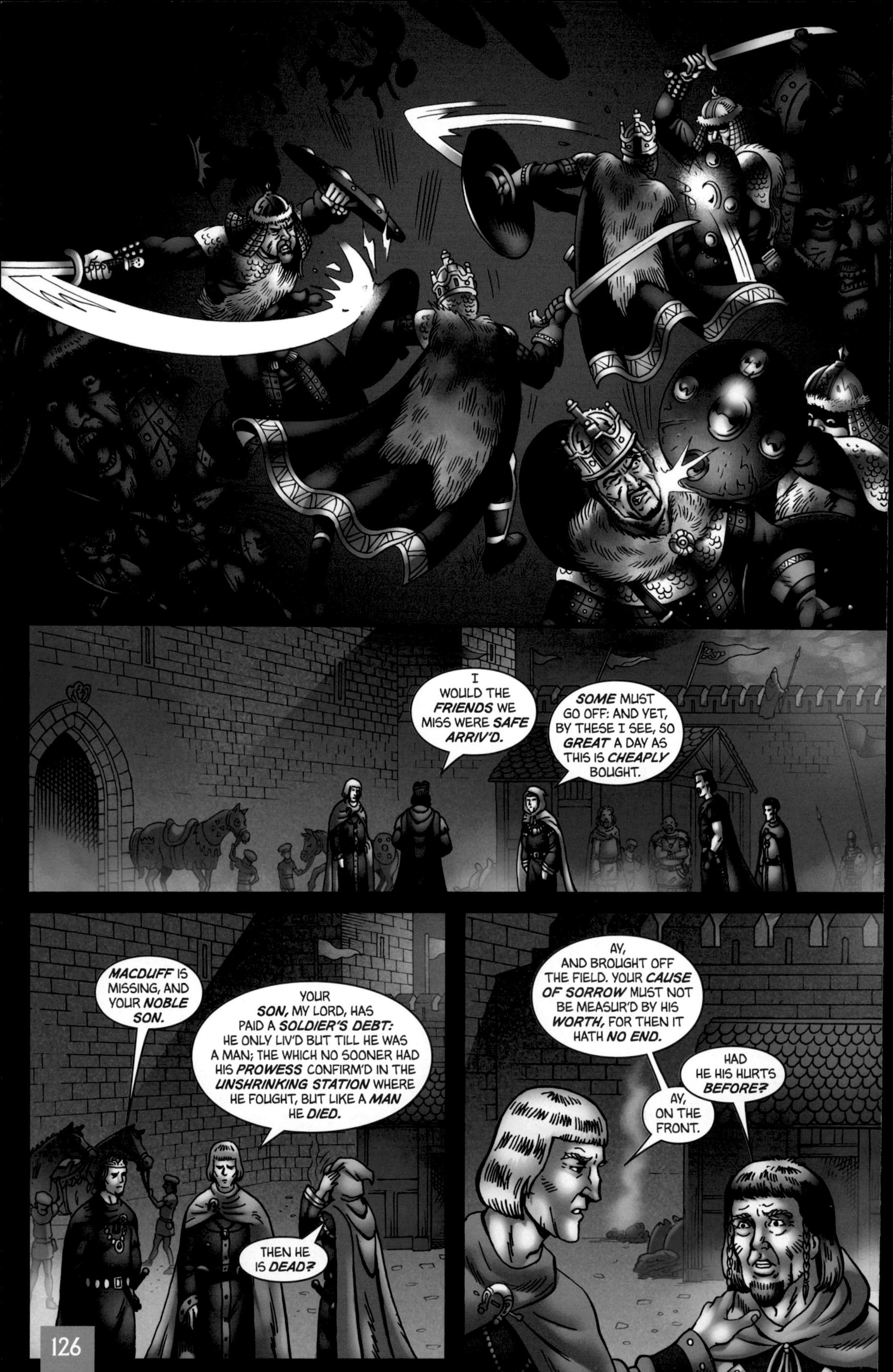
I WOULD THE FRIENDS WE MISS WERE SAFE ARRIV'D.
SOME MUST GO OFF: AND YET, BY THESE I SEE, SO GREAT A DAY AS THIS IS CHEAPLY BOUGHT.
MACDUFF IS MISSING, AND YOUR NOBLE SON.
YOUR SON, MY LORD, HAS PAID A SOLDIER'S DEBT: HE ONLY LIV'D BUT TILL HE WAS A MAN; THE WHICH NO SOONER HAD HIS PROWESS CONFIRM'D IN THE UNSHRINKING STATION WHERE HE FOUGHT, BUT LIKE A MAN HE DIED.
THEN HE IS DEAD?
AY, AND BROUGHT OFF THE FIELD. YOUR CAUSE OF SORROW MUST NOT BE MEASUR'D BY HIS WORTH, FOR THEN IT HATH NO END.
HAD HE HIS HURTS BEFORE?
AY, ON THE FRONT.

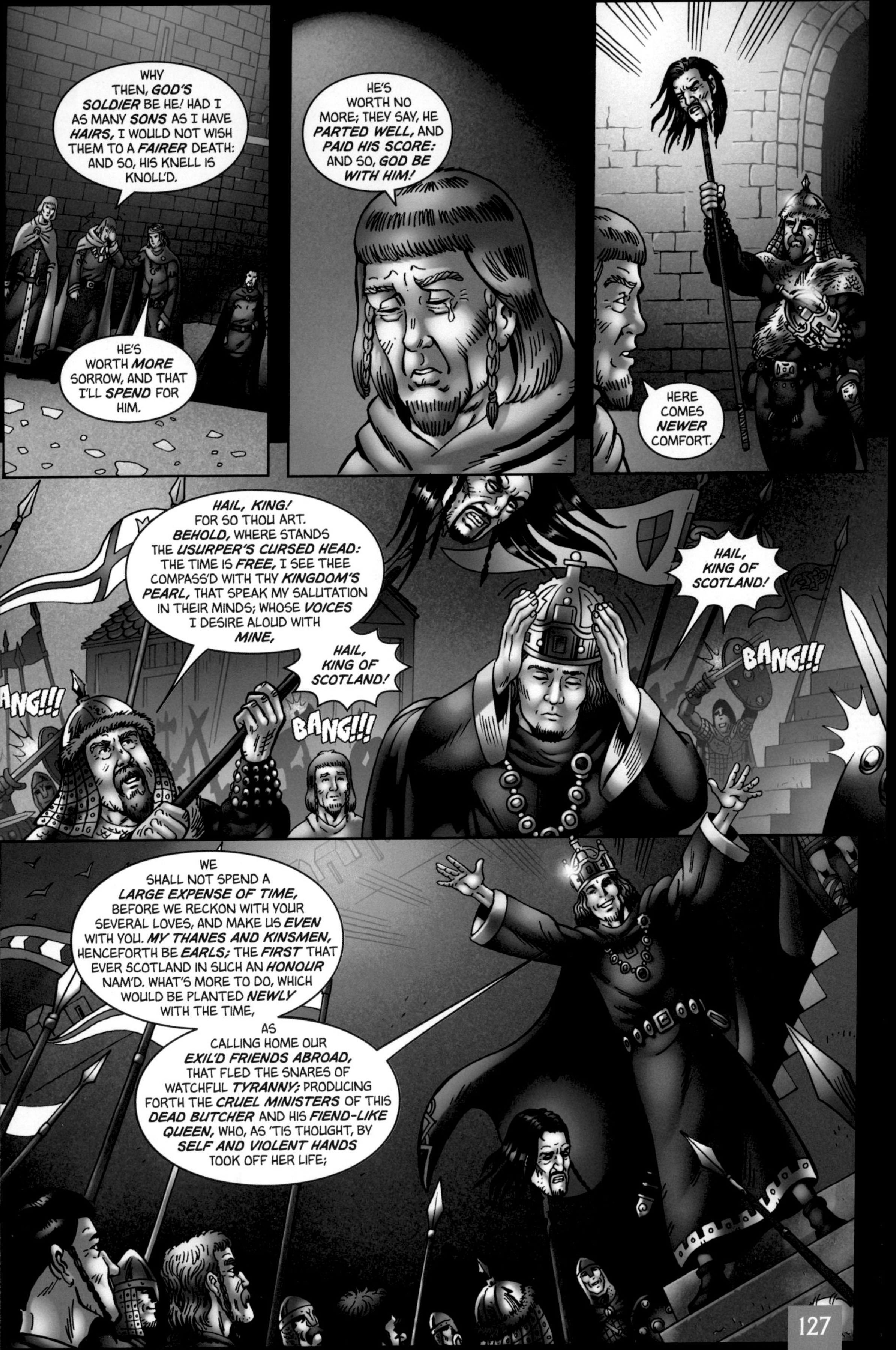
WHY THEN, GOD'S SOLDIER BE HE! HAD I AS MANY SONS AS I HAVE HAIRS, I WOULD NOT WISH THEM TO A FAIRER DEATH: AND SO, HIS KNELL IS KNOLL'D.
HE'S WORTH MORE SORROW, AND THAT I'LL SPEND FOR HIM.
HE'S WORTH NO MORE; THEY SAY, HE PARTED WELL, AND PAID HIS SCORE: AND SO, GOD BE WITH HIM!
HERE COMES NEWER COMFORT.
HAIL, KING! FOR SO THOU ART. BEHOLD, WHERE STANDS THE USURPER'S CURSED HEAD: THE TIME IS FREE, I SEE THEE COMPASS'D WITH THY KINGDOM'S PEARL, THAT SPEAK MY SALUTATION IN THEIR MINDS; WHOSE VOICES I DESIRE ALOUD WITH MINE,
HAIL, KING OF SCOTLAND!
HAIL, KING OF SCOTLAND!
BANG!!!
BANG!!!
BANG!!!
WE SHALL NOT SPEND A LARGE EXPENSE OF TIME, BEFORE WE RECKON WITH YOUR SEVERAL LOVES, AND MAKE US EVEN WITH YOU. MY THANES AND KINSMEN, HENCEFORTH BE EARLS; THE FIRST THAT EVER SCOTLAND IN SUCH AN HONOUR NAM'D. WHAT'S MORE TO DO, WHICH WOULD BE PLANTED NEWLY WITH THE TIME,
AS CALLING HOME OUR EXIL'D FRIENDS ABROAD, THAT FLED THE SNARES OF WATCHFUL TYRANNY; PRODUCING FORTH THE CRUEL MINISTERS OF THIS DEAD BUTCHER AND HIS FIEND-LIKE QUEEN, WHO, AS 'TIS THOUGHT, BY SELF AND VIOLENT HANDS TOOK OFF HER LIFE;

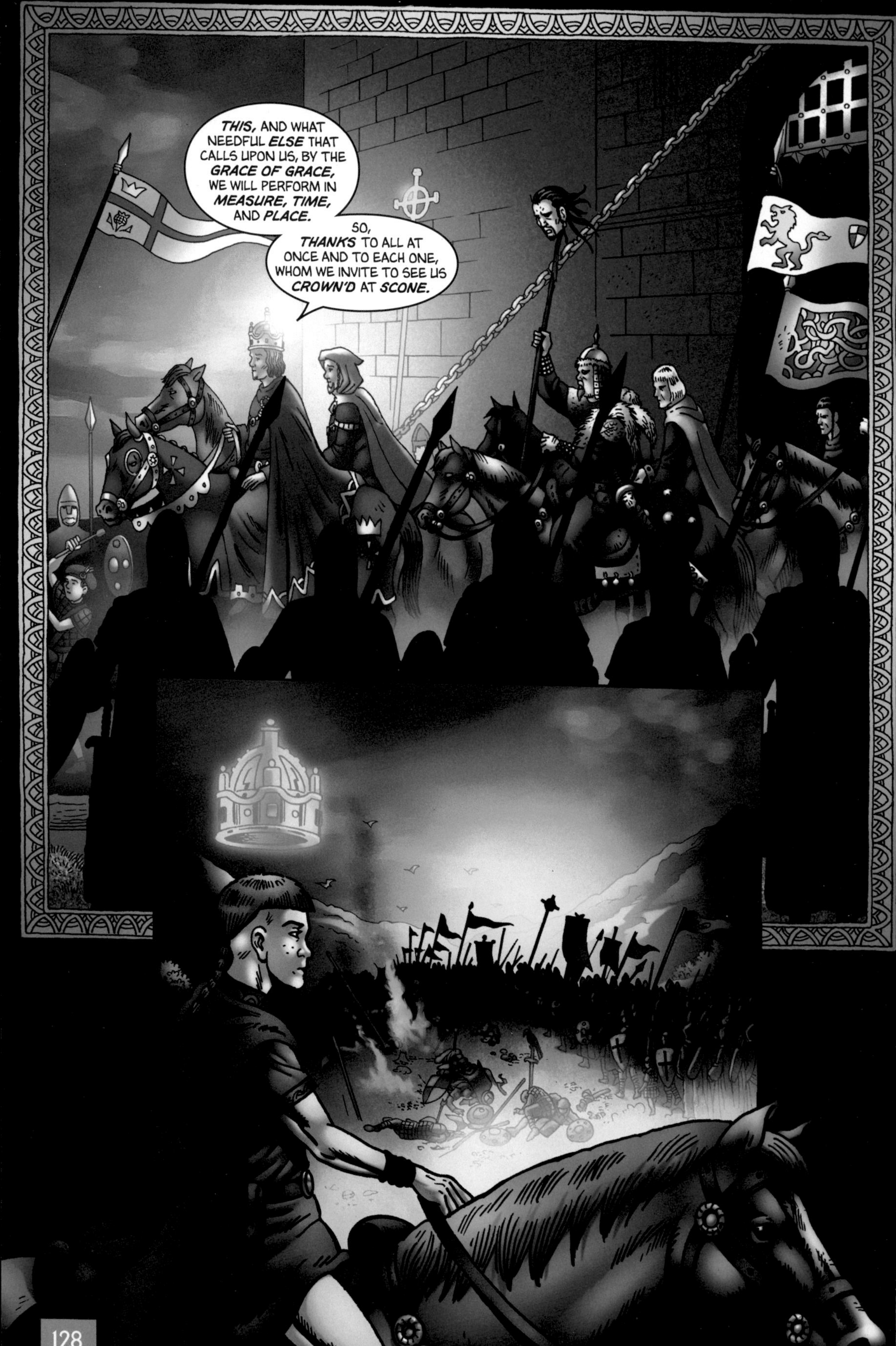
THIS, AND WHAT NEEDFUL ELSE THAT CALLS UPON US, BY THE GRACE OF GRACE, WE WILL PERFORM IN MEASURE, TIME, AND PLACE.
SO, THANKS TO ALL AT ONCE AND TO EACH ONE, WHOM WE INVITE TO SEE US CROWN'D AT SCONE.

Macbeth

End

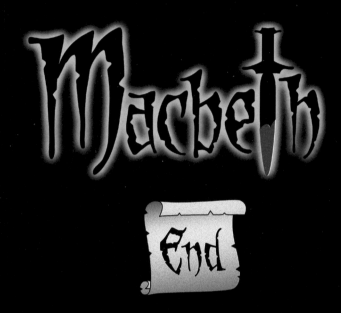

William Shakespeare

(c.1564 - 1616 AD)

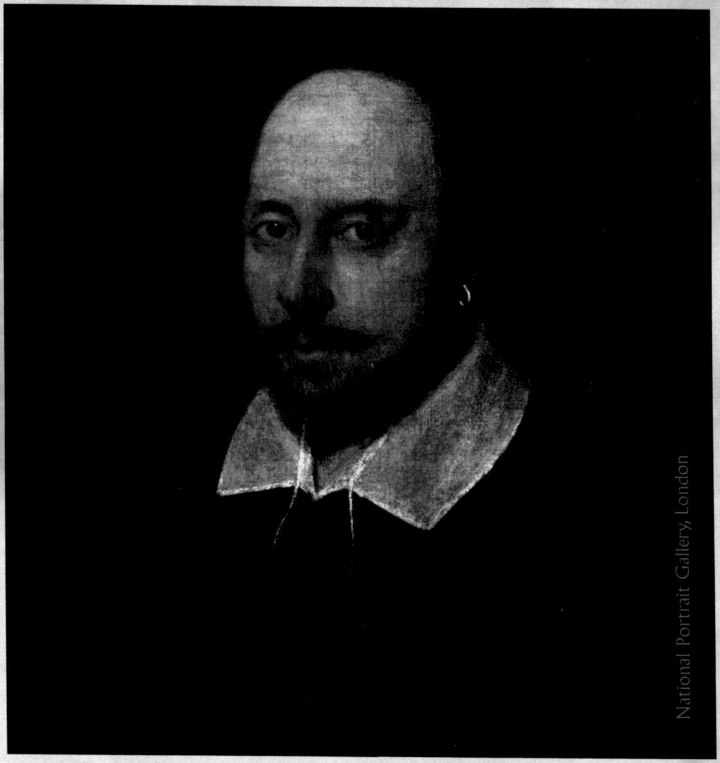
National Portrait Gallery, London

William Shakespeare is one of the most widely read authors and possibly the best dramatist ever to live. The actual date of his birth is not known, but April 23, 1564 (St George's Day) has traditionally been his accepted birthday, as this was three days before his baptism. He died on the same date in 1616, at the age of fifty-two.

The life of William Shakespeare can be divided into three acts. The first twenty years of his life were spent in Stratford-upon-Avon, where he grew up, went to school, got married and became a father. The next twenty-five years he spent as an actor and playwright in London. He spent his last few years back in Stratford-upon-Avon, where he enjoyed his retirement in moderate wealth gained from his successful years in the theater.

William, the third of eight children, was the eldest son of tradesman John Shakespeare and Mary Arden. His father was later elected mayor of Stratford, which was the highest post a man in civic politics could attain. In sixteenth-century England, William was lucky to survive into adulthood: syphilis, scurvy, smallpox, tuberculosis, typhus and dysentery shortened life expectancy at the time to approximately thirty-five years. The Bubonic Plague took the lives of many and was believed to have been the cause of death for three of William's seven siblings.

Little is known of William's childhood, but he is thought to have attended the local grammar school, where he studied Latin and English Literature. In 1582, at the age of eighteen, William married a local farmer's daughter, Anne Hathaway, who was eight years his senior and three months pregnant. During their marriage they had three children: Susanna, born on May 26, 1583, and twins, Hamnet and Judith, born on February 2, 1585. Hamnet, William's only son, caught Bubonic Plague and died at the age of eleven.

Five years into his marriage, in 1587, William's wife and children stayed in Stratford, while he moved to London. He appeared as an actor at "The Theatre" (England's first permanent theater), and gave public recitals of his own poems; but he quickly became famous for his playwriting. His fame soon spread far and wide. When Queen Elizabeth I died in 1603, the new King James I (who was already King James VI of Scotland) gave royal consent for Shakespeare's acting company, "The Lord Chamberlain's Men" to be called "The King's Men" in return for entertaining the court. This association was to shape a number of plays, such as ***Macbeth***, which was written to please the Scottish King.

William Shakespeare is attributed with writing and collaborating on 38 plays, 154 sonnets and 5 poems, in just twenty-three years between 1590 and 1613. No original manuscript exists for any of his plays, making it hard to accurately date any of them.

However, from their contents and reports at the time, it is believed that his first play was *The Taming of the Shrew* and that his last complete work was *Two Noble Kinsmen*, written two years before he died. The cause of his death remains unknown.

He was buried on April 25, 1616, two days after his death, at the Church of the Holy Trinity (the same Church where he had been baptized fifty-two years earlier). His gravestone bears these words, believed to have been written by William himself:-

"Good friend for Jesus sake forbear,
To dig the dust enclosed here!
Blest be the man that spares these stones,
And curst be he that moves my bones"

At the time of his death, William had substantial properties, which he bestowed on his family and associates from the theater. Most went to his eldest daughter, Susanna. Curiously, all he left to his wife Anne was his second-best bed!

William Shakespeare's last direct descendant died in 1670. She was his granddaughter, Elizabeth.

The Real Macbeth

(c.1005 - 1057 AD)

Macbeth is one of Shakespeare's most famous characters. It is a name that's known the whole world over, but many people don't realize that the story is linked to actual historical events — even if those events have been heavily embellished and altered for the sake of entertainment.

Shakespeare obtained his information about the real Macbeth from Raphael Holinshed's book *The Chronicles of England, Scotland and Ireland*, published in 1574 (which Shakespeare used as a primary resource for all of his historical plays). Holinshed himself derived his information from a variety of sources, most notably Andrew of Wyntoun's *Orygynale Cronykil* (Original Chronicle) which traces a history of Scotland from Biblical times, and Hector Boece's

Scotorum Historiae (Scottish History), published in 1526 and translated from Latin into English by John Bellenden in 1535.

Macbeth, or Mac Bethad as he would have been called, was King of Scotland from 1040 to 1057 (although in Shakespeare's play, his reign is made to appear significantly less than seventeen years). The name "Mac Bethad" means "son of life" and is actually Irish, rather than Scottish, in origin.

Eleventh-century Scotland was a barbaric land where war and ruthless slaughter were a fact of life. Survival depended on having a strong and capable local ruler or chieftain to protect both life and property. Such a leader would provide a strong paternalistic rule, guarding the family, community and land from all enemies.

Some of these enemies could be, and often were, collections of distant family members challenging the current leadership.

A number of local rulers would often unite under the nominal leadership of one "king" to promote their common interests and to wage war on more distant clans. Interestingly, in those times, kings and rulers could name their own successor – it wasn't a privilege that was handed down from parent to eldest child as the English monarchy operates today. However, family linkage tended to be respected, and the title usually passed to a relative of the king, selected as being the one most suitable for immediate rule and not necessarily the natural heir. Understandably, this selection process would have been challenged, especially by those individuals who felt that they had a greater right to become king than the person taking on the title. Such grievances were often dealt with or pre-empted by the murdering of family members judged unsuitable for power, to ensure that the "favorite" won the race.

Macbeth was the son of Findláech mac Ruaidrí (who was a High Steward of Moray) in the north of Scotland, around 1005. His mother's name is unknown, and indeed her own parentage is inaccurately recorded. It is uncertain whether she was the daughter of King Kenneth II or King Malcolm II. However, that is largely immaterial as whichever man was Macbeth's grandfather would be a strong enough family link for him to make a claim for the throne.

In 1020, Macbeth's father Findláech died. It is thought that he was killed, most probably by his brother Máel Brigté's son Máel Coluim (Malcolm). Findláech's title of High Steward went to his nephew Gille Coemgáin. In 1032, Gille Coemgáin and fifty other people were burned to death as punishment for the murder of Findláech. This act of retribution could well have been carried out by Macbeth and his allies. Following Gille Coemgáin's death, Macbeth took the title of High Steward of Moray.

It was around this time that he married Gille Coemgáin's widow, Gruoch, and became step-father to her son, Lulach (which explains why Shakespeare has Lady Macbeth talk about motherhood, whereas at no time does Macbeth make any reference to being a father. Moreover, Macduff states that Macbeth has no children in Act IV Scene III (page 102)). Macbeth's marriage to Gruoch was significant, because she was the grand-daughter of Kenneth III. Therefore through their combined

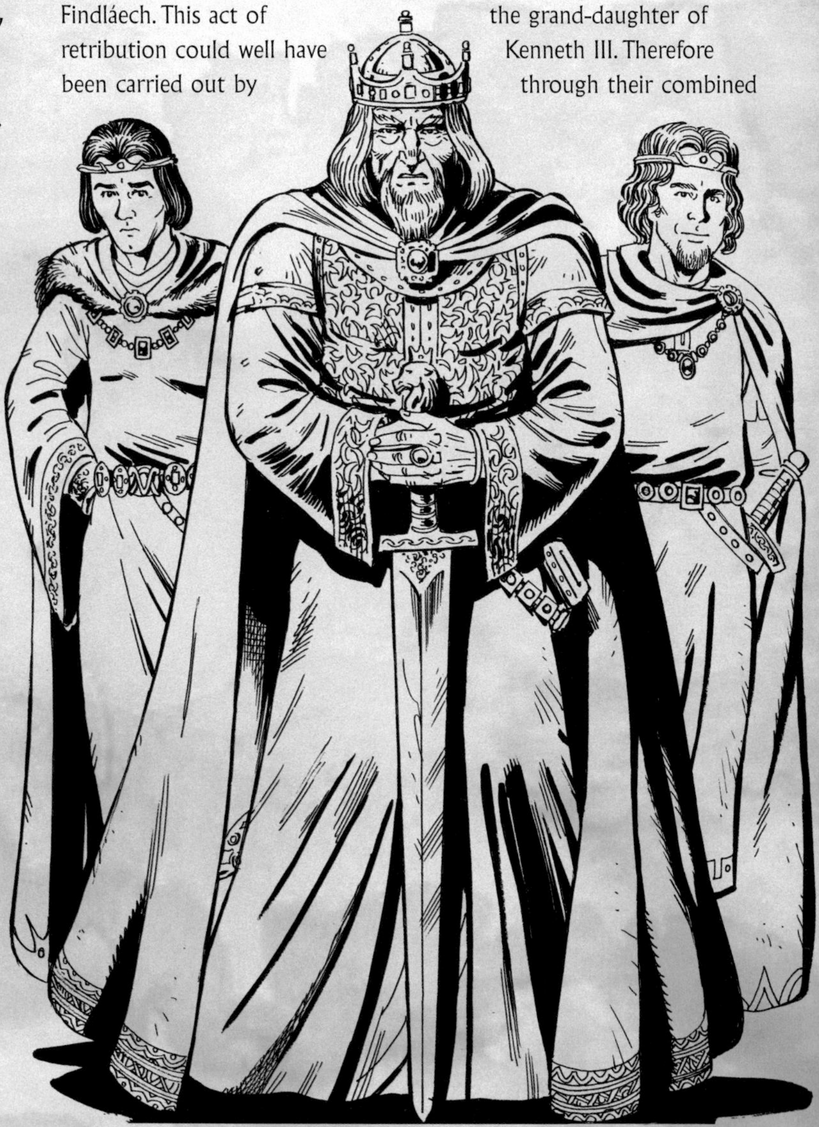

ancestors, the marriage ensured that Macbeth had a strong claim to the throne.

Within a very short space of time, Macbeth's rival Gille Coemgáin had not only lost his life, but his title and his widowed wife had gone swiftly to Macbeth.

While Macbeth was a high-ranking lord of Moray, the King at the time was Donnchad mac Crináin (King Duncan I). Duncan succeeded to the throne when his grandfather, King Malcolm II, died at Glamis. It is thought likely that Malcolm had engineered the succession through the tactical assassination of any family members who might have felt they had a stronger claim to the crown.

Given the circumstances, it would have been a sensible course of action for Duncan to make peace with his remaining family, in particular his cousin Thorfinn the Mighty (Earl of Orkney), his cousin Macbeth, and the person closest to his throne in terms of lineage, namely Gruoch, the wife of Macbeth. Duncan appears to have been unsuccessful in uniting the "royal family", and Macbeth pressed his own claim to the throne with the help of that same cousin and ally, Earl Thorfinn of Orkney. He eventually won the crown by slaying Duncan at Bothgowanan near Elgin in 1040.

Macbeth has been judged by history to be a more able king than his predecessor. Under his rule the kingdom became relatively stable and reasonably prosperous, so much so, that by 1050 he was confident enough to leave the country for a number of months and make a pilgrimage to Rome. At this time he was said to have been so wealthy that he "scattered alms like seed corn". As Wyntoun's ***Orygynale Cronykil*** says:-
"In pilgrimage þidder he come,
And in almus he sew siluer"

All was not peaceful, however, and in 1054 Duncan I's son, Máel Coluim mac Donnchada (Malcolm Canmore, nicknamed "big head"), challenged Macbeth for the throne of Scotland. He did so in alliance with Siward, Earl of Northumbria (who also happened to be the cousin of Duncan's widow) and they took control of much of southern Scotland. Three years later, on August 15, 1057, Macbeth's army was finally defeated at the Battle of Lumphanan, in Aberdeenshire. Macbeth was killed in battle. He is believed to be buried in the graveyard at Saint Oran's Chapel on the Isle of Iona, the last of many Kings of Alba and Dalriada to be laid to rest there. This site is also supposed to be the final resting place of King Duncan I.

Unlike in Shakespeare's play, the killing of Macbeth didn't result in the crown going straight to Duncan's son Malcolm. It first went to Macbeth's step-son Lulach, on the basis that Kenneth III was his maternal great-grandfather. Lulach was a weak king, and people called him "Lulach the Simple" or "Lulach the Fool". After a few months of rule, he was murdered, and Malcolm, son of Duncan I, became King Malcolm III of Scotland.

No-one knows what happened to Lady Macbeth. Dramatically, Shakespeare has her losing her sanity and taking her own life – however, there is no record of that happening, or even of her falling to a bloody death. Having lived through the murder of her first husband, the killing of her second husband in battle, and the murder of her son, even if she was to outlive them all, it's unlikely that she enjoyed any form of happiness.

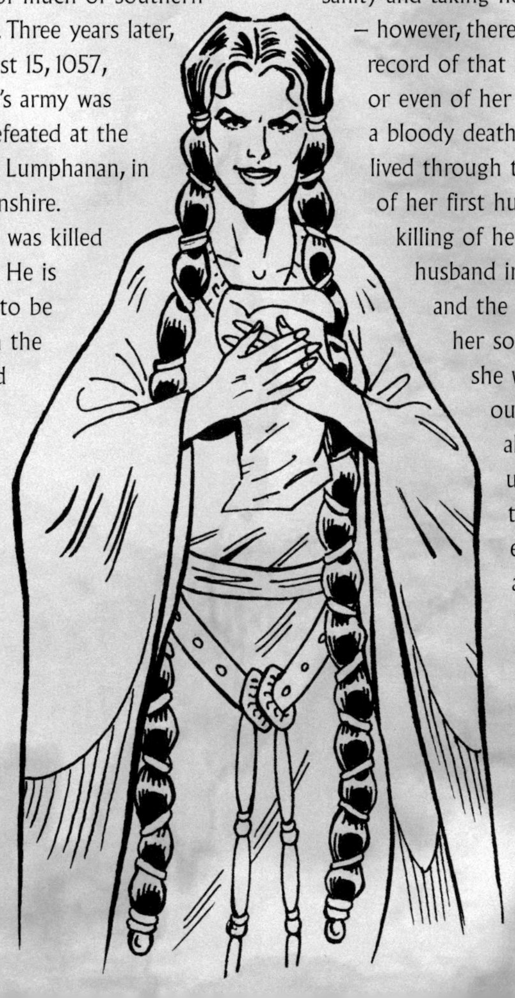

Macbeth and the Kings of Scotland

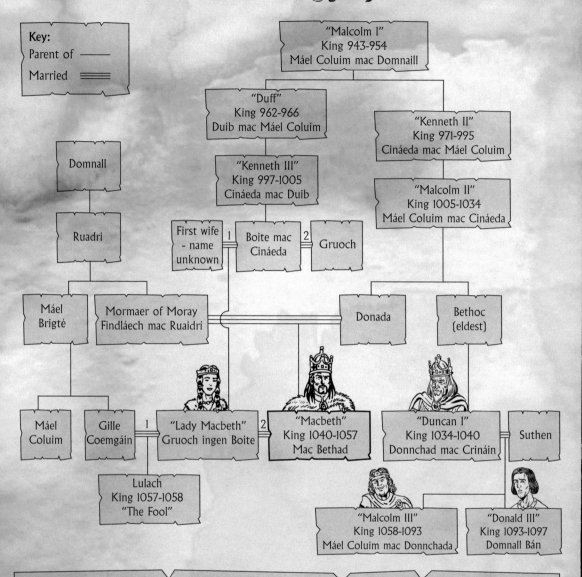

Key:
Parent of ———
Married ═══

"Malcolm I"
King 943-954
Máel Coluim mac Domnaill

"Duff"
King 962-966
Duib mac Máel Coluim

"Kenneth II"
King 971-995
Cináeda mac Máel Coluim

Domnall

"Kenneth III"
King 997-1005
Cináeda mac Duib

"Malcolm II"
King 1005-1034
Máel Coluim mac Cináeda

Ruadri

First wife - name unknown | 1 | Boite mac Cináeda | 2 | Gruoch

Máel Brigté

Mormaer of Moray
Findláech mac Ruaidrí

Donada

Bethoc (eldest)

Máel Coluim

Gille Coemgáin | 1 | "Lady Macbeth" Gruoch ingen Boite | 2 | "Macbeth" King 1040-1057 Mac Bethad

"Duncan I"
King 1034-1040
Donnchad mac Crináin

Suthen

Lulach
King 1057-1058
"The Fool"

"Malcolm III"
King 1058-1093
Máel Coluim mac Donnchada

"Donald III"
King 1093-1097
Domnall Bán

The Macbeth Murder Trail

1020 – Macbeth's father Findláech died – thought to have been killed by his own nephew, Máel Coluim. His title of High Steward went to Máel Coluim's brother, Gille Coemgáin.

1032 – Gille Coemgáin and 50 other people were burned to death as punishment for the killing of Findláech. This may have been carried out by Macbeth and his allies as retribution for killing his father. Macbeth then took Coemgáin's title (that had belonged to Macbeth's father) and took Gille Coemgáin's widow, Gruoch, for his wife. There is also a theory that Gille Coemgáin killed Boite mac Cináeda because he had made his wife the heiress to his estate. As retaliation for this murder, Boite's wife,

Gruoch (the stepmother of the Gruoch that married Gille Coemgáin and later Macbeth), mustered an army to kill Gille Coemgáin.

1040 – Macbeth killed King Duncan I at Bothgowanan.

1050 – Macbeth went on a pilgrimage to Rome.

1054 – Máel Coluim mac Donnchada (Malcolm, son of King Duncan I) staked his claim to the throne and challenged Macbeth in the first of a series of battles.

1057 – Macbeth's army was finally defeated by Malcolm's army at the Battle of Lumphanan. Macbeth was killed in battle. Macbeth's step-son Lulach then became King.

1057 – After only a few months of rule, Malcolm killed Lulach to become King Malcolm III of Scotland.

The History of Shakespeare's Macbeth

When comparing the play to the actual historical events, it is clear that those events were merely inspiration for Shakespeare's own take on the story. It is unlikely that he deliberately intended to misrepresent the facts; however, it is important to recognize that as a playwright, Shakespeare had a responsibility to entertain his audience with his works. Therefore, what takes place on the stage is an artistic modification of what took place in history; to give the best portrayal of the plots and motives of the characters in order to arrive at a worthy spectacle. Among other things, Shakespeare possessed good business sense — and a successful play would draw in the fee-paying public to provide him and his troupe with an income.

But money was not his sole concern. His position in society was paramount, and of prime importance was the need to pander to the monarch.

Macbeth is thought to have been written to be performed in honor of a royal visit by the King of Denmark to King James I in 1606. King James I became King of England in 1603 when Elizabeth I died. He was already King of Scotland (King James VI of Scotland). Interestingly, James I was a keen scholar and had such a deep interest in witchcraft that in 1597 he wrote a book on the subject, which he called *Daemonologie*. In it he advocated severe punishment for witches. In addition, he was a keen supporter of the arts, having the title of "The King's Men" bestowed upon Shakespeare's acting company soon after his coronation. In return, The King's Men were expected to perform at court whenever they were asked, which amounted to around a dozen performances each year.

Setting the play in Scotland and including elements of witchcraft appears to be a deliberate attempt by Shakespeare to please the new King. But he can't take the credit for including witchcraft in the tale of *Macbeth*: we have Holinshed to thank for that. Raphael Holinshed's *Chronicles of England, Scotland and Ireland*, first published in 1574, was a primary source of reference for a number of Shakespeare's plays, and *Macbeth* is no exception. The following extract from Holinshed's *Chronicles* demonstrates just how closely Shakespeare borrowed from his version of events:

"It fortuned as Makbeth and Banquho iournied towards Fores, where the king then laie, they went sporting by the waie together without other company saue onelie themselues, passing thorough the woods and fields, when suddenlie in the middest of a laund, there met them three women in strange and wild apparell, resembling creatures of the elder world, whome when they attentiuelie beheld, woondering much at the sight, the first of them spake and said: All haile Makbeth, thane of Glammis (for he had latelie entered into that dignitie and office by the death of his father Sinell). The second of them said: Haile Makbeth thane of Cawder. But the third said: All haile Makbeth that heereafter shalt be king of Scotland.

Then Banquho: What manner of women (saith he) are you, that seeme so little fauourable vnto me, whereas to my fellow heere, besides high offices, ye assigne also the kingdome, appointing foorth nothing for me at all? Yes, (saith the first of them) we promise greater benefits vnto thee, than vnto him, for he shall reigne in deed, but with an vnluckie end: neither shall he leaue anie issue behind him to succeed in his place, where contrarilie thou in deed shalt not reigne at all, but of thee those shall be borne which shall gouern the Scotish kingdome by long order of continuall descent. Herewith the foresaid women vanished immediatlie out of their sight."

In those days, the Stuart Kings of Scotland (King James I was a Stuart) were believed to have descended from Banquo (this is unproven but may have some truth in it). The witches "predicted" a long line of kings, and this is dealt with in the play verbally in Act I Scene III (page 15) and visually in Act IV Scene I (page 85), when Macbeth is shown a large number of kings in a line, all of whom bear a resemblance to Banquo. The "bloodline" is only made possible by Fleance escaping when his father is attacked. Holinshed describes how Walter Steward, the founder of the Stuart royal family who married the daughter of Robert Bruce, was a descendent of Fleance and therefore Banquo. This ancestral connection must have been behind a change that Shakespeare made to Holinshed's accounts, namely that in Holinshed, Banquo was an accomplice in Duncan's murder; to portray an ancestor of the King as murderous would have been rather

foolhardy on Shakespeare's part. Other pandering includes the reference to the English King (Edward the Confessor) having God-given powers to cure "the evil" in Act IV Scene III (page 99), also known as Scrofula. Edward was believed to have that power, and King James I revived the custom of sufferers being "touched" by the monarch as a cure for it.

But it is with his portrayal of the witches where Shakespeare really aimed to please the King. In his book, King James denounced witchcraft absolutely. It was his belief that witches were mostly women who had masculine features such as facial hair. They were in league with the devil, could summon up spirits, and could even curse images of people to control their destiny. These were early days in the understanding of witchcraft, and the very subject was a threat to King James' belief of divine right of kingship. In his world,

witchcraft was a devil-based display of evil that was an ever-present challenge to the sanctity of his God-given rule. It is a general fear of witchcraft, then, that is the possible reason why neither Holinshed nor Shakespeare ever refers to the women as witches. In fact, the elements of witchcraft that exist in the play, particularly the spells and the appearance of Hecate, are now believed to be later additions, made by Thomas Middleton following on from his own play, *The Witch*. The term only appears once, in Act I Scene III (page 12*), and even then it could be an insult being reported by the speaker.

Beyond the belief that it was written for the visit of the King of Denmark in 1606, a number of other elements point towards it being authored in that year. The Porter's ramblings in Act II Scene III (page 38*) make mention of equivocation:

*Original Text version only

The line "O, come in, equivocator" may refer to the verbal cunning displayed by Father Garnet, one of the Gunpowder Plot conspirators in the trial of 1606. Also that year, a ship called The Tiger returned to England after a terrible two year voyage, and that ship is named in Act I Scene III (page 12*). However, as the first printed version of the play didn't appear until the Folio printing in 1623, the true dating and authenticity of each of the parts of the play are difficult to establish. For certain, a version of the play was first performed at The Globe Theatre in April 1611.

The Scottish Play

Macbeth is steeped in superstition, so much so that actors consider it the height of bad luck to even utter the name, unless they are rehearsing it at the time. Often, people will make references to "The Bard's Play" or "The Scottish Play" simply to avoid saying the "M"-word. There are a number of theories about the origins of the "curse" of *Macbeth*:

- It is thought that the witches' incantations are taken from real rituals and are believed to cast actual spells on the players.
- Legend has it that in 1606, Hal Berridge, the boy playing Lady Macbeth (remember that all the parts, male and female, were played by males at the time) died backstage.
- Another gruesome legend reports that in 1672 an actor playing the part of Macbeth substituted a real dagger for the blunt stage one, and actually killed the actor playing King Duncan in full view of the audience.

The more rational explanations are easier to accept.

- The majority of the play takes place in darkly lit scenes, and this tended to lead to a lot of accidents backstage.
- Because *Macbeth* is a short play, and so well known, theater groups would perform the play when they were in some financial trouble. Of course, a single play is rarely enough to save an ailing company, and therefore the performance of *Macbeth* became associated with failure, misery, and being out of work.

Whether any of those reasons are true or not is open to much speculation; what is beyond any doubt is that the story of *Macbeth* is a powerful, timeless tale of ambition, of the evil that is embedded in ill-gotten gains, and a question that lies at the heart of life itself — are we all the subjects of fate and destiny? Or do we carve out our own existence on this planet?

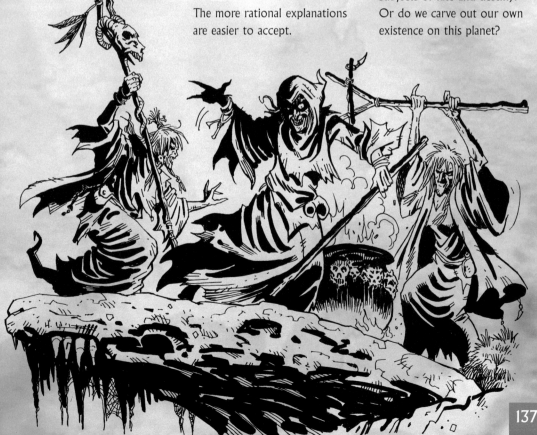

Page Creation

In order to create three versions of the same book, the play is first adapted into three scripts: Original Text, Plain Text and Quick Text. While the degree of complexity changes for the dialogue in each script, the artwork remains the same for all three books.

SWIRLING MIST
BLACK BALLOON WITH RED LETTERING

On the left is a rough thumbnail sketch of page 73 created from the script (below). Once the rough sketch is approved, it is redrawn as a clean finished pencil sketch (right).

HOT HOT HOTTER THAN HELL..
HECATE BRIGHT GREEN EYES HER WORD BALLOON BLACK WITH RED GREEK TYPE FACE

ACT 3 – SCENE 5

249. Somewhere far beyond the light of the sun, the three Witches huddle. Strange weather and strange landscapes surround them. They sense the approach of Hecate, the Queen of Darkness and they're frightened.

250. BIG. Suddenly she's there! Hecate appears as a triple goddess, with three heads (women's in this frame, all identical, harsh-looking, but not ugly) and three bodies, standing back-to-back. She towers over the three Witches, piercing the gloom with her fierce stare. They cringe and make frightened animal noises.

	QUICK TEXT	PLAIN ENGLISH TEXT	ORIGINAL TEXT
WITCHES (2 & 3)	WHIMPER! WHINE!	WHIMPER! WHINE!	WHIMPER! WHINE!
1ST WITCH	Hecate…you look angry.	Hecate! You look so angry.	Why, how now, Hecate! you look angerly.
HECATE	I am! You dared to meddle with Macbeth In riddles and affairs of death	Have I not reason, chaos that you are, Impertinent and rash? How did you dare To trade and traffic with Macbeth, In riddles, and affairs of death;	Have I not reason, beldams as you are, Saucy, and overbold? How did you dare To trade and traffic with Macbeth, In riddles, and affairs of death;

251. BIGish. The Witches scuttle round Hecate like dogs round their master. Hecate's three heads metamorphose into the heads of a horse, a dog and a boar.

HECATE	You did it without me! And now I clearly see That all you've managed to do Is use him as he has used you.	And I, the mistress of your charms, The true instrument of all harms, Was never called to play my part, Or show the glory of our art? And, which is worse, all you have done Was only for a wayward son, Spiteful, and hateful; who, as others do, Wants all he can get and nought for you.	And I, the mistress of your charms, The close contriver of all harms, Was never call'd to bear my part, Or show the glory of our art? And, which is worse, all you have done Hath been but for a wayward son, Spiteful, and wrathful; who, as others do, Loves for his own ends, not for you.

From the pencil sketch, an inked version of the same page is created (right).

HOT HOT HOTTER THAN HELL..
HECATE BRIGHT GREEN EYES HER WORD BALLOON BLACK WITH RED GREEK TYPE FACE

Inking is not simply tracing over the pencil sketch; it is the process of using black ink to fill in the shaded areas and to add clarity, cohesion, depth and texture to the "pencils".

The "inks" give us the final outline, which is checked for accuracy before being passed on to the colorist.

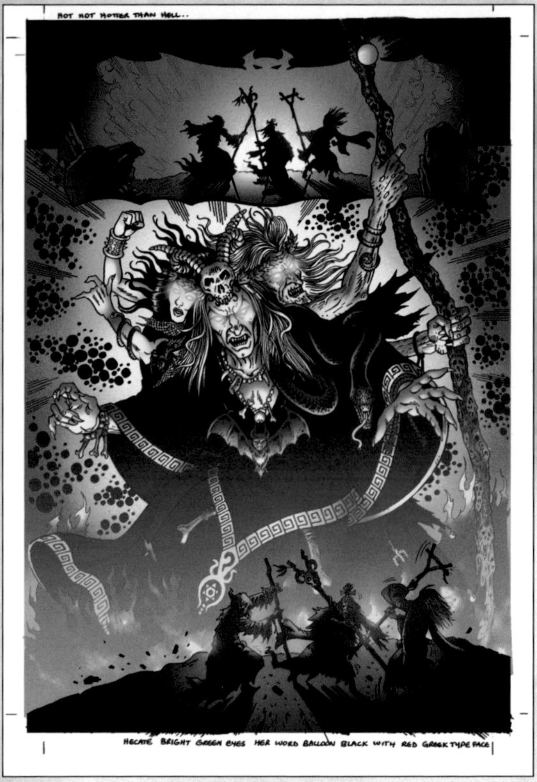
HOT HOT HOTTER THAN HELL..
HECATE BRIGHT GREEN EYES HER WORD BALLOON BLACK WITH RED GREEK TYPE FACE

Adding color brings the page and its characters to life.

Each character has a detailed Character Study. This is useful for the artists to refer to and ensures continuity throughout the book.

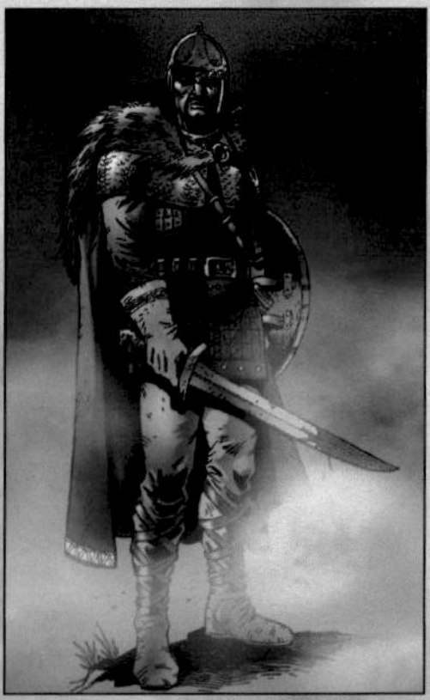

Macbeth character study

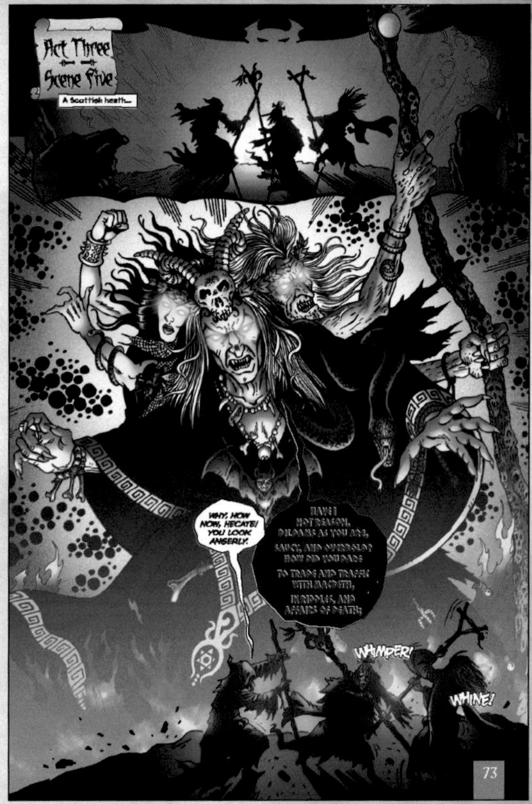
Act Three
Scene Five
A Scottish heath...
WHY, HOW NOW, HECATE! YOU LOOK ANGERLY.
HAVE I NOT REASON, BELDAMS AS YOU ARE,
SAUCY, AND OVERBOLD? HOW DID YOU DARE
TO TRADE AND TRAFFIC WITH MACBETH,
IN RIDDLES, AND AFFAIRS OF DEATH;
WHIMPER!
WHINE!
73

The last stage of page creation is to add the speech bubbles and any sound effects.

Speech bubbles are created from the words in the script and are laid over the finished, colored artwork.

Three versions of lettering are produced for the three different versions of *Macbeth*. These are then saved as final artwork pages and compiled into separate books for printing.

Original Text

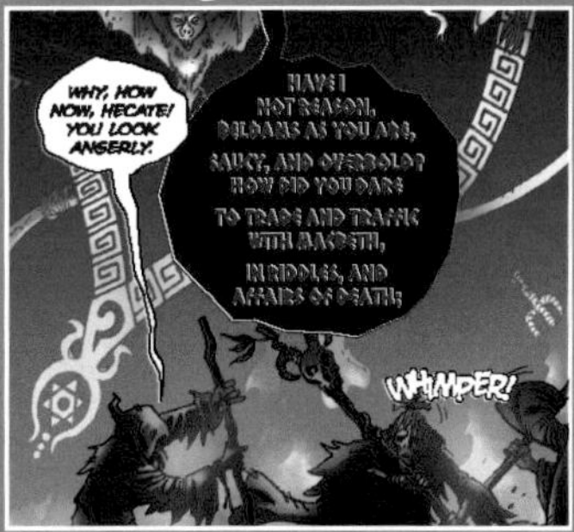
WHY, HOW NOW, HECATE! YOU LOOK ANGERLY.
HAVE I NOT REASON, BELDAMS AS YOU ARE,
SAUCY, AND OVERBOLD? HOW DID YOU DARE
TO TRADE AND TRAFFIC WITH MACBETH,
IN RIDDLES, AND AFFAIRS OF DEATH;
WHIMPER!

Plain Text

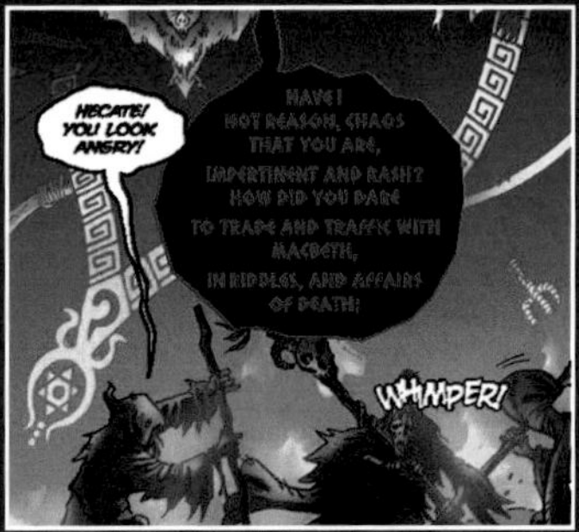
HECATE! YOU LOOK ANGRY!
HAVE I NOT REASON, CHAOS THAT YOU ARE,
IMPERTINENT AND RASH? HOW DID YOU DARE
TO TRADE AND TRAFFIC WITH MACBETH,
IN RIDDLES, AND AFFAIRS OF DEATH;
WHIMPER!

Quick Text

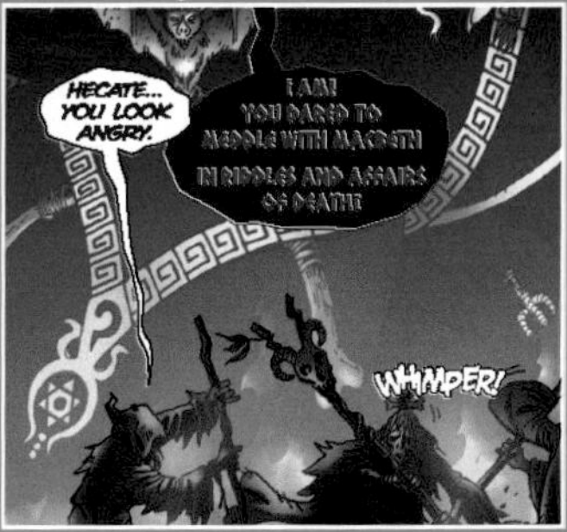
HECATE... YOU LOOK ANGRY.
I AM! YOU DARED TO MEDDLE WITH MACBETH
IN RIDDLES AND AFFAIRS OF DEATH!
WHIMPER!

Shakespeare Around the Globe

The Globe Theatre and Shakespeare

It is hard to appreciate today how theaters were actually a new idea in William Shakespeare's time. The very first theater in Elizabethan London to show only plays, aptly called "The Theatre," was introduced by an entrepreneur by the name of James Burbage. In fact, "The Globe Theatre," possibly the most famous theater of that era, was built from the timbers of "The Theatre." The landlord of "The Theatre" was Giles Allen, a Puritan who disapproved of theatrical entertainment. When he decided to enforce a huge rent increase in the winter of 1598, the theater members dismantled the building piece by piece and shipped it across the Thames to Southwark for reassembly. Allen was powerless to do anything, as the company owned the wood - although he spent three years in court trying to sue the perpetrators!

The report of the dismantling party (written by Schoenbaum)

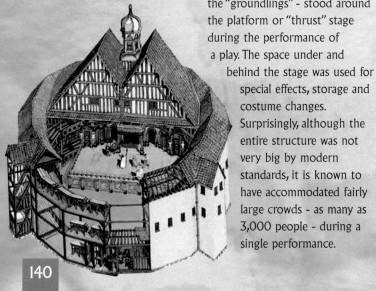

says: "ryotous... armed... with divers and manye unlawfull and offensive weapons... in verye ryotous outragious and forcyble manner and contrarye to the lawes of your highnes Realme... and there pulling breaking and throwing downe the sayd Theater in verye outragious violent and riotous sort to the great disturbance and terrefyeing not onlye of your subjectes... but of divers others of your majesties loving subjectes there neere inhabitinge."

William Shakespeare became a part owner of this new Globe Theatre in 1599. It was one of four major theaters in the area, along with the Swan, the Rose, and the Hope. The exact physical structure of the Globe is unknown, although scholars are fairly sure of some details through drawings from the period. The theater itself was a closed structure with an open courtyard where the stage stood. Tiered galleries around the open area accommodated the wealthier patrons who could afford seats, and those of the lower classes - the "groundlings" - stood around the platform or "thrust" stage during the performance of a play. The space under and behind the stage was used for special effects, storage and costume changes. Surprisingly, although the entire structure was not very big by modern standards, it is known to have accommodated fairly large crowds - as many as 3,000 people - during a single performance.

The Globe II

In 1613, the original Globe Theatre burned to the ground when a cannon shot during a performance of *Henry VIII* set fire to the thatched roof of the gallery. Undeterred, the company completed a new Globe (this time with a tiled roof) on the foundations of its predecessor. Shakespeare didn't write any new plays for this theater. He retired to Stratford-Upon-Avon that year, and died two years later. Performances continued until 1642, when the Puritans closed down all theaters and places of entertainment. Two years later, the Puritans razed the building to the ground in order to build tenements upon the site. No more was to be seen of the Globe for 352 years.

Shakespeare's Globe

Led by the vision of the late Sam Wanamaker, work began on the construction of a new Globe in 1993, close to the site of the original theater. It was completed three years later, and Queen Elizabeth II officially opened the New Globe Theatre on June 12th 1997 with a production of *Henry V.*

The New Globe Theatre is as faithful a reproduction as possible to the Elizabethan theater, given that the details of the original are only known from sketches of the time. The building can accommodate 1,500 people between the galleries and the "groundlings."

www.shakespeares-globe.org

Shakespeare Birthplace Trust

Shakespeare's Birthplace

As so few relics survive from Shakespeare's life, it is amazing that the house where he was born and raised remains intact. It is owned and cared for by the Shakespeare Birthplace Trust, which looks after a number of houses in the area:

• Shakespeare's Birthplace.
• Mary Arden's Farm: The childhood home of Shakespeare's mother.
• Anne Hathaway's Cottage: The childhood home of Shakespeare's wife.
• Hall's Croft: The home of Shakespeare's eldest daughter, Susanna.
• New Place: Only the grounds exist of the house where Shakespeare died in 1616.
• Nash's House: The home of Shakespeare's granddaughter.

www.shakespeare.org.uk

Martin Droeshout's engraving of Shakespeare

Formed in 1847, the Trust also works to promote Shakespeare around the world. In early 2009, it announced that it had found a new Shakespeare portrait, believed to have been painted within his lifetime, with a trail of provenance that links it to Shakespeare himself.

It is accepted that Martin Droeshout's engraving (left) that appears on the First Folio of 1623 is an authentic likeness of Shakespeare because the people involved in its publication would have personally known him. This new portrait (once owned by Henry Wriothesley, 3rd Earl of Southampton, one of Shakespeare's most loyal supporters) is so similar in all facial aspects that it is now suspected to have been the source that Droeshout used for his famous engraving. www.shakespearefound.org.uk

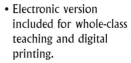

MORE TITLES AVAILABLE FROM

Shakespeare's plays in a choice of 3 text versions. Simply choose the text version to match your reading level.

Original Text — SHAKESPEARE'S ENTIRE PLAY AS A FULL COLOR GRAPHIC NOVEL!

Plain Text — THE ENTIRE PLAY TRANSLATED INTO PLAIN ENGLISH!

Quick Text — THE ENTIRE PLAY IN QUICK MODERN ENGLISH FOR A FAST-PACED READ!

Romeo & Juliet: The Graphic Novel (William Shakespeare)

- Script Adaptation: John McDonald • Linework: Will Volley
- Colors: Jim Devlin • Letters: Jim Campbell

168 Pages • $16.95

ISBN: 978-1-906332-61-7 — ISBN: 978-1-906332-62-4 — ISBN: 978-1-906332-63-1

A Midsummer Night's Dream: The Graphic Novel (William Shakespeare)

- Script Adaptation: John McDonald • Characters & Artwork: Kat Nicholson & Jason Cardy
- Letters: Jim Campbell

144 Pages • $16.95

ISBN: 978-1-907127-28-1 — ISBN: 978-1-907127-29-8 — ISBN: 978-1-907127-30-4

The Tempest: The Graphic Novel (William Shakespeare)

- Script Adaptation: John McDonald • Pencils: Jon Haward
- Inks: Gary Erskine • Colors: & Letters: Nigel Dobbyn

144 Pages • $16.95

ISBN: 978-1-906332-69-3 — ISBN: 978-1-906332-70-9 — ISBN: 978-1-906332-71-6

Henry V: The Graphic Novel (William Shakespeare)

- Script Adaptation: John McDonald • Pencils: Neill Cameron • Inks: Bambos
- Colors: Jason Cardy & Kat Nicholson • Letters: Nigel Dobbyn

144 Pages • $16.95

ISBN: 978-1-906332-41-9 — ISBN: 978-1-906332-42-6 — ISBN: 978-1-906332-43-3

OUR AWARD-WINNING RANGE

Classic Literature in a choice of 2 text versions. Simply choose the text version to match your reading level.

Original Text	THE CLASSIC NOVEL BROUGHT TO LIFE IN FULL COLOR!
Quick Text	THE FULL STORY IN QUICK MODERN ENGLISH FOR A FAST-PACED READ!

Dracula: The Graphic Novel (Bram Stoker)

- Script Adaptation: Jason Cobley • Linework: Staz Johnson
- Colors: James Offredi • Letters: Jim Campbell

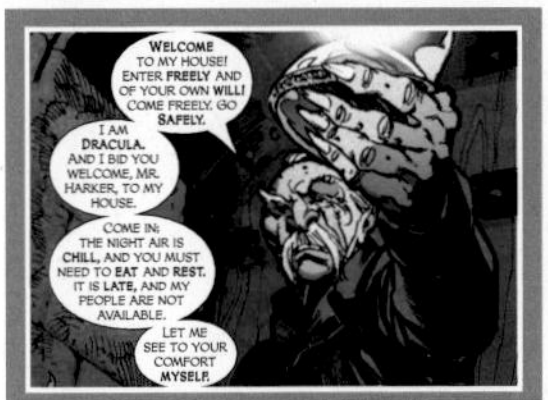
WELCOME TO MY HOUSE! ENTER FREELY AND OF YOUR OWN WILL! COME FREELY. GO SAFELY.
I AM DRACULA. AND I BID YOU WELCOME, MR. HARKER, TO MY HOUSE.
COME IN; THE NIGHT AIR IS CHILL, AND YOU MUST NEED TO EAT AND REST. IT IS LATE, AND MY PEOPLE ARE NOT AVAILABLE.
LET ME SEE TO YOUR COMFORT MYSELF.

ISBN: 978-1-906332-67-9

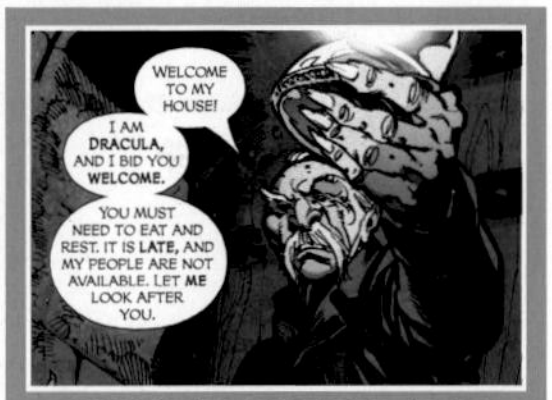
WELCOME TO MY HOUSE!
I AM DRACULA, AND I BID YOU WELCOME.
YOU MUST NEED TO EAT AND REST. IT IS LATE, AND MY PEOPLE ARE NOT AVAILABLE. LET ME LOOK AFTER YOU.

ISBN: 978-1-906332-68-6

"I went down into the vaults. There lay the Count! He was either dead or asleep, I could not say which."

• 152 Pages • $16.95

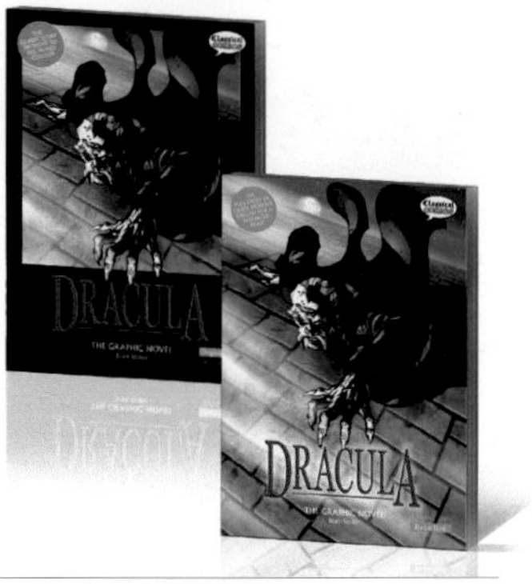

An Inspector Calls: The Graphic Novel (J. B. Priestley)

- Script Adaptation: Jason Cobley • Linework: Will Volley
- Colors: Alejandro Sanchez • Letters: Jim Campbell

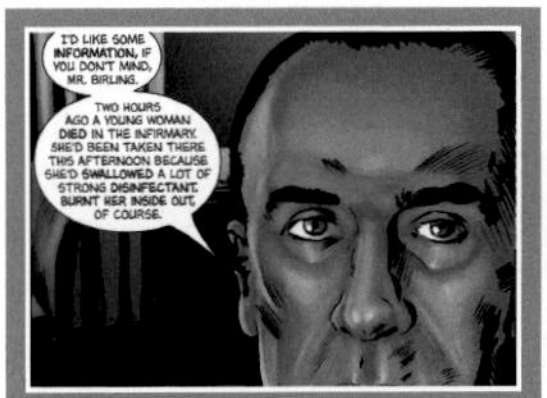
I'D LIKE SOME INFORMATION, IF YOU DON'T MIND, MR. BIRLING.
TWO HOURS AGO A YOUNG WOMAN DIED IN THE INFIRMARY. SHE'D BEEN TAKEN THERE THIS AFTERNOON BECAUSE SHE'D SWALLOWED A LOT OF STRONG DISINFECTANT. BURNT HER INSIDE OUT, OF COURSE.

ISBN: 978-1-907127-23-6

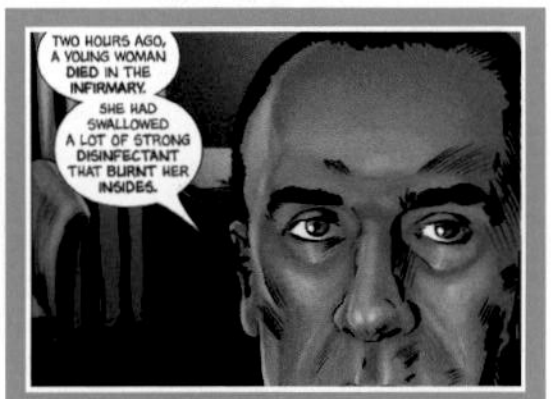
TWO HOURS AGO, A YOUNG WOMAN DIED IN THE INFIRMARY.
SHE HAD SWALLOWED A LOT OF STRONG DISINFECTANT THAT BURNT HER INSIDES.

ISBN: 978-1-907127-24-3

"But don't you see, if all that's come out tonight is true, then it doesn't much matter who it was who made us confess."

• 144 Pages • $16.95

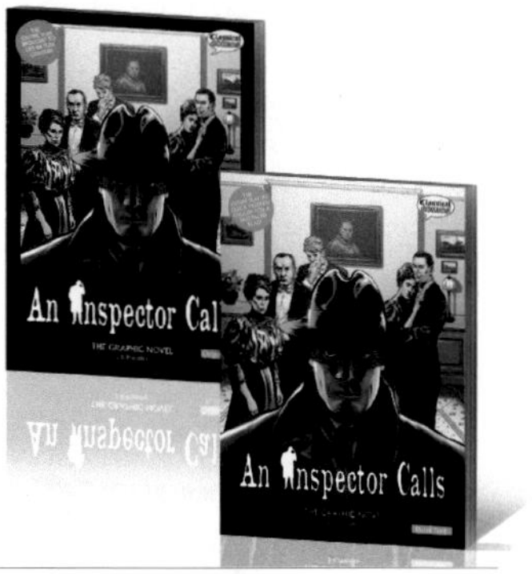

Sweeney Todd: The Graphic Novel (Anonymous)

- Script Adaptation: Seán Michael Wilson • Linework: Declan Shalvey
- Colors: Jason Cardy & Kat Nicholson • Letters: Jim Campbell

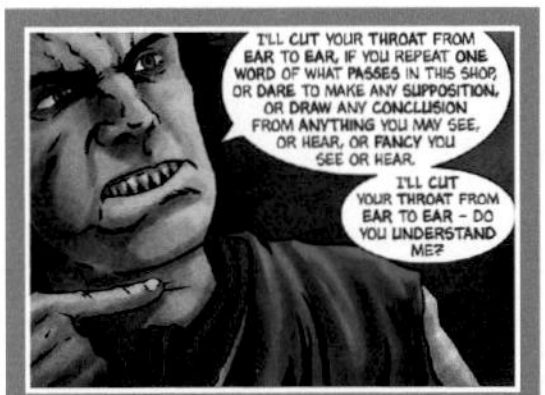
I'LL CUT YOUR THROAT FROM EAR TO EAR, IF YOU REPEAT ONE WORD OF WHAT PASSES IN THIS SHOP, OR DARE TO MAKE ANY SUPPOSITION, OR DRAW ANY CONCLUSION FROM ANYTHING YOU MAY SEE, OR HEAR, OR FANCY YOU SEE OR HEAR.
I'LL CUT YOUR THROAT FROM EAR TO EAR - DO YOU UNDERSTAND ME?

ISBN: 978-1-907127-09-0

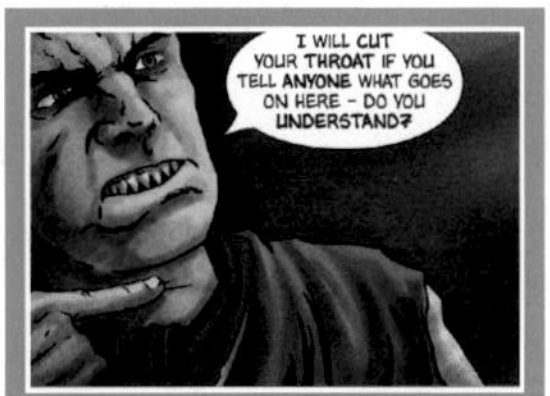
I WILL CUT YOUR THROAT IF YOU TELL ANYONE WHAT GOES ON HERE - DO YOU UNDERSTAND?

ISBN: 978-1-907127-10-6

"Oh! to be sure, he came here, and I shaved him and polished him off."

• 168 Pages • $16.95

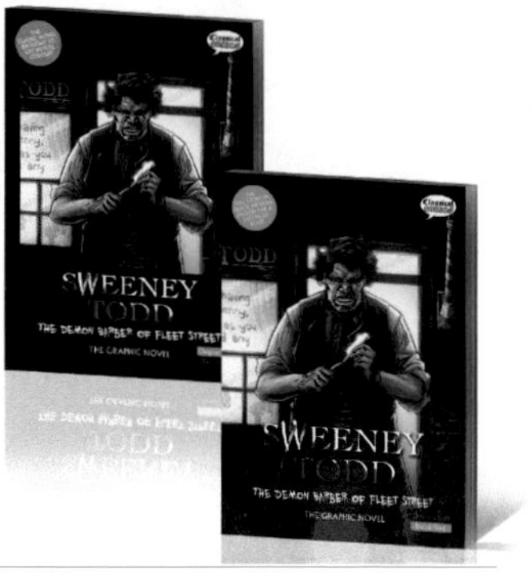

Wuthering Heights: The Graphic Novel (Emily Brontë)

- Script Adaptation: Seán Michael Wilson • Artwork: John M. Burns
- Letters: Jim Campbell

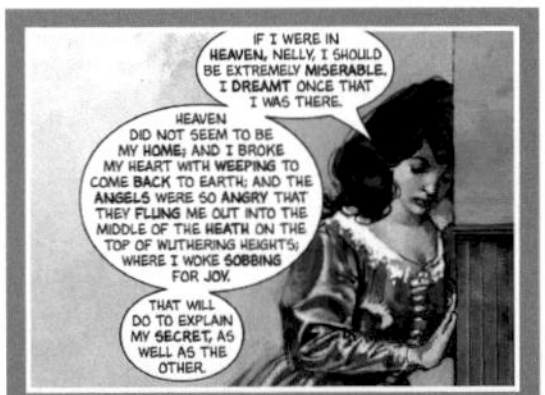
IF I WERE IN HEAVEN, NELLY, I SHOULD BE EXTREMELY MISERABLE. I DREAMT ONCE THAT I WAS THERE.
HEAVEN DID NOT SEEM TO BE MY HOME; AND I BROKE MY HEART WITH WEEPING TO COME BACK TO EARTH; AND THE ANGELS WERE SO ANGRY THAT THEY FLUNG ME OUT INTO THE MIDDLE OF THE HEATH ON THE TOP OF WUTHERING HEIGHTS; WHERE I WOKE SOBBING FOR JOY.
THAT WILL DO TO EXPLAIN MY SECRET, AS WELL AS THE OTHER.

ISBN: 978-1-907127-11-3

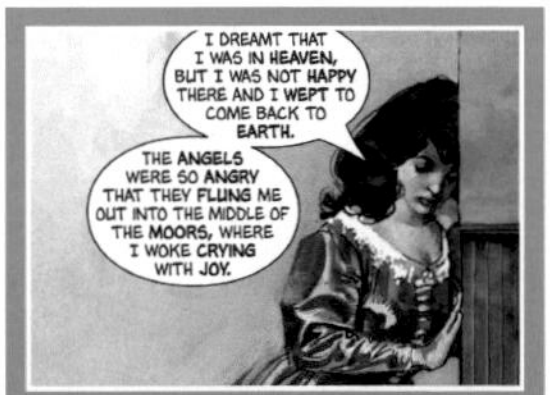
I DREAMT THAT I WAS IN HEAVEN, BUT I WAS NOT HAPPY THERE AND I WEPT TO COME BACK TO EARTH.
THE ANGELS WERE SO ANGRY THAT THEY FLUNG ME OUT INTO THE MIDDLE OF THE MOORS, WHERE I WOKE CRYING WITH JOY.

ISBN: 978-1-907127-12-0

"That minx, Catherine Linton, or Earnshaw, or however she was called – wicked little soul!"

• 160 Pages • $16.95

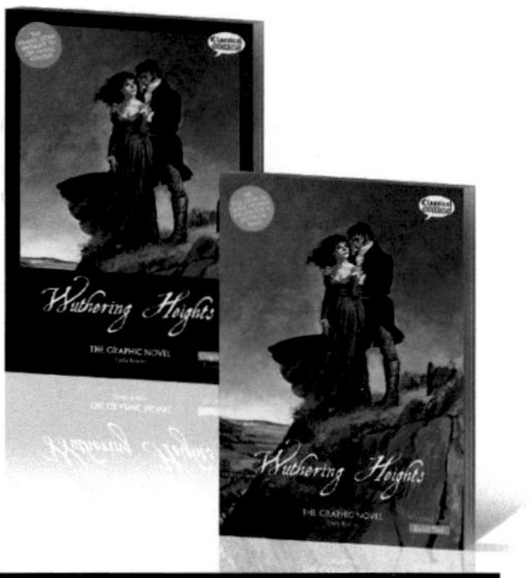

To see the complete range, and to view samples online, go to www.classicalcomics.com